Bound in Fate

The Fallen Guardians Series:
Book 2

Written By:

E.F. Rose

Bound in Fate
The Fallen Guardians Series, Book 2

Written by E.F. Rose
www.facebook.com/DarkestRose13

ISBN: 978-0-9898906-5-6

Edited by: Kim Young

Cover Design by: Diana M. Photography
www.facebook.com/DianaMuniz.Photography

Warning

This book is intended for mature audiences only
(18+). This book contains some explicit
language, some sexual content, and paranormal
mischief

Dedication

This book is dedicated to my 4th grade teacher, Mrs. Harrington, who told me to: "Always nurture my imagination, write my own story, and follow my dreams." Her advice was the building blocks that made my work possible. I will never forget her.

RIP - Mrs. Harrington (2016)

Prologue
May 3, 1984

Hayley ran through the quiet streets of the city, the slapping of her tennis shoes against the wet pavement the only sound. Icy rain beat against her face, causing the already cold night air to chill her to the bone as she frantically made her way from one block to the next.

Hayley didn't know exactly why she felt so frantic, why she continued to run. All she knew was the need to hurry hit her so strong, she couldn't ignore it. A scream, which had been building within her for some time, caught in her throat as she blindly continued down the street. Her chest hurt from the strain of trying to breathe, lungs burning from the exertion. Still, she refused to slow down.

Hayley knew this was a dream. That she would wake up at some point and find herself safe in her room. She knew this just as she knew the fear pushing her was not for her own safety, but for another's. Yet everything felt so real.

As her mind warred over the reality of what she was going through, Hayley found herself at a corner. Coming to a sudden stop, she glanced around. This was familiar, giving her a strong sense of déjà vu. Looking up at the street signs, she couldn't seem to make out the names. No matter how hard she tried, the lettering remained too blurry to read.

Looking around wildly, Hayley wasn't exactly sure whom or what she was looking for, but she could feel tears running down her cheeks as she looked back and forth.

After several minutes, harsh yelling shattered the silence. Turning, she ran towards the sound. There were so many voices, each seeming to build on top of the last. For a time, they blurred together, like a constant drumming. Occasionally, she could hear deep growling over that steady drumming, cutting like a knife through the air. Chills ran down her spine as she pushed herself down the street and into an alley.

The closer Hayley got to the voices, the more two of them began to stand out. One sounded deep and gravelly, causing her stomach to clench. The other, a mere whisper, hissed though the air like a snake. It vibrated with evil, crawling along her skin and warning her away. Both voices...so different, yet similar...sounded angry.

Rounding a corner, Hayley skidded to a stop. Before her, she could see a group of shadows. They were all huge, an impressively masculine quality about *them. One in particular stood out, having a familiar feel to it. A warmth she couldn't quite describe. Hayley watched as he fluidly moved around another shadow, seeming to taunt him, each move mimicked by the looming shadow he circled. This deadly dance was almost beautiful.*

A gasp escaped as their power rolled towards her. The one she was drawn to paused, turning slightly, as if startled by her presence. The emotion hitting her was foreign, not a feeling she had ever felt or one she could put a name to. Hayley just stood there, unable to move, as she watched the shadow engulfing the figure start to clear. She could feel her eyes widen as she began to make out some of the features of this mystery man.

Just as Hayley was about to put a face to the man, she noticed the shadow behind him, the one he had been taunting just moments earlier, lunge forward. She screamed for him to turn around, to defend himself, but it was too late.

The shadow collided into his back, the attacker looking up. His glowing silver eyes stared right at her, as if he were laughing at her anguish. Hayley felt another scream building. Her need to stop this vile creature, this demon, from harming the other man was strong.

Taking a couple steps forward, she contemplated what to do.

Hayley could feel the shadow's satisfaction and glee as he suddenly threw his head back, unleashing his power. Although she could feel it like a car hitting a brick wall, she knew the brunt of it was aimed at the man beneath him. She heard the other men around them yell out. Their screams became ones of anger and disbelief, causing Hayley to cry as a feeling of loss overtook her.

Then she felt the rush of power knock her backwards. The scream that had been building inside her came rushing from her lungs. She couldn't die like this! She couldn't let him die!

"Hayley?"

She began to struggle under the weight of the shadow's power. Squeezing her eyes shut, Hayley could feel the evilness upon her, repeating her name over and over as he taunted her failed attempt at saving him - at saving any of them! She struck out with her hands, continuing to scream, each coming out more strangled and frantic than the last.

"Hayley... Hayley!"

"No!" she screamed.

"Hayley... Wake up, Hayley! Wake up!"

"No... No...," she mumbled, twisting her head back and forth. Her body quieted as she gradually became aware of her surroundings. Still shaking her head, Hayley opened her eyes slowly. Darkness greeted her as she looked around. Blinking rapidly, she felt her fear beginning to build again. Opening her mouth to scream, she felt a sudden warmth on her arm.

"Hayley... It's okay, child. It was just a dream."

Hearing her Aunt Jenny's voice, Hayley sat up. Blinking again, she was able to make out her furniture, her bed, and her aunt standing over her. Gasping, she felt a tear slide down her cheek.

"It was that dream again," she whispered.

"The one with the shadows?" Her aunt sat on the edge of the bed.

Hayley sniffed, nodding. The soothing feel of her aunt's hand on her back made her heart finally begin to slow.

"Well, remember what I told you about your dreams, Hayley," her aunt whispered, reaching up to smooth her hair behind her ears. "Each dream means something. Some are obvious, while others will not make sense until you need them to."

"But, Aunt Jenny, what could this dream mean?"

"I'm not sure, child, but someday, maybe even years from now, you will know." Her aunt leaned down, placing a light kiss upon her forehead. "You go back to sleep now. You're safe."

Hayley smiled slightly, cuddling back down under the covers. Her aunt gave her one last kiss. "Good night, Aunt Jenny."

"Good night, Hayley," she replied, making her way to the bedroom door. "Sweet dreams."

Hayley watched as her aunt quietly closed the door. Pulling her covers up beneath her chin, she stared up at the ceiling, her mind still going over the events from the dream, desperately trying to hold onto every detail.

Her last thoughts before finally drifting back to sleep were of the fight in the alley... The mysterious man who had brought about a warmth in her she had never known... And the need to find him.

Chapter 1
Present Day

It was well after four when Manuel pulled his black Dodge Charger to a stop. This was the third house he stopped to check out that day, the eighth one that week. He shook his head. When he offered to be the one to check out the listings, he thought he would end up seeing two, maybe three houses before finding something. But no. Seven houses later and he was still on the hunt.

It's easier to find demons than a house, he thought.

"Eighth time's the charm," Manuel muttered sarcastically. Looking out his windshield, he gazed at the large iron gates sitting protectively across the driveway. None of the other houses had gates, and he had to admit that he liked them. From the road, they were all you could see. The rest of the property was lined with a sturdy brick wall covered in vines, completely hiding the land from view.

The rest of the estates he looked at had been in the open, standing proud for the world to see. Not exactly what he and his brothers were looking for. Manuel guessed he couldn't really blame the other properties for this seemingly endless search, although he would like to. He would also like to blame his pushy, yet lovely realtor, Joyce. The female who, as soon as she heard the words "money's not an issue", shoved every mansion she could find within a fifty mile radius at him.

But he couldn't blame either of those things, could he?

No.

There was a laundry list of specific requirements he had been sent to look for. Every one of his brothers had something he wanted, needed in the house.

Darren wanted a full office with room for all their books. Nicholas wanted a larger pool room than what they now had. Cyrus wanted a room that could be turned into a gym. Christian wanted a full kitchen, one equipped with a fire extinguisher or two, just in case Cyrus wanted to cook. Shit, even Ella had put in her two cents and asked that it have a nice garden. She had really grown attached to the quiet of their rose garden in the back, wanting to have a place like that in their new house.

Of course, Manuel couldn't tell her no. He smiled, remembering the conversation. He had told her he would make sure there was a garden, one with huge rose bushes, lilacs, and lilies. The smile she had given him, well... That alone made the search worth it. Ella had been through a lot. If a garden was what she need to have some inner peace, then a garden she would have.

Christian definitely found himself a truly amazing girl. The lucky bastard.

All Manuel wanted in the house was security. Things had been quiet lately, but he had a feeling Andras was up to something. If he could, he would surround their house with a mote and set in on fire. Maybe even line the mote with trees that would bat the demons back the way they came. Not that those were real, but Manuel could dream. He would settle for a good security system, though, so the impressive gate he was looking at was definitely promising.

"Point one for the house," he said, adjusting his sunglasses.

Seeing movement in his rearview mirror, Manuel glanced over his left shoulder. He watched as the realtor's sleek little red Fiat came pulling up next to him. *Right on time*, he thought, glancing down at his watch. Manuel looked over as she rolled her passenger window down, signaling for him to do the same. Sighing, he hit the button.

"Hey, Manuel! Glad to see you found the place okay," Joyce said with an overly-friendly smile.

Returning it, Manuel shifted slightly in his seat. "Well, with such detailed directions like yours, Joyce, how could I get lost?" He watched as a faint pink tinge began to spread across her tanned face.

Well into her forties, Joyce was still a truly stunning female. With her black dress, her equally black hair pulled into a tight bun, she looked like she had just stepped out of a business magazine. She had curves in all the right places, high cheekbones, and legs that went on for days. Joyce was too eager, though. Eager for a sale. Eager for attention. He didn't have to feel it radiating off her to sense it. It was written all over her face.

He watched as she tapped a well-manicured nail on her steering wheel. "Well, um... I'm going to pull up to the gate and punch in the code. You just pull in behind me and follow me up to the front of the house."

"Sounds good to me, doll. Lead the way." He grinned as another blush bloomed across her face. Smiling, she mumbled something, pulling ahead of him. Manuel was never one to mind giving someone a little attention. The sale she was craving, though... He'd have to see about that.

Pulling behind her, Manuel watched as Joyce punched in the code, the large gate slowly opening. Driving through, his jaw dropped. "Holy...," he whispered. The property was huge. The gravel driveway was lined with some of the tallest, most beautiful trees he had seen in a long time.

They all had rich, green leaves covering their branches, orange and yellow blossoms drizzled amongst them. Magnificent! Then, just when he thought it couldn't get any better, the house came into view.

Now this is a mansion, he thought. It was massive, the most impressive two-story house around. Looking past it, he saw the grounds were vast, every inch completely covered in rich, green grass.

As they pulled up to the front of the house, the driveway opened into a large oval space, the gravel by the side of the house narrowing and disappearing around the corner. *Probably going to a garage out back*, he thought, his eyes scanning from the driveway to the front entrance.

Pulling up next to Joyce's car, Manuel gazed up at the house. He couldn't even begin to count the number of windows set into the red brick walls, but there were many. *How many rooms are in this place?* He really should have paid more attention to the listing.

Getting out of the car, he focused on keeping his features as relaxed as possible, even though he was grinning like an idiot on the inside.

Joyce got out of her car and smiled at him. "So... As you can see, this property is quite large. The house is three stories, built on about twenty-five acres of land. You are only looking at the top two floors.

See where the driveway goes around the corner over there? It actually goes down to a three-car garage and the first floor."

"So the front door is on the second floor?"

"Yes. The first floor consists of the garage and a large room that could be used for storage, a workshop, or-"

"A gym," Manuel finished, feeling his excitement growing.

"Yeah. You could put a gym down there. It's definitely a large enough space. There's also another smaller room with a full bathroom," Joyce said, beginning to make her way towards the front door. "I'll show you that floor last. Let's head in and take a look at the third floor first. That is where most of the bedrooms are."

With a grunt, Manuel followed her up the couple concrete steps leading to the large, dark wood French doors. The keys jingled as she let them inside. Walking through the front door, he was awestruck. The entrance opened into a large foyer with a high ceiling and chandelier hanging in the center. Standing just inside the door, he glanced around. The walls were all cream-colored with a stunning white molding. To say it was elegant was putting it mildly. He glanced ahead of them and gazed at what was surely the largest staircase he had ever seen.

Joyce turned, glancing his way. "This is the foyer. The chandelier was added by the last owners, saying something about this area being too dark at night and looking too empty during the day." She gave a small shrug, pointing towards her right. "To your left is a walk-in closet and the entrance to the family room. To your right is the entrance to the living room. Both will lead you into the kitchen and dining room in the back portion of the house. There's also a bedroom and a full and half bath on this floor. We'll look at those later. Let's head upstairs."

Joyce chatted about the history of the house, the last owners, and the fact that it would be perfect for a large family. Manuel really wasn't listening, though. His mind was already making a note of the floor plan. He had decided the spare room on the first floor, depending on the size, could be turned into their weapon room. Installing a nice metal door with a good lock, then putting a cage on the inside would work perfectly. Right now, their weapons were scattered throughout the house, hidden in various spots.

This place might really work out.

Reaching the top of the stairs, he saw hallways leading out from either side of him, a closed double door straight ahead.

"The room right in front of us could be called the master."

"Could be?" Manuel asked, raising his brow.

"Well, all the rooms in this house have their own bathroom. Something about the family that built it enjoying their privacy... Anyway, the room in front of us is the largest, so we call it the master." Joyce stepped forward, swinging the double doors wide open. "This bedroom was built with two walk-in closets, a reading nook by the back window, and... See over there? That's a short hall that leads to a full bathroom. It has a standup shower, a whirlpool tub, and his and her sinks."

The whole time she talked, Manuel walked around. The room was impressive. If all the others were built like this, the house would be perfect.

"Let's head out and walk through the-"

"Does this house have office space?" Manuel asked, turning to her.

Joyce stopped, flipping through the papers in her hands. "Um... Yes. Yes, it does. It's on the second floor next to the stairs leading down to the garage and first floor. It's a rather big room with-"

"Big enough to be an office and library in one?"

"Well... Yes, I suppose you could," she mumbled, her eyes widening slightly. "As I was saying... It's really quite large and-"

"How about a bar?"

Planting one of her hands on her hip, Joyce tilted her head. He could see a look of annoyance flashing through her pretty blue eyes, but he knew she wouldn't say anything and risk losing this sale. She forced a smile.

"Actually, there is a bar in one of the rooms downstairs. I think it was where the last tenants entertained their guests. It's a gorgeous dark wood bar with a wine rack and mini fridge that can hold-"

"So it's probably big enough to hold a pool table and still be able to move around?" He raised his eyebrow as Joyce slowly nodded.

"Sure. We can go down and see-"

"No. That's okay, Joyce. How about the kitchen?"

"The kitchen? Oh, it's fabulous. Cherrywood counters. Large center island with stainless steel sink and several barstools. It has an oven, gas stove, dishwasher, microwave, and a large stainless steel refrigerator with freezer."

Manuel nodded as she checked off all the perks in the kitchen. The list seemed to go on and on. Making his way past her, he glanced to either side. "Exactly how many bedrooms are in this house?"

"Let me see..." He watched her shuffle through the papers in her hand. "Here it is. There are eight bedrooms, each with walk-in closets and their own bathroom, as I mentioned earlier."

Eight rooms! Manuel could hardly stop the large grin threatening to spread across his face.

Looking back at Joyce, he felt her nervousness. He could almost see her worrying over the questions he asked. Sure, he was asking all the right ones, but at such a speed, she could barely keep up.

This house was definitely perfect. Manuel knew it as soon as he had stepped through the front door. He just had one more question.

Smiling, he tilted his head slightly. Already feeling a possessiveness for the house, he took note of his surroundings again. It had everything they needed, right down to the large pool room for Nicky. There was just one more thing that would truly make this place theirs.

Clearing his throat, Manuel looked toward the nervous woman behind him. "Joyce, one last question. This house wouldn't happen to have a garden, would it?"

She looked at him for a second. Nibbling on her bottom lip, she ran a hand over her papers, glancing down. The smile on his face must have told her all she needed to know because she slowly looked up, beaming at him. "Why, yes, Manuel! Yes, it does."

Chapter 2

He couldn't believe it!

Darren was smiling like crazy as he walked quickly out of the den. He had just talked to Manuel, the stress already lifting off him. They had a house! From what his brother told him, it had everything they wanted. The price was steep, but Darren had a feeling it was going to be worth it. *Wait until I tell everyone the good news,* he thought happily. After the last couple months, this was definitely needed.

Darren walked down the quiet hall. The light in everyone's eyes had been dimming more and more ever since Ella's rescue. As successful as it had been, being "down there" had really taken a toll on all of them. For instance, he spent a lot of time with Ella in that first week after their return. While there had been a lot of progress with the depression that had hung over her like a black cloud, there was still the question of the darkness curling around her soul. It was buried so far under the surface, if he hadn't known what to look for, he would have missed it.

Damn Andras, that demon POS!

Even thinking his name made Darren want to growl. That demon had his claws in Ella for an hour, maybe two, and whatever he had done still rippled through her. However, he kept it to himself. As far as everyone else was concerned, especially Christian, she was going to be just fine. Until he knew otherwise, that was exactly what he was going to believe, too. Thinking anything else right now would be maddening. Thanks to Ella, they had just gotten Christian back from the proverbial edge. Darren would be damned if they lost him, or Ella, again.

Hearing laughter coming from the yard, he headed in that direction. It shouldn't surprise him that they were all outside. Before, unless they were running errands or hunting, they used to just stay indoors. But since Ella came into the house and found their small garden out back, it had become the place to be. Darren had actually forgotten about their little garden. When Ella and Christian were back there and she saw it, it was a wonder any of the plants were even still alive.

God, that had been the day everything got turned upside down in the house. Ella blowing out the windows, she and Christian hooking up...although, if you asked Darren, that had been a long time coming...and Manuel and Nicholas going up against some real shitty demons. There never seemed to be a good day anymore. There was always a little crap thrown into the mix. Shaking his head, Darren tried to return his thoughts to the here and now.

The garden had become their new hangout. They had even bought a few new chairs so everyone had a place to sit. Well, everyone except Cyrus. He still preferred the pool room with the bar. A glass of whiskey had become a constant companion of his ever since they got back from rescuing Ella from Andras.

That name again!

Giving his head another shake, Darren forced himself to put the demon out of his mind. Now was a time for celebration. Stepping out onto the back porch, he cleared his throat. Looking around, he watched as Ella tapped Christian on the shoulder. When he didn't turn, she smiled at Darren and nudged Christian again. He and Nicholas seemed to be in a friendly debate, but with Ella's last nudge, they both paused and looked his way.

"Where's Cyrus?" Darren asked, although he had a feeling he already knew the answer.

"Where do you think?" Christian responded with a roll of his eyes.

Ella smacked his arm playfully, earning her a half-hearted scowl. She chuckled lightly before glancing at him. "He's in the pool room, Darren."

Darren smiled at her as he leaned back through the door. "Cyrus! Can you come out here for a sec?" Waiting, he listened for the sounds of Cyrus moving around the house, ice clinking in his glass, and sighs that always escaped him when he was pulled into a meeting...even for good news. When he heard nothing, he raised his voice. "Cyrus!"

"I'm coming," Cyrus growled from the pool room.

Darren just smiled at the sound of ice clinking as Cyrus poured more whiskey into his glass. His heavy footsteps echoed through the house as he made his way to the door.

Seeing his brother come around the corner, Darren moved aside to allow him to step out onto the porch. He watched as Cyrus took a long drink of his whiskey, his black eyes glinting in the afternoon light as he glanced around.

"What now?" Cyrus drawled.

"Well, I got some great news," Darren started, smiling at each of them. "Manuel just called. He found a house."

Everyone was silent for a minute, each staring at him as if they were waiting for him to say he was kidding.

"Really?" Ella whispered, her pupils dilating as her excitement grew.

"Yes, and he said it has everything we want in it."

"Well, shit," Nicholas murmured. "I was beginning to think he would never find anything!"

"Manuel said the house has *everything*?" Ella asked, her gaze hopeful. "Does that mean it has a garden, too?"

"And a tricked-out kitchen?" Christian chimed in with a grin.

Darren grinned. "Well, from what I hear-"

"How about my pool room?" Nicholas cut in. "I sure hope he found a house with a huge room that I can put my pool table in."

Darren tried again. "Manuel said the house-"

"I should call Cindy and let her know," Ella said, reaching for her phone. "She's been wondering when we were going to get into a place with more space."

Darren finally gave up on trying to get a word in. Everyone was so excited, he doubted they would want to stop and listen to him right now anyway. Glancing toward Cyrus, who wasn't saying anything, Darren watched him look back and forth between the excited faces. "You okay?" he asked, leaning towards him. He could feel his brother tense up. Other than that, there was no outward sign of how he was feeling.

After a few moments, Cyrus slowly turned his head and looked at him. "Of course... Why wouldn't I be?"

"You're just so quiet and withdrawn lately," Darren said softly. "I just want to make sure you're okay."

"I'm fine, Darren. I'm glad Manuel found us a house. I'm sure it'll be great." While his tone didn't sound sarcastic, Darren still got the feeling he was not quite as happy about this news as everyone else. Cyrus turned back toward the others, slowly taking another sip of his drink. "Change is good."

He said it so quietly, Darren wasn't sure whether to respond. Choosing to just nod, he looked back toward the group. Ella had now moved from her seat and was standing out in the yard, her right hand waving in the air as she talked on her phone. Knowing she was talking to Cindy, he shook his head. *That woman...* She'd been driving him crazy since the first moment she stepped into their home like she owned the place. And all those questions! God, he thought she would never stop talking.

For the first couple days after she had graced their household with her presence, she'd come with a notebook full of questions. Most of them he couldn't answer; some he just didn't want to. Why she only bothered him with them, he didn't know, but he refused to hide in his own house.

Darren watched as Ella finally hung up, turning, a wide grin on her face. He would never tell her just how much he couldn't stand Cindy. Well, that wasn't entirely true. It wasn't that he couldn't stand her. He just didn't know what to do with her. She had him so mixed up, he wanted to scream. Plus, he liked Ella too much to put her in that kind of position. He wouldn't want her to think she had to tell Cindy she wasn't welcome in their home. She was welcome...just not all the time.

Ever the balancer, he thought.

Thankfully, Ella must have sensed his mild irritation because, ever since those first few days, she had kept Cindy occupied whenever she was over. So busy, in fact, that she had not been able to track him down with another one of her "I just have one more question. This won't take long. Just four hours" chats. *Females!*

Darren sighed, clearing his throat. "Manuel said we can start moving in as soon as the paperwork is done and the down payment clears."

"How soon will that be?" Nicholas asked.

"A week...maybe two." Darren shook his head. "I don't really know how long this is going to take. In the meantime, we have a lot of packing to do."

"Yeah, we do," Christian said as he stood up, stretching his back with a grunt, his eyes never leaving Ella. She stood by him, her eyes sparkling with excitement.

They really are meant for each other. Darren hadn't been too sure about the whole soulmate thing when Manuel had first brought it up. With every day, though, he could practically see their bond getting stronger. A fallen angel finding his soulmate on Earth... Who would have known?

However, Darren knew the reason for Christian always keeping his eyes on Ella was not just because of their bond. He worried about her. They all did. *Maybe Cyrus was right*, Darren mused, watching them all began to talk about packing up their rooms. Even Cyrus joined in, saying he'd take care of packing the liquor, which brought on a lot of friendly joking.

Seeing all of them so happy, so excited, Darren knew what Cyrus had said was exactly right. Change was definitely good for all of them.

Chapter 3
5 Days Later

"You guys are going to love this house!" Manuel said with a smile as he looked out the passenger window. Darren drove their H3 through the streets, heading towards the house. Earlier that morning, Manuel got a call from Joyce. It had only been five days since she put their application through escrow, but it was done.

They got the house!

He knew they would. He just hadn't expected things to move so quickly. By the sound of things, the bank was afraid that, if given too much time, they may change their mind and back out. Which, of course, wasn't going to happen, but they hadn't known that. Joyce had been so excited to tell him that everything was done. That they had been able to get all of the paperwork approved with no problem.

It had been a long time since he felt this kind of rush. He could sense his connection to the new house growing, could practically feel how good this was going to be for all of them. People didn't believe in houses having souls, but Manuel knew differently. Every house held onto a little of each and every soul who passed through it, and this house's soul called to him. Just as he knew it would call to his brothers once they drove through the gates.

"Yes, but *how* much are we going to love it? I mean, are we going to love it like we love fighting? Or are we going to love it like Cyrus loves his whiskey?" Nicholas asked, breaking into Manuel's musings. He leaned forward in his seat, eyebrow raised to emphasize his questions.

Manuel rolled his eyes when he heard Cyrus give a low growl from the back. He looked over his shoulder with a sigh. "Like I said, you'll love it, so stop being such a pain the ass."

He watched Nicholas' eyes widen. Placing his hand on his chest in mock surprise, Nicholas gave him his best innocent look. "I have no idea what you speak of, Manuel. I am not now, nor have I ever been, a pain in *anyone's* ass!"

Christian began laughing next to Nicholas. Shaking his head, Manuel watched Christian gasp for air. "Right, Nicky! You're not a pain in the ass at all."

Manuel chuckled as his brother reached over to give Christian a punch in the arm. "Whatever," Nicholas laughed.

Gazing past the two as they laughed and joked, Manuel glanced at Cyrus. He had chosen to sit by himself in the back, his long legs stretched out over the seat, head leaning back against the window. His eyes were closed as if he were sleeping, but

Manuel knew better. The guy hardly ever slept anymore. He wasn't sure if the others were aware of Cyrus' horrible sleeping habits, or lack thereof, but he was. He started noticing it a week or so after they had gotten back from rescuing Ella. Sure, Cyrus had been confident when it came to dealing with those demons. However, deep down, Manuel had a feeling being there had touched on a sore spot. The way Cyrus was sitting, Manuel had a clear view of his scar, chills taking over as unwanted memories rippled through his mind.

Manuel flew home as fast as he could. He'd just received a call from Darren that there was trouble and he was needed ASAP. Soaring high into the clouds, Manuel flapped his wings furiously. Darren's voice had been strained. That was never a good thing, especially seeing as he was one of the calmest of the brothers.

Something was wrong. He could feel it. His thoughts tumbled with every worst case scenario that there could be, praying none of them were true.

They had been investigating this horrible group of Shadows for weeks. The filthy mongrels had not only been seen by humans, but had been the cause of many horrible deaths. Three humans had been killed before Manuel came across their files and connected the dots. Christian had gone out searching, but these Shadows were smart, covering their tracks completely. However, he and his brothers hadn't given up. It had taken months to track them, but as of a couple days ago, they were finally able to catch their scent.

The last couple nights, they had been on the hunt, each of them taking a section of the city to search. Darren hadn't been happy about everyone splitting up, but it had made the most sense. The more dark corners and alleyways they could cover at once, the better their chances of finding the fuckers.

Judging by the sound of Darren's voice over the phone, it had worked.

But why were they meeting back at the house instead of somewhere in the city? That was the question repeating itself in Manuel's head as he finally landed in the backyard.

Making his way towards the back door, he could hear his brothers' voices, each one trying to talk over the other. Reaching for the sliding glass door, he paused for a moment when he heard Darren's voice over the others.

"Please, just try and calm down."

"How can we calm down, Darren? How are you even calm?" Nicholas yelled, his voice shrill.

"If we get ourselves all worked up, we won't find him. We won't be able to

think clearly, and...and we...we can't lose our heads right now!"

Manuel had heard enough. Throwing the door open, he stepped into the room. "Find whom?"

He stood there looking from one face to the next. Nicholas and Christian both looked his way, their eyes black with anger. Darren's eyes also held anger, but he was doing what he could to keep his emotions in check. So instead of a coal black gaze, Manuel was met with cool, dark blue eyes. Glancing around the room, Manuel realized somebody was missing.

"Should we wait for Cyrus before getting into whatever has you all riled up?"

Darren closed his eyes, looking away. The emotions in the room spiked, and Manuel felt a chill as their anger rolled over him. Looking around, he realized none of his brothers were looking at him. Nicholas and Christian were staring at Darren, seemingly waiting for him to say something. When Manuel glanced at him, he noticed his brother was looking his way, but not really seeing him. He seemed to be gazing right through him.

Clearing his throat, Manuel took another step into the room. "Where's Cyrus?" When he got no answer, Manuel felt his anxiety grow. "Darren? Darren... Where. Is. Cyrus?"

When Darren finally really looked at him, what Manuel saw in his eyes made his blood run cold. Inside, Manuel willed him not to say it, not to tell him what had happened to put that look in his eyes and had brought about the anger in his other brothers. Blinking several times, he watched as Darren began to slowly shake his head.

"Manuel...they have him. They have Cyrus. We don't know how yet, but the Shadows...the fucking Shadows got him."

Manuel shook his head as Darren's words repeated over and over in his mind. This couldn't be happening. They couldn't have gotten Cyrus. Rage began to fill him, burn through his body like a wildfire. How could this happen? "What do we do?" he finally asked though clenched teeth.

"We get him back!" Christian stated with force, Nicholas nodding in agreement. "We hunt them down and get...him...back!"

"Manuel?"

Manuel shook his head as the memory began to fade. Glancing over, he noticed they were stopped outside the gate of their home. Darren was staring at him, a questioning look in his eyes.

"I'm sorry. What?"

"Are you okay?" Darren asked. Manuel just nodded as he mentally chased away the memories of that horrible day.

Obviously not believing him, but choosing not to push, Darren rolled down the window. "What's the code to get in?"

"Oh, right. It's pound followed by 092315," Manuel responded, watching Darren lean out and punch it into the machine. As he hit the last digit, the large gate gave a shudder and began to slowly slide open. He felt the Hummer rumble as Darren eased it forward. The trees looked just as beautiful, the house just as breathtaking.

There were low murmurs as they pulled to a stop in front of the entrance. Climbing out, they all stopped and stared at the house. Manuel glanced around, smirking at the awe in everyone's faces. Even Cyrus seemed pleased with what he saw.

"What did I tell you." Manuel smiled.

"You weren't kidding about the size of this place," Christian said, smiling. "This is enormous!"

"Yeah. It's huge," Nicholas exclaimed. Stretching his arms out wide, Manuel watched as he turned in a circle. "And look at all this land!"

Manuel laughed as he started to walk towards the door. "Just wait until you see the inside."

Glancing over his shoulder, he met Cyrus' coal black gaze. His brother was looking at him with the calm respect he'd always had, but his eyes also now held a distance to them. A distance that was new and unnerving. Cyrus gave him a small smile. Manuel nodded at him as he unlocked the door. Hearing the click of the deadbolt, he turned the handle, feeling the cool air from within rush past him as he stepped over the threshold.

"Open sesame," he murmured. Turning, Manuel watched as the rest followed close behind him, their eyes getting even wider than they had been outside. Standing in the center of the large foyer, Manuel gestured around him, a huge grin spreading across his face. "Welcome home, my brothers! Welcome home!"

✝

Ella glanced through the various apples on the grocery store stand. Each one looked more delicious than the next. The boys were all fans of the red Fuji apples. Something about their sweetness had the guys always wanting more. Personally, she preferred the Granny Smith apples, but seeing as they all made sure to keep chocolate in the house for her, she supposed she could get them their apples. Ella smiled as she grabbed a couple good ones and put them into the plastic bag.

"What else do we need?" Cindy asked from behind her. Ella turned to see her best friend looking over their shopping list. "Steak, potatoes, milk...*ten* boxes of mac n' cheese! Geez... These guys sure do eat a lot, don't they?"

Ella gave a little laugh in agreement. Glancing back at the different fruits and vegetables lining the wall, she couldn't help but smile. Cindy had been such a big help the last few weeks. Weeks! It felt like years since she had been kidnapped by Andras, then rescued by Christian and the boys. It had also felt like years since she had first met Christian in that dark alley. *How time does fly*, she mused, sifting through the various peppers. These last months had been the toughest.

Every night, Ella dreaded going to sleep. Her mind never seemed to rest, and when she did sleep, her dreams were haunting. Andras never really left her. She could feel him around her every second of every day. Even now. In her dreams, though, he would talk to her, try to coax her into letting him in. She would refuse, her will seeming to be getting stronger every day. Ella could sense that he knew it, too. Still, she dreaded these encounters, no matter how strong she felt. She couldn't risk underestimating him.

Then there was her constant battle to understand her new powers and control them. She figured she was doing pretty good. She hadn't blown out any more windows, so she figured that was a good sign. She also hadn't slammed anyone into a wall or started any fires in the house. *Also a very good sign*, she thought. Dealing with her powers, both new and old, was taxing, which didn't help with her nightly battles. She wished she could practice more; however, when the chance did come up, she would usually change her mind. She was so afraid of losing control, she would just freeze up, which didn't help her stress.

This had been going on ever since the first day Christian brought her back. She couldn't tell him, though. He was already worried about her, watching everything she did. Ella knew he wanted to help her, to be there for her, but she felt it best not to worry him more than he already was. There was really nothing he could do anyway, so she kept her fears and dreams from him. That was where Cindy came in.

Sure, she needed to leave out a couple details, but Cindy got the gist of what had happened. Ella knew it was really only a matter of time before her friend learned what had been going on and exactly who and what the boys were. She just couldn't deal with all the questions right now, so she told Cindy what she could. With the dreams, she hadn't needed to hold a whole lot back, and Cindy had been a great listener.

Cindy, seeming to sense her distress from the first day she walked into the boys' house, had hardly left her side...much to the guys' dismay, especially Darren. Ella smirked, remembering his expression after Cindy had come by for the third day in a row. She couldn't quite put her finger on it, but she sensed something between Cindy and Darren. Well, something besides the constant bickering and questions.

"So... Have you seen the new house yet?" Cindy asked suddenly.

Ella glanced over at her, mentally shaking her head to clear her thoughts. "No, not yet."

"It's a shame you won't be in there in time to decorate for Christmas."

Ella furrowed her brows. "Christmas?"

"Yeah. It's only a week away."

Feeling lost, Ella could only shake her head. With everything that had gone on, the holiday had completely slipped her mind. *Did the guys even celebrate Christmas?* she wondered, glancing back towards the shelves. After her grandma passed away, she had stopped celebrating it. She didn't exactly hate the holiday. She just hadn't really felt like celebrating the last five years.

"There's been so much going on, Christmas completely slipped my mind. I'm sure we'll be in a better position to celebrate next year."

Cindy nodded. "I get that. I can't wait to see what the house looks like. Once you see it, you'll have to let me know so we can start planning the decorations." She smirked, her eyes gleaming. Her love for Christmas was both endearing and concerning, bordering on obsessed. "Have the guys gone to see the house yet?"

"Actually, they were going to head over there while we shopped."

"I'm surprised Christian didn't come with us."

"He was going to," Ella admitted as they made their way towards the cereal, "but I told him we'd be fine. That we were just going grocery shopping and he should go see the house. It had taken a little work, but he finally agreed there was nothing to worry about." *He hoped,* she silently added.

"Well, I'm glad. You need a break from him every now and then."

"Cindy, we've talked about this..."

She raised her hand in mock surrender. "I'm not getting into how quickly you two moved in together, or how I think it's a little strange that he watches you like you're going to vanish. I'm just saying that every couple needs a few hours away from each other so you can have some 'you' time." Cindy shook her head, continuing to push their cart. "I'm not going to say I understand what's going on between you two, but he makes you happy and that's all that counts. Right?"

"Right." Ella sighed. "I think we're going to go to the house tomorrow so I can see it. Maybe take a couple things over that we won't need with us over the next couple days. Do you want to come?"

"I don't know," Cindy chuckled. "I don't think Darren would like me snooping around your guys' new home already."

Ella stopped and looked at her. "You know he doesn't mind you being around, right?"

"Could have fooled me, what with his sulking and brooding."

Ella just laughed. She knew Darren could be a little moody, but hearing Cindy say it was hilarious. "That's just the way he is. It's not you. Promise."

"If you say so," Cindy replied, rolling her eyes.

Ella stopped by the Lucky Charms, reaching up to grab a box. Holding it, she remembered that first night in the kitchen with Christian. Even then, she had felt such a connection with him. Looking up, she spotted Cindy chewing on her bottom lip, her eyes distant as she gazed at the boxes next to her. *I wonder if she's felt any kind of connection to any of the guys. Darren maybe?* Ella thought with a secret smile. It would be nice to have another woman around the house. Someone else to help keep the boys from getting too crazy. Before she could think of a way to bring it up, though, Cindy turned to her in a sudden huff.

"What's with Darren anyway?"

"Darren?" Ella asked, barely suppressing a smile. Reaching up to grab a second box, she waited for Cindy to elaborate.

"It's just... He's just so... I don't know. He just makes my blood boil. I try to talk to him, ask him some questions-"

"*Some* questions?" Ella cut in, raising an eyebrow.

"Fine! I may have asked him a *lot* of questions. I just figured I could ask him, get to know him... I mean, he just seemed like the one to ask!"

"And did he answer your questions?"

"Kind of. With some questions, he just talked in circles. With others, he completely ignored them. He's just so...so...frustrating!" Cindy blew a breath of air out, causing her cheeks to puff, her eyes flashing in frustration. Well, frustration accompanied by what looked like desire.

Ella had to turn away because she knew she wouldn't be able to hold back her laughter much longer. Making her way down the aisle, she just shook her head. "I don't know what to tell you, Cindy. Maybe you just need to try harder. Or maybe start over again, but don't bombard the poor guy with your questions this time."

"I didn't bombard him," Ella heard Cindy mumble.

Ella turned to look at her briefly before continuing on. "A fresh start can change everything."

"I don't know why I should even bother," Cindy said behind her. "It's not like he likes me anyway."

Ella just kept walking, silently listening to Cindy talk herself out of, then back into trying to get to know Darren. If that hint of desire in her eyes held any weight, Ella didn't think she would need to try convincing herself for very long. Getting Daren on board, well... That could prove to be a challenge. On top of that, Cindy would find out he was actually an angel.

This could get interesting, Ella thought as she turned down the next aisle. *Very interesting.*

Chapter 4

Hayley looked out her car window towards the library. She loved coming here. Today, though, everything felt different. She couldn't put her finger on exactly why. It was just a tingling in her mind. Sweeping some hair out of her eyes, she blinked furiously. The sun was bright this morning, casting a harsh glare that blurred her vision and caused her eyes to water. Nothing looked out of the ordinary, though. *It's probably just me*, she thought with a huff. The past couple weeks, although uneventful, had left her feeling tense.

If she were being honest, she had felt this way ever since Manuel first popped into her life. *Manuel*. That name rolled through her mind like a stormy wave. The minute she saw him, sparks of recognition flashed through her mind. Hayley couldn't be sure, but she had a feeling she was going to be seeing a lot more of him. He was her perfect sex dream come to life. Walking, talking, and smelling delicious. Feeling her cheeks flush, Hayley gave her head a quick shake.

Casting one last glance out the window, she opened her car door. The smell of flowers and freshly cut grass washed over her as she made her way toward the side entrance of the library. The breeze was just strong enough that as she walked through the door, the smells followed her in. Inhaling deeply, she drew the scents into her, pulling their calming essence around her like a blanket.

Walking through the library, she watched the volunteers moving quickly through the aisles, making sure every book was in place before the doors opened for the day. Every shelf was dusted, every table wiped down.

Hayley moved through the various aisles. She liked to take her time in the mornings and walk among the books, calmly making her way towards the stairway leading to her space below.

When she moved to town, she had been happily surprised to learn of this local library's hidden gem. Hayley had known immediately that she was meant to be here. Not only in this town, which she had been drawn to, but working in this library. She needed to be here. So, after settling into her new apartment, Haley set up a meeting with the gentleman who watched over the oldest section of the library. Thomas had been a little standoffish upon their meeting, but she quickly won him over. Nothing like having a comfort charm on hand to set the most defensive people at ease.

Once she had him smiling and laughing, it was fairly easy to get him to realize she was exactly what he needed. He was overworked and in need of a break. Hayley told him how he owed himself time off to take it easy and enjoy what life had to offer. She told him how she had a deep love for books and that it would be a dream come true for her to work among the library's hidden treasures. After promising him she would watch after his books, care for the library as he had, Thomas had eagerly agreed.

The very next day, Hayley had shown up to her new job.

Slowly making her way down the stairs that she'd already come to know by heart, Hayley ran her fingers along the brick walls. They were cool to the touch, but vibrated with a life not many could sense.

Hayley had always been closely in tune with the world. Her aunt had often commented on her ability to sense and commune with everything around her. Much of her life had been difficult. Hayley had gone through her fair share of ups and downs. This side of her, though...her "true side", as she liked to call it...had always come naturally.

Stepping onto the thick carpet at the bottom of the stairs, Hayley glanced around the dark room. With a flick of her wrist, she smiled as the air around her shivered and the lights flickered to life. *That never gets old!* she thought, making her way towards her desk. Gazing over the stacks of paperwork and unsorted books, she let out a sigh. As much as she loved working here, she sometimes hated the paperwork. Sifting through a couple pages, she pushed the pile to the corner of her desk. Nothing that can't be taken care of later.

Sitting in her chair, Hayley leaned back for a moment and closed her eyes. She felt her body relax immediately. Now if only her mind could be at ease, too. Her soul felt content, she was warm inside and grounded, yet her mind kept going a hundred miles a minute. Her thoughts kept jumping from that nagging feeling of something being wrong to Manuel.

Manuel.

Opening her eyes, Hayley sat back up. Ever since he had shown up, she hadn't been able to stray far from thoughts of him. What was it that drew her? Why couldn't she stop thinking about him? Better yet, why did he seem so familiar?

I need some clarity, she thought. Reaching into the bottom drawer of her desk, Hayley sifted through her various candles. "I just need...," she mumbled, going from one to the other. "Here we go." Pulling out a light blue candle, she sighed. Holding it in her hands, she already felt comforted by its weight, the coolness of its wax, the beauty of its color. "I'm in need of your wisdom," she whispered, reaching into the drawer to remove a small dish, setting it before her, delicately placing the candle upon it. Speaking softly to the air around her, she reached into the top drawer for her matches.

"Any help clearing my troubled mind would be welcome," Hayley said with a smile as she felt a light breeze tickle the back of her neck. Striking the match, she held it out in front of her. The golden flame licked the air as it grew. "I ask for your guidance."

Touching the flame to the wick, she watched as it ignited, its flame reaching high as she breathed in the candle's ocean scent. "Thank you for being with me," she whispered, blowing out the match. Sitting back, she watched the candle's flame dance, enjoying the light tingles on her arms from the air around her responding to her words. She always loved communing with the world around her. Everything had a spirit, a soul. Each had its own voice, and with air being increasingly helpful when it came to finding clarity, it was this that Hayley invoked.

Resting her head back, she closed her eyes, feeling the air move calmly around her. Taking in one breath after another, she focused her thoughts on Manuel. He was the cause of her inner turmoil and was all she could think about.

What do I do? Does he need my help, or should I stay away? she mentally asked, an image of him materializing in her mind. His amethyst eyes flashing, his short dark hair a sexy contrast against his pale skin, a small smile playing upon his lips. She smiled, recalling the warmth that had radiated off him when he stood next to her. The wonderful scent of leather and oak that had curled around her. How it had taken everything she had not to react to him.

A breeze began to swim through the room as his image became clearer. Breathing deeply, she licked her lips. *Hayley.* Although it was but a whisper, his deep voice rolled through the quiet room, sending delicious shivers down her spine. At the same time, a tingling sensation began in Hayley's fingertips as she rested them on the desk. Feeling the cool wood, she lightly ran her fingers back and forth. Reaching out farther and farther with each swipe, she suddenly touched the edge of a book. A slight vibration tickled her fingertips as she ran them along the binding.

Hayley opened her eyes and gazed at the book. "*Dierum Immortlibus,*" she whispered. The book Manuel had checked out. Pulling it from beneath the pile, she placed it before her. Hayley's eyes lingered on the old Latin writing scrolled across its cover. *It's so beautiful*, she thought.

Tracing the golden letters, she allowed herself to connect with the book. "What secrets do you hold?" she asked, gently opening it, holding her hands above it. "*Ostende mihi.*" Her palms warmed, the pages slowly beginning to flip until it finally came to a stop. A piece of loose paper fluttered up from between the pages, landing gracefully in her lap.

She picked it up, her eyes widening as she read through it. "Why would you be looking up the different levels of demons?" she muttered. She saw the word "Shadow" listed, then crossed off. The words "Missing People" were circled repeatedly, almost on an obsessive level. Shaking her head, Hayley kept reading, scanning over the random notes until she came to the last one at the bottom. "Castigo." Pausing, she felt a chill slide down her spine. Even though she had never heard that name before, it seemed to have a deep impact on her. The name also obviously held great significance for whatever Manuel was searching.

Castigo.

It tugged at her mind as it repeated itself.

Castigo.

Suddenly, like a bolt of lightning, memories began to rise to the surface. Dark alleys, suffocating fear, and heart-stopping pain. She had suppressed those dreams for so long, there was no detail to it anymore.

Closing her eyes, she watched as blurry images swam behind her eyelids. Images swarmed in and out of the light, barely making themselves known long enough to register. But one image stood out in an almost greyish glow, its essence giving off a feel of evil and destruction.

"Castigo," Hayley whispered.

Just as she started to open her eyes, another blurry image swept across her mind. This one was hued in shades of purples and white. A feeling of comfort and familiarity ran through her, giving her a sudden need to reach out to the figure, to embrace it. The purple was so vibrant, so bold, her mind immediately associated it to the first thing the color reminded her of.

"Manuel."

Her eyes flew open and she stared down at the paper before her. She needed to get to Manuel. He was going to need her. She could feel it. It was clear to her, as real as the desk beneath her hands.

Closing the book, the paper safely inside, Hayley looked at the candle, its flame still dancing. Breathing deep, she thanked the air around her for its guidance and clarity.

"I know what I need to do now. For this, I thank you."

With that, Hayley leaned towards the candle, smiling as she softly blew out the flame.

Chapter 5

"Where did I get so much shit?" Manuel grunted as he lifted another box onto his growing pile. Four boxes for his books, three for his pictures, and three for his movies...and he wasn't even halfway done yet. Looking around his room, Manuel went over and began unfolding yet another box, taping the bottom shut. He had even picked out the largest ones Nicholas had brought home. *Wonder if everyone is having this much trouble?* he thought as he walked into his closet.

His eyes wandered over all of his dress shirts, slacks, and jeans, finally landing on his leather jacket in the corner. Walking over, he smiled, running his right hand down the soft black leather. He had owned this jacket for years, longer than he cared to remember, and it was still his favorite. Of course, it had been the favorite of the thug he had taken it from, too. Manuel snickered as the memories of that day came back to him.

Walking out of the local convenience store in Buffalo, New York, after grabbing some Reese's peanut butter cups, he heard a commotion coming from behind the store. Making his way around the side of the building, he listened. He could make out a female's voice. It was high-pitched and scared, begging for the mystery offenders to leave them alone. Manuel could only assume the person with the female was the male telling the offenders to just take the cash and go.

Thieves, Manuel thought with a sneer. There was nothing he hated more than individuals who thought they could take whatever they wanted, using whatever amount of force they deemed necessary, and that their actions were justified. Most of these lowlifes had never done an honest day's work in their lives.

Coming around the corner, he found exactly what he thought he would - two want-to-be thugs holding up a couple.

One of the thugs wore his pants down around his knees, causing him to sway back and forth like a penguin as he held them up with his left hand, waving a gun in front of the couple with his right. The other thug, who was in a rather stunning leather jacket, was also brandishing a gun. Whereas the one waddling like penguin was waving his gun in every direction, the leather jacket guy was pointing his steadily in the couple's general direction. Probably the brains of the operation, *Manuel thought, rolling his eyes. He watched as Penguin gave a little hop, his voice raised. Manuel could see the thugs getting more and more agitated, the blackness of their souls practically glowing as they both continued spewing out their demands.*

The couple was in hysterics. The male tried to comfort the female, holding her behind him as he kept looking from one gun to the other. Manuel watched as the male held out his wallet, begging the thugs to take it and leave them alone. Unfortunately, Manuel could smell the excitement coming off Penguin and Leather Jacket. They were looking to get more than just cash out of this couple.

He heard Penguin laugh. It was a sickening sound, one laced with too much eagerness. Manuel watched as the man protecting his loved one jerked back in reaction. Realization darkened his eyes as he pushed the female further behind him.

Knowing things were about to get really ugly, Manuel felt the need to intervene roll through him. Moving forward, he stepped quietly so as not to startle them. He could hear the woman trying to muffle her cries into her man's back, fear radiating off her in waves almost to the point of being suffocating.

Within a split second of him beginning to move forward, Manuel saw Penguin reach out and grab onto the woman's arm. A loud scream erupted from her, cut short as she tripped over her own feet from the sudden movement, landing hard upon the ground. The male moved towards her prone figure, but Leather Jacket stepped between them, pointing his gun to force him backwards. Manuel picked up his pace, reaching them just as Penguin roughly grabbed the back of the woman's shirt, attempting to yank her up.

Moving silently, Manuel reached out and yanked Penguin back, tossing him into the concrete wall. He hit it with a sharp crack and, after a huff of breath was forced from his lungs, fell to the ground, motionless.

Turning towards Leather Jacket, Manuel was only faintly aware of the female scooting away from him. Her eyes were large as she held a hand over her mouth so as not to yell out.

"What the fuck?" Leather Jacket said, his gun still trained on the defenseless man, his eyes staring daggers at Manuel.

"Put the gun down," Manuel said. He knew this request would not be met, but figured he'd give him a chance.

Ignoring him, Leather Jacket waved his free hand towards Penguin. "Who the fuck are you? What the fuck did you do to T-Man?"

"T-Man? What's your name? Q-Man?" Manuel laughed. Glancing over towards the prone man, he smirked. "Well, it seems I threw your friend, T-Man, into the wall."

"No, fucker! My name is Pain, bitch, 'cause that's what I bring," Pain snarled. "Now, before I take you out, what's your name, fucker?"

Manuel watched his pupils dilate. He was talking a good game, but his body screamed panic. Taking a deep breath, Manuel could smell the sudden change in Pain's chemistry. "I don't think you're going to be taking anyone out...Pain."

"Listen, fucker..."

Manuel saw the gun waver in Pain's hand. His fear was spreading. Manuel contemplated savoring it for a moment longer, maybe playing with him a bit to see if he could make him pee himself. This idea was cut short when the male in front of Pain shook a little, his eyes still glued to the business end of the gun pointed at him. Resigning himself to ending this quickly, Manuel allowed his anger to seep into his eyes.

He knew the minute they changed from their deep purple to a black onyx because Pain reacted. His spine went rigid, his eyes got wider than one would think possible, and his gun hand slowly began to lower.

"Wha... Wha...," Pain stuttered as Manuel took a couple steps towards him.

In a flash, Manuel was on him. Grabbing Pain by the collar, he lifted him into the air, giving him a violent shake, the *gun dropping to the ground with a clink. Pain flailed his arms and legs as Manuel brought him close, their noses only inches from each other.*

"Don't kill me, man!" Pain gasped.

"I'm not going to kill you, you filthy piece of shit," Manuel hissed, his eyes traveling over the man. "Well, at least I'm going to try not to...but I will be taking your jacket."

Confusion mixed with fear as Pain moaned pitifully.

With one last shake, Manuel turned and effortlessly threw Pain into the wall. He heard a loud crack when his head connected with the concrete. Falling into a heap next to his pal, T-Man, his body twitched a couple times before falling still.

The male stood in shock for a moment before launching himself towards the woman. Manuel watched as she curled into a tight ball, burying her face into him as the male wrapped his arms around her.

Manuel listened to the soft murmurs as the male attempted to comfort his distraught female. Deciding to leave them to their moment, Manuel began to walk back the way he had come. Pausing, he looked over his shoulder at the two idiots lying at the base of the wall.

"I almost forgot," he whispered.

Walking towards them, he reached down, grabbing the back of Pain's leather jacket. Giving him a soft shake, he pulled it free of the unconscious body within it. Sliding the jacket on, he reveled in the feel of it against him. The material sliding along his arms, hugging his shoulders... Perfect!

Pulling his Reese's from his back pocket, Manuel left the man and woman to their own devices.

Looking at the jacket hanging in his closet, Manuel couldn't help but smile. It was still as stunning and soft as that first day.

A ringing interrupted his thoughts. With a frown, Manuel turned and walked back into his room. *Who could that be?*

He paused, looking around, his phone continuing to ring. He had so much stuff strewn all over the place, he couldn't remember where he had thrown it. Closing his eyes, he keyed his body into the sound. After the fourth ring, he opened his eyes. Walking to his bed, he reached under his pillows and pulled out his phone.

Glancing at the screen, he frowned. It was a number he didn't recognize. He would usually just ignore it, but he gave a little grunt and answered.

"Hello?" His voice sounded irritated, even to his own ears. A sharp gasp was the only response. Manuel's frown deepened. "Hello? Who's this? If this is a telemarketer, trust me when I say you have the wrong fucking-"

"Manuel?"

Manuel's breath caught. It wasn't just the sound of his name that caught him off-guard. It was the voice saying it. "Hayley?"

"Hey. I, um... I know this is kind of out of the blue, but, um... I really need to talk to you."

Manuel sat on his bed. To say this phone call was unexpected was putting it lightly. It was unreal. So much so, he never thought it would happen. Ever! "Sure, baby girl. What's goin' on?"

"I found the notes you made in the book you checked out."

"Notes?" he asked, although he knew. *Shit!* His mind went into overdrive as he tried to remember what he had written on them. Had there been anything about him or his brothers? About Ella? He didn't think so, but just to be safe... "What notes?"

He heard Hayley sigh. "Notes concerning all the missing people...and Castigo."

Manuel ran a hand through his short hair. "What about them?" His voice came out a little harsher than he intended, but he was alert now. Last thing he needed was twenty questions from a librarian...no matter how freaking hot she was.

"Listen, I can help you."

"Help me with what exactly? Those notes were just for a research paper I was working on."

"A research paper involving all the people who have gone missing over the past month or so? Research about a demon named Castigo?"

Manuel sat up straight. "How do you know about Castigo being a demon?"

"Please, Manuel. Like I said, I can help." He could hear her heart beating through the phone. "Just meet me and hear what I have to say."

Manuel opened his mouth to tell her no. To tell her that this was of no concern to her and it would be best if she just forgot about him and whatever it was she thought she knew. Before he could utter a single word, though, she cut through his thoughts.

"Please, just hear me out. If... If you don't need or want my help afterwards, I'll back off."

Something in her voice caught him. He could almost picture her green eyes narrowing as she waited for him to answer, one of her hands running through that gorgeous auburn hair of hers. It would be nice to see her again. He could use this as an excuse to be close to her, even if it were only for a short moment. Then, like she said, he could just tell her he wouldn't need her help and she would drop it.

After a moment more hesitation, Manuel finally gave in. "Okay, Hayley. Where do you want to meet?"

"Yeah?" He could hear the slight lift in her voice. "How about at the coffee shop on Main in, say, a half-hour?"

"Yeah. Sounds good, baby. I'll see you then." Slowly pulling the phone away from his ear, Manuel just stared at it as he hit END.

"Who's Hayley?"

Startled, Manuel jumped up to find Darren leaning against his door. "I didn't hear you come up."

"Obviously," he answered with a smirk. "So, who is Hayley?"

"She works at the library," he stated as he walked over to start moving some more boxes around. He needed to find his keys. Glancing back at his phone, Manuel figured if he left in ten minutes, he could get to the coffee shop before her. Looking around, he realized Darren was still standing in the doorway, staring at him. "What?"

"That's it? She's a librarian? That's all you're going to give me? Because, from what I heard of your conversation with this *librarian*, there should be a bit more of an explanation than that."

Reaching for his shoes, Manuel stopped. "Listen, I met her at the library and she wants to talk."

"About?"

"Why the twenty questions, Darren? Can't I just go and have coffee with someone without getting drilled?"

Darren frowned. "No, actually, you can't. Mainly because you've never just gone out for coffee...especially with a woman."

Now it was Manuel's turn to frown. He shook his head. "Come on, Darren. I'm just going to meet up with this chick, then I'll be back." He tried to give Darren his best shit-eating grin.

Darren looked at him for a minute, finally letting out a sigh. "Fine. I know there's more to this than you're letting on. She obviously really wanted to talk to you about something, but if you don't want to tell me what's going on, fine. Just try not to bring whatever this..." Darren waved his hand towards him in a suggestive manner, "is home with you. We're trying to get our shit packed up. Cool?"

"Yeah," Manuel mumbled, putting his shoes on. "No worries. Like I said, I'm going to meet with her, then I'll be back. I won't even be gone long enough for anyone to miss me."

"Right," Darren said, turning to leave, his unspoken thoughts giving away his doubts. "Have fun."

"Will do," Manuel said as he watched him go. After he finished tying his shoes, he reached for his keys. *I'm going to meet with her, see what she has to say, then bounce,* he thought as he headed into the hall. *Nothing more!*

Chapter 6

Dev sat still as he listened to the construction around him. It had been over a month, but the work was still going on. Rubbing his temple, he tried to fight off the headache threatening. They were way behind schedule and the boss was going to be pissed - if he weren't already.

I finally catch a break, get put in a position where I can really prove myself in this miserable existence in which I've landed, and it's all going to go up in fucking smoke because nobody knows how to stick to a fucking schedule! he thought with a groan.

Maybe there was still time to save this. If he could just get a few more workers, maybe pull a couple all-nighters, they would be able to make their grand opening deadline. Two weeks was all he had to get this club up and running. Sighing, he leaned back. Maybe his boss, Andras, would understand. *Right!* he thought, rolling his eyes. *Yeah, he'd understand. He'd understand he put the wrong person in charge and that will be the end of me.* Dev looked up at the ceiling.

Suddenly, a loud crash jolted him from his chair. "What the fuck?!" he exclaimed, running into the hallway. His temper rose with every step he took until he found himself out in the front of the bar. Dev couldn't believe his eyes. Last he had checked, a member of his team had been working on finishing the molding on the ceiling. Now all he could see was a dusty mess all over the floor, a ladder on its side, and his guy lying in a heap.

Making his way over, Dev glared down at the man. "What the fuck happened?"

Groans of pain were the man's only response. Dev looked him over, noticing both the man's legs bent at funny angles and a bone sticking out of his left arm. By the look of his head, Dev assumed the idiot had cracked it pretty good in the fall because blood had already begun to pool beneath him. The smell of it was so strong and metallic, he cringed as it tickled his nose. Dev had never been a fan of blood, no matter how much its importance fascinated him. He watched it now, almost mesmerized as the puddle grew. Blinking, he realized the amount of blood had tripled in size within a matter of seconds. Seeing it inch towards him, he moved back a bit so as not to get any on his shoes.

What a mess! he thought. Grinding his teeth, he watched the man before him whimper in pain. "We don't have time for this," Dev hissed, looking around them.

Everyone else must be working outside...or on another break, he thought with a frown.

Looking back down at the man, Dev noticed his breathing beginning to get shallow, his heart slowing. Taking a deep breath of his own, Dev concentrated on the power within him. Crouching down, he focused it on the human. Dev could feel the churning within him as he held his hands in the air. It grew steadily, sliding through every cell of his being until he was completely engulfed by it. His body vibrated for a brief moment before a calmness settled upon him. It always felt like this when he used his powers...the powers he had left anyway. Shaking away the sudden chill spreading across his skin, Dev forced his thoughts back on the body before him.

The human groaned louder as Dev violently shoved his power into the man. The sound of bones snapping, then mending reached his ears as he watched a dark glow form around them. The human began to shake violently. Normally, Dev would not push this hard to heal, but time was not on his side. Sweating profusely, the human cried out, then became still. Except for some light bruising, he was probably healthier than he had been before his fall. The man's eyes opened slowly and, with a mixture of fear and relief, he looked up at him.

"Now, get back to work." Dev stood and began to make his way back to his office. The human began to stutter, muttering about this being a miracle. Spinning back around, Dev glared at him. By the look on the human's face, he could tell that his eyes most likely were no longer their normal brilliant blue, but were now a deep black. "I said," he growled, watching the human scoot backwards, shaking as he slowly pulled himself to his feet, "get the fuck back to work."

"Ye...yes, sir!" he stammered, hurrying to retrieve his downed ladder.

"And clean this mess up!" Dev bellowed before turning and leaving the stunned man to his job. *Probably have to fix that human's memory before I let him go home*, he thought with a shake of his head. *If I allow him to head home.* He hadn't exactly hired these people with the idea of letting them go once they were done. His boss had hinted at that anyway. *What a mess!* he thought as he walked back into his office.

He was just sitting down at his desk when the phone began to ring. Still annoyed, he grabbed it without looking at the caller ID. "What?" he growled.

"Is this Dev Trissel?" a man's gravelly voice asked.

"Yes. Who's asking?"

"This is Inspector Gregors. I'm scheduled to come by and do an inspection on your club in two days."

Dev's teeth clenched as he leaned back in his chair. Damn it! How had he forgotten about the fucking inspector's visit? Damn humans and their red tape bullshit! "Right, Mr. Gregors. What can I do for you today?"

"Well, I'm hearing you may not be ready for me, which would truly be unfortunate. You see, if you're not ready, I will not be able to come back to do my inspection for another couple weeks. I would *hate* to have to push you off until then. You are supposed to be opening in two weeks, right?"

"Yes, but you're hearing wrong, sir. I will be more than ready for you. May I ask who told you I wasn't going to be ready?"

"Oh, just people." Dev could hear the smirk in the inspector's voice.

"People?"

"Yes, Mr. Trissel. People. People who have a lot riding on this club being a success."

Of course. Those sleazy investors were going to start getting their panties in a twist. Why his boss even decided to go the traditional route with this business venture he had no idea. Dev let out a sigh as he leaned forward in his seat. "Well, you tell these *people* that they have nothing to worry about. I'll be ready."

"Good. I'm glad to hear that. As I said, I would hate to have to put off your opening, just as I would hate to have to tell your boss the reason why. I don't think the outcome of that conversation would be a very good one...for you." The last words were said with a soft chuckle.

"I'll be ready," Dev hissed. When he heard the line go dead, he slammed his phone on his desk. "Fuck!"

If there was anything he hated more than being behind schedule, it was being threatened. He couldn't even go kill the bastard. The inspector was bought and payed for by Andras, along with all the other "people" he had mentioned. All of them would be more than happy to snitch to the boss if he fell short, each wanting to get their kudos and pats on the back. He hated this, but he couldn't exactly tell the boss no when he got pulled into his office, especially when he was told to lead this little project. Nobody told the boss no.

Things used to be so much different for him, so much easier. If only... Dev shook his head. He found out a long time ago that there was no use dwelling on the past. He just needed to make the best of the situation. In order to continue moving forward, continue surviving in this personal hell of his, Dev realized he was going to need help. *Double shit!*

Picking up his cell phone, he looked at it for a minute. He needed more workers if he was going to have this place ready in time. He couldn't leave to go do any recruiting, though. Asking for help was not one of his best qualities, but Dev didn't think he had any other choice. Not that he wanted to put much weight into Mr. Gregors' not-so-subtle threat, but, well... He'd seen Andras mad before, been in the line of fire more times than he would like to think about. He had no desire to end up the focus of his rage.

Scrolling through his contacts, he came to one of the few names he felt any kind of kinship with. Who or, rather, what this male was made this kind of closeness rare.

He listened to it ring once, twice, three times. "Pick up," he whispered as he stood and began to pace around the room. Finally hearing a soft click, he let out a sigh.

"Dev?" said a harsh voice.

"Hi, Sy."

"To what do I owe the pleasure of this unexpected phone call?"

"I, uh... I need some help."

"You need help?"

"Yes. Listen, I..." Dev paused as he tried to find the right way to ask the demon for a favor. He knew it was the only way this would work, but he really didn't want to do it.

"Listen, I am really busy right now, so I suggest you spit it out. I have my own...business to attend to."

"Yeah, sorry. I just really need your help with something," He listened for a response. When none came, Dev took a deep breath. "Listen, Sy, I know you're busy, but if you could just give me a hand, I, um..." Pausing by the wall, Dev turned and rested his forehead against the cool cement. He couldn't believe he was going to do this. It was not only a step just above begging, but it was the same shit that got him here in the first place. "Listen, I - I would owe you one."

"A favor, huh? You must be in a real mess to need something bad enough to be in my debt. Is that not the reason you are among us demons, my friend?" Sy asked slowly, the term "friend" being said in a whisper.

Dev ground his teeth. He didn't need a reminder of how he had gotten here. "Yes," he said slowly. "You know I don't ask for help easily, let alone place this kind of offer on the table."

"What do you need?"

Still not allowing himself to feel at ease, Dev turned and slid down the wall, sitting roughly. He contemplated the deal he could possibly be making. Sure, he felt a connection, almost something resembling trust, with this other male, but being in a demon's debt was never a good place to be. Also admitting to possibly falling in a bad way with Andras was not information to be shared lightly. In fact, depending on whose hands the information fell into, it could be downright dangerous, but he needed Sy's help.

"I'm falling behind schedule. Without some help, I don't think I'm going to be able to have this club ready in time. You know how Andras is when he gets disappointed."

"What exactly do you need from me, Dev?"

"I need some workers, but I can't go find them on my own. I need them here and ready to work as soon as possible. If I don't come through, if I fail..." Licking his lips, Dev tightened his grip on his cell. "Shit, Sy. I'm running out of time, and I can't land in a bad way with the boss. Not again."

"So if I do this for you, if I get you the help you need so you can have Andras' club open on time, you will be in debt to me? Whenever I call and whatever I need of you, you will do?"

Dev definitely didn't like the demon's wording, but... "Yes, whatever you need."

He heard a soft chuckle come across the line. "Well, how can I say no to that? I will help you, Dev, and you will open on time. Just do not forget this deal of ours as you bask in the glow of Andras' good graces. I *will* collect, and when I do, you cannot, no matter what I ask of you, say no. Do we have a deal?"

Licking his lips again, Dev ran a hand through his hair. This was not good. What the hell was he doing? The last time he made a deal with a demon, his world had been turned upside down. Not that he would ever regret his decision, even if he hadn't been fully aware of what he was getting himself into, but the fallout from it had been horrific...far worse than he could have prepared for. That deal had been made about one hundred years ago, and Dev had been paying for it ever since. The only decision he'd made since that deal was when he pledged his allegiance to Andras, swore to do whatever was asked of him, but he hadn't really had a choice in the matter. It was either pledge himself to the demon or remain in Andras' dungeon.

Shuddering, Dev pushed unwanted memories from his mind. This was different. It had to be. Could he do this without Sy's help? The answer to that, much to his dismay, was a resounding no. *Shit.*

"Yes, Sy. I will be in your debt."

"Swear it, Dev."

"I swear, upon my very existence, that I will be in your debt, that I will owe you a favor, and that I will continue to be in your debt until the time in which I can repay this favor."

"That's a good little fallen angel," Sy said softly.

Dev closed his eyes as he allowed the significance of what had just happened to fall upon his shoulders like a lead weight. It was happening all over again. This time, he had gone into the deal knowing exactly what he was doing. It was no wonder He had sent him here. Dev could still hear the amusement in the demon's voice.

"You will have your help before night's end.

"Thank you, Sy," Dev whispered.

"No, Dev... Thank *you!*"

With that, the line went dead. Placing the phone next to him, Dev took in a gulp of air, his throat suddenly feeling tight. Letting his head fall forward, he sent out a silent apology to the heavens and the very air around him...something he had been doing every day since he was banished.

Chapter 7

Manuel stood outside the coffee shop. The early afternoon breeze swirled around him, bringing with it the delicious scents of coffee and freshly baked pastries. Inhaling deeply, he relished in their enticing aromas. *Speaking of enticing*, he thought with a smile as he looked at Hayley through the window.

It had taken him a bit longer to get out of the house than it should have. Everyone was suddenly so curious about where he was going, like he'd never left the house by himself before. Hayley, on the other hand, had obviously made it here in record time. She hadn't noticed him yet, which was fine with him. It just gave him a chance to watch her, commit her beauty to memory, before he headed in to tell her to forget all about him and this crazy idea she had about helping him. If she refused, he would just have to make her forget.

Cringing, Manuel ran a hand through his hair. He didn't like messing with a human's mind, but if need be... Personal feelings aside, he did what he had to when it came to protecting his brothers and himself.

Manuel watched as she brushed her hair out of her face, the sunlight causing the red to shimmer. She was so beautiful, and not just physically. Even from this distance, he could see her pureness, her light. His very core yearned for that light. For so long, he and his brothers had known nothing except the bleakness of this world. How he would love to go in there and take her with him, finally having someone bring some light into his darkness. *If only things were different*, he thought as he watched her. Sighing, he mentally shook himself. He didn't have time for daydreams.

Manuel could tell Hayley was nervous. She rolled the coffee cup in her hands as she stared down at the table, occasionally biting her bottom lip. Almost unconsciously, he watched her reach down to the bag hanging off her chair.

Must be where the book is.

For the tenth time in so many minutes, Manuel berated himself for forgetting his notes. He had been in such a rush to get the book back to her, so concerned about how late he was and worried that she was in trouble for his carelessness, he hadn't even given his notes a second thought. With everything going on, he should have been more careful.

Growling in frustration, Manuel moved towards the door. Better to get this over with. He still had to finish packing, get his family moved somewhere safe, and get the security system up and running.

Walking into the coffee shop, he watched as her head shot up, their eyes locking as he walked over to her table. The impact her gaze had on him almost caused him to stumble.

"Hayley," he said simply, taking a seat across from her.

"Manuel," she whispered back. Her voice came across breathy, causing him to shiver.

Trying to hide his body's sudden reaction, Manuel shifted in his chair. "So, you wanted to talk." He eyed her as she licked her lips.

"Yes, I... This is going to sound silly, but I think I'm meant to help you."

"What do you mean 'meant to help me'?"

She closed her eyes briefly. He could almost see the uncertainty on her face. Waiting, Manuel noticed she had gone back to rolling her coffee cup in her hands, squeaking it against the worn table. Reaching out, he laid his hand upon hers, stopping her nervous motion. Her eyes flew open, first staring down at his hand on hers, then up to his face. Manuel sucked in a breath as her green eyes flashed.

Pulling back his hand, he felt his cheeks warm. *I'm freaking blushing*, he thought with a mental shake. *This is ridiculous.* "Sorry," he mumbled.

Hayley just smiled. Slowly, she took a sip of her coffee, her shoulders relaxing. "No, Manuel. *I'm* sorry. I shouldn't have called you like that. It's just... When I found those notes, things started to stand out..."

"Like the name Castigo?"

"Yes. I know this sounds crazy, Manuel, but when I saw your notes, I knew I needed to talk to you. To help you."

"And how exactly do you think you can help me?" Manuel asked, getting more and more confused by the minute. "Look, Hayley, I'm really busy right now. I have no idea where this conversations is going, so-"

"I grew up dreaming about you... About you and the demon Castigo!"

Blinking several times, Manuel frowned. "I'm sorry... What?"

Manuel watched Hayley run her fingers through her hair, her green eyes darting from the table to his face and back. "I told you it sounded crazy, but it's true. All I ask is you just hear me out." She paused for a minute, her eyes searching his. Frowning further, Manuel gave her a slight nod. He watched her let out a breath before continuing. "In my dream, I'm running through a city. I'm not sure where, but the streets are deserted. I run several blocks until I come to an alley and hear a lot of yelling. I see you...or, rather, your aura, and I just know I am there to help. I think you and Castigo are fighting, and there are others around you.

"I haven't thought about that dream in a long time. I mean, when I saw you the other day, I knew I had seen you somewhere before. I haven't been able to stop thinking about you. It's like I'm drawn to you or something. When I saw your notes, everything just came rushing back."

Manuel's mind raced as he went over everything she had said. *She's dreamt about me?* That was, well... He didn't really know. It was definitely a first. *She was drawn to me? Couldn't stop thinking about me?* Hearing that was probably the hottest thing... Shit, if he weren't so baffled by this whole thing, he would probably take her right here. He was sure he looked like an idiot because he kept opening his mouth to say something but, for the life of him, he had no idea what to say. Hayley must have sensed that because she rushed on.

"I know you're probably wondering how I'm going to be able to help you," she said nervously.

Manuel watched as she slowly licked her lips, causing a heat to rise in him as her pink tongue disappeared back into her mouth. Images of taking her bottom lip into his mouth flashed though his mind. *Damn!* Barely stifling a groan, he suddenly realized she had continued talking.

"Hmm?" he hummed, meeting her brilliant green eyes. "What did you just say?"

She smiled at him. "I said I have a gift of sorts that I think could be really helpful. I mean, I wouldn't normally tell anyone this, but given your, um...interests, I figured you would believe me."

His mind clearing instantly, Manuel leaned back in his chair. "What kind of a gift? And what do you mean by my 'interests'?" If she knew he was a fallen angel, this conversation was about to take a totally different turn.

"Castigo, the demon," Hayley whispered, leaning forward slightly. "Like I mentioned on the phone. So you must be a... What? A demon hunter? I mean, I have never heard of anything like that before, but..." She laughed a little, her eyes searching his.

Demon hunter? Manuel tapped his finger on the table. That was another new one, but why not? Why wouldn't she think he was a demon hunter? It wasn't like there was anything in his notes that screamed fallen angel.

Thank the heavens for that!

Deciding that allowing Hayley to think he was a demon hunter would probably be the best for now, Manuel just nodded.

Smiling, she took a deep breath, seeming pleased with being right about what he was. Manuel smiled back.

"So," he said slowly. "Back to this gift of yours..."

"I'm a witch," Hayley said matter-of-factly, her green eyes staring into his, almost daring him to not believe her.

"A witch." Manuel's mind flipped through any information he and his brothers had come across concerning witchcraft. Of course, a lot of it were myths. The whole flying around on a broomstick, although funny, was not real. Neither was the green skin and warts. Although Manuel was sure there were some out there with a wart or two decorating an already pimpled mug, it wasn't due to being a witch. Having never come across one in person, Manuel could only go with what he had heard and, if his memory served him right, there were two types of witches...those who practiced dark magic and those who practiced white.

Nicholas had talked briefly about a run-in he had with a witch over twenty years ago. A run-in that, if he were remembering correctly, hadn't exactly ended well. Something about hexes and crows with red eyes. Definitely not the kind of witch Manuel had any desire to ever run into, let alone deal with. Now, a white witch, on the other hand... Who knew? Could be helpful.

So the question was if Hayley were indeed a witch like she claimed to be, exactly whose side did she really stand on? Well, there was one way to find out.

Taking a deep breath, Manuel reached out with his senses. Instantly, he could feel her nervousness. Like a storm, it washed over him in waves. Not that he needed his heightened senses to know that. Her anxiety was practically written all over her face. Lowering his eyes to the table, he concentrated on looking deeper, past her outward emotions. He felt for her soul, hoping it was pure because if it wasn't... Well, he didn't really want to think about that. He'd seen her light from out on the street, but not knowing much about witches, he had to take a closer look. What if that enticing light had been a cover, something to hide behind? He allowed her warmth to surround him as his power flexed and flowed over her.

Manuel paused for a second in his search as a sudden burst of energy shot out. *What the...?* Confused, he grasped onto this power, curling his around it as he tried to get a feel for what kind it was. It was definitely Hayley's, but that was all he could tell. Manuel could sense the resistance as her power reacted to his, trying to fend him off, but he pushed on. Then, with a sudden jerk, he hit a wall. Her power shot up around her, shoving him out. Blinking, he pushed harder, attempting to get past this sudden barrier. Nothing.

Hearing Hayley clear her throat, Manuel glanced up and focused back on her.

"Manuel?" she asked. He couldn't tell if she were aware of the inner battle they just had, but as he watched her eyes travel over his face, Manuel saw nothing but worry across her beautiful features. She was probably looking for some reassurance that she hadn't been wrong in telling him what she was. He wanted to give it to her, but the worry beginning to build in him was undeniable. She was strong...and definitely not a normal human.

"Um...," he started, then stopped. *What do I say?* he thought. *Should I just tell her she should forget all this, send her on her way, and save my brothers and myself from getting into a possibly sticky situation? Or should I just say "screw it" and take her with me?* Taking another deep breath, he studied her as she sat across from him. Her green eyes flashed, her bottom lip pulled in slightly between her teeth as she nibbled at it. Manuel's guard was still down, so he could now feel her power swirling around her, but it wasn't trying to reach out to him, attack him. It was almost...protecting her. "Hayley, I..."

He stopped when she reached out and laid a hand on his arm. The warmth from her fingers trickled across his skin. He tensed slightly, waiting for her power to rip through him. When nothing happened, he glanced from her hand to her face. Hayley's eyes held his as she gave him a soft smile.

"Please, Manuel. I really do want to help."

"Shit," he whispered, causing her smile to grow a little. Darren was going to kill him. Hell, they were all going to kill him. Looking into her eyes, though, feeling her calming warmth surround him, he just couldn't say no. "Okay, Hayley... What did you have in mind?"

She leaned back and gave him an award-winning smile. "Why don't we start by telling me why you were looking for this Castigo character?"

Grunting, Manuel glanced around the coffee shop, then back at her. "I really can't go into details, but let's just say I think he's involved in a string of recent disappearances."

"How recent?"

"The past month or so. People have just been disappearing, weird shit, and I think it's demonic." His voice was just above a whisper as he watched the humans around them go about their day.

"Do you think it's just him behind it, or are there others?"

Images of Cyrus diving into a group of demons, and Andras, with help from Castigo and another unknown demon, attacking him and his brothers down in Hell flashed through Manuel's mind as he looked back at her. "I think there may be a few others," he stated flatly.

"How many?"

"At least ten, if not more," he sighed.

"Ten? Please tell me you aren't the only one trying to hunt them down." Her voice rose slightly as she tried to keep her emotions under control. "My god, Manuel. They could kill you."

"Naw, I'll be fine," he replied quietly, smiling slightly. "Anyway, it's not just me. I have my brothers."

Chapter 8

Hayley watched as Manuel's eyes flashed. The deep purple seemed to take on a soft glow, but only for a split second. It happened so fast, if Hayley hadn't been staring right into them, she wouldn't have seen it. *Interesting.*

They had been staring at each other for some time now. Since Manuel told her he had help tracking down the demons, Hayley felt a tightness she hadn't even been aware of loosening in her chest. The thought of him having to go up against these demons alone had not only angered her, but scared the hell out of her. What if something happened to him? What if they took him? Killed him?

A shiver ran down her spine and she gave her head a quick shake. There was no way she would let him do this alone. Even with his claim to have help, she silently vowed to be by his side, as well. Not that she didn't think he could take care of himself. He was by no means a small man, nor did he look weak. Hayley's eyes traveled from his face to his wide shoulders and muscular arms.

No, not weak at all.

However, she also knew he had a secret. She had sensed a power flare out from him, wrapping around her with a strength she had never felt before. It had happened so quickly, pushing against her barriers like a tank, that if she hadn't been used to keeping her wall tightly in place, he would have broken through. There was definitely more to Manuel than met the eye.

An urge to confront him had instantly taken over, but when she opened her mouth to question him, the quick look of uncertainty crossing his face had given her pause. Whoever he was would have to remain a mystery, at least for the time being. It was obviously a secret he didn't seem eager to share.

So she attempted to steer her mind towards other, more immediate concerns. Questions kept forming, though. Like whether she had been a little too eager to jump to the conclusion he was a demon hunter. It had made sense at the time. To a certain extent, it still did. Now, though, Hayley was starting to reconsider.

Seeing his muscles tense slightly, she looked back up at his face. Hayley felt her cheeks warm at the directness of his gaze. She hadn't realized she had been staring at him. Not that she should be surprised. Ever since he walked through the coffee shop door, she had hardly been able to look anywhere else. He was, by far, the sexiest man she had ever seen. This idea was only heightened by the fact that everything about him, from his boots to his piercing gaze, screamed danger. He was the kind of man she had always stayed clear of, yet she wanted nothing more than to tackle him to the ground and not let him up until she knew every inch of him intimately.

Snap out of it, she thought. She didn't really know anything about him. For all she knew, his dangerous outward appearance could be an all-too-real fact. *What if* he *were a demon?* Shaking her head, she dismissed that thought right away. There was no way she would be meant to help a demon. No way at all.

"How exactly do you plan on helping me?" Manuel asked, his voice growling through her thoughts. His face remained completely impassive, almost bored, and if she hadn't just seen the briefest flash of amusement in his amethyst eyes, she would have sworn he was about to doze off. Maybe even begin humming and tapping a little tune on the table to show her how unimpressed he was with what she was offering...or maybe with her in general. Hayley had tried to look nice for this meeting, changing her outfit a good five times before finally throwing her hands in the air in frustration. She didn't even know him, but looking nice for him pleased her for some reason. Suddenly realizing he was still talking, Hayley gave herself a mental shake.

"I'm just not clear," Manuel was saying, "on how you working with herbs is going to get me any closer to solving my problems."

Blinking, she felt her eyes get wide as she stared at him. Was he serious? He really thought all she did was play with herbs all day? Sighing, Hayley reached for her coffee, attempting to hide her irritation. "I assure you... I do a lot more than work with herbs all day."

"Really?" His gaze traveled lazily over her. "What exactly do you do then? Chant over cauldrons? Fly on broomsticks?"

Choking, Hayley practically spit her coffee all over him. "*Broomsticks*?" He shrugged. "I hardly ride around on a broom!" she replied with a grunt.

Manuel raised his hands, palms toward her. "I was only kidding."

"Right."

"Seriously...," Manuel said, coughing to cover up his laugh. "How do you plan on helping?"

"I don't really feel like going into all of that here. There are too many people around, and there are certain things that need to be shown rather than explained. Let's just say I have a lot of...talents."

"Fair enough. These *talents* are going to help me then?"

"Yes."

Hayley watched as he leaned back in his chair, a look of contemplation on his face as he studied her. She couldn't tell if Manuel believed her or not. There was a chance he was just continuing their conversation to humor her. Hell, he still hadn't told her how he even got involved in looking for Castigo or what his notes meant. Hayley didn't even know if he had found what he needed from the book now in her bag.

One thing Hayley did know was she needed him to take her seriously, to show him she could help. Thinking fast, she leaned forward. "Listen, just give me a chance. Let me show you how much of a help I can be. We can go out and I can lead you to a demon-"

"A demon?"

"Yes, a demon. I'll lead you to a lower-level one, a Shadow, so you can see that not only can I help you track them, I can also help you deal with them once we have."

"You want to go on a hunt with me?" The question came out laced with uncertainty, his eyes narrowing slightly.

"Yes, I want to go on a hunt with you and your brothers."

"Why?"

"Why what?"

"Why are you so determined to do this? To prove yourself?" He shook his head. "Why do you want to help me?"

"Because..." Hayley licked her suddenly dry lips. "You're going to need me with you, to help you...just as much as I *need* to help you."

Holding her breath, she watched him sit quietly across from her. She could practically see his mind working. Seeming to come to a decision, he sighed and ran a hand through his hair. When he opened his mouth to respond, a sudden ringing made him pause. Reaching into his pocket, Hayley watched as he took out his cell. Swiping his finger across the screen, he gazed at it, his eyes narrowing as he read over whatever message had come through. Hayley saw several different emotions cross his handsome face, irritation and uneasiness being the more prominent ones. She was just about to ask if something was wrong when he began to stand.

"I have to go," he simply said, his eyes never leaving hers as he began to step away from the table.

"Wait. You can't just leave... I mean, you *can,* I'm not going to try to keep you here, but we haven't finished talking yet. You never said-"

Raising his hand, Manuel interrupted her. "Listen, Hayley, I appreciate your desire to help. I truly do. I'm just not sure this is a good idea."

"Manuel," she started, slowly rising from her seat. "I know you don't know me, don't trust me-"

"Hayley, I-"

"No. It's okay, Manuel. I understand," Hayley rushed out in a hushed voice, still trying not to draw too much attention to them. "I don't know a thing about you and, under normal circumstances, I would just walk away from this. But these aren't normal circumstances. My very being is telling me I need to help you. That this is what I have been moving towards ever since I was born. I can't deny my instincts. I learned a long time ago that fate is a very real factor in this world, and my fate has lead me to you. Just give me a chance to prove it."

Manuel stood there for a moment. She watched him shift slightly as he pushed his chair into the table. Bracing himself against the back of it, Hayley held her breath as he stared down at the table like it was going to give him whatever answer he was searching for. "Okay, Hayley. I'll give you a chance." Looking off to the side, he seemed to become briefly lost in thought, his features tight, as though the thought of her helping was more painful than anything else.

"I really *will* be able to help you. I promise not to get in the way, either."

"I'm not worried about you getting in the way, Hayley," he said, glancing back at her.

"Then what are you worried about?" she whispered, her breath catching.

His features softened slightly. "I'm worried about *you*. I would never forgive myself if I dragged you into this and something happened to you."

Shaking her head, Hayley gave him a small smile. "First off, you aren't *dragging* me into anything. I'm practically throwing myself at this..." Hayley waved her hands between them, "whatever *this* is. Secondly, I can take care of myself." As a look of doubt flashed over his handsome features, she pressed on. "Really, Manuel. I'll be fine. Listen... If and when things start to get too crazy, I'll back off. I promise. Okay?" Not that she really planned on leaving when he needed her most. However, if it put his mind at ease and made him feel better about bringing her along, she would make this promise.

When he nodded slowly, Hayley let out a breath she hadn't realized she'd been holding.

"Okay, Hayley. I still need to talk to my brothers about this, but I'll give you a call in, say, three days. We'll go out, try and set things up, and see what you can do for us." He stared as her a second more before turning to leave.

Hayley watched as he made his way out of the coffee shop, noting how every female in the building had her eyes on him, following his departure...including her.

As he walked out the door and disappeared from view, she slowly sat back down. Her body relaxed slightly as she thought over their conversation and what she needed to do now. She wasn't even angry that he hadn't said goodbye. In a way, she supposed he had, promising he'd call. She would take what she could get.

First things first, she needed to stop by the store to pick up some supplies. Finding demons took a lot more than just wishful thinking on her part. A few days was all she had to get ready. She didn't need to make a huge show of it. Manuel seemed more like a factual, the end result was what mattered kind of guy. He was going to be tough, skeptical, and obstinate. He would learn, though. She would show him she could be trusted.

Baby steps with this one! she thought, taking a sip of coffee. She had gotten him to agree to give her a chance. She had actually been prepared to bribe him into letting her help. If he shut her down, she had even considered stalking him until he needed her. So this was more than she had hoped for.

She would get ready, make sure everything she needed was in order, then wait for his call.

Three days.

She wasn't used to going by someone else's schedule, but she would for him.

Hayley felt her lips twitch at the corners as she lifted her coffee cup. "Okay, Manuel... Okay."

Chapter 9

Manuel pulled up to the curb. Staring out the window, he gazed at the aging one-story house. A couple days from now, they would be moved into their new home. This one, and everything that had happened since they moved into it, would become nothing more than a memory.

They were all overdue for a fresh start; hopefully, the new house would be the beginning of that. As much of one as they could get anyway. He was sure their problems would not be far behind them. If the feeling in his gut was any warning, Manuel didn't even think they would get another week. Maybe with Hayley's help, if she could help, they would be able to find the demons before the demons found them.

Hayley.

How in the hell was he going to tell his brothers about her offer, let alone convince them it would be worth giving her a shot? Shaking his head, he turned off his car. Crap. He didn't even know if it would be worth it. Telling her they would give her a chance to prove herself had been a knee-jerk reaction to the pleading look in her eyes. He just couldn't seem to tell her no, even when he knew he should. The text from Darren reminding him that he needed to get home had come at both the best and worst time. The longer he'd sat across from Hayley, the more he'd wanted her. Putting space between them was what he needed to get his mind working again.

Getting out of the car, Manuel was just closing the door when he felt a wave of energy rush over him, hitting him hard. It would have knocked him flat on his ass if he hadn't been holding onto the door handle. It was so strong, he could practically see the house windows begin to bow, the wood frame around them cracking as it expanded. Gritting his teeth, Manuel braced himself, his back muscles bunching as his own power began to respond. He needed to stay in control, not lose it in the middle of the street. His very bones ached under the strain, sweat running down his face and back as he willed himself to calm down. Then, just as suddenly as it started, the pressure vanished.

"What the hell?" he muttered, pushing away from his car. His breath came out in short, ragged bursts as he attempted to slow his racing heart.

Quickly walking towards the door, he shook his head when he heard yelling. Several voices seeped through the walls and reached his ears. Manuel paused, his hand hovering just above the doorknob. He already had so much on his mind. Did he really need to step into what sounded like a war zone? He should just turn around, get back in his car, and drive away. Pulling his hand back, he was ready to do just that when he heard Ella's voice raised above the chaos. Fear and anguish laced every one of her words, ripping at his heart. Throwing the door open, Manuel stepped into the house just as Ella came around the corner.

"I told you this was a bad idea!" she yelled, coming to a quick stop and spinning around. Her hands waved in the air as Christian came into view.

"Ella, sweetheart-"

"I almost blew the windows out of the damn house, Christian. Again!"

"But you didn't."

"The whole house shook!"

"Yes, but everything is fine. Listen, darling, it's going to take time. I told you I would be right by your side to help you."

"Great! Be by my side so that the next time my powers go all *mass destructo* on me, you'll be there to take the brunt of it." Her face scrunched up as a tear rolled down her cheek. "I don't want to hurt you. I don't want to hurt any of you."

"You're not going to hurt us, honey. I promise. We're going to be fine. You do need to practice, though."

"But-"

"Ella, sweetheart, everything's going to work out," Christian said softly, slowly walking towards her.

Manuel watched quietly as his brother walked up to Ella, pulling her into his arms as she released a strangled sob. She had been trying so hard to get her powers under control. Well, the ones they knew about anyway. According to some of the research he had done, her powers would reveal themselves to her in stages, supposedly coming out when she was in a stressful situation. Her first ability, the gift of sight, came when her friend had been abducted back in high school.

Her second gift appeared during an argument between Christian and Cyrus. Manuel hadn't been there for that incident, he and Nicholas had their hands full at the time, but he heard it had escalated quickly. They had all thought her blowing out the windows was the extent of it, but they were wrong. Her new gift was why, when they were in Hell, she was able to stop a bullet meant for Christian, as well as throw Andras and his demon posse around like rag dolls.

It had been quite a sight.

Since their return from Hell, Ella wanted to practice her newfound abilities. However, every time they started to do just that, she changed her mind. Her fear of hurting someone or losing control would always stop her, overshadowing the good that could come out of it. Sure, she had a few small power flares, like when she had stubbed her toe in the middle of the night and shattered the bathroom mirror. But, for the most part, she had been able to control those. It was controlling her powers in a larger sense, being able to call them forth when she needed them, that was the giant elephant in the room.

It looked like Ella had decided to put her fears aside and give controlling her power another try. Obviously, practice hadn't gone well.

Manuel watched as Christian rocked her a little bit, running his hands up and down her back in a soothing motion. He glanced towards Manuel, a plea in his eyes. Sighing, he quietly closed the door.

"Maybe we can reinforce the walls of one of the rooms in the new house so Ella can practice without worrying about windows and such," Manuel said slowly, taking a step towards the couple. At the sound of his voice, Ella turned her head to peer at him.

"Do you think that would help?" she asked, her voice sounding slightly shaky. Her bloodshot eyes searched his as she pulled her head away from Christian.

"Ella, for you, we'll *make* it work," Manuel promised as he glanced up and met Christian's gaze, giving him a small nod. Relief instantly radiated off his brother.

Thank you, Christian mouthed before pulling back and holding Ella's face in his hands. "See," he said with a soft smile. "I told you everything's going to be fine. We'll get a room fixed up for you and get you practicing with your powers. Before you know it, you'll be so in control of them, it'll be like they've been with you all along." Leaning forward, Christian placed a kiss on her forehead.

Hating to break up this moment, Manuel almost decided to wait until another time to gather his brothers and tell them about Hayley. A sudden tightening in his chest changed his mind. He didn't know why, but he just knew he shouldn't wait. Maybe it was his need to just get this conversation out of the way, God knew it was probably going to be anything but smooth, or maybe it was that he had a feeling something was coming - something for which they would need to be prepared. Gazing at Christian and Ella a minute longer, Manuel let out a soft cough.

Christian, his blue eyes still dancing with relief, glanced his way. "And where have you been?" he asked.

Manuel opened and closed his mouth a couple times, attempting to figure out where to even begin. "Out."

"Out?" Christian frowned.

By now, Ella had turned her head to stare at him, too. Her curious look caused him to feel an unfamiliar warmth in his face. "I may have found someone who can possibly help us with our demon problem."

"Really?" Christian asked with a raised eyebrow.

"Who?" Ella asked at the same time.

Looking between the two of them, Manuel suddenly realized he wanted to run this past his brothers before bringing Ella into it. It wasn't that he didn't want her input on this matter. He just had a feeling some of the boys might not be so happy to hear about his little meeting with Hayley. If an argument did happen, he didn't want Ella there, especially after the last argument she was witness to. No need to bring on another power rush so soon after calming her down from the last.

As if reading his mind, Christian gave him a knowing look, then turned his loving gaze to Ella. "Honey, why don't you go take a nice bath. I can feel the tension still radiating off you."

Ella glanced back and forth between the two of them. Manuel watched as the confusion flitting across her face slowly turned into a frown as she looked ready to start arguing. Sensing this, Christian gave her a quick kiss and turned her towards their bedroom. "Okay, but don't think you two are going to leave me out of whatever is going on," she said with a huff, narrowing her eyes at both of them to further show her unhappiness about being dismissed.

"I promise, Ella. As soon as we're done, I will personally fill you in," Manuel said.

"Okay," she replied slowly. "I expect to be filled in...on *everything*!"

"Of course, love." Christian gave her ass a playful little tap. "Now, off with you."

Ella rolled her eyes and turned to head down the hall, although not before Manuel saw a smile play upon her lips. He just shook his head. She was a feisty one, and he didn't know where his brother would be without her.

"So, what's going on?" Christian asked, his voice pulling Manuel's attention his way.

"Let's get everyone together," Manuel answered with a sigh. Running a hand through his short hair, he ground his teeth, tension building in his shoulders. He was not looking forward to this. "If you wouldn't mind going to find Nicholas and Cyrus, I'll go find Darren."

"Yeah. No problem, brother," Christian said, concern in his voice.

Manuel watched him make his way through the house. Taking several deep breaths, he stood there a moment longer before heading towards the office. Even down the hall, he could hear the clicking of keys as Darren typed away on their computer. He almost spent more time on that old thing than Manuel did. Almost.

Lightly tapping on the door, Manuel reached down and let himself in. "Darren?"

"Back so soon from your little get-together with the librarian? I take it you got my message?" Darren asked with a chuckle, not even looking up.

"I *told* you I wouldn't be long. Your little text to remind me wasn't needed."

Darren laughed, turning from the computer to look at him. "So you did. How'd it go?"

"That's kind of why I came to see you."

He lifted an eyebrow and leaned forward in his chair. "Really? What's going on?"

"Well, I was actually hoping to get everyone together so I only have to go over it once."

Darren looked at him. Manuel could practically feel his brother trying to figure out what was going on. Moments felt like hours as they stood there. Finally, with a nod, Darren stood up and made his way towards him. "Okay, Manuel. Let's get everyone together."

Manuel moved to the side as Darren walked past him. He could feel the confusion and curiosity radiating off his brother as he lead the way towards the dining room. Entering behind Darren, Manuel could feel tension in the air. It had been a while since they had all gotten together like this. The last time was when Darren had linked together a bunch of strange disappearances. That felt like ages ago. Moving to take his seat, Manuel looked up to see everyone watching him. Cyrus, glass of whiskey in hand, glared at him. Not that he would expect anything else. It could be the most gorgeous day out and he would find something to scowl about. Nicholas, on the other hand, was studying him, his red eyes flashing as he looked at him curiously. Hearing a throat clear, Manuel glanced over to find Darren eyeing him thoughtfully.

"So, brother, what's going on?" he asked.

Licking his lips, Manuel pondered on where to start. Shaking his head, he figured there was no place like the beginning. "So, you know when I got the book *Dierum Immortalibus* from the library a couple weeks back?" He looked around the table. "Well, there was this librarian who took over Thomas' position, and she-"

"*Please* tell us this is not about some female you have a thing for!" Cyrus exclaimed in a growl.

"Thomas isn't there anymore?" Nicholas asked. "I really liked that guy."

"You just liked the fact that he would laugh at your sorry ass jokes." Cyrus glanced at Nicholas with a scowl.

"Hey, my jokes are funny," Nicholas said with a smirk, lifting his chin, his red eyes flashing. "And you know it. Just because you always need to be Mr. Doom and Gloom, refusing to laugh, is on you. It definitely doesn't mean my jokes aren't funny. It just means you need to lighten up."

Christian, who had been quiet up to this point, slammed his hand down on the table as he let out a loud laugh.

Cyrus just shot him a glare before looking back at Nicholas. "Listen here, you little shit-"

"That's enough," Darren bit out, causing all of them to look at him. He glanced around the table, his gaze finally landing back on Manuel. "What about this librarian?"

"She... Well, after I dropped the book back off, she..." Pausing, Manuel shook his head, attempting to get his thoughts in order.

"She what, Manuel?" Christian asked, his head tilted slightly to the side.

"I forgot some notes in the book when I returned it and she found them."

"What kind of notes?" Darren asked.

Glancing down at the table, Manuel lightly drummed his fingers on the cool wood top. Taking a deep breath, he looked up, meeting Darren's gaze. "They had to do with the possible connection between the missing people and the different levels of demons. They were just random notes, page numbers, keywords..." Sighing, he glanced around the table. "I also had a couple notes written down about Castigo. It seems she recognized his name on some level."

The silence in the room was deafening. He saw Darren's eyes narrow. Waiting patiently for any of them to say something, Manuel just sat there, glancing briefly from one face to another.

"Like, she's *met* him?" Nicholas asked quietly.

"No, not in person."

"What do you mean by that?" Cyrus asked, his face tight with anger. "What did they do? Skype?"

"What? How the hell do you know about Skype?" Raising his hand, Manuel growled. "Never mind. No. She...she said she had a dream about him. More precisely, about him and *me*."

"What?"

Manuel shook his head. "I don't know how to explain everything she told me. She called me up and asked to meet. Said she found my notes and that she thinks she can help. When I went to meet with her-"

"You went to meet with this stranger?" Christian hissed. "Alone?"

"Yes. We met in the coffee shop downtown," Manuel said quickly before pushing on. "Anyway, when we met up, she told me she would be able to help me, help us, and that she has been dreaming about me since she was young."

"Now I've heard everything," Cyrus bit out, standing.

"Sit down!" Darren said, anger flashing though his eyes.

"But this is fucking ridiculous."

"Cyrus!"

"You really want us to sit here and entertain the notion that there is some nutjob out there who claims to be able to help us? Not only that, but she's been dreaming about our dear Manuel since she was a kid? Are you kidding me?"

"She isn't some nutjob," Manuel hissed.

"Oh, really? And you know this from a conversation over a latte? Is that it? You sit down with some chick and, all of a sudden, you think you know everything about her? Is that how this works?"

Manuel felt his muscles clench as a wave of anger swept through him. "You have no idea what you're talking about."

"Oh, wait! It must be because she claimed to have dreamt about you. Yeah, that's it. You're so fucking desperate to have someone in your life that when the first bitty shows you any attention and claims to see you in her dreams, you get so twisted up, you don't see her for the fake she is!"

"Fuck, Cyrus-" Christian started.

"No! You said she knows about Castigo. Well, who's to say she isn't working for him? Did you think about that when you were gazing lustfully at her from across the table? Shit, why didn't you just bring her home? Wouldn't be the first time someone's decided to bring home a new pet!"

Christian stood up with such force, his chair flew back into the wall. "What...in...the...*fuck*...is...that...supposed ...to...mean?!"

"You'd better watch your fucking mouth!" Manuel spit out as he also stood up, rolling his shoulders as tension built.

"What are you going to do about it, pretty boy?" Cyrus hissed at Manuel, his black eyes glowing. He looked at Christian. "And you know *exactly* what I mean."

Before Manuel could blink, Christian was across the table. He slammed into Cyrus so hard, they both crashed into the next room. When Manuel and Nicholas moved forward, they were stopped by Darren. Shaking his head, Darren eyed the two as they rolled around on the floor, exchanging punches as they slammed into the surrounding furniture.

"You sorry piece of shit!" Christian bit out, slamming his fist into Cyrus' face, the impact sending his head bouncing solidly off of the floor. "You fucking take that back!"

A growl from Cyrus was the only response as he violently twisted around, sending Christian over his head and into the wall behind them.

"Fuck you!" Cyrus yelled, blood running down his face from the fresh gash on his cheek. Jumping to his feet, he started to lunge at Christian.

"*Enough!*"

Jumping, they all turned around. Ella stood there with her arms crossed, her eyes flashing as she took in the scene before her. Manuel watched as Christian slowly got to his feet.

"Really? This is how you guys have a family meeting?"

"Honey," Christian started, his words coming out a little rough. "It's just a little disagreement."

"A little disagreement?" She shook her head. Turning her gaze towards Manuel, he felt her power licking out around her. "And what, pray tell, was this little disagreement about?"

Before Manuel could even think of a response, Cyrus gave a low growl. "It's about Manuel's new female friend and how she wants to *help* us."

Ella glanced at him, then back at Manuel. "Why would you guys be fighting over that?"

"It's not really over that, per se," Nicholas started. "What they were fighting about is a little more...personal. Right now, I think we need to figure out what to do about... What did Cyrus call her? Manuel's new friend? We just don't know if we should trust her or not."

"Why? Who is she?"

"Her name is Hayley. I *know* we can trust her," Manuel spoke up. He could feel his anger slowly receding as he thought about his conversation with Hayley. She had been so honest when she talked about helping them. He knew she really wanted to. He wasn't sure about her helping, but trusting her? He just knew they could do that. He could feel it.

"How Manuel?" Darren asked.

"I just know," he said with a shrug.

"And how do you know she isn't some kind of demon?" Cyrus asked, his lips twisted into a snarl. "She may just be playing you for a fool."

"I know for a fact she's not a demon," he responded, squaring his shoulders as he faced his angry brother.

"How?" Cyrus snarled.

"Because, brother," Manuel stated slowly, "she's a witch."

Chapter 10

"That went well," Manuel muttered as he stormed into his room, slamming the door behind him. Not that he had really expected the conversation to be a walk in the park, but he also hadn't expected it to feel like a war.

Once he had revealed she was a witch, all hell broke loose. Cyrus had blown up, and Nicholas, much to his surprise, had turned into an instant asshole, saying how he couldn't believe Manuel would be stupid enough to fall for some witch's lies. He had gone on and on until Manuel thought the veins in his head were going to burst from the amount of anger pulsing through them.

He couldn't believe it. They were acting like he had just told them they should make a deal with the devil. Then there were Darren and Christian. For all their opinionated, loudmouth qualities, they had just stood there, staring at him, their mouths opening and closing.

Absolutely no help at all.

Even Ella had just stood there. He knew this conversation was a bit out of her depths, but shit. She could have at least attempted to stand by him.

Seething, Manuel began to pace. All he asked was that they just give Hayley a chance. He may have reservations about her helping them, but those uncertainties had nothing to do with her intentions.

His bedroom window shook as his pace quickened.

When he looked at Hayley, Manuel could tell she truly felt she could help. He didn't sense any darkness around her or that she was harboring any secret agenda. It wasn't like they were getting anywhere on their own. Manuel had been through all their books a hundred times over. There was nothing in them about any of the shit that was now going on, so why not let someone else try? If Hayley could help, they would be closer to taking care of this mess. If not, well... It wasn't like it would hurt anything.

After what just happened, he wasn't just going to consider her request to help them. He was going to push for it. Hell, he was going to demand it out of principle. After all he had done, how could his brothers be so quick to write his opinion off? He'd never asked them for anything, not even a fucking dollar. One would think they would at least be willing to listen to what he had to say. Once the word "witch" left his mouth, he should have just left the house. It would have saved him the trouble of standing there while he was talked down to.

"Assholes," he breathed out as he paused in his pacing.

Feeling tension running through his back, Manuel closed his eyes and took a deep breath. He could hear the walls around him beginning to crack in reaction to his anger. Power rolled across his skin as he let his head fall back. Standing in the middle of the room, he could practically feel the paint splitting, the plywood beneath it shuddering under the pressure. After a second more of allowing his anger to control him, he started concentrating on his breathing, willing himself to calm down. It would do him no good to wreck the house, giving the guys, especially Cyrus, any idea of just how much their meeting had gotten to him.

This was ridiculous!

Finally, he felt his muscles start to relax. The tension in the room, which had been extremely thick, finally began to lessen. Opening his eyes, he saw a long crack running the length of his ceiling.

"Wonderful," he growled.

Hearing footsteps coming down the hall, Manuel rolled his eyes. *Round two,* he thought, walking over and plopping down on his bed. Stretching out, placing his arms under his head, he stared at the crack in the ceiling, listening as the footsteps drew closer. The hair on his arms began to stand up as his bedroom door flew open. Not looking, Manuel closed his eyes.

"What do you want, Nicholas?"

"You can't just leave in the middle of an argument!"

"Actually, as far as I was concerned, it was already over."

"And how in the hell did you figure that?"

"Well, when a simple discussion turns into an argument, I feel it's best to walk away."

"A simple discussion? Is that what that was?" Nicholas' humorless laugh echoed in the room. "There was nothing fucking simple about any of the shit you just laid on us!"

"What the fuck did you come back here for?!" Manuel yelled as his eyes flew open. "Because I don't feel like listening to you tell me how stupid I am. I heard enough of that in the dining room. Plus, as you said, I *left*!" As the last words left his mouth, he felt a wave of power roll over him, the walls shuddering violently. Slowly climbing to his feet, he looked at Nicholas. "I think you should leave."

Nicholas' red eyes flashed as he shook his head. "I'm not leaving until we finish this!" The air stirred around them, lifting some papers off Manuel's desk as Nicholas took a step closer. "And I wasn't calling *you* stupid. I was saying that to just readily believe anything a *witch* says is stupid." The word witch left his lips like a dirty word.

"You weren't there. You have no idea whether or not I just accepted what she said. If you had just fucking heard me out-"

"I *did* hear you, Manuel... We all heard you. You want us to work alongside a witch. To trust her when she says she's here to help us. That she won't screw us over with her dark magic and black heart. What more is there for us to know?"

"You don't even know her," Manuel hissed, the wall splintering behind Nicholas as he felt his power lash out. "How dare you assume anything about her magic...or her heart. You...don't...know...shit!" The floor shifted with a growl beneath their feet as Manuel rolled his shoulders. Even though his head told him he needed to calm down, his wounded pride was winning. Taking a step towards Nicholas, he met his glare.

"I don't *need* to know her!" Nicholas yelled, a wind beginning to howl around them as his red eyes darkened. "I've dealt with witches before...and all of them have been evil shrews. So no, I don't need to know her. All I need to know is that she is a witch. That alone tells me she's bad news. I guarantee she's just like the rest of them, Manuel."

"Come on, Nicholas-"

"No, Manuel. Start thinking, will you?"

"I *am* thinking, damn it! I seem to be the only one around here looking past any personal issues to see the bigger picture."

"You're not looking at any fucking big picture. You're looking at some chick who's giving you attention. You're thinking with your dick instead of your head."

"Really?!" Manuel yelled. He could feel his back muscles shiver as he teetered on the edge of completely losing control. "Do you not know me at all? When the hell have I ever thought with anything other than my head?"

"There's a first for everything."

Manuel stood there, staring at him. He couldn't believe his brother really had that little trust in him and his judgment. Shaking his head, he turned from Nicholas. He could feel the tension leaving him as he looked down at the floor. "Hayley's different. I know you don't believe that, but she is. She's not like the other witches you've dealt with."

"Manuel, I'm sorry. I really am. But I'm afraid you're wrong." Manuel could hear the anger in Nicholas' voice draining away. "Trust me. They're all the same."

"I *have* trusted you, all of you, even when I didn't agree with what was happening or being said. Why is it so hard for you to trust me now? To see that, just this once, you might be wrong." Manuel turned and met Nicholas' angry gaze. "I know she isn't evil." He pointed aggressively at his own chest. "I can feel it."

"And can she help us?" Both Nicholas and Manuel gave a start, turning to find their argument had attracted the rest of their brothers. Darren was looking pointedly at Manuel. "Well, Manuel? Can she help us?"

"I don't know, Darren," he stated slowly, holding his brother's stare. "But I want us to give her a chance, allow her to try."

"And if she can't?" Christian asked, sliding past Darren in the doorway to lean casually against the wall. "Let's say we give her a try and find that she can't help us. What then?"

"Then I'll deal with her," Manuel answered. "She won't remember anything."

They were all quiet. He watched as they glanced at each other, then back towards him. Nicholas looked between Manuel and Darren as he shook his head.

"This is a bad idea," Nicholas said. "We shouldn't trust this witch. We shouldn't trust *any* witch."

Manuel began to argue, but Darren raised a hand to stop him. "I heard you two in here. While I understand where you're coming from, Nicholas, I also know that Manuel wouldn't bring this to us unless he felt confident she is who and what she claims to be." Nicholas opened his mouth, but Darren shook his head. "When Manuel brought this up, I admit I had my own reservations about the idea of working with a witch. The ones I have known have left a bad taste in my mouth, causing my stomach to tense when I think of trusting one. However, Manuel has never steered us wrong. He's also had each of our backs, even when most wouldn't have."

"I can definitely vouch for that," Christian piped up. Manuel glanced his way with a smirk.

"Yes," Darren went on with a small grin. "I'm sure we all can. What I'm saying is that I believe he has earned our trust." Darren gave Manuel a hard look. "Know that, if this should all go wrong, you will be responsible to clean it up."

"Of course," Manuel said, tilting his head up.

"Then I don't see why we can't give this Hayley a shot, see if she is able to help us."

"I agree," Christian said, glancing past Darren to a dark shadow hovering in the hall. "Cyrus?"

Manuel looked at Cyrus as he stepped into the room. His brother's black eyes glinted as he looked at Christian. "I still don't think this is a good idea," he grumbled. "We know nothing about this chick. Nothing about why she wants to help, or even where in the hell she came from. I seriously think we should just fog her memory and move the fuck on."

They all started talking at once. Manuel, Darren, and Christian telling him he should just give her a chance. Nicholas further telling them his misgivings and agreeing with Cyrus. The whole time, Cyrus just shook his head, driving Manuel crazy. He had finally felt like he was getting the support that he needed. Nicholas was not going to get on board with this anytime soon, but Manuel thought with the other three backing him, Nicholas would at least stop fighting him.

Nicholas looked pleased with himself. That Cyrus hadn't agreed right away proved, to him anyway, that he must be right. As Darren and Christian continued talking to Cyrus, Manuel turned towards Nicholas.

"What the hell are you smirking about?"

"I'm just glad there's someone else in this house who has the balls to stand up and say no. I'm sorry, Manuel, but there is no way we should trust this witch. It would be best if you did what Cyrus suggested and go-"

"I never said no," Cyrus bit out. Everyone stopped talking and turned to look at him.

"But you said this wasn't a good idea. That we should get rid of her memory and move on!" Nicholas said in exasperation.

"No, Nicholas," Cyrus said in a gravelly voice. "I said I don't *think* this is a good idea and I *think* we should fog her... I never said I wasn't going to agree to give her a chance."

"Really?" Manuel asked uncertainly, turning towards him.

Cyrus just looked at him. Manuel couldn't tell what his brother was thinking, but he swore he saw something sad cross his features before Cyrus shook his head. "Listen, I know we all disagree sometimes-"

"Sometimes?" Christian mumbled.

Cyrus paused long enough to send him a dirty look in response before looking back at Manuel. "Like I was saying... Setting our disagreements aside, if giving this chick a chance really means that much to you, well... Why the hell not?"

Nicholas shook his head. "Am I the only one who knows this is all going to end horribly?"

Cyrus looked at Nicholas. "My decision, the one I feel is the right one to make, is to let this girl-"

"This *witch*," Nicholas cut in.

"Yes, this *witch* help us. Let's just to see what she can do." Cyrus looked back at Manuel and pointed at him, his black eyes gleaming slightly as he sneered. "But if this little experiment of yours blows up in our faces, it's on you, brother."

"I know," Manuel said slowly, looking around at all of them. "Like I said, if this goes south, I don't want any of you to worry about it. I'll handle it."

"Fine!" Nicholas bit out. He took a step towards Manuel, narrowing his eyes. "I'll stand by you as this witch does her thing, but I refuse to like it. And don't expect me to get chatty or any shit like that with her."

"Then it's settled," Darren spoke up. "Manuel, go give Hayley a call. We'll meet her three nights from tonight. I sincerely hope you know what you're doing."

"Me, too, brother," Manuel muttered as each of them made his way out of his room. Blowing out a breath, he ran a hand over his face. "Me, too..."

Chapter 11

"Yes! Oh god!"

"Shh..." Dev reached up and grabbed the woman's shoulders. Driving harder into her, he pushed her head into the couch cushion. Her moans became muffled as she gasped into the fabric. The heat from her core was intoxicating. Leaning over her, Dev picked up his speed. He could feel her muscles gripping his dick, feel himself getting closer with every thrust.

Turning her head, the woman looked at him over her shoulder, her dull brown eyes heavy from sex and alcohol. Her lips curled into what he was sure she thought was a sexy smile as she let out a gasp. "Yes, Dev! More... More..."

The smell of alcohol flew through the air with each breath that left her. Dev wrinkled his nose as the scent assaulted his senses. "Turn your head away!" he grunted, his grip tightening on her shoulders.

Her short hair flew around her face as her body rocked violently. "But-"

"I said, turn... Shit! Just... Don't look at me!"

"Whatever you say. Just don't... Ahh... Don't stop what you're doing!" she panted. Looking away from him, she threw herself backwards to meet each of his thrusts.

Dev moved his hands from her shoulders to her hips. He looked down at the span of her back, the colorful butterfly forever tattooed onto her skin, her black skirt bunched unceremoniously around her hips. His stomach muscles tightened as he released a low moan. Gripping the fabric in one hand, Dev rolled his shoulders, his rhythm faltering as he neared his release. Closing his eyes, he felt her body beginning to shudder. Dev knew she was as close as he was. He could hear it in her breathing as it begin to take on a frantic rush.

Rolling his hips, Dev allowed his power to rise to the surface. Its energy instantly added to his rush. Some of it flowed off him to play across her skin, goosebumps rising to the surface. Leaning down, he let out a moan as he ran his tongue up her spine, causing the woman's back to arch, allowing him to bury himself deeper. She screamed out as he drove himself into her with an animalistic fever, chasing his own release.

So close, he thought.

An instant after his power engulfed her, Dev felt the woman's body shudder. Like a storm, her climax rolled through her, causing her to buck and groan beneath him. Her core clenched tightly around him, pulling his cock further into her until he felt his tip hit her wall.

This was the sensation he craved. The moment when she reached the peak of her climax and fully opened up beneath him. Her mind, her very soul, was bared to him in these moments as her body begged him to take her. All of her.

With a snarl, Dev threw his head back. The couch rocked violently as he moved in her, allowing the sensation of her trembling to bring on his own release.

Digging his fingers into her soft flesh, Dev gave one final thrust as he erupted within her, his dick pulsing, his seed shooting out of him to bathe across her inner walls. Waves of euphoria ran through him as he let his head fall forward. Closing his eyes, he felt his power uncurl around him, hovering just above his skin. It didn't flow outward, reaching out towards the woman beneath him as it had mere seconds ago. This time it was just...there. Surrounding him.

Holding himself above her, he relished the slight chill running through him. In this moment, this brief second, Dev felt free. All of his stress, all of his fear, all of his regrets vanished. In this moment, he could pretend he wasn't living this nightmare, this personal hell he had been cast into. He allowed himself to feel safe.

It never lasted, though.

Feeling movement beneath him, Dev sighed and opened his eyes.

"That was amazing," the woman purred, her cheeks flush as she looked back at him.

Dev stared at her for a heartbeat, a quiet darkness washing over him as the high from his climax began to dissipate. Moving off the couch, he reached down and grabbed his pants. Pulling them up with a jerk, Dev walked towards his desk.

"Hey, aren't you going to say anything?"

He plucked his shirt from the desk chair and began to slide it on.

"Dev? What's wrong, baby?" the woman cooed.

He looked over as she started pulling herself up. Her skin was tinged a light pink from the rush of blood, her sides red from his fingers gripping into her. Several of the marks upon her flesh were sure to bruise, which he regretted. Human women were so delicate. Almost too delicate for his form of play. Even in his roughest moments, he held back, but he couldn't get enough of them. More truthfully, he couldn't get enough of their lust. He loved the female figure...its softness, its curves. This woman, regardless of her muddled soul, was beautiful...and she knew it.

Tracing a hand seductively up her thigh, she looked at him. "It's crazy. We

just finished and I already want you again."
Her voice came out breathy.

Dev stood there silently as he
watched her hand slide over her stomach,
coming to rest over an already taut nipple.
He wanted to go to her, to need this woman
the way she obviously needed him. Hell, he
wished he needed any of the women the
way they did him. He marveled at the look
in their eyes, the heat coloring their skin,
and the lust saturating the air around them.
He just couldn't, though. Those moments
of pleasure, those mere seconds of release,
were like his unicorn...a mythical creature
he was always looking for. A feeling that
made him think the world wasn't as dark as
he knew it to be. However, this window of
bliss would be immediately followed by a
feeling of regret that would rise within him
and he would be done. Sure, he would find
himself hunting for his next release within
a day or two, but not now. Now, he would
allow the feelings of regret and despair to
wash over him, just like he deserved.

She reached out towards him,
crooking her fingers, beckoning him closer.
"Come here, baby. Let Mommy take care of
you."

"I think you should go."

"Now, honey-"

"Now," Dev hissed as he began to
button his shirt. Pulling his chair back, he

sat down, straightening the stack of files before him.

"Whatever you say, lover," she said with a playful pout. He glanced up to watch her pull down her skirt, then slide her hot pink tank top over her head. "Remember, I'm just a phone call away." She sauntered towards him. Resting her hip against his desk, she leaned down, her hands smoothing down the front of her skirt. "You just call..." She reached over and touched the side of his face, running her fingers over his cheek and lips, "and I'll come running."

Dev pulled back slightly. Reaching down into his drawer, he began to retrieve his wallet.

"No, sweetie." She smiled. "Trey said this was on the house because you're such a good *friend* of his."

He glanced up. "Yeah, well, you'll have to tell Trey I said thanks. It was a pleasure, um..."

"Candy," she said with a wink. "And it was most definitely a pleasure, Dev." His name left her lips on a silky whisper. Making her way out of his office, she sent him one last wink before disappearing.

"Candy," he murmured. Running his hands over his face, he looked towards the wall. *Fuck, it's hot in here.* Willing the wall fan on, Dev sighed as cool air rushed over him.

Shaking his head, he began going through his files. Most were bills, a couple applications... Mostly junk. This past month-and-a-half had been chaotic. Even with the help of Sy and his workers, who never stopped working, he still felt stressed...and was running out of time.

Luckily, they were far enough along that inspector dipshit couldn't give him a hard time. Sure, he had threatened to call his boss, although Dev felt that would be a nifty trick since he knew Andras made the calls. He didn't receive them. *More like couldn't*, Dev thought with a chuckle. The only thing he really had to be thankful for right now was that Andras couldn't get topside...yet. That fancy trick he pulled with the priest only severely weakened the veil, much to Andras' dismay. Dev knew that would soon change, though. It was already weak enough to let most of Andras' soldiers through. Little by little, it was dropping. God help this world when it was gone.

A knock on his door pulled Dev from his musings. Glancing up, he spotted Sy leaning on the doorframe.

"Smells like you've been having a good time in here, my friend," he stated with a click of his tongue.

"Well, I have to have some where I can," Dev said, suppressing a frown at Sy's crude observation. "It's not like I can leave." Leaning back in his chair, he looked the demon over, feeling a slight chill. Sy was an imposing figure. "I'm surprised to see you so soon."

The demon smiled as he walked into the room, taking a seat across from him. Sy glanced around the office, his eyes sparkling in amusement as he looked back at Dev. "It seems things are moving right along for you. Were my workers able to get you where you needed to be?"

Clearing his throat, Dev glanced down, gathering all his papers into a small pile. Noticing his fingers shaking slightly, he quickly clasped his hands together in front of him. "Yes, they have been a great help. I know I said it before, but thank you."

"Oh, Dev, there is no reason to thank me. I am just glad that I was able to help in your time of need."

Dev looked at Sy. He wasn't sure what to make of the demon's sudden appearance. He had briefly stopped by when the workers had first shown up, but that had been a couple days ago. For Sy to show up now, unexpectedly, had Dev feeling uneasy. He shifted slightly in his chair.

"Sy, I was just about to-"

"Have you talked to Andras lately?" the demon cut in.

Hearing that name, Dev sat up a little straighter. "No. Not in a few weeks."

"Interesting..."

Dev stared at him, waiting for him to continue. Had he missed something? Was there a reason he should have talked to Andras lately? He couldn't think of anything. Then a chill went through him as thoughts of Andras showing up flashed through his mind.

"Why... Why is that interesting?"

"Well, there has been quite a commotion going on down there. I have heard whispers the veil is thinning out enough that Andras can get through."

Dev swallowed. "I thought it had to be completely down for him to get through."

"Well, yes, that would be true if Andras were to come over here with all his power."

Dev frowned. "How else would he come over here, Sy? It's not like he's just going to leave some of it sitting back in his office while he comes topside."

"Of course not. That would not work at all, would it?" Sy said with a grin. "But who says he has not already sent some of it up here?"

"That's impossible!"

"Is it?"

"I mean, I've never heard of... It's just..." At a loss for words, Dev shook his head. "How?"

"Nobody has been clear on the *how*," Sy stated slowly. "It seems he was able to part with some of his power, sending it away from him until he needs it."

"Until he's topside?"

"That is the rumor." Sy shook his head. "Who is to say that there is any truth to this? Some just say Andras has lost some of his power, which is why he's been so...moody lately."

"He's always moody."

"True, but it seems he has been more so as of late." Sy shrugged. "Ever since the chaos in his building. Remember the little mishap that happened not even two months ago?" As Dev shook his head, Sy let out a small laugh. "Oh, that is right. You were... How did I hear it? Still rather *occupied* around that time."

Dev felt his pulse quicken. That was the one and only time since his fall he had ended up on Andras' bad side. It was a period of time he would never forget or ever get over. Images of blood, memories of pain began to push to the surface. Refusing to allow his mind to go there, Dev blinked quickly and cleared his throat.

"Yes, you could put it that way. I do remember hearing of something happening, though."

Sy nodded. "Yes, well, I guess Andras had a mystery female as his 'guest' for a short time. One who was able to get away from him. He has not been the same since."

"How did she get away? I mean, from the sound of it, her escaping was what he wanted, but...she was down in Hell." Dev shook his head. "How in the world did she get back up here?"

"How indeed?" Sy responded with a sly grin. "I would imagine she had a little help."

"Help? Help from whom?"

Sy sat there silently for a moment. The longer the demon sat there and grinned at him, the more Dev's unease grew. Finally, with another click of his tongue, Sy leaned forward. "I believe her rescuers were some old friends of yours."

Dev's mind raced. Friends? He hadn't had any real friends in a very long time. None of the demons he knew could be considered a friend. Sy and maybe one or two others were the closest, but Dev knew better than to completely let any of them in. Besides demons, and maybe a few Grimms, Dev really didn't know whom Sy could be hinting at.

Leaning back in his chair, he tapped his fingers on the desk. Not a single name, face, or evil soul came to mind. Even if he knew of someone, even if he had any kind of suspicion on whom it could be, why would they help Andras' "guest"? There was no reason a demon would want to go against Andras...not unless they enjoyed having their flesh ripped or melted off.

He couldn't believe that anyone he had any sort of connection with would knowingly pit themselves against Andras. Dev shook his head slowly as he eyed Sy. "I have no idea what you mean, Sy."

"Really?" Sy asked, his grin growing even wider. "Think harder..."

"Sy, I don't-"

"Come now, Dev! Who would be powerful enough to get in and out of Hell? Who would have anything to gain from upsetting Andras? Who could cause that level of destruction, of chaos, in Andras' own building...and get away?"

Dev started to open his mouth to tell Sy he was out of his mind, that he had no idea what he was talking about, when he felt a slight pull on his memory. Names he hadn't thought of in centuries began to manifest themselves in his mind, growing until Dev felt the burning in his chest from the breath he hadn't realized he'd been holding. Slowly letting the air out, he looked down at his desk. Judging from the holes in Andras' building and the demons sprawled along the streets, he should have known as soon as he heard. It had been so long ago, though. Dev had thought them long gone...at least that was what he had told himself when he had been chained up in the very deepest part of Hell, writhing in pain with no end in sight.

With no sign anywhere of his so-called friends.

If they were truly back, though, if they were close by... Shit, if they were here...

Licking his lips, Dev glanced back up at Sy, forcing his eyes and face to remain emotionless, even as his mind whirled with the possibilities.

"So you *do* know whom I am talking about?" Sy asked, his black eyes boring into Dev's as he studied him. "You understand why I would assume Andras has been in touch with you then?"

Dev sat for a moment, silent and completely still. Of course. Andras would come to him for his knowledge. A chill ran down his spine. If Andras did come to him, he would just have to come up with something, get creative. Tilting his head slightly, Dev considered the demon across from him. If Sy were here on Andras' behalf, if he had merely been toying with him, he already knew the answer.

Sy, seeming to read his mind, shook his head. "If you are wondering, the answer is no, I have not been in touch with Andras, and no, I do not work for him...if I can help it anyway." He chuckled, leaning back in his chair. "So, Dev, do you or do you not know who has been causing trouble with our false king?"

"Yes, Sy," Dev said slowly. "I believe I do..." Sy nodded for him to say it. For him to say the name of not only the ones going up against Andras, but the ones he had once called brothers. The ones who had once regarded him as their own. With a sigh, Dev glanced away from Sy's knowing stare. "The Guardians," he whispered. "It has to be the Guardians."

Chapter 12

"Are you nervous?"

Christian's voice shook Manuel from his thoughts. Looking over at his brother, Manuel just nodded, his thoughts running a million miles a minute. They were only hours away from meeting Hayley, but he wasn't sure whether he was excited or scared shitless about seeing her and going through this little "trial" of theirs. The twisting in his stomach suggested the latter.

Silently, he watched Christian lean against the doorframe of his room, crossing his arms over his chest. "Okay, so you're nervous. I get that." When Manuel raised his eyebrow. Christian raised a hand. "Really, I do. So...let's talk about it. Are you nervous for Hayley? Or yourself?"

Opening his mouth, Manuel started to answer, but stopped. What was he really nervous about? Sure, this was a bigger risk than he would normally take, but hadn't they all been taking big risks lately? Christian and Ella... They had hardly known a thing about each other, but they had taken a risk, trusted when others wouldn't have. So what was he so tied up about? Maybe he was still worked up over the argument...or maybe he was just anxious about tonight.

Sighing, he glanced down at his sword, its sharpened edges catching the light as he slightly twisted it. With little to no strain on his part, Manuel flexed his hand around the hilt, watching it pulse with a faint glow. Hearing his brother shift, he glanced back his way.

"I don't know, Christian."

"What did Hayley say?"

Laying his sword beside him, Manuel ran his hands threw his hair. "She said she'd be ready, that she is glad we're willing to give her a chance, and that we wouldn't regret it."

Christian looked to be mulling that over. Manuel watched as his brother glanced away, seeming to lose himself in thought as he stared at the window. "How did she sound?" he finally asked.

"A little nervous, but she sounded fine otherwise." Manuel stood and walked over to his jacket thrown across his dresser. "Maybe that's what I'm feeling. Maybe I'm reacting to the nervousness I heard in her voice." He recalled her slight pause after he told her it was a go, the breathiness in her voice as she said she'd be ready, and the nervous laugh that left her when he said he'd see her soon. Her feelings must have affected him. Hell, they were radiating so strong off her, he could practically feel them. The more he thought about it, the more it made sense. That had to be what was wrong with him.

"Maybe," Christian said slowly.

Pulling his jacket on, Manuel turned. "You think it's something else?"

He smirked. "I just think it's more than that. I think you're nervous about seeing her."

"Why would I be nervous about seeing her?" Manuel shook his head. "I've seen her before. This time shouldn't be any different."

"But it *is* different," Christian said, stepping into the room. "This time, it won't just be the two of you. Darren and I will be there, too."

Manuel looked away. They had made the decision that Cyrus and Nicholas would stay behind tonight. Not only because of the arguments that had erupted between them, but Darren felt Hayley may be a little more comfortable with only three of them meeting her the first time. Manuel had felt Darren was definitely right in this, although that wasn't the only reason he had agreed. There was also a powerful need to keep Hayley away from Cyrus and Nicholas for as long as he could. The feeling to protect her had kicked into overdrive just seconds after he had first told them about her. Yes, they were his brothers and he trusted them with his life, but he just didn't feel comfortable having them around her right now.

However, he was unsure of the whole situation. Maybe he should just meet with her alone, filling everyone in later about how things went. That way, if this little test goes wrong, he could just handle it. He wouldn't have to worry about her being nervous because she wouldn't have a reason to.

Looking back at Christian, he gave a small grin. "I think you're right." Christian nodded slowly. "Maybe it would be best if I went alone tonight."

He watched his brother's eyes narrow. "Manuel, we talked about this-"

"I know, but what if things go wrong tonight and it's because she's nervous around you guys. I just..." Manuel trailed off.

"Darren and I won't do anything to make her feel threatened." He raised his right hand. "I promise." He gave a small smile. "I had a feeling that was what you were worrying about, which is why I came back here." Christian sighed, stepping closer. "Listen, Manuel, you need to chill. If she gets nervous tonight, it won't be because of us. It will be because she feels *you* are."

Blinking, Manuel let out a low sigh. Although the need to get defensive and lash out at Christian came over him, he knew his brother was right. Sure, he could blame how he was feeling on his brothers or the fact that he was taking a huge risk. In the end, though, it came down to the fact that he didn't want her to fail.

"You were the one who said we all needed to give her a shot, to let her prove to us that she is here to help. I admit I wasn't too keen on the idea at first, but I trust you, brother." At his words, Manuel looked back. His brother's deep blue eyes seemed to bore into his. "So now it's your turn."

Confusion ran through him. "My turn to do what?"

"Trust *us*," Christian said with a smirk. "We aren't going to sabotage your girl, Manuel."

"I never said you would," he answered quickly as Christian turned to leave.

"But you were thinking it," Christian said over his shoulder.

Even though that may have been true, Manuel wasn't going to say so. He watched his brother walk into the hall, thinking about what he had said. He needed to get his head on straight for tonight. This whole "what if" crap had to go if he were going to let them all go through with this.

Suddenly, he felt himself frown. Glancing sharply at the now empty door, he yelled, "And she's not my girl!"

The sound of Christian's laughter was his only response.

✝

Two hours later, Manuel found himself standing at the edge of town. Thick clouds blanketed the sky above him, making visibility impossible...for most. For Manuel, though, it was as clear a night as any other. Looking around, he gazed at the fields spreading out before him. Corn grew to his left, rustling softly as the night breeze washed over it. Besides that, it was quiet.

He had left the house a bit earlier than his brothers, wanting to get to the meeting site sooner so he could check it out. They all agreed this would be the perfect spot to start. No innocents to worry about, no traffic to dodge...and, most importantly, no buildings for Castigo or his like to hide in. The last thing he and his brothers wanted was to run into any of them tonight.

Hearing a sharp whistle, Manuel glanced up. Smirking, he watched Darren and Christian fly into view.

Darren's white wings were a sharp contrast to the black sky. Silently, he glided through the air, his wings held out straight beside him as he cut sharply to the left, then threw himself into a tight corkscrew.

Show off! Manuel thought with a soft chuckle.

Christian, on the other hand, blended into the night, his black wings hidden as he soared above. With a twist of his shoulder, he began his descent, his body at ease as his wings worked easily to lower him to the ground.

Manuel took a slight step back as both landed before him, a small cloud of dust lifting from the ground. Almost immediately, Darren took a step toward him, his wings soundlessly vanishing. "You left without us," he said.

Even though it was a statement and not a question, Manuel still felt the need to respond. Darren just had that effect on him. "I just wanted to get here early to check the place out."

"And?" This question came from Christian, who still seemed to be enjoying stretching out his wings.

"I think this place will work, just like we thought it would," Manuel remarked.

He watched Christian give his wings a good shake before a flash hid them from view. As the light slowly faded, Manuel stared at the empty space where the wings had been. Christian's face showed the slightest hint of sadness as he rolled his shoulders.

Manuel sighed. "You haven't really been able to get out to stretch them lately, have you?"

"No. With everything that has been going on..." Christian gave a slight shrug. "Hopefully, with the new place and the land that comes with it, I'll be able to get out more."

"Definitely," Manuel said with a smile. He was about to say more when a flash of headlights caught his attention. His thoughts stopped as he watched the little red Toyota drive down the dirt path, causing a cloud of dust to rise in its wake.

"Here we go," Christian murmured beside him.

They stood there as the car pulled up, the headlights shining brightly in their direction, making it impossible to see the driver. Manuel stood there a moment longer before slowly making his way towards the car. Stepping up to the driver's side, he watched the window open. He leaned down. "Hey."

Hayley looked at him then, her big green eyes taking his breath away as they met his. "Hey," she said with a small smile. He could feel the nervousness radiating off her like electricity. She licked her lips a couple times before nodding her head in Christian and Darren's direction. "Your brothers?"

"Two of them," he replied softly.

She nodded slowly, then glanced around. "Where's your car?"

Manuel blinked. *Shit. Hadn't thought about that*, he thought furiously. "It's, um... It's with one of our other brothers. He needed to use it, so we just had him drop us off." Her eyebrow raised slightly. "I told him we'd let him know when we're done here so he can pick us up."

"Okay... Um..."

"You sure you want to do this?"

"Of course," she answered immediately. "I'm just... It's just..." She blew out a breath. "This is the first time I've done something like this with an audience...well, besides my Aunt Teresa, but she's family so I don't think that really counts. I mean, of course it counts... That wasn't what I meant to say. See, she's the one who taught me everything I know, so she was with me when I practiced. I mean-"

Manuel reached in and laid his hand on her arm. He watched as she took a deep breath and gave him a lopsided smile.

"I'm rambling, aren't I?"

He just nodded, grinning as he gazed down at her. "It's going to be okay."

"Of course it is," she said, reaching down to turn off her car.

Stepping back, Manuel waited for her to roll up her window and get out. She had her red hair pulled back into a ponytail, her soft curls cascading lusciously down her neck and over one shoulder. God, how he wanted to reach up and release her hair, running his fingers through it as it flowed wildly around her. Biting the inside of his cheek, his eyes continued to travel over her. Greedily, he looked at the thin black tee hugging her chest, her tight blue jeans clinging to her hips and thighs. Everything showed off her deliciously curvy figure.

Hearing a throat clear, he quickly glanced up. Hayley, seemingly unaware of his staring, was busy silencing her phone. Looking at his brothers, he couldn't help but frown at their raised eyebrows and smirks.

Great.

"Well...," Hayley said, bringing his attention back to her. "Aren't you going to introduce me?"

"Yeah. Sorry," he muttered, leading her away from the car. "Guys, this is Hayley. Hayley, these are my brothers, Christian and Darren."

He watched her eyes widen as she gazed up at them. Quickly recovering, she smiled and stuck her hand out. "It's very nice to meet you both." Taking each of their hands it turn, she just shook her head.

"What?" Manuel asked when he saw her expression grow thoughtful.

She glanced between the three of them a couple times before turning his way.

"It's just..." She paused, a slight shade of pink creeping up her cheeks.

"Just?"

"Well, are all of your brothers so...large?"

Chapter 13

The sound of the men chuckling only caused Hayley to feel even more embarrassed. The moment the question left her mouth, she wanted to pull it back. It wasn't that she wasn't curious, but she hadn't really meant to voice her curiosity. They were just huge men. Not that she was a short woman by any means, but these guys had to be well over six feet tall. The sight of them had, quite literally, stopped her when she had pulled up.

It wasn't until her brain registered Manuel walking towards her that she remembered she needed to breathe. Now here she stood, in front of three of the largest, sexiest, and probably most dangerous men she had ever been around, and all she could think about was how she was glad she didn't wear her sweats.

The one named Christian had the most amazing steel blue eyes. They were intense, seeming to see right into her soul as he gazed at her. The other one, Darren, seemed equally intense. His eyes, a much darker blue, had a very knowing feel to them. They both smiled at her, trying to show they were happy to meet her, but she knew better. The tenseness in their postures spoke volumes. Even their chuckles at her question sounded forced. The quicker she could get the ball rolling, the sooner they would realize she was on their side.

Licking her lips, she turned and faced the fields. *First things first*, she thought, closing her eyes.

"So..." Manuel's voice shivered over her skin. Opening her eyes, Hayley turned her head slightly to look at him. "How does this work exactly?"

"Well...," she said, looking at the field. "It's hard to explain. I'm able to, um...communicate with the world around me." Judging by the silence, Hayley realized she might need to expand. Chewing on her bottom lip, she attempted to put into words what she had always been able to do naturally. "Okay. I need to locate a Shadow. Although they are lower-level demons, they are devious - *very* devious. To hide themselves, they move amongst the shadows." A smile crossed her lips. "Hence their name, I assume. Anyway, to find one, I will open myself up to the air and the Earth. With their help, I will know where we need to start."

"That's it?" Christian asked from behind her. "I don't mean to sound disappointed... Well, no, I guess I do. I thought there would be more..."

When his voice trailed off, Hayley turned to see him looking back and forth between Manuel and Darren. He seemed to be at a loss, searching for words. Darren also seemed to be confused, although he features held a slight look of amusement, as well. Manuel, on the other hand, was glaring at Christian. He seemed to be silently yelling for him to shut up.

"What were you expecting?" she asked quietly. They all turned to look her way, Manuel's eyes softening. Christian and Darren looked at her as if she were going to sprout another head. *Or maybe a big hairy wart*, she mused. "Okay, let's get some things straight. I assume Manuel informed you that I am a witch?" They both nodded. "Good. Is it safe for me to assume the news was not taken well?" At this, they seemed to frown.

"We didn't mean to-" Darren started.

Holding her hand up, Hayley just smiled. "Listen. I know you are trying and it's okay. Really. I know how witchcraft is usually perceived, and I've met my fair share of witches over the years who couldn't be trusted. But I was raised differently. From a very young age, my aunt Teresa told me that the greatest joy a witch can get from her gifts is to always use them for what is right. Something I have remembered and live by."

"So you want us to believe you have never used your gifts for anything except helping others? That you've never used them for anything evil?" Christian asked. His questions came out carefully, trying not to be rude.

"Yes. Well, unless you want to count the time I caused my ex's pants to drop in front of the family of the girl he was cheating on me with... Or the couple times I caused beer to spill on some jerk who wouldn't take no for an answer... Oh, then there was that one time I made this girl's hair start to fall out right before prom!" She laughed softly at the memory, stopping when she saw the strange looks each of the men were giving her. "Oh, come on, guys! I *was* a teenager once. Anyway, I let her hair grow back the day before the dance. I'm not *that* cruel."

Finally getting a true laugh, even if it was just a small one, from each of them, she smiled. *Just go slow*, she told herself. "So, as I said, I'm not evil. I've never used my gifts for evil, and I sure don't plan on starting now." Turning her attention to Christian, she let the amusement reach her eyes. "Now, back to what you were expecting..."

"Listen," Christian started, looking down. "It's just... I've never worked with a witch before-"

"It's okay, Christian." Hayley laughed. "So, let's see... Will there be some spell casting? Yes. A physical response to everything around you? Most likely. Do I need a cauldron, frog legs, or anything that would resemble a Halloween favor to pull this off? 'Fraid not." She watched as he glanced down at the ground again. "I know... I'm sorry to disappoint you." As he looked back up at her, she smiled. "I don't even have a broom!"

At that, he laughed outright. Really laughed. He was soon joined by both Darren and Manuel, who just shook his head as he gazed at her. His look held multiple meanings. She felt a warmth spread through her as she smiled back at him. Being able to put his brothers at ease had obviously earned her some major points.

"Okay, so how do you get started?" Darren asked, his tone softer now.

"I just need to open myself up," she said, turning back to face the field. *And hope there's something out there to find.*

Taking a deep breath, she closed her eyes. She could feel the cool breeze tickling her skin, the ground feeling solid beneath her feet, and the strong energy of the men at her back. They truly had a power about them, each having a different feeling. That was something she would definitely have to explore later. Now, though...

"I'm in need of your help," Hayley whispered. Raising her hands slightly at her side, she felt the air begin to change. It curled around her fingers as she let more of her power out. "Your guidance in finding an evil that plagues our land." As her power began to spread out, she was instantly aware of the flair of energy behind her. It gave her pause. Frowning slightly, she shifted her power to move closer to it, feeling a comfortable warmth. Letting a slow breath escape her lips, she immediately got a vision of Manuel. A purple haze swirled around him, calling to her.

Oh, the questions I'm going to have for him, she thought, willing her power to move on.

Reaching up above her head, Hayley felt the air around her shudder. "I call upon the air," she breathed out. The soft breeze began to pick up, her hair lifting from around her shoulders and twisting out behind her. "I call upon the birds in the sky to be my eyes. Show me this demon I am looking for. Show me the Shadow that hides within this world so I may find it and send it back to where it spawned." She felt a fire beginning to burn behind her eyelids, its heat spreading throughout her irises as she continued to silently call out. Hayley could feel her hair whipping around her face, the ends stinging her skin. The feelings slowly subsided as she began to sense a connection. Her breath left her again as the burning within her eyes flexed, taking on a power all its own.

"*Ostende mihi,*" she murmured, the air around her suddenly stilling.

Opening her eyes, she was no longer looking at a field. Now, through the tunnel vision of a bird, she was looking down at the town, soaring high above the cars, passing quickly over houses and streetlights. The feeling was disorienting. Not being something she did often, it was definitely taking its toll on her power.

A little longer, she thought.

The buildings were a blur as she flew. She could practically feel the bird's wings as it glided through the night.

Landing on top of a streetlight, Hayley had a clear view of a quiet suburban home. The lights were off inside, except for one downstairs. Watching closely, she could just make out a figure behind the curtains. The person seemed to move around the house quietly before settling into what looked like a chair by the window.

Hayley was so focused on the person, she almost missed the movement coming from the side of the house. Zeroing in, she felt her excitement bloom. *A Shadow*. The demon twisted through the shadows, moving lazily from one house to the next as it went down the street.

Probably looking for its next victim, she thought with a sneer.

The bird's attention turned from the demon to the street sign down the way. Lifting from its perch, it soared closer, shifting until the sign came into view. "Hansen Road," she whispered.

Smiling, Hayley once again closed her eyes, sending out a silent thank you to the bird as she felt the warmth begin to leave her. As her power calmed and her mind cleared, she slowly opened her eyes.

"Shit," she exclaimed, jumping back when she saw Manuel and his brothers crowded around her. They had the decency to look ashamed as they all held up their hands, stepping back. "What the heck, guys?"

"You were completely out of it," Christian stated.

"Yeah. The wind went crazy, you mumbled things, and..." Darren's voice trailed off.

"And when you opened your eyes, they were white!" Manuel finished.

"I told you I was going to have to reach out, open myself up."

"We didn't expect your eyes to do that, though," Christian said curiously. "I mean... Does that happen all the time?"

"Listen, we can go over all of this later," Hayley said. "I promise. Right now, there is a Shadow slinking around a rather nice-looking neighborhood on Hansen

Road. So, if you guys still want to go hunting, we should really get moving."

"The wind told you it was on Hansen Road?" Darren asked, slightly tilting his head.

"No..." Hayley turned and began to head towards her car. "I saw it through the eyes of a bird on a nearby streetlight."

"What?"

"Really?"

"No shit?"

Shaking her head, she unlocked her car. The guys' words blurred together as they shot out their questions behind her. Turning around, she saw them still standing where she had left them, their eyes wide, jaws hanging open. "Are you guys going to just stand there and stare at me all night?" she said with a laugh. "Or are you going to get in the car so we can go bag ourselves a demon?"

When they still didn't move, she thought she might need to push them a little more. Suddenly, Manuel grinned. "Shotgun!" The other two, seeming to snap out of their stupor, glared at him.

"Damn it," she heard Christian mutter as they made their way towards her car. "I hate cramming into the back."

Laughing softly, Hayley sat down in her car, marveling at her passengers. *Men!*

Chapter 14

Manuel stared out the passenger window at the trees flying by, his mind still reeling over the events in the field. In truth, he hadn't known what to expect when Hayley showed up, but her power had been, well...surprising. He knew she would have some power within her, he had felt it at the coffee shop, but he hadn't anticipated the level she would be able to unleash.

Who knows if she has even shown us her full power, he mused.

Even now, he could feel the remnants of it clinging to his skin. Running his hands over his jeans, Manuel felt the tingle in his fingers. Judging by the look in his brothers' faces when she had started, they had a similar response.

Darren had seemed rather intrigued, taking what came in stride as she pushed out her power.

Manuel had felt his power flair in response, no doubt an automatic defensive move, but it had quieted instantly. Hayley's power had felt warm, enticing, as it rolled over him.

Christian, on the other hand, had stayed tense throughout, his body throwing off warning flares. It had radiated off him in waves, making Manuel feel like he was watching a tennis match. His eyes had constantly scanned back and forth between the two, as if one or both of them would suddenly blow.

Right now, though, the feeling in the car was rather subdued. Not as hyped as it usually was during a hunt. He figured it came from the fact that neither he nor his brothers had any idea what to expect next.

Turning his head slightly, he could just see Hayley out of the corner of his eye. Her eyes, now back to emerald green, stared straight ahead as she navigated through the city. Flashes of her eyes going white crossed his mind. Shaking his head, Manuel looked back out the window.

Now that *had been a surprise!* he thought with a laugh.

"Penny for your thoughts?"

Hayley's soft voice drifted through the car. Glancing at her, Manuel saw her look over. Blinking, he just smiled. "Just thinking about what we're going to do when we find the Shadow."

"Is that all?" she asked calmly.

"Yeah. Is that all?" Christian cut in before Manuel could answer.

Shooting an annoyed glare over his shoulder, seeing Christian's smirk, Manuel ground out, "Yes. That's all." Softening his tone, he looked back at Hayley. "I was just wondering what you had planned for us next." She shook her head. He could tell that she wasn't exactly buying it, so he pushed on. "I mean... After what you did in the field, I really don't know what to expect. Between the wind, your eyes going white, and telling us that you literally got a bird's-eye view, what else do you have in your bag of tricks, Ms. Hayley?"

Hayley's laughter filled the car. Like her power, it rolled over him. Looking over his shoulder at his brothers, Manuel could only grin. Darren just smirked at him, while Christian rolled his eyes.

"I have plenty of tricks," Hayley said with a chuckle. "One of which is being able to track demons down and send them back to Hell."

"Do you do this often?" Darren asked.

"Um... I've done it a few times before."

"How often is a few?" Christian inquired, leaning forward.

"Twice," she answered softly. "Both were lower-level. I've only tracked one down once, though. Well, twice if you count tonight."

"Twice," Christian spit out. Manuel glanced back and saw his brother's eyes narrow. "That's hardly enough experience to be qualified for this hunt, don't you think?"

"Well... Maybe I don't hunt down as many as you guys," she said with a huff, pausing when her response was met with sounds of dismay coming from the back. "But I can handle myself just fine. You guys can judge me on my experience, or lack thereof, all you want. However, I promised to track down and bag a demon tonight, and that's exactly what I plan to do."

"What exactly do you know about Shadows?" Darren asked.

"Other than the fact they like to move in the shadows to hide themselves," Christian bit out.

"Well, I know they're lower-level demons. The weaker ones can manipulate humans, while the stronger ones can physically harm them." She glanced towards Manuel, then in her rearview mirror at his brothers.

"And?" Darren asked.

"And they can be rather hard to find..."

Judging by the tension suddenly filling the car, Manuel could tell his brothers were doubting her again. He understood their irritation. Sure, by the way she had talked about hunting demons, he thought Hayley would have more experience, and yeah, he hoped she had more knowledge of what they were going up against, but he still felt she could do what she claimed. His instincts pushed him to believe her, regardless of what his mind said.

"How many have you guys hunted?" Hayley asked, breaking through his thoughts. "I imagine there have been quite a few...being demon hunters and all."

Manuel's mind raced as he tried to remember if he had told his brothers what she thought they were.

"Um...," Christian started. Manuel twisted around in his seat, meeting his brother's confused gaze, trying to convey that he should just go with it. "Yeah... Demon hunters..." He shook his head and looked over at Darren.

Darren, the same confused look on his face, glanced between the two of them before clearing his throat. "Yes, well, I would say we have definitely hunted down our fair share."

"At least two dozen," Manuel piped up, giving his brothers a grateful glance before looking over at Hayley.

"Two dozen?!" she exclaimed. "That's a pretty impressive number. How long have you been in the business?"

"Since we were made," Christian mumbled.

"What?" she asked, glancing in the rearview mirror.

"Since we came of age," Manuel rushed out. "Our Father was a real stickler for, um...the family business."

"Oh... So your Father was a hunter, too?"

"No. Our Father isn't really the hunting type," Darren said slowly.

"Really? I thought you said it was a family business."

"It is. He's just more of our..." Manuel paused, searching for the right word.

"Teacher," Darren said.

"Leader," Christian offered at the same time.

"Yeah... When it comes to hunting, he's our teacher and leader," Manuel agreed, looking over his shoulder, then back at Hayley.

"So your father... What? Taught you about demons, then told you where to hunt them?" she asked with genuine interest.

Manuel frowned slightly. Technically, she was right, but he had never really put it that way. They had never really been taught what to do. Not in the general definition of the word anyway. He and his brothers had just known. Just like they had never really been told where to go. The direction had just kind of been installed in them. Not that any of this was something he wanted to go over with Hayley at the moment because he'd have to reveal they weren't really demon hunters. Frowning more, Manuel looked out the window. He guessed they kind of where, but he would like to think he and his brothers were more than that. Thinking back over all they had done since falling, he felt his lips curl. Only hunting really came to mind.

Shit, she's right, he thought with a sigh. *We are glorified demon hunters with wings!*

"Manuel?" Hayley asked.

Realizing the conversation must have gone on without him, Manuel shook off the sudden feeling of hollowness that had washed over him and turned back to her. "Sorry. What?" He could hear his brothers' shift in their seats, but didn't bother to look their way.

"I was just saying that if all you guys did growing up was hunt demons, if that's all you knew, it..." Her voice trailed off as she looked over, briefly meeting his gaze.

Instantly, he felt his defenses rise. "It what?" he asked, his voice coming out a little sharper than he meant it to. "Not that you really know us enough to have formed an opinion on how we were raised. I mean, you met me... What? Three times, two of my brothers once, but you feel you know us well enough to give us your two cents on how sad our childhood must have been? Please continue. I can't wait to hear your take on my life."

"Sorry... It's nothing," she murmured, seeming to concentrate harder on the road in front of her. "I'm just nervous about finding this Shadow. I talk a lot when I'm nervous. Just forget I said anything."

Feeling a twinge of guilt flutter through his chest, Manuel watched her nibble on her bottom lip. Her hands gripped the steering wheel so tightly, he could see her knuckles turning white. Hayley's eyes had even taken on a misty look, as though she were trying to hold back tears. Considering he had just released his inner asshole on her, she probably was. Why did he act like that? Because he didn't like the fact she was probably closer to the truth then he cared to admit. Part of him wanted to apologize. The other part felt that she should feel bad. Even if she were right, it wasn't her place to say anything.

Shit. He wanted to get out of here. Manuel had never been like this. He had always known what he felt, what needed to get done, and how to handle those around him. However, in the course of a couple weeks, Hayley had completely turned his world upside down. Glancing over his shoulder, he was meet with glares. After his little outburst, both his brothers looked at him like they didn't recognize him. Christian looked away, his lips tight, as if he were trying to rein in his anger, while Darren still glared at him. Feeling even more like crap, Manuel turned back around and slid down a bit in his seat. He could feel Darren's and Christian's anger, mixed with something like disappointment, radiating through the car...and they didn't even truly like Hayley yet.

Well... Shit!

Chapter 15

Turning onto Hansen Road, Hayley's body seemed to relax. Since the conversation had come to a complete halt, it had been as quiet as a coffin in the car. When Manuel snapped at her, she had been hurt. Of course, she understood how he felt. Hell, if they were to try and make assumptions about her past based on what little they knew, Hayley was sure she would have acted the same way.

Then again, she would like to think that if their situations were reversed, she would have quickly realized any comments made hadn't been said to hurt her, and she would have apologized or explained why she had acted that way. But she got nothing. Not even another glance from Manuel the rest of the drive. *Well, fine*, she thought with agitation. If he wanted to act like that, so be it. At least the other two had the decency to look apologetic when she caught their gazes in the rearview mirror.

With a mental sigh, she pulled her car up to the curb, quickly looking at the house as she turned the key. It looked like nobody was home.

What a relief.

Climbing out of the car, Hayley slowly made her way toward the sidewalk.

She could hear the doors on her car closing as the men climbed out. Looking around, she smiled at the well-kept lawns and lovely houses. Neighborhoods like these always charmed her. Maybe it was the *Leave it to Beaver* feel they had. Whatever it was, Hayley loved it.

Turning in a circle, she noticed the neighborhood seemed darker than usual. Frowning, Hayley turned towards the boys. She opened her mouth to say something when she saw all three of them stop, frowns on their faces. She was just about to ask if they saw something when a sudden flash of movement caught her attention. Spinning to the right, Hayley made out a shadow curling along the back of one of the houses.

"Did you-"

"The Shadow's over there," Darren interrupted, shrugging apologetically at her glare.

"Yeah... That's what I thought I saw," she remarked, turning to walk towards the house in question. She could hear their heavy footsteps as they began to follow her, Manuel still not saying a word. Just thinking about him increased her pace.

"Hold up," she heard Christian say. Pausing, she turned around and placed her hands on her hips in irritation. "We haven't gone over what we're going to do once we find this Shadow."

"We send him on a one-way ticket right back to where he came from," Hayley stated simply.

"Yes, but how?" Darren asked, his eyes narrowed.

"Well...," she said, looking from one pair of uncertain eyes to another. Hayley could feel their power simmering on the surface. She knew they were eager to go after this demon, even if it wasn't showing on the outside. She also knew they were uncertain of what was going to happen. "It's simple. I'm going to curse him."

"Curse him?" Manuel said with a small level of amusement.

"Yes, Manuel. Curse him," she said with a huff. "Listen, while we stand here trying to strategize, our Shadow demon...you know, the one we are trying to hunt down...is getting away."

Just as the last word left her lips, she heard a deep chuckle come from behind her. The sound was like oil rolling across her skin. Her spine stiffening, she spun around.

"What the fuck?" she heard one of the guys murmur as they watched a large shadowy figure slide around the side of one of the houses. The demon's form, devoid of any true detail, was massive. Even with only getting a glimpse of it, they were able to see that the Shadow towered well over the house's second story.

"Shit." The hiss came from Manuel as he stepped up next to her. "I forgot how big these fuckers can get."

Hayley looked at Manuel, sure that her eyes were wider than ever. "I have never seen any that big!"

"Surprise," Christian said sarcastically as he and Darren stepped up to her other side.

"Funny. Can we get this show on the road, or do we still need to discuss things?"

Without saying a word, Manuel began to walk towards the building, the rest of them falling into step behind him. Trying to watch for the Shadow, Hayley made sure to keep scanning around them as they went. She could feel her hands shaking by her side as they walked up to the side of the house. Her heart beat so hard, she was certain the Shadow could hear her coming.

I need to calm down, she thought, concentrating on her breathing. Repeating a five count for every inhale and exhale, Hayley didn't see that Manuel had stopped moving...until she slammed into his back. "Oh," she breathed out, taking a step back, her hands still resting against him. His muscles flexed beneath her touch. *Thank God it's dark out*, she thought, her cheeks heating up. Hoping to play it off, Hayley quickly glanced behind her, hoping to make it look like she had been pushed. However, the smirks on Darren's and Christian's faces told her they weren't planning on letting it slide.

"You okay?"

Manuel's deep voice smoothed across her skin, causing her body to hum. Turning around, she planned on giving some snide remark...something about him needing to warn people when he was going to stop and to watch where he was going. Instead, her breath left her when she suddenly found herself mere inches from his face.

"Fine," she whispered, her eyes widening as she stared into his deep amethyst gaze. They almost seemed to have a glow about them as they traveled down her body, then back up to her face. A knowing look filled them as he smirked down at her.

"Are you sure?" Even his voice held a hint of cockiness as he tilted his head.

"Yes." Her voice shaking slightly, Hayley willed herself to remember to breathe. Taking another step back, she forced her eyes to narrow. "I said I was fine. So continue doing...whatever it was you were doing."

A twitch of his lips was his only response as he pulled back. The need to pounce on him and press her lips to his took her by surprise as she watched him turn back towards the house. What the heck was wrong with her? She wasn't the type to just go around and jump the bones of any hot guy who crossed her path. Although, if Hayley were being honest with herself, she had never come across a man with Manuel's...raw sexiness. She had been doing so well pushing these thoughts aside, but when she had turned and found him so close to her...

No! Now is definitely not the time or the place.

When the guys' voices broke through her warring mind, Hayley snapped herself out of her thoughts and looked around. "What's going on?"

"Welcome back." Christian raised his eyebrow.

"Whatever," she mumbled, gaining her a cheesy grin from him. Smiling, she looked back at Manuel, who was watching her intently. "So, what are we doing?"

"Well," Manuel whispered, glancing over his shoulder. "The Shadow is in the backyard. I don't think we're going to be able to get him away from the houses, so we're going to have to confront him here."

"Here?" she asked incredulously, looking at the three of them. "What about all these people? I'm sure the houses aren't empty. What if they hear us? See us? I mean-"

Darren raised his hand. "Don't worry... Nobody here will know a thing."

"How can you be so sure?"

"Hayley-" Manuel started.

"What happens when he fights back?"

"Hayley," Manuel said a little louder.

"Because he *will* fight back, things will get loud, and everyone in this block will know something's going on, and-"

"Hayley!" Manuel snapped.

"What?" she asked angrily.

"Stop worrying so much." His voice got softer. "It's going to be okay."

"Yeah, Hayley," Christian chimed in. "I got this." His statement caused the other two to chuckle. Her gaze swept over them as she felt her jaw drop.

"You *got* this? What does that even mean?" she whispered.

The guys just smiled at her as they turned to make their way to the backyard. She watched as Darren walked up to the corner and peeked around it. Christian leaned against the wall behind him, Manuel following. Seeming to notice she had yet to move, he turned to look at her.

Shaking her head, she could only whisper, "What does Christian mean by 'I got this'?"

Manuel just smirked, motioning for her to hurry.

With a huff, Hayley moved in behind him. She just couldn't understand how they could be so nonchalant about doing this in a neighborhood. How could they just laugh it off? This was ridiculous. Dangerous. They should try to lure the Shadow out and away from all these innocent people. Just as the thought crossed her mind, she began to hear Christian mumbling. Hayley thought he was saying something about the Shadow or what they should do next, but the more she strained to hear him, the more she realized whatever he was saying wasn't English.

Hayley moved a step closer, leaning around Manuel. Christian's back was to her. She could see his tension as he shifted from one foot to the other. She could sense it, just as she could feel the power beginning to roll off Manuel and Darren. When she opened her mouth to question what they were up to, she was hit with a force so strong, it made her stumble back. She would have fallen had it not been for Manuel. He grasped onto her arm and pulled her roughly into him. Looking up, she gasped at their closeness.

"Wha-" Her voice came out so quietly, she wasn't sure she had even made a sound.

"I got you," Manuel whispered, smiling down at her. His arms tightened around her body before releasing his hold.

The loss of contact caused her to shiver as she felt him step back. She wanted to ask about the sudden rush of power, but before she could utter a word, they heard a loud growl coming from behind the house.

"Shit," Christian hissed.

Manual spun around, pushing her behind him. Hayley stepped to the side and found the boys all facing the Shadow...and the demon was huge! She honestly thought her eyes had been playing tricks on her earlier, but seeing him towering over the men in front of her, men who were all large in their own right, was daunting.

"Did the little Guardians decide to come out to play?" the demon growled.

Guardians? Hayley glanced around, then back at the demon. *Just gonna add that to my growing list of questions.*

"And is that a little witch you have hiding back there?" the demon continued, his voice sounding like gravel scraping along the ground. "My, my, my... This is a treat!" The air shuddered with a sudden pulse of power as the demon let out chuckle.

Manuel slid over, blocking the demon's view of her. "Watch it, demon."

"Or what?" the demon hissed. "Tell me, Guardian. What is it you think you can do to me? Are you going to... What did I hear your little witch say? Curse me?" At their silence, the Shadow just clicked his tongue. "How amusing."

"I'm going to send you back to that oily black pit from which you spawned," Hayley ground out.

At this, the demon growled. "We shall see."

Hayley felt the demon's power start to flow around them, its darkness causing goosebumps on her skin. The air around them grew colder by the second, making it painful to breathe. This Shadow's power was intense. He was definitely at a higher level than what she'd dealt with before. The boys all shifted their weight in front of her, seemingly ready to fight. With what, she wasn't certain. Hayley hadn't seen them bring any weapons. Then again, wasn't *she* the one who was supposed to be fighting the demon? Maybe they had left their weapons behind because they trusted her to handle this. Shaking her head, she felt the demon send another wave of power towards them.

Well, I'm not here just to watch, she thought. *Time to get started.*

Moving quickly around Manuel, she was immediately met with the Shadow's hostile gaze. He smirked, looking down at her. His power shuddered violently around them as Hayley watched his form shift. A gray mist began to swirl around him as he seemed to shrink in on himself, his eyes blazing as they remained fixed on hers. Seeming to enjoy her shock as he pulled his form into a more human appearance, he chuckled.

Gasping, Hayley watched him take a step towards them. Although looking like a human, he still had a very demonic air about him. If that didn't give her pause, there was also the fact that he looked like he had just stepped out of an old film noir. It might have been humorous, but he now looked like a nightmare come to life.

Hayley's fingers twitched slightly as she felt her own power begin to rise. Stepping in front of Manuel, she felt his power brush hers, his warmth giving her more strength.

"Hello, little witch," the demon breathed, his hands rising slightly at his sides. "Were you looking for me?"

"Yes," Hayley whispered, her power building as she moved towards him slowly.

"Well, here I am." His head tilted down slightly as a glow appeared to emanate around him. His black eyes took on a shine as they tracked her movements. "So now that you have found me, little witch, what do you plan to do next?"

"I plan to send you back to Hell," she stated simply.

"Oh, really? You think between you and your little *Guardian* friends you can beat me?"

"No," Hayley responded with a smirk. "Just me." Facing the demon, she mentally began to pull her power into her, silently calling on the air around her.

His grin widened as he flexed his own power. "Really? You think you can take me on all by your lonesome? How very brave of you." His eyes narrowed as he bared a rather impressive set of sharp teeth at her.

Hayley crouched down slowly, never breaking eye contact, resting her right hand upon the ground. She felt it warm beneath her touch as she silently called to it. A breeze began, her hair whipping around her face as she listened to the demon continue to spew out his vanity-laced words. With each remark, she inwardly smiled. The one thing that would always be a demon's downfall was their vanity. They all thought they were so untouchable, so beyond reproach. This demon was no different. She watched as he puffed his chest out, throwing his power around him, as if that proved he should not be messed with. Well, Hayley knew better. Sure, it would take a little more effort on her part, and she'd probably be close to fainting once she was done. However, like the old saying goes...

The bigger they are...

She threw her power towards him, testing to see how serious he was taking this so far. Upon impact, she felt her power come up against a wall. It was impressive, but not immovable. Gritting her teeth, she called on the wind to aid her. It blew over her in a gust, causing her hair to curl around her face as she pushed its strength into the demon. For a split second, she felt a sense of victory when the demon's eyes widened in shock.

He took a step back before being pushed down to the ground. The demon hit with a thud, letting out an owl-like shriek as he fought against her.

She watched as the demon pulled himself up, his power now vibrating around him as his anger rose. There were no more empty threats, no more childish jabs. Now she really saw him. His black eyes narrowed into slits, his teeth shining in the moonlight.

With no warning, he lunged at her. Hayley felt the rush of power as the guys fought their need to jump in. She was ready for this, though. Pulling her power back into her like a breath of air, she raised her hand and thrust it towards him. *"Sistete!"* she shouted. Her power crashed into him, halting his advance.

Standing slowly, she kept her hand raised, focused, holding him in check. He snapped and growled at her as he fought against his invisible restraints. "Witch!" he half screamed and half growled. "Release me! Now!"

She watched him a second more, noticing how his form began to shudder as he lost his control to maintain his human form. Tipping her head to the side, she raised her other hand. "So be it," she whispered, feeling her power tighten around him. He threw his head back in response to her deadly grip. His screams chilled her to the bone as he intensified his attempts to get free.

"I call upon the powers of the world to give me the strength I need. Strength to remove this unholy disease, this demon, from our sight and return it to the firepit from which it rose. Strengthen me to send it, to keep it there, never able to rise and set foot upon our soil again."

The demon became wild at that point, thrashing his arms and legs hysterically. "You will not win, witch!" he screamed into the night. His human form dimmed in and out as he began to resort back into his shadowy self. "Do not think you can beat me!"

"I call upon the Earth beneath my feet to swallow up this foul demon. To remove it from your surface, returning the balance that is ever in the light." She felt her power burning from the pressure. "Be gone from my sight, from this plane, falling into that oily vat from which you rose."

"You...will...never...beat...me!" he screamed. The demon was now nothing more than flashing black eyes and a

shadowy image, like black smoke caught in the wind.

"But I already have," Hayley stated calmly as the wind growled around her. "Be gone, demon! *Recedemus! Recedemus!*" Her voice rose to a scream as she fought to be heard over the wind. She felt the moment the power around him changed. With wide eyes, she watched as the demon ceased his movement. His angry eyes promised revenge right before he threw his head back one last time, his image twisting as a red light started in his center. The light grew and grew until it was shining out all around him. Then, as quickly as the light had appeared, it exploded with a sudden brilliance, then was gone, leaving nothing of the demon in its wake.

Looking down as the last bits of black smoke whispered out of existence, Hayley felt her power recede, only somewhat aware of movement behind her. It wasn't until she felt herself being lifted from the ground that she even realized she had collapsed.

"I got you," a warm voice whispered in her ear. *Manuel.* Closing her eyes, she welcomed his warmth and strength as he carried her away. "You did good, darlin'. You did really good."

She felt a small smile on her lips as she nestled into him. Her last thought before sweet oblivion took her away was that at this second, in his arms, she was right where she was supposed to be.

Chapter 16

"Christian, you coming?"

Christian turned to see Darren standing by Hayley's car, Manuel tucking her into the back seat. Shit! After what she had just done, he wouldn't be surprised if she were in a coma for a week. Between the wind growling, the ground moving, power rolling over them like a locomotive, and the demon's fucking combustion... Dammit, *he* was tired!

Christian smirked, remembering the look of pride on Manuel's face when Hayley took the demon down.

As soon as the act was done, they had all noticed Hayley sway. Manuel had gotten to her just as she was about to collapse. Memories of catching Ella raced through his mind as Christian watched Manuel scoop Hayley protectively into his arms. And the similarities of that act weren't lost on Manuel. They had made eye contact as he carried her towards the car. Christian had laughed out loud at the realization in Manuel's eyes. He wasn't going to give his brother a hard time about it...yet.

Darren had stopped by Christian before following Manuel to the car. "Can you take care of the Shade, brother?"

"Sure thing," he responded, turning to concentrate on the power still surrounding them. If he allowed his power to roam freely, he could follow the full arc of the Shade. It was as little or as big as they wanted. In this instance, it was enough to cover the back and side of the house. Sending his power out, he felt the Shade shiver beneath his invisible touch. This cover had saved their asses more than once...not to mention the countless fragile human minds.

As Christian began pulling his power back and calling down the Shade, a sudden sound made him pause. It had been at that instance Darren had called out to him.

Staring at Darren, he watched his brother slowly walk away from the car, a frown forming on his face as his eyes narrowed. "Christian?"

The smile that had been on his face as memories had washed over him was replaced with a sneer. A slight drumming sound began to echo through his mind. It was a sound Christian had not heard since the night they rescued Ella from Hell.

Looking away from Darren, he glanced around. Christian could just barely make out the drumming, but he would know it anywhere.

The wind curled over him as he whispered for the Shade to drop, falling around him like the Earth itself sighed.

Holding still, he waited for the power to quiet so he could better search for the demon behind the drumming. He had a few guesses on which demon it could be, but he only needed one.

As the air stilled around him, Christian held his breath. It had to be Castigo. Andras was still stuck below, and the other demon there that night, well... Christian really didn't know much about that one, but he was certain he wasn't the one watching them now. No. This had to be Castigo.

Curling his fingers into a fist, Christian felt rage start to build within him. How dare he follow them here. Turning in a slow circle, he listened. The drumming, which had been soft, sounded louder, stronger when he faced north. Christian took several steps in that direction, pushing his power out before him.

He was so caught up in his hunt, he jumped when Darren suddenly appeared beside him. "What's wrong?" he whispered, his eyes scanning the area in which Christian had been staring.

Looking towards the houses, Christian opened his mouth to tell Darren about the drumming, tell him they were being watched, but just as suddenly as the drumming started, it stopped.

His frown deepened as he took a couple more steps forward, confused.

"There was drumming. It stopped, though. I was sure it was getting stronger, but..." Shaking his head, Christian turned to look at Darren. His brother's eyes were filled with worry.

"You mean like the drumming you and Ella heard?" he asked, his voice low.

"Yes... I think Castigo was nearby." Christian could still feel his muscles tensing with anger. *The fucking coward*! Why did Castigo take off? Looking at the houses again, his eyes scanned the dark corners and shadowed rooftops. Why didn't he face him? Not that he should be surprised. That piece of shit was probably too scared.

Giving himself a mental shake, Christian realized Darren was talking to him. "Sorry. What?"

"I asked if you can still sense him anywhere. I would ask Manuel to check it out, but he's with Hayley."

Christian nodded. Sending his power out one last time, he took a deep breath and turned back to Darren. "I don't sense him or anything else around here now. He must have taken off and is probably long gone by now."

Darren glanced around again. Christian watched as he unconsciously ran one of his fingers over his gold ring. Since the events with Andras, he had started wearing it every day. He eyed the cross boldly engraved on the top, roughly carved into the gold with black ink soaked into it, causing the contrast between black and yellow to be readily noticed. Of course, the ring was more than it appeared...but so was most of what Darren owned, as well as the man himself.

"Well, let's get out of here. Hayley woke up a bit ago and asked if we could take her home."

"She's awake? Already?" Christian couldn't believe it. He was sure she would be out for days.

"Yeah. She's a tough one. Anyway, Manuel promised her we'd get her back to her place to rest. Plus, we need to get back and fill everyone else in." Darren looked around again before turning to walk back towards the car. "With the Shade down, we should probably leave before someone sees us anyway," he remarked over his shoulder.

Christian just nodded as he began to follow. Making his way slowly through the yard, he glanced over his shoulder, looking around one last time before jogging to catch up with his brother.

Chapter 17

Well, that almost sucked, Castigo thought with a groan. Leaning around the house's chimney, he watched the Guardians pile into that little witch's car. Where did they get a witch? And such a powerful one? She may still be a little green, but shit. After the way she took care of that Shadow, she was well on her way to being a serious force with which to be reckoned.

And she's working with them!

Andras was going to be pissed. Then again, he may appreciate getting a heads-up. Castigo smiled as he thought of finally getting back on Andras' good side. Sure, his boss had trusted him to come up here again, but this taste of freedom hadn't come without some...reminders.

Just the thought of their last meeting caused the wounds on his wrists to flair. Barely suppressing a growl, he watched as Christian glanced around before getting into the car. No doubt looking for him.

He had just happened upon their little hunt after the rush of power in the area had caught his attention. It had tasted different than any he'd come across before. All power has a distinct flavor to it, changing from one to another. This power had tasted earthy, wild.

As he had come upon the group, he quickly realized what was happening, managing to slide in just as they had enabled the Shade. Keeping himself close to its edge, Castigo had been able to hide himself amongst its pulsing power. Moving to the rooftop, he had been able to see the whole show...and what a show it had been!

Afterwards, he had gotten careless. Leaning over the edge to get a better look at the fiery redhead, he had practically slid down the fucking side of the house. Luckily, he was able to catch himself and move back before Christian spotted him.

The Guardian may not have seen him, but he sure as hell knew he was there. Castigo had been so wrapped up in what was happening, he had forgotten about Christian's annoying ability to sense them.

He was like fucking demon radar.

As the car slowly pulled away from the curb, Castigo rose to his feet. Never taking his eyes off the shrinking vehicle, he quietly made his way to the edge of the roof. Crouching on the ledge, he tore his gaze from the street the Guardians had disappeared down. After pausing to make sure he was alone, Castigo quietly leapt to the ground.

Making his way to the backyard, he couldn't help but notice the remnants of the little witch's power still clinging to the air around him. Reaching the spot the Shadow had been, Castigo knelt down, hovering his hand over the still smoking grass.

"Fool," he muttered as tiny lines of smoke curled around his fingers. Shoving his power into the ground, he searched for a direct line to where the Shadow had been sent. Finding nothing, he sighed. Not that he had really expected to find anything, but he figured he'd give it a shot.

Time to give the boss the good news.

Closing his eyes, Castigo sent out a mental call to Andras. Seeing that he didn't normally contact Andras, usually waiting for him to reach out first, an instant sense of unease fell over him. A shiver of power raced through him. His only warning before Andras' voiced hissed through his mind.

Castigo. His name sounded more like an irritated statement than a question.

Although his first instinct was to wait for Andras to say more, he decided keeping silent would do his cause more harm than good. *Sir, I have some information that may be of great importance to you.*

Really? And what information do you have that is so important it could not wait?

Licking his lips, Castigo got right to it. *I saw the Guardians working with a witch, sir. She cursed a Shadow into the Nether Realms as the Guardians held the Shade around them.*

Castigo felt Andras' power rumble through him as he growled. *A witch? Did you recognize her as one we have dealt with before?*

No, Andras. She is not. She is quite powerful. I can still feel it clinging to the ground around me, and the spot the Shadow was is still smoking.

You saw it all?

Yes, sir.

And did the Guardians know you were nearby?

Castigo felt his blood chill. He knew Andras would ask this. The demon was just waiting for him to mess up again. Yeah, Christian probably sensed him, and yeah, he probably knew Castigo was in the area, but did he really need to tell Andras?

Castigo? Did they know you were there?

Making up his mind, Castigo took a deep breath to calm his nerves. *No, Andras. They did not.*

Good.

Would you like me to look into the witch, sir?

No. I will get another to do that. I need you to do something else for me.

Frowning slightly, Castigo nodded. *What would you like me to do?*

I think it is time someone checks on our own little fallen angel. He has been on his own, unchecked, for some time now. I wish to know how my club is doing.

Of course. I will head there straight away. Castigo could feel Andras' power flexing.

I trust you will make sure everything is in order for my arrival there. Tomorrow night, I plan to send up some of my close guards to serve as security. I will follow them soon after.

Is Dev not doing what you asked of him? Castigo asked. He didn't exactly care for the little shit, but he had seen some of what Dev had been put through. Castigo's stomach turned at the memories.

I do not doubt that Dev has followed my orders. He, more than most, knows what happens if he does not. No. I simply want you to check on my...investment. Make sure I will be happy when I finally arrive. Andras paused, Castigo feeling a sudden shift in his boss' power. It flared briefly, causing him to break out in a cold sweat as he fought to not pull back. Bracing both hands firmly on the ground, Castigo waited for Andras to continue. *Then,* Andras' voice whispered dangerously through his mind, *remind him whom he belongs to and that, once I am there, I expect his unquestioning loyalty when it comes to dealing with the Guardians.*

Of course, Andras, Castigo instantly responded. He felt Andras mentally smirk before closing their connection.

Finally alone, Castigo slowly opened his eyes and let out a soft sigh. He had not been to Andras' club, The 9th Circle, since he found the location, but he had heard a lot about it. It was a massive project. One Andras insisted be complete before he came topside.

It was to be a nightclub in the truest sense. The 9th Circle would open as the sun began to set, closing when it rose. It would serve the best alcohol and, unbeknownst to the public at large, the best drugs on the market. Then there would be music. The more sexually charged, the better. However, Castigo was sure all this club was going to offer was not purely for their human customers' benefit.

What his boss truly intended to get out of it, nobody seemed to know. There was a lot of speculation, but it could be anything.

Looking down, he noted the ground beneath his hands had cooled. All power left over from earlier was gone. There wasn't even a bent blade of grass as a reminder that anything had even taken place. It was as if the true keeper of the balance was the Earth herself, cleaning up after their run-ins.

A sudden sound behind him pulled Castigo from his thoughts. Standing slowly, he turned around and came face-to-face with a rather frightened human male.

"What's goin' on he..." The human's voice trailed off as he watched Castigo rise to his full height.

The male was probably no older than forty. He stood there, staring with wide eyes and a gaping mouth. His skin was unusually pale beneath the moon's soft light. Castigo couldn't stop the grin from spreading across his face. He could smell the fear in the human like a heavy perfume.

"Wh-who are you? What are you doin' in my backyard?" the human finally stuttered.

Castigo cocked his head, debating on what to do with him. He could always wipe his memories, erase the last few hours from his life completely.

That's too boring.

He could steal his soul with a quick twist of his power. Castigo frowned.

Too clean.

He could always just play with him a bit, then let him go. He would take pleasure in the fact that this human would live in fear for the rest of his life with the knowledge that there really were creatures out there that went bump in the night.

Hmm... That one definitely has potential.

His silence must have unnerved the human further because he released a low whine as they stared at each other. His eyes were so wide now, they looked as though they would pop right out of his head. Castigo watched with amusement as the human fought to pull himself together.

"I...I think you need to leave. I'm going to call the cops!" he threatened.

Castigo laughed. "And do you think they will be able to help you? Truly, what do you think they will do? You will be dead long before the first ring."

"You're gonna kill me?"

"Well, the thought *had* crossed my mind."

His words seemed to hit the human physically because he took several unsteady steps back, sweat dripping down his face, his eyes beginning to move around wildly as he looked for a way to escape.

I really don't have time to play with him, at least not enough to truly make it worth my while, Castigo thought with disappointment. He watched as the human's muscles began to flex, his need to flee growing.

"Please, you don't have to do this," the human whined. "I won't tell anyone. Nobody would believe me anyway."

"You are right," Castigo agreed quietly. "You will not tell anyone."

"I swear I won't... Just, please, let me go."

Castigo reached into his coat, his fingers brushing the various blades he liked to use. A thrill ran through him as he touched upon his favorite, its steel cool beneath his fingertips. The feel of the blade caused his fingers to twitch with a need to use it. *It has been a while*, he mused.

"That will not be happening, either," he stated calmly.

"Then... Then I'll scream," the human retorted, his voice shrill.

In a flash, Castigo was on him, the human collapsing beneath his strength. Rolling the man beneath him, he pinned him down with a knee to his back. Castigo's blade was already in his right hand, glinting dangerously as he held it over the human. With his left hand, he shoved the man's face into the soft ground beneath them.

Muffled whines and whimpers rose from the human as he thrashed wildly. Castigo pressed the tip of the blade to his neck, hissing sharply when he saw the first drops of blood pool around it. Sliding his knife across the man's skin, he felt the human still, his body shuddering as he yielded to Castigo's will.

Leaning closer, the scent of blood and fear filled his nose, causing Castigo to pause before releasing a soft chuckle. Maybe he could play for just a bit, have a little fun before ending the human's life. "I cannot promise you will enjoy the next few moments, for what I plan to do with you will be for *my* enjoyment, but I can promise you this." Licking his lips, he slid the knife down the man's spine, slicing cleanly through his shirt's thin material to the delicate skin beneath. The human's shudders were now so violent, he could feel each one humming through his bones. "In the end...," he whispered, willing his grip on the human's head to tighten as he increased the pressure of his blade, "you *will* scream."

Andras unconsciously tapped his finger on his desk. His office... Shit, his whole building was quiet. Almost too quiet compared to how chaotic it had been the last few weeks. With most of his demons already gone, there weren't as many around to constantly bother him. Well, there was still Agalon, but he was busy getting himself ready and taking care of the last few errands Andras needed him to do down here.

With a content sigh, he glanced around. It was almost time for him to leave. Within a matter of days, he would finally find himself out of Hell and standing on the streets above for the first time. It was no longer a matter of waiting for the veil to drop because that had happened some time ago. Now it was just the simple act of making sure any loose ends down here were taken care of before heading out. Not that there was that much to do. He had been sure to keep the knowledge of his entire plan to just a select few, careful not to have any sensitive information find its way to the wrong individuals...like Lucifer.

Andras frowned at the thought of his boss. Saying Lucifer had a temper was an understatement. Andras had been witness to it first-hand on several occasions. Hell, he had been on the wrong end of his anger more times than he would like to admit. In this case, it wasn't that he thought his boss would be against what he had planned, but he would probably be a bit unhappy that he'd been kept out of the loop, more than likely demanding to be in charge of things from now on.

And that wouldn't do.

So, to keep things going the way he wanted them to, and to keep his ass out of the proverbial frying pan, Andras kept things close. That way, should they blow up in his face, there was a short list to go down to find out who caused it.

Simple, just the way he liked it.

And, like his club, things were falling into place.

Leaving the care of his club in Dev's hands had been a hard decision. One that, thankfully, had panned out. Since he sent Dev topside, things had been moving along with little to no problems. At least no problems he'd heard about. Not that he wouldn't put it past Dev to try and hide any issues from him, especially since Andras had been very specific on what would happen if he were to be disappointed. There was always the chance of a slip up, a possibility of things falling through. That was why he told Castigo to check on him.

Ever since that little angelic pain in the ass had landed in Hell, he'd been a thorn in Andras' side, but it was nothing that a little time in his personal dungeon hadn't been able to fix.

Smiling at the memory, Andras leaned back in his chair. Sure, it had taken some time to break him, but it had been worth it.

Just the thought of Dev's screams brought forth an almost giddy laugh. That first time had been a while ago. He had held Dev down in that pit for years, breaking him. *It had to have been... What? At least thirty years,* he mused with a grin. Andras had been sure he had taken all the fight out of him. For years after letting him out, Dev had been a good little soldier, doing everything Andras asked of him without question.

Then, out of nowhere, the little bastard had decided he was going to pull a one-eighty and start acting like a little shit again. Needless to say, that didn't go over well...with Andras or any of his demons. So, to get control of the situation, he had Dev dragged back down into his dungeon.

This time, though, it hadn't taken years to bring him to heel. Remembering what had done the trick the first time, he had made sure Dev was dealt with quickly and thoroughly. It wasn't until the fallen angel was completely broken and begging for his torture to end that Andras had let up. But he needed to make sure the lesson stuck this time. That Dev understood any disobedience from him in the future would not be tolerated. Period.

Even with Dev's promise of obedience, Andras had left him down there for another twenty years to really grind in his point. *Literally*, he thought with a laugh.

So did Andras feel Dev was going to mess up with his club, disappoint him in any way? No. Did he think they may have a problem when it came time to deal with his brothers? Absolutely.

Dev may not defy him outright, but the angel would probably need to be reminded a couple times about whom he now belonged to. With any luck, Castigo already paid him a visit and started planting the proper...incentives. They had enough with which to concern themselves. Adding a rogue angel into the mix would just be a headache Andras would prefer to avoid.

His immediate concerns were getting to Ella and finding that little witch with whom those pesky Guardians were now working. A snarl ripped from his throat. Getting the news about that had been an unwelcome surprise, yet it was one he could definitely capitalize on if he could get his hands on her. The inconvenience of this new information didn't matter, though. What mattered to him now was getting to the witch and his beautiful Ella before the five cocky bastards got in his way...again.

Once back in his care, dealing with Ella would be a snap. Having left her with a part of himself to keep her tethered to him, ever so slightly, had been draining. He hadn't realized how taxing it would be to part with even just the smallest amount of his power. Even now, he didn't feel quite right, slightly off-kilter. Once she was back with him, not only would he feel complete again, but that small bit of power residing in her would help bond her to him. And, this time, she would find her desire to fight him off wouldn't be what it was. In fact, if the worries in her dreams proved true, he had a feeling she may not fight him much at all.

The witch, on the other hand, may be a problem. He could definitely make use of her if he could break her, bend her to his will. If not, well... He had ways of dealing with a defiant witch. The main thing was to get her away from the Guardians. Not only would that break them a little with the failure of losing yet another female in their care, but it would keep her from being able to help them.

To be able to completely break them, to see the hope and light fade from their eyes... That would make all his recent headaches worth it. Maybe he would even put Dev back in the pit for fun, lining up his brothers right beside him. Their own little family reunion down here in Hell.

Andras smirked. *Oh, this is going to be fun.*

Hearing a throat clear, Andras swung his gaze to his office door, Agalon standing patiently in the entrance. The demon's normally ice blue eyes were now black, and had been ever since he'd ended up on the wrong end of his own bullet. Although it only had the power to kill an angel, not a demon, it turned out to still pack quite a punch. Even after all the time that'd passed since that day, Agalon's power continued to remain present, flaring against his will just below the surface. Andras watched that power swirl through his eyes now.

"Agalon."

"Andras, I have done all you asked of me. We should be ready to leave soon."

"Good."

"Has there been any news?"

"No. Last I heard, all was moving along just as I planned." At that, Andras heard Agalon scoff. Giving his second-in-command a low growl, he watched Agalon immediately cast his eyes to the ground. "Do you feel I am being lied to? Or maybe you feel I am not aware of what is going on with my own demons?"

"Of course not, Andras."

"Then what? You obviously have doubts, so tell me."

Agalon gave a small shrug. "It is that fallen angel. Dev. I do not trust him."

"You think he will defy me?"

Agalon lifted his gaze to meet Andras'. His black eyes took on a soft grey glow as he released a throaty growl. "Yes. Maybe not right away, but I think he will turn on us, on you, the first chance he gets."

Andras watched his second for a moment. He could not fault his concerns, seeing as he felt the same way. For now, though, they needed Dev to take care of the club. Once it was up and running, Andras was sure they could easily find someone else to take the angel's spot. Until then, though...

"Well, Agalon, I guess we will just have to keep an eye on him. Make sure he never forgets whom he now answers to."

At that, Agalon's lips twitched. "I am sure I can help with that. I have enjoyed all the...*time* I have been able to spend with Dev over the years."

Grinning, Andras leaned back in his seat. "Yes, I am sure. Do not worry, Agalon. All will be well. As soon as we get topside and I have everything going the way I want it, you can have all the time you wish with Dev." Watching the demon's eyes light up, he chuckled. "I would hate to deprive one of my most loyal demons of something he so enjoys. Yes. I believe putting Dev in your...care will keep him in line."

"It will be my pleasure." Agalon's chin dipped a bit. "Truly."

Chapter 18

Manuel let out a soft moan as he walked into his room and spotted his bed. Crap, he was tired. After getting Hayley back to her house, making sure the place was secure, and checking on her several times before leaving, he felt like he had been up for days. As soon as he and his brothers had walked a good distance from her house, they had dematerialized to their own...just as the sun was rising.

Can't believe I've been up for almost twenty-eight hours, he thought.

The day after tomorrow, they were supposed to start moving their things into the new place, and he needed to get some sleep.

Falling face-first onto his bed, he turned and looked at all the boxes on the floor. *If only they could move themselves.* Reaching out, he snapped his fingers a couple times. When nothing happened, he proceeded to try different ways to get them to move. He wiggled his nose, squinted his eyes, and tried to will them to move with his mind. If he could just get them to move across the room, he felt confident he would be able to send all his belongings to the new house while lying in his bed.

He tried everything he could think of, but the boxes didn't move, mocking him. Hell, they were practically laughing at him. Well, not actually laughing, but definitely taunting.

"I can bring down entire buildings and open up holes in the ground so large, a small town can get swallowed up in it...all with a single thought. But I can't move these fucking boxes," he mumbled, glaring at them.

Flopping onto his back, Manuel gazed up at his ceiling. Frowning, his eyes traveled over the crack running the length of it. *Damn, Nicholas!* That was going to need to be fixed before they turned over the keys. Of course, the crack wouldn't even be there if Nicholas had just trusted him.

Releasing a frustrated sigh, Manuel decided to close his eyes and try to get some sleep. The sun felt warm against his skin as it shown through his window. Curling onto his side, he began to doze off.

Images of a spirited redhead with gorgeous green eyes ran through his mind. She smiled at him seductively as her fingers curled, beckoning him to come to her. With an uncharacteristic eagerness, he reached for her. His fingers skimmed over her blouse, releasing the buttons one by one. Her shirt slowly opened, revealing a lacy green bra and cream-colored skin to his hungry gaze.

Not being able to hold back, he leaned down, running his tongue above the lace, goosebumps rising in his wake. A delicious smell of honey and sugar filled his nose as he hovered against her. His lips brushed over her taut nipples, the lace a thin barrier between them. A throaty moan was her only response as he felt her fingers threading through his hair.

"Manuel," she gasped as he moved up her neck. His name on her lips sent a shock through him as he dove in and captured her mouth. She opened immediately for him, sucking his tongue into her mouth as she pulled roughly on his jeans, pulling him closer, her need matching his.

Suddenly, she pulled back. Her cheeks were flushed, lips already swollen from their kissing. "We need to stop."

"Why?" he murmured, attempting to pull her back in.

"Manuel, we can't. Not like this." Her voice was breathy.

"Like what?" he asked. He ran a hand across Hayley's neck and over her chest, her skin quivering beneath his touch. "Like this?" He curled his hand slightly so he could run it in between her breasts, eliciting another moan from her as he continued over her stomach, toward her jeans.

"Stop, Manual... Oh... We need to stop." Her hand grasped his, stopping him.

"Do you really want me to? I don't think you do. I think... No. I know you want this as much as I do. You want me to rip these clothes off you and do everything I've been wanting to do since I first laid eyes on you." Gazing into her bright green eyes, he watched them dilate. Her lips parted slightly as she shivered. "Just say it, Hayley. Tell me you want me, you need me, and I'll make you fly so high, you may never come down."

"I do. I want you so bad, but not like this." Tilting her head up, she pulled his mouth to hers. This kiss was softer, filled with frustration, need, and regret. Manuel tried to keep her there, her soft lips pressed tenderly to his. After a moment, though, she pulled back. "You need to wake up, Manuel."

"But-"

"Shh." She placed a finger across his lips. "Wake up, Manuel. We'll be together soon."

"Hayley." He reached for her as she stepped back, her image becoming unfocused as he called her name. "Hayley!"

Manuel.

His name began to echo through his head. A feeling of imbalance came over him, causing his body to shudder.

Manuel.

Fighting against the darkness around him, Manuel felt an invisible tug pulling him unwillingly through the night.

"Manuel!"

Bolting up in bed, he looked wildly around his room. *What the hell?* he thought, his heart still pounding. Rubbing his hand over his chest, he took in a shaky breath. Glancing at his clock, he grimaced. He had only two hours' sleep. Moving to the edge of the bed, he glanced down, taking in his rumpled shirt and extremely noticeable hard-on. Shifting his pants, he felt his pulse quicken as his dream drifted over him. "Damn," he grunted.

"Manuel, brother!" Christian's voice boomed. "Get up. Darren called a meeting."

"I'm up!" he snapped, taking in one deep calming breath after another. *Think of something non-sexual*, he thought with another deep breath. *Like sports, or the weather, or the million boxes I still need to pack.* Standing, he reached down and shifted his thankfully relaxing dick as he moved towards the door...only to have it thrown open as Christian stepped into his room. "Please, Christian, come on in." He rolled his eyes.

"Don't mind if I do." Christian grinned. As he took another step forward, Manuel saw him frown. Christian glanced around the room, confusion flashing across his face. He raised his eyebrows at Manuel.

"What?" he asked as his brother continued to stare at him.

Sniffing the air, Christian gave him a smirk. "You sneaking women into your room now, brother?"

"What?" Manuel laughed. "No. Why would you say that?"

"It smells too sweet in here to be just you." Christian smiled. "Unless you're not telling us something."

Rolling his eyes again, Manuel tilted his head and took in a deep breath. His chest tightened instantly as the smell of honey invaded his senses. Frowning slightly, he looked around. "Hmm..."

"So you really didn't smell that a minute ago?"

"No. I..." Manuel paused as he began to silently question his dream. If it had even been a dream. If it weren't, that would mean she was able to get into his head. *Shit!* "I guess I was just too tired to notice."

"I hear ya. As soon as this meeting is over, I'm heading to bed...if Ella doesn't send me out of the room again."

Manuel watched his brother's face fall. Ella had been acting strange lately. One moment, she would be her sweet, caring self; the next, she would be irritable, bossy, and sometimes downright mean. At first, they had all chalked it up to normal mood swings. It had made sense, and even Ella had gone with it. But it had gotten worse day by day. Last night, before they had left to meet Hayley, Ella had completely flipped. After their fight about Hayley helping them, she had gone from reasonable to crazy in a flash. Christian had taken the brunt of it before they headed out. Once they got in this morning, though, she had been her usual spunky self. Something was off with her, though, and had been since they brought her back. It was starting to become more noticeable. Manuel knew Christian saw it, too. He was just either denying it or hoping things would start to calm down. Either way, Manuel was certain the question of her well-being was going to eventually come to light. He hoped it was sooner rather than later.

"I'm sure she'll be fine," he said. Even to him, his words sounded flat.

"Yeah," Christian murmured, uncertainty radiating off him as he stood there.

Clearing his throat, Manuel decided it was best to change the subject. "So, you said Darren called a meeting?

"Oh, um... Yeah. He wants to go over what happened with Nicholas and Cyrus."

Sighing, Manuel made his way towards Christian. "I don't see why we need to do this now."

"Darren wants to get it out of the way. Plus..." Christian's voice trailed off as he looked towards the window.

"Plus what?"

"Well, I didn't want to tell you this when we were out there, but I think Castigo was nearby."

"What?!"

Christian looked back at him. Manuel could see the anger lurking within his blue eyes. "I *know* he was nearby," he all but snarled. "I heard those fucking drums in my head, but when I started looking for him, the sound faded away." Shaking his head, he stepped away from Manuel, moving to the door. "I don't know how. It's like he was able to shield himself or something."

"So he was there? He knows about Hayley?" Manuel fired out. He was angry at himself for not knowing. He was supposed to be a great tracker, for fuck's sake. How had he not known that demon piece of shit was nearby? What if he had attacked and hurt Hayley?

"We'll figure it out, brother. Darren knows. That's part of why he's calling the meeting."

Manuel glanced at him, watching as Christian stood just inside the doorway. Trying to calm himself, he made his way over and grasped his brother's shoulder. He could feel the emotions rolling off him, knew he was stressed and probably berating himself for letting Castigo get away.

If Manuel were being honest with himself, it was probably for the best. They hadn't been prepared to go up against him. Not yet anyway. "Listen, Christian. It's cool. I mean, we knew they were still lurking around somewhere, trying to get a bead on us. We'll just have to figure it out."

"Yeah." Christian sighed. "Let's just get this meeting over with." His voice sounded as tired as Manuel felt.

"Yeah, brother. Let's go."

Once the meeting was over, he was going to call Hayley. If Castigo knew about her... Fuck! A sick feeling began to curl through him. Shaking his head, he followed Christian down the hall towards the dining room. Their brothers were all at the table, waiting. Darren looked tired, while the other two just stared at him expectantly, as if waiting for him to say they had been right about Hayley. Rolling his eyes, Manuel took a seat. As Darren began talking, all Manuel could hear was the dull throbbing of a headache coming on. This was going to be a long meeting.

Chapter 19

Long didn't exactly describe the meeting. Neither did the term "meeting" for that matter. It was more like a battle, Nicholas fighting them at every turn.

It had started off well. Darren had run through the night's events, from meeting Hayley to hunting down the Shadow. It wasn't until he suggested having her go on more hunts with them that Nicholas spoke up, and once he got started, he wouldn't stop.

He had gone on and on about how working with the witch was a horrible idea. That it may seem good in the beginning, but she would only turn on them. It had taken everything in Manuel to not launch across the table at him. Instead, he sat there, concentrating on his breathing, reminding himself that killing his brother would not be a good idea. Cyrus, on the other hand, had remained silent the whole time. He just stared at him, his black eyes narrowed, as if he thought if he stared long enough, he would be able to figure out what Manuel was doing with her.

In the end, after what felt like hours, they had all parted ways...with nothing being resolved.

The only positive thing that had come out of the meeting was Christian promising him Castigo had not followed them to Hayley's. Manuel felt uneasy when Christian started telling everyone how he had sensed the demon near them in the neighborhood. This news had sent all the brothers into a whole different argument. With Christian's promise, though, Manuel could at least rest for a bit without worrying about the demons going after Hayley. As soon as he got to his room and got some much needed rest, he was going to figure out some reason for Hayley to stay with them. That way, he would know she was safe.

Manuel groaned as he made his way down the hall. Rest. They all just needed some rest, then they could talk about it again. He was hoping Nicholas would actually be willing to listen then. Walking up to his door, he paused and looked across the hall at Christian and Ella's closed door, a soft light radiating from underneath it. Concentrating, Manuel stood there quietly, listening for sounds of an argument. He could hear movement coming from inside, but it was quiet.

Good. No fighting tonight! he thought, heading into his room. *Well, maybe tonight isn't the right term seeing as it is noon.*

The fact they weren't fighting was definitely a good thing. Not only for them, but for him since that meant a sound sleep was in his future. Looking at his bed, he saw Holly curled up by his pillow. "Hey, little girl," he murmured as he sat on the edge of his bed. She yawned and stretched, looking at him curiously as he reached out to pet her. Her black fur was soft beneath his touch. "Did you get kicked out of your room again?" Holly's soft purrs were her only response as she curled back up.

He watched her for a moment, her purrs becoming soft snores as she drifted off to sleep. *Sleep.* He rubbed a hand over his face. He just wanted to go to sleep. Looking over towards his nightstand, Manuel noticed the notification light on his cell was blinking.

Checking the screen, he saw a text from Hayley.

Thank you for taking such good care of me today. It means a lot. Call me after you get some rest.

He stared at it for a bit. Memories of his dream washed over him and he smiled. Little minx had some explaining to do. Between her crazy amount of power, ability to curse that Shadow, and getting into his dreams... Yeah, he was definitely going to have a talk with her. But first, he needed to sleep.

Will do, doll. Thanks for the sweet dreams!

Hitting SEND, he placed the phone back on the table and laid down, falling into a relaxing sleep seconds after his head hit the pillow.

✝

The blush that had spread across her face when Manuel texted her back had been intense. Hayley was sure she had looked like a tomato. That had been four hours ago, but seeing that she still held a heat to her cheeks, she was worried it was permanent.

That had been so stupid, she mentally berated herself. She shouldn't have reached out to him like that. It had been too risky, going into his dream the way she did. The worse part was he *knew*!

Pacing around her living room, Hayley glanced at her cell. It was still on the couch where she had tossed it. Still no messages. She'd been glancing at it often over the last couple hours.

"This is ridiculous," she huffed. Blowing her hair out of her face, she glanced around the room. "If he calls, he calls! If not..." Her voice trailed off as she felt her chest tighten. *What if he doesn't?* "No." She started pacing again. "He'll call."

She was sure he had a lot of questions. Who wouldn't? She had been in his head, in his dream, practically throwing herself at him, for heaven's sake. His response to her, though... That had taken wet dream to a whole new level.

Just as things were getting really hot, though, she realized how wrong it was. God, she had wanted him so bad. Still did, if she were being honest with herself. And when he had growled his promise of pleasuring her, she had almost fallen apart right then.

Feeling a warmth spread through her at the memory, Hayley stopped by the couch, slowly sitting, her body sinking into the cushions.

She was in trouble.

She should be worrying about how the hunt went, whether Manuel's brothers would allow her to help, and what would happen next if they did. Instead, Hayley was sitting here wondering whether or not Manuel was going to call. Whether he truly wanted her the way she wanted him. And on Christmas Eve no less! Not that she had any family to celebrate with, but still. What was wrong with her?

Feeling slightly disgusted with herself, Hayley rose and headed into the kitchen to get a drink. Not even five steps away from the couch, she paused when she heard her phone. Racing back, she grabbed it, smiling when she saw his name on the screen.

Hey, baby girl. You up?

Smiling, Hayley quickly replied.

Yes. Did you sleep?

Like the dead!

That's good.

You?

I slept a bit.

Good dreams? :)

Hayley felt her cheeks warm. It would probably be best to just deny she had dreamt of him. If she said she had, it would open it up for him to bring up his dream. Chewing her bottom lip, her finger hovered over the keypad. Just as she was about to type, her screen lit up with an incoming call. Manuel. After two rings, she answered.

"Hello?" she said hesitantly.

"You didn't answer my question." His voice rumbled through the phone.

"Oh, um... Yes, I did." She sighed. She just couldn't lie to him.

"Yeah? Me, too."

"Yeah?" Her voice came out breathy.

"Do you do that often?"

"Do what often?" She frowned, sitting slowly on the couch.

"Have good dreams, Hayley. Do you often have good dreams?" He chuckled softly.

"Oh." Looking down, she smiled shyly. "No, not often at all."

"Hmm... We may have to remedy that." Before she could respond, he continued. "Another time, though. I was actually calling to see if you were okay."

"I'm fine. I mean, I'm still kind of tired, but other than that... Why?"

"Nothing... Just checking." There was something else. Hayley could hear it in his voice.

"Just tell me, Manuel." She pushed. "What's going on?"

"It's nothing, I'm sure. It's just that Christian said Castigo may have been in the area."

"What?" Her mind started working furiously. If Castigo had been in the area, he saw her...with the boys...taking on a Shadow. Shit! If he did see them, he knew she was a witch. "Oh no."

"Hey, it's going to be okay." He paused. "Hayley, would you consider staying with me...with us...for a bit?"

"Um... Manuel, I'm not sure-"

"It would just be for a while. Listen, we're moving into a new house the day after tomorrow and you could, you know, help us with moving, and you could also maybe give Christian a hand with something."

"With what?"

"Well, his girl, Ella... She's been having a hard time of it lately. I was kind of hoping you could, well...do something to see if you can figure out what's going on with her."

"What do your brothers think about me staying with you?" she said uncertainly. "Plus, it's Christmas Eve. Don't you guys have plans?"

"No, um... We don't have plans." She could hear the hesitation in his voice.

"Do you not celebrate Christmas?"

"No, we do... We just don't go out or anything. What about you? I guess I should have asked that before I asked you to come over tonight."

"No. I don't have anyone to celebrate with," Hayley whispered. This wasn't usually something that bothered her but, at this moment, the thought of spending yet another Christmas alone made her sad.

"Then all the more reason for you to come over," Manuel said. She could practically see the smile crossing his face. "Then you won't be alone."

She definitely liked the idea of spending time with Manuel rather than being alone. Even if it weren't to celebrate the holiday, it would still be nice to be someplace other than on her couch watching reruns. But still... "What about your brothers?" she finally asked.

"My brothers? They'll be fine." He paused again. She could almost feel his uncertainty flowing through the phone. "Do you want me to come get you, or..."

"That's okay, Manuel. I can drive over."

"So you'll come?"

She smiled softly. "Yes. I'll be over in a few. I just need to pack some things."

"Okay. So... Yeah. I'll text you the address. Just let me know when you're on your way and I'll meet you out front."

"Sounds good, Manuel. I'll see you soon."

"See you soon, Hayley." A moment later, the line went dead.

Hayley set her phone down and looked around the room. Her anxiety from earlier seemed to double from one heartbeat to the next. She had been hoping to be accepted by Manuel and his brothers, to be able to help them and stay close to Manuel. Staying with them, though... Staying with Manuel, even if it were only temporary, could definitely end up being more than she had bargained for. Standing up, she could only shake her head.

Well... This should be interesting.

Chapter 20

The liquor burned as it slid down his throat. He had never been really big into drinking...until recently. Even with the club almost ready to open, Dev felt anxious.

Sitting at the bar, he watched Trix make her list of what she needed. "What do you think, Dev? Two cases of tequila? Or three?" Her green eyes flashed his way.

"Whatever you think, Trix." He took another sip of his drink, the honey-colored bourbon practically glowing in the soft light. *If only everything could be as simple as bourbon*, he thought with a sigh. The ice clinked against the glass as he raised it to his lips, downing what was left. "Make sure you get more of this, though," he commented, setting the glass down. Trix just nodded, making some more notes on her notepad.

He sat there watching her a bit longer before deciding to head back to his office. "I'll be in the office," he muttered. "Call if you need me."

"Sure thing, Dev."

Nodding, he began to make his way down the hall, his mind already going over what else needed to be done. All the signs were scheduled to arrive in two days. The booths, chairs, and tables should be delivered tomorrow. Once the furniture was in, the interior of the club would be done.

He looked through the open doors of the many VIP rooms lining the hallway. Each room was soundproof, decorated and furnished to Andras' exact specifications. He wasn't exactly sure what they would be used for, and he hadn't asked. All he knew was those who paid big, were powerful, or were on Andras' "list" would make it back here. Glancing into one room, he took note of the leather and chains adorning the walls.

Not sure I want to know, he thought, barely suppressing a shudder.

It wasn't his job to ask questions anyway. He just needed to make sure the club was ready and set up the way his boss wanted it. Feeling a sense of disgust creep through him, Dev sharply rounded the corner towards his office only to come to a dead stop. His office door, which he was sure he had closed and locked, stood partially open. *What the fuck?!* Stepping quietly, he breathed in the air around him, attempting to discern who was in the room. Only one smell, one that had become as well-known to him as his own, assaulted his nose. Sulfur!

Well, it's not Sy, he thought, trying to figure out who could be in his office. Sy had been by earlier to check on him. That was what the demon had said anyway. Dev was pretty positive he had been making sure he wasn't going to try and disappear on him. Not that he could do that even if he wanted to. Then there was Andras' security crew...Rave, Vhin, Lakmi, and Kanibal. Dev glanced at his watch. They weren't supposed to show for another twelve hours - give or take.

Shit! Shit! Shit!

Dev stood there, staring at the door. A line of sweat ran down his back as he felt his chest tighten. He hated the constant feeling of fear and uncertainty that warred within him every day. He had done this to himself, though. This was his reality, and had been for some time now.

Rocking slowly back on his heels, Dev let out a soft hiss. *Just go in there and get it over with*, he thought harshly. *Stop standing in the hall, putting off the inevitable.*

With a deep breath, he squared his shoulders and made his way towards the door. He cursed softly when he reached out to push the door open and noticed his hand shaking. He wasn't even through the doorway before he heard a deep chuckle. Closing his eyes briefly, he walked around the open door...pausing when he saw Castigo sitting at his desk.

"I was wondering how long you were going to stand out in the hall, Dev," he said with a laugh. "For a moment, I almost thought you weren't going to come in."

Dev stood there silently, his pulse hammering as he watched the demon. Castigo's silver eyes flashed as he smiled, waiting for him to say something. Not knowing how to respond, Dev decided to remain silent.

"The club looks good, Dev," Castigo finally murmured, leaning forward in the chair, tapping a finger upon the desk. The soft tapping echoed through the quiet office.

Dev gave a brisk nod. "Just getting it ready."

"Ah, yes! For Andras." Castigo smirked.

"Yes." Dev felt his eyes narrow slightly. "Are you here to check up on me, Castigo?"

Castigo titled his head, his eyebrows drawing into a frown. He seemed to be deciding what to tell Dev, his silver eyes traveling over him from head to toe. Dev's pulse began to speed up the longer Castigo stayed quiet. Finally seeming to decide on what to say, Castigo gave a shrug. "Yes...and no."

Dev opened his mouth to ask what the hell that meant, but quickly changed his mind. Moving into the room, he kept his eyes on Castigo.

"You see, Dev," Castigo continued, "Andras sent me here for a couple reasons, one of which is to check on his club."

"And the other?"

Dev watched Castigo raise an eyebrow. "The other reason, well... We'll get to that soon enough." He leaned back in the chair. The wheels rolled across the ground as he stretched out his legs. "So, tell me, Dev. How has it been going around here?"

Dev shifted slightly. "Fine. Everything has been coming along as planned."

"Really? No problems then?"

A sudden sense of panic washed over him. Did Castigo know about his deal with Sy? *He couldn't know that...* Dev mentally shook himself. No, he had been very careful, and Sy wouldn't have said anything. Would he?

Still holding the demon's gaze, he forced a tight smile. "No... No problems at all."

Castigo stared at him. Dev had the feeling the demon was seeing the lie like it was written across his face. Keeping himself still, Dev just stared back.

The strained standoff went on for several minutes before Castigo finally gave a sharp nod. "Good. That is very good, Dev. Andras will be pleased to hear that. I had feared I would be delivering bad news to our boss, the outcome of which I am sure you would not have enjoyed." Castigo's top lip twitched slightly. "If I remember correctly, you almost did not make it through the last time you ended up on Andras' shit list."

"Yes, well..." Dev licked his suddenly dry lips. "As you can see, everything is good here."

"Yes, it is," Castigo said slowly.

Dev shifted his weight. "So..." He cleared his throat. He was starting to get the feeling he didn't want to know the other reason Castigo was here. Dev's stomach clenched as he watched the demon. Castigo wasn't giving off any threatening vibes. He actually seemed relaxed, almost reluctant to continue, which made Dev feel even more unsettled. He needed to know, though, especially if the real reason behind his visit had to do with what he thought it did. His brothers. Because, regardless of how long it had been, he still felt a deep loyalty to them. Something he was sure would not go over well with Andras if it came out. Suppressing yet another shudder, Dev started to ask about it, but was stopped by the ringing of his cell. Not sure if he should answer it or not, Dev paused and looked questioningly at the demon. A lift of Castigo's eyebrow had him reaching for the phone, not even glancing at the screen.

"Yeah?"

"Hello, my friend."

Keeping his expression blank, Dev turned slightly. *Why does Sy have to be calling now?* he thought furiously. "Yes, hello." He hoped Castigo didn't figure out who it was.

"So snappy today. Are you not alone, Dev?"

"I'm actually in a meeting right now. Can I call you back?"

"A meeting? My, my. You wouldn't happen to be chatting with a certain silver-eyed demon, would you?"

Dev suppressed a groan. "That's correct. If there is nothing else..." His voice trailed off, a sudden movement catching his eye. Turning, he found Castigo now standing, leaning against the front of the desk, his arms folded across his chest. "If there is nothing else," he continued slowly, "I really must be going."

"Of course, Dev. I only called to pass on some information I have received concerning some long-lost friends of yours. I feel you should call me once you are finished with your...meeting." Dev heard Sy let out a soft hiss. The demon was obviously frustrated they could not talk at the moment, although all Dev could worry himself with was the demon in front of him. He started to end the call when Sy suddenly spoke up. "And, Dev, do be careful with that one. Castigo is not known for being...pleasant to deal with if he is looking for information, which I fear is why he came to see you."

Watching a sly smile begin to spread across Castigo's face, Dev shivered. He knew exactly of what the demon was capable, especially if he wasn't getting what he wanted. "I understand," Dev said as evenly as he could. "I will be in touch."

"Goodbye, my friend."

"Bye," Dev said, hanging up. He kept his eyes focused on Castigo, watching his grin widen.

"Business or pleasure?" Castigo asked politely, although Dev had a feeling he already knew.

"Business," he responded quickly. "Sorry about that. Um... You were saying?" At Castigo's questioning look, Dev rushed on. "The other reason you've come to see me."

"Oh. Yes," Castigo said, his smile tightening. "Tell me, Dev. You've been here for a while now... Have you been in touch with your brothers?"

He felt his spine stiffen. "No, I haven't."

"Oh, come now. You honestly want me to believe that, after all this time left on your own, you did not reach out to them? Even to just tell them you are alive?" Castigo clicked his tongue. "I truly find that hard to believe. You know, you can tell me if you have."

"I haven't."

"But you know they are around?"

"I had heard, but I haven't seen or talked to them in a long time. Not since before..." Dev's voice trailed off. He was telling Castigo the truth. He had not been in contact with his brothers. He had wanted to reach out to them, though. He'd sat in his office for hours at a time, contemplating. Dev didn't even know if they would want to talk to him. Why would they? It wasn't like he could say they had parted on good terms. No matter how much he wanted to, Dev knew staying away from them was for the best...for all of them.

Glancing down, he let out a sigh. "I doubt they would talk to me, even if they knew I was here, which I honestly don't think they do."

"I see," Castigo said. The doubt in his voice caused Dev to look back at him. "So I guess you wouldn't know where they are or what they are up to?"

Shaking his head, Dev remained quiet.

"If you did, though, you would tell us...," he asked, although it came across more like a statement. Dev tried to mask his aversion to the idea. Castigo must have seen the defiance in his eyes because he slowly pushed off the desk. Dev tensed as he watched Castigo take several steps towards him. "Now, Dev, I feel you may be under the impression you have a choice in what you tell us. Do you need to be reminded to whom you now belong to? Whom you answer to?"

Dev held still as the demon stopped in front of him. The smell of sulfur was almost suffocating as he pulled in one shallow breath after another. "No," he choked out. "I...I don't know anything."

"If you did, though?" Castigo hissed, his silver eyes glowing dangerously as he leaned closer.

"If I did, I would tell you," Dev whispered, hoping the demon couldn't sense the lie.

Castigo stared at him for a heartbeat. His power whipped out around him, pushing against Dev as a warning and a promise of the pain to come. "I hope so," he finally said. "Andras will want to question you further about them when he arrives. He was very adamant about your...obedience when it comes to this matter. He will not tolerate any hesitation, or silence, on your part." He tilted his head, his eyes darkening as he glared at him. "They are not worth the pain you will suffer if you choose to go against Andras in this."

Dev nodded slowly as he felt Castigo's power finally begin to pull back. Looking at the ground again, Dev could only hope the demon was done. His mind raced as images of his brothers rushed through it. Tensing, he felt Castigo lean in, his breath warm against his ear.

"They cannot save you," he hissed. "You are damned. For that alone, they will turn against you given half the chance. But if you do choose them, even knowing they no longer see you as one of their own, if you defy Andras, you will never be free. Never feel the rain against your face, enjoy a glass of your favorite drink, or relish in the feel of a warm female beneath you. Andras will make you his own personal toy and you will spend an eternity knowing nothing but pain." He paused, pulling back slightly. "Would *they* risk that for *you*?" Without waiting for an answer, Castigo took a step back and quietly left his office.

Dev listened to the door close softly behind the demon. Releasing the breath he had been holding, he moved backwards, only stopping when he bumped against the couch. Slowly sitting on it, Dev rested his head in his hands. He wouldn't give up his brothers. Whether they still saw him as such or not, he would protect them as best he could. He just needed to figure out how to protect himself at the same time.

Not that he had illusions on where he would end up once this horror movie played out, but it would be nice to remain intact for as long as he could. Rubbing his hand down his face, he sat back. Shit!

Looking at his cell, he scrolled until he found Sy's number. His finger hovered over the screen for a second before hitting DIAL. "Sy," he said once the demon answered.

"Dev, I was worried you would be unable to call."

"Yes, well, it looked questionable."

"Did he ask about your brothers?"

"You know he did," Dev responded, suddenly feeling tired. "You called with information earlier?"

"Yes. What do you think about witches?" Sy asked.

Dev frowned. "Witches?"

"Yes. Witches. More importantly, Dev, what do you think about your brothers working with one?"

Chapter 21

Hayley pulled up to the curb. It had taken her a little longer than expected to get here. Every time she had started to leave her house, she remembered something she needed, or needed to check to make sure everything was turned off. It had happened so many times, she thought maybe the world was telling her not to go. She had even paused to really think about what she was doing. In the end, the warmth she felt when she thought of Manuel, her desire to be there for him and his brothers, was what had her walking out the door and getting into her car.

Looking out her window now, she gazed at Manuel's house. It was nice. White trim with blue shutters, green grass, and a large tree reaching proudly towards the sky out front. It wasn't what she had expected, but it was cute. Pulling out her phone, she sent him a quick text saying she was out front. To say she was nervous about going in would be putting it mildly. She felt downright nauseous.

Seeing the front door open a second later, she watched Manuel walk out, closing the door behind him. The few rays of sun streaming through the clouds gave a glow to the air around him as he walked towards her car. His eyes looked black, so dark against his skin, but Hayley knew better. Up close, the amethyst color was so vibrant, you thought you were looking at the gem itself. Everything about him called to her, pulled her, and she wanted it.

Taking a deep breath, Hayley got out of her car. Feeling the chilly air immediately flow across her skin, she shivered. "Hey." She smiled as he stepped off the curb.

"Hey." He smiled, his eyes flashing as he looked her over. "Do you need a hand with your stuff?"

"No. I just have my tote and backpack." Moving away from the car, she attempted to hide the flush warming her cheeks. All he had to do was look at her and she felt herself turn to putty. *Get ahold of yourself,* she thought with a mental shake. Opening her back door, she started to grab her things, but Manuel beat her to it.

"It's cool. I got them," he said, grinning down at her.

Shaking her head, she locked the car and followed him towards the door. "Um, Manuel?"

"Hmm...?"

"Are you sure this is okay?" she asked quietly, stopping when he turned towards her.

"I told you, Hayley. It's going to be fine."

"It's just... With you guys moving the day after tomorrow and everything, I don't want to be in the way." She looked away, suddenly feeling the uncertainty of her decision weighing down on her.

She felt him step towards her. "Hayley, look at me," he demanded softly. Looking up, she watched as his eyes lit up, his smile warming her to her toes. "I want you here."

Hayley let out a low gasp. Searching his face, she looked for a sign that he didn't really mean it. Finding none, she smiled back. "I want to be here, too, Manuel."

"Stick with me then. Everything will be good. Anyway, you already know Christian and Darren." Getting to the door, he shuffled her bags from one hand to the other. "Oh, just do me a favor, though."

"Um, sure. What's up?" She watched as he paused, his hand resting on the doorknob.

"Stay clear of Nicholas. At least until he warms up to you. Cool?"

Hayley opened her mouth to ask why, but he was already pushing the door open. A comfortable warmth and the sounds of laughter washed over her when she stepped over the threshold. Looking around, she followed Manuel as he walked toward the hallway.

"We'll get you settled, then we can-"

"Hayley?" The sound of Darren's voice stopped her.

"Hey, Darren," she said.

"What's going on?" He stopped in front of them, glancing between her and Manuel. "Did something happen?"

Her mouth dropped open. Manuel hadn't told them? How could he not tell his brothers she was coming? Spinning around, she glared at him.

Looking at her, he grinned sheepishly. "Oh, yeah." Clearing his throat, he glanced at Darren. "I asked Hayley to stay with us for a bit."

Rolling her eyes, Hayley looked over to find Darren scowling at him.

"Manuel, can we have a word?" Darren ground out. He was obviously trying to keep his cool in front of her, but Hayley could feel his anger rolling off him.

"Let me just-" Manuel started.

"Manuel," Darren hissed.

"Darren," he shot back, "I'm not about to leave her standing in the hall. I'll get her settled, then I'll be out."

Darren let out a sigh. "Fine." He glanced her way, his expression softening. "It is nice to see you, Hayley. It's just..."

"Unexpected," she quietly finished.

"Unexpected," he agreed, smiling tightly at her before heading back the way he had come.

She silently followed Manuel down the hall. When he turned left into his room, she walked in behind him, then paused. His room was huge compared to hers. Looking around, she took in the king-sized bed, maple furniture, and big screen TV. The walls had several movie posters on them, and there were boxes marked **BOOKS** that lined, well, almost every flat surface she saw.

Turning, her eyes landed on Manuel. He stood by his bed, watching her closely. For the first time, he seemed unsure of himself. Whether it was because of his decision to invite her here or bringing her into his room, she didn't know.

She was definitely upset about him not telling his brothers she was coming, but she didn't want to argue with him about it right now. Hayley had a feeling he would be going through enough when he went back out there. She was sure everyone now knew she was here because the laughter had stopped about the time Darren had walked away. If that weren't a sign of their unease at having her here, she wasn't sure what was.

"So... I'll stay out in the living room or the library, and you can bunk in here," Manuel stated, slowly looking around his room. "Sorry it's a mess. You know, with moving and all..." He cleared his throat. "But I haven't packed everything yet. I have a stereo over there if you want to listen to some music." He pointed to the right. Following his gaze, she spotted an impressive stereo system, stacks of CDs on either side. She wanted to see what he had, figuring she'd have plenty of time to snoop when she was alone. "And over there..." His deep voice drew her attention back to him. He was looking admiringly at his TV, "is my TV. I have cable and tons of movies, so there's plenty to watch if that's what you're in the mood for."

"And plenty of books," Hayley chimed in.

"What?" he asked, turning to look at her. Hayley just smiled and waved her hand towards all the boxes of books stacked around his room. Still seeming confused, Manuel looked around, then laughed. "Yeah." He ran a hand through his hair. "I have a couple books in here, too."

"A couple?" She chuckled. "I think I could be set for months just looking at everything."

Manuel grinned. "Well, I wouldn't want you to get bored."

"I have no fear of that happening," she replied, walking over and slowly sitting on his bed.

She knew he watched her sit down. Hayley could feel his gaze upon her as a sudden change in the air around them sent a shiver up her spine. Looking over her shoulder, she watched him make his way around the bed. Manuel moved through the room, his body tense, as if he were concentrating on holding himself in check as he walked to her. How she wished he would lose control. Just the thought of him pushing her down on the bed made her insides tighten. As he stood in front of her now, Hayley chewed on her bottom lip, gazing up at him.

Manuel seemed at a loss, taking a step towards the door, then back. She could see that he was battling with himself. Hayley was also warring over what she wanted to happen and what she knew was the right thing. They hardly knew each other. As much as she wanted him, had been thinking about him, she knew now wasn't the time.

"You should go see Darren. I'm sure they're all waiting for you," she said softly, even as a small voice in the back of her head screamed for him to stay.

"Yeah... You gonna be okay?"

"I'll be fine. I'll be here when you're done."

"Okay," he said with a nod. Making his way to the door, he glanced at her again, his gaze holding hers before disappearing into the hall.

Sighing, she flopped back onto the bed. *I did the right thing*, she thought. *This is where I'm supposed to be.* Now if only the others would accept her, it would make her helping them so much easier.

Manuel had said he wanted her here. Snuggling down into the bed, she smiled at the thought. That had to be one of the sweetest things a guy had ever said to her. It had cemented her decision, even with her dismay at finding her arrival a surprise to his brothers.

Rolling over, Manuel's scent engulfed her. All of the thoughts running rampant through her tired mind faded as she curled around his pillow, taking a deep, calming breath. *I think I'll just nap while I wait*, she thought, closing her eyes. Images of Manuel lying next to her sprang to mind as she took another deep breath. Her body had just started to relax and she began to drift off when an angry yell startled her. Sitting up quickly, Hayley strained to hear what was going on.

Several male voices rolled over each other as their aggression electrified the air. Slipping off the bed, Hayley walked to the door. With each step, she felt the air thicken as a power had begun to build within the house. She could feel goosebumps rising along her arms as she reached for the doorknob, the door opening without a sound. She walked slowly into the hall.

Her hand flew to her mouth when a black blur streaked past her, taking off into one of the rooms down the hall. *Just a cat,* she thought with a nervous chuckle.

Shaking it off, she closed her eyes, concentrating on the power humming through the air, mentally testing it with her own. To her surprise, she realized it was actually the combination of several powers. One, in particular, held a warmth to it, flowing teasingly over her skin.

"Manuel," she sighed.

Then there were two that were familiar to her. Images from their previous night's hunt crossed her mind. *Darren and Christian.* She nodded. Their powers held anger and irritation. She was sure most, if not all, of that stemmed from her presence.

Frowning, she reached out for the ones she didn't know. There were three powers she came across. Two were filled with anger. They whipped through the air, sending shivers down her spine as they lashed out. Hayley knew Manuel's brothers may not be happy she was around, but this aggression took her by surprise.

Yet it was the sixth power, the one that was building at a dangerous rate, that had her the most concerned. This power seemed to pulse through the house with complete abandon. The others, although aggressive and powerful, still had a sense of control to them. This, however, felt wild and unstable. Hayley's eyes flew open when she felt that power suddenly spike.

Manuel's power, along with everybody else's, was quickly becoming overshadowed by the darker one. Making her way down the hall, all thoughts of the argument gone, all Hayley could think about was getting to the source of this wild power before the owner of it lost control. Her skin tingled as she made her way past the kitchen and towards the commotion. As she got closer, the voices became more and more distinct. The argument reached her ears as she raced towards them.

"Don't give me that shit," Manuel's voice growled through the air.

"I don't care that she's fucking here," she heard Christian respond. "It just would have been nice to get a little heads-up. That's all."

"A heads-up?" Manuel laughed. "Like you did when you brought Ella here?"

"Don't bring me into this, Manuel," a female's voice rang out, her tone sounding slightly off. With every word leaving this woman, the power rolling across Hayley's skin intensified.

That was whom she needed to get to. Ella. When Hayley walked around the corner and into the room, she felt Ella's power shudder. She spotted her instantly, the woman's brown eyes flashing as she scanned the room. Hayley could see her power pulsing around her. It was a wonder there weren't sparks flying with how volatile it felt. Hayley moved faster as she ran to her, her brain only vaguely registering the men.

"Hayley?" Manuel's voice called to her, but she couldn't stop. She needed to get to Ella.

Hayley knew the woman was about to lose control, sending her power out around her like a nuclear bomb. The worst part was she didn't think Ella had any idea. Hayley began to push her power out around her, shivering when it came into contact with Ella's. Their powers collided with a metaphysical bang, and Hayley saw Ella stagger from the sudden hit. Whereas everyone else's power was warm, Ella's was a muddle of warm and cold, causing the perfect storm to rise up within her. She had never come across someone with such warring powers before.

Meeting her gaze, she saw fear and uncertainty flash through her eyes. She was almost to her when she saw Ella's body shudder, then start to sink to the floor. Her power was now lashing out so wildly, Hayley feared for everybody in the room, including Ella. With this level of intensity, she could only imagine what the poor woman was going through.

Out of the corner of her eye, Hayley saw Christian start to move towards Ella. Fearing what would happen if they touched, she threw her arms out, forming

an invisible circle around them, stopping
Christian from getting too close. She could
feel his instant rage. Later, she hoped he
would understand why she had to keep him
away.

Practically falling to the ground in
front of Ella, Hayley felt a sudden pressure
build within the protective circle she had
cast. A wind created by both their powers
grew, lifting their hair to whip wildly in the
air. Looking at Ella's face, she could see a
light swirling in her eyes. It seemed to be
fighting a dark shadow dancing around it.

"Please...," Ella mumbled, her eyes
tearing. "It hurts."

"Shh...," Hayley whispered.
Reaching up, she placed her hand on Ella's
cheek. "It'll be better soon."

Pushing her power into the woman,
she heard her gasp. Ella attempted to pull
back, but Hayley slid her hand to the base
of her neck and held her still. Sending more
of her power into her, Hayley called to the
air around them, asking it to calm, to ease,
to comfort Ella, willing her power to quiet.

"Calm," Hayley whispered. Leaning
closer, she started her spell. Her words
wove through the air as she called for Ella's
spirit to quiet, her power to recede.

With each word, she concentrated
on soothing Ella's nerves. It took some time
but, eventually, Hayley watched in
satisfaction as Ella's face relaxed and she

felt her power calm. Relaxing her grip, she eased her back so the woman was sitting against the wall.

Pulling her own power back into herself, Hayley became aware of just how quiet it was around them. "Are you okay?" she asked.

She watched as Ella blinked a couple times. "Yes. I... It came on so fast." She took a deep breath, seeming to try and collect herself. "Thank you. I'm not sure how you did that, but thank you."

Hayley smiled. She looked at Manuel, seeing him gazing down at her, a look of respect, and something else, blazing in his eyes. "Everyone," he spoke, his voice carrying through the quiet room. Hayley felt her cheeks redden as he steadily stared at her. Manuel grinned broadly, nodding in her direction. "This lovely creature is Hayley. Hayley, meet my family."

Just like that, she knew she was right where she was supposed to be.

Chapter 22

Even after several hours, Manuel was still in awe of how Hayley had calmed Ella down earlier. It had all happened so fast. When he left Hayley back in his room, he knew he was heading into a fight. The tone Darren had used told him as much. The level of aggression from the moment he stepped foot into the front room, though, had been staggering. Of course, Nicholas and Cyrus had been upset, starting in on him immediately. What he had not been prepared for was getting hit from all sides. Darren, Christian, and Ella had all felt now was not the time for him to bring Hayley here, especially since he hadn't run this past any of them first.

So to say everyone's emotions were running high would be putting it lightly. The room had almost felt suffocating with all the power pulsing through it. Because of the sudden power battle erupting around him, he hadn't noticed Ella's slipping from her control. None of them had. They had all been so involved in their argument, it wasn't until Hayley came running into the room that everyone realized something was wrong.

Hayley had immediately taken control of the situation. Before any of them had been able to catch up to what was happening, she had calmed Ella down, helping her to get her power back under control. Even though it happened so fast, the whole event would forever be ingrained in Manuel's memory.

The moments afterwards had gone by in a blur. After he had introduced Hayley, everyone immediately started talking at once. She had done the best she could to answer the questions. He marveled at how she handled his brothers, especially Nicholas.

Not that Nicholas had been rude. He had actually been quite calm, which surprised the hell out of Manuel. He had asked several questions, most centering around her witchcraft and why she wanted to help them. Then, of course, there had been Cyrus, who also wasn't shy with his questions. Like Nicholas, he hadn't been rude, just direct. Hayley had answered all their questions as best as she could, but Manuel could tell she felt a little uncomfortable under their scrutiny.

Ella, on the other hand, was extremely taken by Hayley. Because of that, so was Christian. At least between the two of them, along with Darren, Hayley had felt a little more comfortable. After almost an hour-and-a-half of questioning, Manuel had seen the exhaustion in her eyes. She hid it well, but he knew she was ready to sneak away.

She had been so grateful when he squeezed in between his brothers and took her hand. With several understanding nods from the guys, he had led Hayley back to his room. Once she lay down, it hadn't taken her long to begin to drift off. He had stayed with her until he was sure she was okay. Slipping quietly from his room, Manuel had been relieved to see all of his brothers, as well as Ella, had retired to their own rooms, leaving him to his thoughts.

Since then, he had been sitting in the kitchen, laptop open, checking on recent events and nursing a glass of Crown. Manuel knew he should be finalizing everything for their move, but the day's events had exhausted him. Sighing, he took another sip of his drink, his thoughts constantly drifting back to the gorgeous redhead asleep in his room. *What am I going to do with you?* he thought with a frown. He had only been around her a couple times, but he already knew he was hooked. It shouldn't be possible for it to happen that fast, but it had. Having her come stay with them had just been a thought, but as soon as he had voiced it, he hadn't been able to let it go. Hell, if she had fought him, he had been ready to beg. Luckily for him, it seemed she wanted to be here as much as he wanted her here.

Scrolling through the Fhallon Heights' website, he noticed they had updated the announcement section. Clicking on the link, he found most of it was about the city council. Looked like they were trying to renovate downtown. Some new shops were opening up...music store, bookstore, bakery. He read down the list of places that would be open in the next month or so. Sliding his finger over the mouse pad, he scrolled down. So many random events. Shaking his head, Manuel was just about to sign out when the last announcement caught his attention.

"New club to be open in Fhallon Heights." *Just what we need...* Clicking, he frowned at the vagueness of it. It was so short, he hesitated to even call it an article. It was more like a blurb or a quick note. Frowning, he studied it.

New club to open January 3, 2015.

Located on South Rivers Street, it will be open between 6pm and 6am Monday through Saturday.

It will feature a wide variety of dance music, along with

multiple VIP rooms for private entertainment. The council is excited to welcome this new club and all the jobs it will provide. The club's owner was unable to be reached for an interview, but did send us a message in which he stated:

"I am so very excited to be a part of this growing community. There is so much potential here. A perfect location for me to open my club and share my dream. I do insist you all come by on opening night to see all my employees and I have to offer."

We, too, are looking forward to the opening of this club. It's sure to become our town's hot spot. So, on January 3rd, please join us in welcoming our newest entertainment location, The 9th Circle.

"The 9th Circle," Manuel murmured, scanning the short article again. He found it interesting there was no mention of the owner's name. Tapping his finger against the table, he reached over to take another sip of his drink. The club's name kept echoing through his mind. There was something more to this. He could feel it. He just couldn't put his finger on what.

Hearing a throat clear behind him, Manuel reluctantly pulled himself from his mussing. Turning, he found Nicholas leaning against the counter, staring at him. The emotion suddenly rolling through the room was one of confusion and irritation. Two things he could definitely do without.

Letting out a frustrated groan, Manuel turned back towards the laptop. "I'm not in the mood, Nicholas."

"Listen, Manuel, I-"

"No. I said I'm not-"

"Just hear me out. Please."

Turning back to face him, Manuel let out a sigh. Nicholas had now moved a few steps closer and had his hands out before him. The look in his eyes showed his sincerity. "Okay, Nicholas. But if all you're going to do is give me shit about Hayley, you can just turn around."

Nicholas shook his head and walked over to the table, taking a seat across from him. "I'm not here to give you shit about

Hayley. I just..." He grew quiet and looked down at the table.

Manuel moved his laptop to the side so he could see his brother better. "You just what, Nicholas?"

He glanced up at him, his red eyes flashing. "I just wanted to apologize for earlier. I still have my doubts about working with a witch. What I went through the last time... It's just not something I can easily get over or forget." Holding up a hand when Manuel opened his mouth, he continued. "I still believe I was right in voicing my concerns about this, but I shouldn't have taken things as far as I did."

Manuel took a deep breath. He just couldn't stay mad at him. "It's okay, Nicky. I know you were just looking out for everyone. Pushing for what you felt was best."

"Yeah. So were you, though," he replied with a small smile. "It's pretty crazy how Hayley was able to help Ella."

"It was." Manuel shook his head. "I've never seen anything like it." He watched as Nicholas picked at the table a bit, seeming lost in his thoughts. "I really do think she can help."

"I know you do, and I trust you. I know my actions lately may lead you to believe otherwise, but I do. I just don't trust her...yet."

"But you'll give her a chance?"

Nicholas nodded. "I will. She *did* help Ella, so that gained her some extra points."

"And she put up with all of your and Cyrus' questions."

"True." Nicholas smirked. Hearing a soft meow, Manuel watched as Nicholas leaned down and lifted Holly onto his lap. He ran his hand over her head a bit before looking back up at Manuel with a laugh. "I guess anyone who can put up with all of us at once, for any given amount of time, is worth the chance. Plus, I think Ella would have my head if I didn't at least try."

Manuel chuckled, taking another sip of his drink. "There is that." Looking away, he glanced back at the laptop. "Hey, Nicky? Have you heard about new club that's going to be opening up?"

"Nope," Nicholas said, letting Holly jump off of his lap and standing up to grab a glass. "Why? You feel like hitting the town?"

"Not likely," Manuel muttered, still looking at the article. He had never gotten into the club scene. Each of his brothers, at one time or another, had gone through a phase. Cyrus, for instance, had been very big into the club scene...at least before he had been taken by the Shadows. But Manuel was just never interested in it. There were too many people, and the music was too loud. He could do bars. Someplace he could relax, enjoy a nice glass of whiskey or bourbon, and have a conversation. But clubs were definitely not his thing. Looking at this article, though, the club's name echoing through his head, Manuel started to think he was going to have to get into the club scene after all. "I have a feeling we may need to check this one out."

"Yeah?" Nicholas asked, sitting across from him again. Setting his glass down, he reached across for the whiskey bottle to pour himself some. "Why do you say that?"

"I don't know..." Manuel paused, looking at the screen. Sighing, he could only shake his head. "There's just something about this club..." Looking over at Nicholas, he frowned. "I don't know. Maybe it's nothing. Maybe I'm just getting antsy, waiting for something to happen."

"I hear that. It's been too quiet lately. I think we're all feeling a little anxious."

"Yeah."

They both sat there, quietly drinking their Crown, lost in thought. He didn't know about Nicholas, but the day's events were definitely starting to get to him...and they all still needed to finish packing.

"So what's the name of this club?"

"What?"

Nicholas waved his hand towards the laptop. "The name of the club you're talking about."

"The 9th Circle."

"Seriously? That definitely doesn't sound like your scene."

Manuel smirked as he looked back at the screen. "No, it doesn't. This article on it is just so vague. It feels like whoever wrote this piece on the club intentionally left information out."

"Like what?"

"Like the owner's name. They have a quote from him, but no mention of his name or any other information."

"And his quote?"

Manuel read the quote to Nicholas, pausing before looking back up. "It kind of reads more like an invitation to a country club or something rather than a dance club."

"Or a cult," Nicholas remarked. Finishing off his Crown, he got to his feet. "You said this place isn't open yet."

"Not for another week or so."

"So we have some time to check it out. Let's finish getting the house packed up and move. Then, after we get settled in the new place, we'll go take a look at this new club."

"Sounds good."

He gave Nicholas a nod as his brother left the kitchen. Shutting down his laptop, Manuel stood and put his glass in the sink. His whole body ached from lack of sleep. Stepping out of the kitchen, he took a couple steps towards the den and stopped.

Images of Hayley sleeping in his bed came to mind. Smiling, he looked down the hall. Why sleep on a couch when there was plenty of room in his bed for two? In fact, there was so much room, she might not even notice him there. It would definitely be more comfortable than the couch. Tapping his finger against his leg, he thought about it. Would it really be a bad idea to go lay down with Hayley? *Next to Hayley, not with her*, he chided himself, although being with her wouldn't be bad, either. If that dream, or whatever it was, told him anything, it was that being with her would be fucking amazing.

Mind made up, Manuel turned and began to make his way towards his room. He could just make out the soft light glowing from beneath his closed bedroom door. He paused, the sound of her soft breathing reaching his ears. Closing his eyes, he listened for a bit before silently opening the door and walking in. Shutting it softly behind him, Manuel stepped towards the bed. She must have woken sometime after he left her because she had fallen asleep, fully clothed, on top of the covers. Now, though, she was curled up beneath the sheets, the majority of her clothes on top of his dresser.

Shrugging out of his shirt, Manuel sat gently on the bed. Hearing a soft moan behind him, he held his breath as he turned, seeing her shift. She didn't wake up, though. She needed her rest, and the last thing he wanted to do was disturb her.

Removing everything except his boxers, he slid under the covers. Lying on his back, Manuel curled one of his arms behind his head. Willing the bedroom lights to turn off, he immediately found himself surrounded by darkness, soft light coming through the window. As he listened to Hayley's steady breathing, savoring the warmth of her nearness, Manuel slowly felt himself begin to drift off.

Just when he felt his body growing heavy, he sensed movement beside him.

"Manuel?" Hayley whispered. "Are you awake?"

He blinked a couple times before turning his head. She had turned onto her side, her arm curled beneath her head, gazing at him. Her emerald green eyes seemed to search his. As she tilted her head a bit, he watched a few curls of her hair fall around her face. The effect of her skin bathed in moonlight stole his breath.

"Manuel?" she whispered again, staring intently at him.

"What is it, honey?" he whispered back.

"Can I ask you something?"

"Sure."

"You and your brothers... You're not really demon hunters, are you?"

He looked away, his body tensing as his mind scrambled to come up with an answer. He knew this would eventually come up. She had heard Christian invoke the Shade when they had been hunting the Shadow. Still, should he tell her? Could he even play it off that they were nothing but regular guys, especially now that she was staying in their house? Probably not.

His frantic thinking stopped when he felt her hand lightly touch his arm. Looking back at her, he saw the worry in her eyes. "You don't have to tell me everything. I just... I just want to know if what I'm feeling, what I'm sensing, is right."

He looked at her for a moment more before giving her a soft smile. "No, Hayley... While we do hunt demons, we are much more than regular hunters."

Hayley smiled at him. "I thought so. Will you tell me later?" she asked, her eyes shining even brighter when he gave her a slight nod. Seeming satisfied for now, she scooted closer to him, curling comfortably into his side. "Is this okay?" Her breath caressed his skin.

Leaning his head down, he breathed in her warmth, the scent of honey soothing his senses. "This is more than okay," he whispered back, placing a soft kiss on top of her head. He felt her sigh beside him, her body relaxing into his as her breathing began to even out again.

Smiling, he felt his eyes begin to close. His last thought before sleep engulfed him was that this was definitely more than okay. It was perfect.

Chapter 23

Waking up slowly, the warm sun shining through the bedroom window, Hayley felt rested for the first time in years. Reaching her hand out, a sense of disappointment washed over her when she found the spot Manuel had slept in the previous night was cold. Sitting up, she glanced around the room. After only being there one night, she was surprised at how comfortable she already felt.

Before Manuel had come to bed last night, her sleep had been restless, visions of demons and blood plaguing her dreams. After some time, she had decided it would be best to just stay awake and rest her eyes. So she knew as soon as Manuel had come into the room. It had taken all her willpower not to move when she sensed him standing in the doorway, watching her. He had been so quiet while he was undressing. It wasn't until he sat down on the edge of the bed that she had finally shifted.

It was his scent that had caused her to move. Once he sat down, it had rolled over her, teasing her senses in such a way, she had moved to get closer to him. As he had stretched out on the bed, she started thinking about the past few days. About the hunt, his brothers, the fight that had happened earlier. So many things pointed to the men in this house being more than what they claimed. She needed to ask. Needed to know if what she was feeling were true.

His response to her question told her a lot. He was obviously uncomfortable with the subject, and although she didn't want to push him, she needed some sort of answer. The excitement that bloomed in her when he said she was right was intense. His promise to tell her about it had appeased her curiosity...for the time being. After that, it just felt natural to curl up next to him. To let his warmth wash over her and allow her to feel a sense of peace, of safety. There had been no nightmares after that. Just a deep, peaceful sleep.

Sliding out of bed, Hayley stretched. She could hear talking as she inhaled deeply, a smile crossing her face. *Coffee!* Throwing on a pair of sweatpants and a zip-up jacket over her tank, she followed the smell. It wasn't until she stepped around the corner and into the kitchen that she realized she should probably have waited for Manuel to come get her.

Ella, Christian, Darren, and Nicholas were all sitting at the table as she stopped in the kitchen entrance. She knew they had been in deep discussion about something, but it was now forgotten as they all turned to look at her. Feeling suddenly self-conscious, Hayley tugged at the bottom of her tank, then pulled her jacket tighter around her. "Good morning," she said shyly.

"Good morning," Darren answered.

"Mornin'," Christian said, giving her a friendly smile.

"Good morning, hon, and Merry Christmas," Ella said as she stood up, walking towards her. "Do you want some coffee?"

"I would love some. Thank you. And Merry Christmas to you, too," Hayley responded. She glanced past Ella and saw Nicholas watching her. Last night, she sensed he wasn't happy about her being here. He and Cyrus had seemed a little uncomfortable about her being a witch, although they had both shown their gratitude for helping Ella. Giving him a small smile, Hayley figured giving him space was the best right now. She just hoped he and Cyrus would come around, realize she wasn't so bad. Looking back at Ella, she realized she was still talking. "Sorry?"

"I was just wondering if you took cream and sugar in your coffee," Ella said, smiling.

"Oh... Yes, please. Sorry. My mind is just all over the place."

"I completely understand." Ella reached over, handing her a steaming cup. "Did you get some sleep last night?"

Taking a sip, Hayley practically moaned. It tasted so good. "I did. Thank you. How about you? Did you sleep okay?"

"Yeah," Ella said, her eyes sparkling. "Actually, I slept better last night than I have since..." As she paused, Hayley watched a shadow cross her eyes. Waiting for her to continue, she leaned against the counter and took another sip of her coffee. Suddenly, Ella seemed to shake herself out of it. Looking back up at Hayley, she smiled. "It's just been a while since I've had a good night's sleep."

"Well, I'm glad." Hayley returned her smile. "Have you seen Manuel this morning?"

"I think he went to the store," Christian spoke up.

"I'm sure he'll be back soon," Ella said as she walked back to the table and sat down.

"Okay, well... I think I'm going to go back to his room and watch some TV while I wait." Hayley smiled, taking another sip of her coffee. As much as she wanted to get to know them all, something about being out here without Manuel just felt off. She was sure part of it had to do with not yet knowing what he and his brothers really were.

Feeling a slight shift in the air, Hayley glanced towards Nicholas. His eyes were boring into hers, causing her uneasiness to grow. Deciding it was time to make her exit, she looked back at Ella.

"You can stay out here with us," Ella said before she could continue. Pointing to an empty chair, she smiled. "That way, we can all get to know each other better."

"No, I... Thank you, but I think I'm going to go lie down and relax for a bit. It's been a long couple days." Hayley looked down at her mug, then back at Ella. "Thank you for the coffee, Ella. We'll catch up later."

Glancing at Nicholas and Christian, Hayley took another sip. Christian seemed confused as to why she didn't want to stay, while Nicholas seemed relieved.

"Okay. I'll chat with you later then. Yeah?" Ella said, drawing Hayley's attention back to her.

"Yeah," she murmured. "Will you please let Manuel know I'm awake?" Hayley heard Ella promise to do that as she turned and made her way back down the hall. The air in the kitchen had seemed to thicken around her, so she couldn't get out of there fast enough. She was certain Nicholas had been the cause. She just wished she knew why he so obviously didn't like or trust her.

Walking back into Manuel's room, she closed the door and sat on the bed.

Taking another sip of coffee, she glanced over at the nightstand. Reaching for the remote, she switched on the TV. Trying to take her mind off Nicholas and the questions she had surrounding the men in this house, she lay back and flipped through the channels upon channels of mindless shows. Finally settling on an *X-Files* marathon, Hayley settled into the bed, dozing off into a restless sleep soon after the second episode started.

Manuel drove slowly through the streets. Because he only needed to head to the store really quick, he could have dematerialized there, but he felt the drive through town would do him good. His thoughts had been racing since he woke up. He just couldn't get the beautiful woman in his bed out of his mind. She invaded each of his thoughts, teased all of his senses. He had felt the tightness in his chest as he lay in bed this morning, watching her sleep. Her red hair pooled around her as she curled onto her side, her eyelashes fluttering against her cheeks as she dreamed.

Manuel's fingers had itched with the need to reach out and touch her, to run his fingers through her hair and over her shoulder. The feeling to get closer to her had been so overwhelming, it had scared the crap out of him.

Then, as if his physical reaction to her wasn't enough, his mind apparently had stopped working, as well. At least that was the only explanation he had for telling her last night that he and his brothers were not demon hunters, but more. Had he really said that?

Running a hand through his hair, Manuel slowed at a stoplight. *What am I doing?* he thought, closing his eyes. He wanted her at the house, had fought with his brothers to keep her there, and now... Now she was lying in his bed, curled beneath the sheets, waiting for him. With all of her questions, he was sure.

Yet that wasn't what was really nagging at him.

It was his dream from the previous day, the one that she had, quite literally, invaded. Ever since he had woken up this morning, it had been replaying in his mind, causing his usually manageable morning erection to be downright painful. Even the cold shower he had taken hadn't helped. Maybe he just needed to go home, press her up against his bedroom wall, and... He could feel the blood warming in his veins. There were too many reasons he shouldn't finish that thought, give in to his need to sink himself deep within her.

"Down boy," he whispered, adjusting his pants.

Turning onto their street, he drove slowly, glancing around at all the lights decorating the houses. So many things had changed within the seventy or so years since they'd fallen to Earth, but the act of decorating for Christmas had held true. He didn't know how this tradition had started, but it was one Manuel always looked forward to. Watching all the lights flash by him as he drove, he began to feel calmer, feel some peace of mind.

Driving up to their house, he pulled into the driveway. Taking several deep breaths, Manuel looked at the house they'd called home for the last seven years. Things were changing, and had been ever since Ella had shown up in their lives. Now, with Hayley, he could feel the change in the air, sense it in his brothers. Hell, he could sense the change in himself. It felt right to him, though. Moving the next day, Hayley being here... One thing he had learned since he and his brothers had fallen to Earth was change was inevitable. The best thing you could do during times like these was hold on tight, stick together, and just go with it. He just hoped they were all still standing in the end.

A sudden rapping on his window jolted Manuel from his thoughts. Whipping his head around, he saw Cyrus staring at him, his black eyes glinting in the morning light.

"Are you getting out of your car? Or are you just going to sit out here the whole day?" His eyebrow raised slightly.

Manuel rolled his eyes as he turned the car off and got out, Cyrus moving back to give him room. "What's up?" he asked slowly.

"Nothing. Just wondering how long you were going to sit in your car." Cyrus looked at him, his black eyes seeming to search Manuel's.

Manuel shifted slightly. "I was just thinking..."

"About?"

"Just how so many things are changing. That I feel like all of them are exactly what should be happening." Looking at his brother, Manuel raised a single eyebrow. "I know you have been against a lot of these changes lately. I also know you aren't too keen about having Hayley here." Cyrus nodded slowly, a slight tick in his jaw giving away his stress in the matter. "I just want us all to be safe, and I believe Hayley will help us."

Manuel watched Cyrus look away from him, staring off into the distance. A low growl finally escaped his lips before he turned back to meet Manuel's gaze. "I'm not against change. These past couple years have been...tough for me." Manuel's eyes grew wide as he opened his mouth, but Cyrus raised his hand, continuing in a rough voice. "I do not wish to go into it right now. All I want to say is I also feel the changes happening. While I may not be eager to accept them so blindly, I do not plan on fighting them, either. If you say this witch-" Manuel opened his mouth, but Cyrus shook his head. "Hayley. If you say you believe Hayley and it is a good idea to have her around, well, then I'll stand by you."

Manuel stared at him for a minute. The gravity of the fact Cyrus was willing to stand by him, even when he didn't agree, was not lost on him. "Thank you." He nodded. "That means a lot to me."

"Don't get all mushy on me, brother," he responded with a grunt, his black eyes narrowing. "But you're welcome."

Manuel looked from his brother to their house. "Now if I can just get Nicholas to come around."

"Hmph... I wouldn't count on that happening anytime soon." Cyrus frowned as he moved past Manuel, heading towards the house. "You'll have a better chance convincing him that Santa or, shit, the fuckin' Tooth Fairy is real."

"Don't I fuckin' know it," he ground out. "Do you know why? What happened to him for him to be so against her? I mean, I know he's had some run-ins, but nothing to explain this level of aggression towards Hayley."

Cyrus glanced over his shoulder, a grim look on his face. "It's not my story to tell, Manuel."

"But there *is* something? There's a reason he's acting this way?" Manuel pushed. He just needed to understand. Sure, he and his brothers had disagreed before, but Nicholas was taking it to another level. He had said he was going to give Hayley a chance, but Manuel had a feeling that wasn't going to last...if he had even tried to begin with.

Cyrus turned to him. "Nicholas has his secrets and they're his to share. If you want to know, ask him. If he wants you to know, he'll tell you. If not, well, I suggest you just let it go." He shook his head. "Maybe letting it go would be the best choice...for all of us."

Without waiting for a response, Cyrus turned and walked into the house, leaving Manuel with more questions than he had started with. *Just what I need. More shit to worry about*, he thought, following his brother inside.

Chapter 24

Walking into the kitchen behind Cyrus, he saw everyone sitting around, drinking coffee and discussing the move. Well, everyone except Hayley. Assuming she was still asleep, Manuel had joined the conversation...or tried to.

He listened as Darren mapped out how tomorrow would go. They all agreed to start early. That way, they would be done sooner, which was absolutely fine with Manuel. However, that was about where his interest in the conversation ended. It wasn't that he felt what Darren or the rest of them said wasn't important. His mind just refused to stay focused on it.

The drive Manuel had gone on to clear his mind had, in fact, only helped bring more concerns to light. They mainly revolved around Hayley. He needed to talk to her, clear up what he said last night. But what should he say? He had a feeling she would know if he lied to her, just like he knew she hadn't believed his demon hunter story to begin with. Plus, he hated lying to her. It had never been a problem before, but it was different with Hayley.

"Manuel?"

Ella's voice pulled him from his thoughts. How many times had she called his name? Blinking, he glanced down at his coffee. *Shit, I didn't even realize I was staring at the kitchen door.* His mind had been so wrapped up in thoughts about Hayley, he hadn't noticed he had been staring towards the door, hoping for her to walk through it. *I must look like a damn lost puppy*, he thought with an inward groan.

Attempting to cover up his embarrassment, Manuel turned to look at Ella, clearing his throat. "Hmm?"

She slowly smiled at him. "I just wanted to let you know Hayley came out for some coffee earlier."

"She's up?" he asked, wondering why she wasn't out here with everyone.

"Yeah. Well, she was. She said she was going to wait back in your room..." Ella's voice trailed off as Christian started nodding.

"We asked her to hang out with us, but she said something about wanting to go lay down." Judging by his tone of voice, Manuel could tell Christian didn't believe her.

Manuel stepped away from the counter he had been leaning on. "That's weird. I mean, I know she's been tired lately, but she slept like a rock last night." A nagging concern began to grow in his chest. He looked at Nicholas, who was looking anywhere but at him. Manuel narrowed his eyes at his brother. Finally pulling his eyes away, he looked back at Ella. "How was she when she came out here?"

Ella frowned. "She seemed fine. A little uncomfortable, but who wouldn't be in a house full of strangers? We asked her to stay out here. I really do want to get to know her, help her feel comfortable, but if she isn't ready for that, I'm not going to force her. I remember what it's like to feel like an outsider. It wasn't too long ago that I was in her shoes." Her voice got higher as her defenses went up. Immediately, he saw Christian tense next to her.

Not wanting to get everyone upset, Manuel quickly nodded. "Of course. I just hoped to be here when she woke so she wouldn't feel that way. I'm mad at myself for being away for so long." It wasn't necessarily a lie, but also not the full reason behind his growing anger. He knew Nicholas had said or done something to make Hayley want to hide in his room. Remembering Cyrus' words, he pushed the anger down. As much as he knew he should let this go, he might not be able to. Nicholas' mood swings where Hayley was concerned had his head hurting. No. He'd definitely be dealing with his brother's issues soon enough.

"Why don't you go get her, bring her out here so she can start getting to know us," Ella said, curling into Christian's protective hug. "That way, she can hopefully start feeling more comfortable here."

"Yeah. I think I'll do that," Manuel said slowly.

"Great-" Ella started, only to be cut off by Nicholas.

"I have some things to do. I'll be back later." Rising from his seat, Nicholas avoided everyone's eyes as he walked quickly from the room, his boots thudding loudly as he made his way through the house.

Manuel felt his jaw clench as he started to go after his brother. Maybe waiting to air this shit out wasn't such a good idea. Nicholas needed to stop acting like a dick, and he needed to stop now. Manuel may be uncertain about his growing feelings for Hayley and his need to have her near, but one thing he was sure of was that he wasn't going to allow any of his brothers to treat her like shit, make her feel like she made the wrong choice coming here.

Manuel was almost to the kitchen door before he knew it, his body humming as his power began to build. The sound of Darren clearing his throat and Cyrus growling his name made him stop.

Looking down, he pulled in one ragged breath after another. Feeling the walls around him give a slight shudder,

Manuel closed his eyes. He knew they were right, even if every part of him wanted to chase Nicholas down, demand an explanation. He needed to see Hayley, the thought of her beginning to calm him.

Taking a deep breath, Manuel opened his eyes and glanced over his shoulder. "I'm going to see if Hayley's awake. If she is, I'll bring her out here and maybe we can all have some lunch."

Murmurs of agreement and understanding reached Manuel's ears as he walked out. Making his way towards his room, he passed the pool room that Nicholas had disappeared into. He didn't even bother glancing his way. If his brother wanted to avoid Hayley, avoid him, Manuel was more than happy to do the same. Nicholas could come to him when he was ready; otherwise, he would do as Cyrus suggested and let it go.

Well, he'd try to anyway.

Chapter 25

As soon as Manuel walked through his bedroom door, Hayley knew he was stressed. He wouldn't talk about it, seeming to want to talk about anything but what was bothering him...which seemed to cover about every topic she was interested in. Not wanting to add to his already aggravated mood, Hayley let it drop.

Instead, she agreed to spend the rest of the day getting to know his family. The relief on his face when she mentioned how she thought spending time with them was a good idea made dealing with her growing anxiety worth it. It wasn't that she didn't like them. Quite the opposite. She was still trying to figure out how to get them to accept her...especially Nicholas. There was something in the way he looked at her that said he didn't trust her, didn't want her around, and she had a feeling the root of his mistrust ran a lot deeper than he let on. Luckily, it wasn't something she had to worry about today.

As they walked into the kitchen, she was sure everyone would be able to hear her heart beating. It was so loud in her own ears, she couldn't see how they wouldn't. If any of them had sensed her nervousness, though, they hadn't shown it.

The day had gone a lot better than she'd hoped. His family was truly amazing, and the love they had for each other was easy to see. The best were Christian and Ella, who seemed to be made for each other. She couldn't take her eyes off them when she first sat at the kitchen table. The way they interacted with each other was adorable, but watching Christian dote on Ella was almost too much. An instant spike of jealousy shot through her at one point, but she had quickly squashed it. Sure, she yearned to have someone love her like that, but knew there was a chance she never would. However, she refused to let herself have any animosity towards someone who did. She liked Ella and Christian. They made sense together. If she opened herself up, she could even see their auras intermingling. The uniqueness of their bond was unmistakable.

Darren, Hayley noticed, was the observer of the family. As they sat there eating lunch, he had been quiet, watchful. There wasn't an uneasiness to him, though. She felt a calmness radiating off him, but like the rest of them, there was also a constant power rippling just below the surface.

Cyrus also made an appearance, but he didn't linger long. Part of Hayley wanted to talk to him. To get a feel of where he was with her being there. But as she watched him step away from the wall he had been leaning against and leave the room, she decided it would be best to wait. It wasn't that she felt the same vibe coming off him that she'd felt from Nicholas, but she also didn't sense he was quite ready to welcome her with open arms.

She was hoping time would change that.

Back in Manuel's room, Hayley placed one of her bags on his bed. He was still sitting with his family, but she had claimed a headache. After promising to be back out for dinner, she headed back to his room to presumably lay down. Of course, she had other plans.

Looking through the contents of her small bag, she pulled out one of her black candles and a holder, placing them on the bed in front of her. Taking her matchbook out, Hayley turned it around in her hand as she stared at the candle. The extra power floating around in Ella last night still bothered her. She had never felt something like that in an individual before. One body holding two separate and very different powers was not just unheard of. It was extremely dangerous.

Hayley was concerned for her well-being, both physical and mental.

Looking at the matches in her hand, she ripped one out and struck it, watching the orange flame crackle to life as she thought about the darkness in Ella. It seemed to twist itself around her white light. She needed to find a way to help before the warring powers within her became too much.

Lighting the candle, she concentrated on the feel of those two powers. The white light was definitely Ella's. It had her essence, her soul, attached to it. Hayley could also see Christian's power bonded to her. The darkness, though, was foreign. Was it placed in her on purpose? If so, by whom?

One question at a time, she thought, blowing out the match, the smoke from it curling into the air. First things first. She needed to figure out how that darkness wound up in Ella.

Thinking back on that power, the feel of it as it moved like oil across her own, she began to get flashes of its owner. Frowning, she gazed down into the flame licking around the candle's wick.

"I need answers," she whispered, her voice carrying through the quiet room.

Leaning down, Hayley pulled a small pouch from her bag. Its weight was familiar in her grasp as she cradled the soft cloth bag in her hands. *Whose power resides in Ella?* she thought, closing her eyes. Rolling the bag between her hands, she could feel the stones rubbing against each other. A warmth began to spread from the bag into her hands, curling around her fingers and up her arm.

As it filled her body, Hayley opened her eyes and brought the bag up to her lips. Blowing softly against the drawstrings holding it shut, she watched as they slowly loosened. The pouch opened as the power of the stones inside called out to her.

Setting it down, she turned it over and watched as seven brilliant gems rolled out...amethyst, amber, hematite, lapis lazuli, moonstone, opal, and diamond. She eyed the stones as they rolled to a slow stop atop Manuel's comforter.

Hovering her right hand over them, she felt a pull as one of the stones began to pulse stronger than the others. Looking at it, Hayley smiled. Reaching down, she felt the coolness of the hematite as her fingers wrapped around it. Its power began flooding her senses as Hayley tightened her grip. Focusing on the question at hand, she closed her eyes.

A shadowy male figure flashed through her mind. She could sense the darkness surrounding him, its essence shivering across her, leaving her with the same bone-chilling sensation the darkness in Ella gave her.

"Who are you?" she whispered, focusing on the dark image. Hayley knew what she was seeing wasn't the actual individual, but she hoped her vision would still give her the answers she was looking for.

The figure twisted, pulsing, going in and out of focus. A light sheen of sweat began to cover her skin as she tightened her grip on the hematite. Its power burned her palm as it responded to her growing demand.

Just as she felt she couldn't hold the vision a moment longer, the shadowy figure darkened and became a solid black silhouette...except for the multi-colored eyes glaring devilishly back at her. One was the brightest blue she had ever seen; the other was a dark forest green. A shiver ran through her as the eyes narrowed. If she hadn't been aware that this was only a vision, Hayley would have sworn the figure was staring straight into her soul. Those eyes suddenly flashed, darkening as they turned a deep shade of red. The intensity of them shot fear right through her veins.

Gasping, Hayley's eyes flew open. Tossing the stone back onto the comforter, she sat there, rubbing her suddenly cold hands together.

"What did you see?"

At the sudden sound of Manuel's voice, Hayley let out a startled yelp. Glancing up, she saw him leaning against the doorframe. *Didn't I close the door?* she thought with a frown. "You scared me... How long have you been standing there?"

He held his hands out before him. "Sorry. I didn't mean to startle you. I've only been standing here a few moments," he said slowly, seeming to study her as he stuffed his hands into his pockets. "I didn't want to interrupt. You seemed to be really into...whatever it was you were doing."

"Yes, um... There is something that has been bothering me. Something I needed to try and figure out." Leaning down, Hayley sent out a silent thank you as she blew out the candle. Watching the smoke curl into the air, she looked back up at Manuel, who was patiently waiting for her to say more. Licking her lips, she gave him a small smile. "When I helped Ella last night, I felt something...off."

"Off?" He frowned, walking into the room. "What do you mean by off? You didn't say anything about this last night." His voice held no animosity, yet she felt her defenses going up anyway. His emotions rolled off him as he stopped by the bed.

"I didn't want to say anything until I had some answers," she explained patiently. "The last thing I wanted to do was come here and start causing trouble. I just... I wanted to be sure there was something to be concerned about before I came to you."

He slowly nodded. "And? *Is* there something we should be concerned about?"

She looked at him for a moment. There definitely was something to be worried about, something that was darker than anything she'd ever come across, but did she really have anything to go off of besides her vision? Sure, she would stand by it a hundred percent, coming to trust them completely over the years. Would everybody listen to her, though? Nobody in this house knew her well enough to take her at her word. The thought of any of them, especially Manuel, looking at her like she was just looking to cause trouble hurt her heart. She may not know Manuel, but she felt a connection to him.

What if he felt it, too? she wondered. If he did, maybe he would listen to her, knowing that she was truly concerned and not just wanting to cause drama.

Licking her lips again, she gazed into his amethyst eyes. Her mind told her to tell him. That he would stand by her. That this was not something she should keep hidden from him. *What if I don't say anything and Ella gets hurt? Manuel would never forgive me*, she thought suddenly.

Hayley took a deep breath and gazed up at him. "When I helped Ella last night, I sensed she had two powers residing within her."

Manuel's eyebrows shot up in surprise. "Two? That's impossible. There's no way Ella could..." His voice trailed off as his eyes narrowed.

Sensing he had just thought of something, her eyes widened. "What?"

"Nothing...," he said slowly. "I don't *think* it's anything anyway." Shaking his head, Manuel sighed loudly. "Is that what you were doing in here? Trying to figure out how she has two powers?"

"Yes. I know one of the powers is definitely hers. It's warm and pure." Smiling, Hayley's eyes traveled over his face. "I could see that power as we were sitting with them earlier. It's mesmerizing. When Christian's next to her, it's constantly curling around both of them. That level of connection is something I have never seen before."

"They're bonded," he said simply.

"Bonded?"

"Soulmates." He smiled at her, a warmth temporarily stamping out the worry in his eyes.

Hayley felt her heart speed up. "How beautiful."

Manuel's eyes flashed briefly. "It is. They were lucky to have found each other."

"Something tells me luck has very little to do with what happens in our lives."

Making a low rumble of agreement, he gazed intently at her. "And the other power?"

"What?" she asked, still gazing into his warm expression. Having momentarily forgotten what they were talking about, her mind raced to get back on track.

"The other power you sensed in Ella... What do you know about that one?"

Feeling a coldness run through her, she unconsciously wrapped her arms around her chest. "It's cold. It's a very dark, cold power."

The frown that had momentarily left his face was now back. "Dark?"

"Yes. It's an evil power, Manuel. I don't understand how she can have that within her." Shaking her head, she took a deep breath before rushing on. "I think it was placed in her. Someone, or something, put that evil inside her. It's fighting her own power."

He seemed at a loss as he stared back at her. "It's not possible...," he repeated again. It was so quiet, he was probably saying it to himself.

Hayley answered anyway. "It is *very* possible. I saw them both inside her. That's why she almost lost control last night. When you guys were arguing, I think the negative emotions rolling through the room fed that dark power in her, strengthening it."

Manuel had a look on his face that she couldn't quite figure out. It was almost like... *He's aware of this?* she thought.

Before she could ask, his eyes began to take on an otherworldly glow.

"Were you able to sense who gave that to her?" His voice came out raspy as he tried to contain his emotions.

"I didn't get a name or anything like that," she said slowly. "But..."

"But?" he pushed, his power suddenly flooding her senses.

Taking another deep breath, she felt her own power beginning to respond to his. Flashes of a darkness with multi-colored eyes coursed through her mind. The evil within them caused her body to shudder again. Staring up into Manuel's face, she put all her fear into her eyes. "This being is powerful, Manuel. More so than anything I've ever come up against. And his eyes..." Licking her lips, she felt the air around her grow cold.

"What about them?" Manuel asked, his voice barely audible.

"They're multi-colored," she whispered, watching in amazement as his eyes darkened to almost black as soon as the words left her lips. Nodding slowly, she leaned forward, curling her arms even tighter around her. "One eye... One eye's blue, and-"

"The other's green," Manuel growled.

Chapter 26

A light rap on his door and his name being whispered had Dev glancing up from his paperwork. "Come in," he said, shuffling his papers back into a pile.

Watching the door open, he smiled as Trix peeked into his office. The slight frown on her face, though, caused his smile to slip. "Um, there are some guys out here wanting to see you. They say they're the club's security?" One of her eyebrows raised as she spoke the last word.

As he sat there, contemplating how to respond, the scent of sulfur tickled his nose. He felt his muscles tense up as he leaned back in his chair. *Fuckin' demons.* Taking a shallow breath, Dev just nodded at Trix, letting her know to send them in. Did he want to see them? No. Did he want to have these demons prowling around the club twenty-four/seven? Definitely not. Sighing, he shifted in his seat as the main question flickered through his mind. Did he have a choice in the matter? That, like everything else in his life, was a resounding no.

Standing slowly, he watched as the four demons stalked through the door.

Kanibal...or K, as he liked to be called...walked in first, his dark brown eyes scanning the office. He was a tall demon, probably about six-three, and thin as a rail. That didn't mean he was any less dangerous than other demons, though.

Next was Rave. His grey eyes zeroed in on Dev as soon as he walked through the door. They had a strange relationship...if that was what you could call it. By no means did Dev consider the demon a friend. However, in a way that only an angel and demon could, he had a level of respect for Rave, and it seemed the feeling was mutual.

Rave may never have stopped any of the horror Dev had gone through after his fall, but he never added to it, either. Because of this, when Dev heard Rave was one of the demons Andras was sending, he felt a little better...very little. He didn't fully trust him because, well, he was a demon. Dev knew better than to completely trust any of them.

Dev watched him walk over and lean against the wall, sending only the slightest nod his way. He nodded back before looking at the door again.

The twins, Lakmi and Vhin, came in next. They were almost completely identical. They had the same build, same height, and same short blond hair. Their eyes were what separated them. Lakmi's were a dark forest green, while Vhin's were an ice blue. They were creepy as shit and probably two of Dev's least favorite demons to be around. Not that it was a small list, but they were definitely near the top.

Frowning slightly, he watched them both cross their arms over their broad chests, glaring at him.

Yep, definitely creepy.

"Dev," Rave's gravelly voice pulled his attention from the twins.

"Rave," he responded evenly.

"Is the club ready for Andras' arrival?" Before Dev could answer, Rave raised one of his hands. "He will be here soon. You are aware that time is running out, yes?"

Grinding his teeth, Dev walked around his desk to lean on the front edge of it. Of course he knew time was running out. Hell, with every hour that passed, he half expected Andras to walk through the door. Looking at the demons, he stopped himself from sighing. "Yes, I'm aware. The club will be ready. I have made sure everything meets with his...specifications."

"So you are ready for him to show up then?" K asked, his lips curling into a sneer as he stared at him.

"Yes," Dev responded tersely. "As I said, I will make sure everything is ready. You just concentrate on what it is you're here to do." His eyes narrowed as his unease grew. "Being security for Andras' club."

"Security for the club," K murmured, taking a step towards Dev. "Yes. That is one of our orders."

"*One* of your orders?" Dev asked in a growl.

"Of course, Dev. Do you really think Andras would put us here to *only* watch over his club?" K tisked.

Dev just glared at him before looking back at Rave. Deep down, he knew they were here for more, but that hadn't stopped him from hoping he wasn't going to need to add them to his ever-growing list of demons to watch out for. Just once in this miserable existence he had landed in, Dev would like to not have to worry about who's around. He wanted to believe these four were just going to watch over the club, make sure nothing got out of hand between the demons and humans who would be traipsing in and out of the joint.

If that were the case, he could easily keep his distance from them, leaving only Castigo, Agalon, and Andras as his main tormentors. But if these guys were also going to be keeping an eye on him, his chances of staying topside for any length of time just got smaller. They would surely find out about his dealings with Sy, the debt he owed him, and the discussions they've had.

Dev blinked slowly as another thought crept up. Maybe they weren't ordered to keep an eye on him. Maybe it was something else entirely and his paranoia was just working overtime. Then again, what if it didn't have anything to do with him, but everything to do with his brothers? What if their other orders were to hunt them down?

"What exactly are you guys here for?" he asked slowly.

Rave blinked, staring back at him. He seemed to be contemplating on how to answer when Kanibal gave a low chuckle.

"What do you think we are here for?" K snapped. "Andras has many plans for this club, some of which will take a lot more than just some sad little fallen angel to oversee." Watching him take another step closer, Dev tensed up. The demon's brown eyes flashed as he sneered at him. "There is also the matter of the...pest problem this town seems to have." K chuckled. "I mean, I'm sure Andras will want them dealt with once he's settled here."

"Yeah," Lakmi laughed. "Maybe they will make it easy on us and show up at the club."

"I hope not," Vhin growled. "What would be the fun in that?"

"Well, we wouldn't need to track them down." Lakmi shrugged.

"The hunt is part of the fun, brother," Vhin glanced at Lakmi, then looked back at Dev with a sneer. "After all, it *is* part of the foreplay."

Dev's breath caught in his throat. *Great. Just fucking great*, he thought. Keeping his face blank, he leaned back, crossing his arms over his chest. What the hell was he going to do now? Maybe he should try to reach out to his brothers, give them a heads-up before they found themselves knee-deep in demon assholes. However, then they'd know he was here, working for Andras. Not that he had a choice, but what were the chances they would care about how he ended up working for the demon? *Shit*.

If he could get word to them without them finding out it was from him... That would probably be the best.

His mind already working on a way to reach out to his brothers, Dev didn't realize Kanibal was talking to him.

"Dev!" K snarled, bring his attention back to the demons in his office.

"Sorry," Dev replied. "I just remembered I need to call the bank back about the credit card machines." *Not quite a lie*. Out of the corner of his eye, he saw Rave raise an eyebrow. He wanted to glance at the demon, but decided to continue holding K's glare instead. "What did you say?"

Dev felt a tiny spark of satisfaction as he watched the demon's jaw muscle twitch. "I said," K ground out through clenched teeth, "we expect you to give us any information you have on your brothers and the females with them."

"Well, seeing as I haven't seen them in several decades, I don't really think any information I have on them would be of any use to you. I mean, a lot can change in that amount of time." He smiled at the demon. "And I definitely have no idea about any females who may or may not be with them."

"I find that hard to believe," Vhin said.

Turning to him, Dev shrugged. "Believe what you want, but I don't have any information. Guess you boys are going to have to get it from someone else."

"Yeah, well, I think you are full of shit, but go ahead and play that card. We have time. Just know that once Andras gets here, *he* will be the one asking you about them, then we will see what you know." Smirking, Vhin turned and walked out of his office, Lakmi right on his heels.

Kanibal chuckled at Vhin's statement as he turned to follow them out. He paused at the door, glancing over his shoulder. "We will see you around, Dev." He grinned before walking out.

Dev stood there, staring at the empty doorway. Another moment passed before he realized Rave had remained behind.

Looking at the demon, he saw Rave standing there, his grey eyes narrowed as he stared at him. Looking at the ground, Dev sighed. "Is there anything you would like to add to your friends' parting comments?"

"They are hardly my friends," he muttered. "But I do have one question."

Dev looked up to find Rave still staring at him. "Yes?"

"When Andras asks you about your brothers...and he will...," Rave started, tilting his head slightly, "do you think you will be able to lie to him better than you lied to us?"

"I'm not sure what you mean," Dev responded slowly.

"Come now, Dev," he chided. "Those three may *think* you are full of shit, but I *know* you are. You may not have been in contact with your brothers, but you know something about them. Maybe even something about their females." He let out a soft chuckle when Dev looked away from him. "Thought so."

"Listen, it's not that-"

"No, *you* listen." His voice was sharp as he stepped closer. "You had better come up with something to tell Andras, or at least a better lie than the pitiful one you just spit out, because we both know what will happen to you if you don't. So, I ask again, will you be able to lie to him when he gets here?"

Swallowing hard, Dev looked back at Rave. The demon was now close enough that he could feel his power radiating around him. It was strong and dangerous, causing him to want to edge closer to the side of his desk. Rave didn't throw his power out at him as Castigo had, but he really didn't need to. The damn demon was one of the more powerful ones he had come across. Why he took orders from Andras, let others tell him what to do, was still a mystery. Dev was just thankful Rave had never used his power against him.

Standing straight, he met the demon's stare. Breathing slowly so as to calm his nerves and keep his own power in check, Dev thought over his question. Would he be able to? The answer came to him instantly, just as it had every time he had been asked about his brothers. There wasn't a question about it. He would have to lie to Andras. He would have to protect his brothers, warning them if he could. There was no other option.

He watched the frown slowly lift from Rave's face. Dev wasn't sure whether the demon saw a change in his stance, a flash in his eyes, or maybe he could just read Dev better than most. Whatever it was, he seemed satisfied. Taking a step back, the demon gave him a knowing look before turning to walk out of the office, shutting the door behind him.

Before the door clicked shut, Dev's mind, which had begun to race as soon as Rave stepped back, had already started forming a plan on how best to reach his brothers.

Chapter 27

Manuel poured himself another glass of Crown. This would be the second one since he left Hayley back in his room to do her thing. After he realized Andras was responsible for all the problems Ella had been having, he wanted to storm right out and tell everyone they were going hunting. He didn't know if he was more pissed about Andras planting some of his power in Ella, leaving it there like a time bomb, or that none of them had figured it out sooner. Poor Ella. To have her power warring with that piece of shit's had to be taking a toll on her.

But Hayley had stopped him, saying they needed to get more information before telling the others. She didn't want to jump the gun only to find out her vision was wrong. Although there was no doubt in his mind that Hayley was right, he could understand her wanting to be sure, so he promised to keep this to himself...for now. There was no way he'd be able to keep this kind of information a secret from his brothers for long, especially Darren. He just had a way of knowing things, which also concerned Manuel. Shouldn't he have been able to tell there was something wrong?

Shaking his head, he took another healthy swig of his drink. He could hear his brothers out in the front room. Cindy had shown up a while ago. Along with a very energetic Ella, she had been cracking the boys up with stories of their past jobs. By the sounds of it, working as a PI and consulting with the local police on their more intense cases led to some downright ridiculous tales, each of which brought rounds of laughter from everyone in the room. Well, at least, Christian, Nicholas, and Darren were laughing. Cyrus, as usual, would only let out a low chuckle every once in a while.

Manuel had been hiding in the office, listening to them and thinking. Even if he didn't tell them right away, he should still be doing something. He wanted to do some research, but he had no idea where to start, let alone what he should be looking for. He could always go back to help Hayley, but knowing nothing about witchcraft, he probably wouldn't be any good to her.

Maybe that's what I need to do, he thought as he took another drink. *I'll do some research on witchcraft.*

Feeling relieved to have some sort of direction, Manuel leaned over and booted up the computer. As icons appeared on the screen, the soft hum of the cooling fans reaching his ears, he added some more

Crown to his glass, downing half while he waited. When everything was finally loaded, Manuel brought up the internet.

His fingers hovered over the keys as he stared at the search engine. Where to start? After some thought, he simply typed in "witchcraft". His screen instantly filled with different sites offering everything from love spells and herbal remedies to the craft's origins and what the term meant in today's culture. Moving his mouse from one link to another, Manuel finally decided that the history was the best place to start.

Two hours later, he groaned and shut the computer down. Manuel wasn't sure if anything he had just read would be of use, but at least he felt like he had done something. He now understood the candles and the stones, Hayley's connection with the Earth, and her need to help.

Standing from his chair, he stretched, then left the office. The house had gone quiet an hour or so ago. His brothers, Ella, and Cindy, who was staying over so she could help with the move, had probably headed off to their respective rooms to either relax or finish packing. Packing. Something he should be doing, but he wasn't sure if Hayley was done yet. Walking into the kitchen, he spotted Nicholas sitting at the table, staring intently at the laptop screen.

"What's going on?" he asked, grabbing a glass for some milk.

Nicholas looked up, his eyes tired. "Just checking out that new club that's going to be opening up."

Manuel frowned. "The one we were talking about earlier? The 9th Circle?"

"Yeah. Sounds like it's going to be an interesting place to check out." Nicholas clicked his mouse a few times. "It says it'll be opening on January third. Maybe we shouldn't wait to go like we had originally planned."

A feeling of uneasiness began to curl through Manuel as he sat across from his brother. "I don't know. I think maybe you were right and we should check it out *after* we get settled. Plus, I have Hayley around, so..."

Nicholas glanced up from the screen. "What? Now that you have your pretty little witch you don't want to go out?"

Manuel felt his temper spike. "Seriously, Nicholas?" He knew his eyes had taken on a slight glow as he glared at his brother.

"Don't give me that look. Just a couple months ago, you would have jumped at the chance to go scope this place out. All of a sudden, you're not sure now? Come the fuck on!"

"Damn it, Nicholas. My being unsure of this club has nothing to do with Hayley.

Like I said, I read up on this place and it gave me a bad feeling. Maybe we shouldn't worry about it at all. At least for the time being."

"Well, *I* just read up on it and my gut is telling me we should go now." Nicholas held his hand up when Manuel opened his mouth. "But you're right. I had originally said we should wait, and maybe that is the best way to go, no matter how much my gut says we should go now. If we wait, we can get in there opening weekend when the club's busy and crowded. Nobody would even bat an eye at our presence. What I don't understand is you suddenly not wanting to go at all. You say your change of mind isn't about Hayley, but because you have a bad feeling about it. I say all the more reason to go, have a drink, and take a look around."

Manuel shifted in his seat. "I don't-"

"Hey, we can take Hayley with us. Yeah? Just you, me, Hayley...and Cyrus, if he wants to go. They'll be so busy opening night, I doubt anyone will even notice we're there." Nicholas' red eyes gleamed as he smiled. "Besides, we'll all be tired from getting the new house set up and be itching to get out for a bit."

"You'd want Hayley to go with us?" Manuel's eyebrows rose. "You, who only hours ago wanted nothing to do with her, would suddenly be okay with her tagging along with us. Really?"

Nicholas shrugged. "I'm under the impression she is going to be staying around...at least for now. If she's still around after New Year's, then yeah, I'm cool with her coming along." He immediately turned back to the laptop, avoiding further eye contact.

Manuel's eyes narrowed. "Why?"

"Hmm?" he hummed, not looking up.

"I said..." Leaning across the table, Manuel reached out and closed the laptop. Nicholas' eyes shot up as it clicked shut. "Why? Why the sudden change of heart?"

Sighing, Nicholas leaned back in his chair. "It's nothing..."

"Nicholas."

"Fine. I talked to Cyrus. Okay?" Nicholas stood up, his chair scraping across the ground. "He came up to me a little while ago and told me it was obvious you really cared about Hayley, and if I cared about you at all, I would give her a chance because she makes you happy. I've been trying, you know. It's just hard to get over the past." Knowing Manuel, he held up his hand and shook his head. "I don't want to get into it right now, but I thought I was doing the right thing by keeping my distance. Obviously, that wasn't the case. The conversation with Cyrus just brought everything into perspective. So..." He shot him a crooked smile, holding his arms out at his sides. "This is me promising to give her a real chance." He chuckled. "Don't get me wrong. I'm not comfortable with her in the let her borrow my books or share my macaroni and cheese kind of way, but I won't be opposed to her being around."

Manuel's jaw dropped open as he stared at his brother. This was the last thing he expected to come out of Nicholas' mouth. If anything, he was expecting him to demand to know when Hayley would be leaving. Not that he had thought about how long she would be sticking around. He had only asked her to stay for a couple days, so he assumed she would head back to her home at some point.

"That means a lot to me, Nicholas, although I'm sure she won't be around for very long. She just came to help us with the move, possibly helping Ella out with whatever's going on with her power." An ache in his chest shot through him at the sudden thought of Hayley leaving. Pushing that feeling down, he shook his head. "It's not like we're together or anything."

"Right," Nicholas murmured. "So you fought this hard to get her welcomed into our lives because you... What? Wanted to be in the *friend zone*? Is that what you guys are now? Friends?"

"What? No. I mean, yes." Manuel growled. "She said she could help us. That's why I wanted her here."

"Right," Nicholas said again, rolling his eyes. "Whatever you say, Manuel. She also said she has been dreaming about you for as long as she can remember, but hey..." He shrugged as he turned to leave. "As long as she wants to help *us*, that's what's important, brother. I'm gonna finish packing."

Eyes wide, Manuel watched as Nicholas left the kitchen. The fact his brother had picked up on the attraction between him and Hayley should have irked him, but it didn't. Hell, he was sure everyone in the house knew. Like Nicholas said, he hadn't fought so hard to get the female here just for her help, had he?

This connection between them was purely out of necessity. Nothing more than a growing friendship. If he were lucky, maybe friends with benefits eventually. But that was all. It had to be. Manuel didn't have anything outside of that to offer.

The thought caused a lump to form in his throat as he got up to head back to his room. God, how he wished he could have what Christian and Ella did.

Maybe I'm just overthinking everything, he thought with a nod. It wasn't like Hayley said anything about sticking around or even wanting anything from him, other than help with the demons. Then again, if her coming to him in his dream said anything, and Manuel felt it spoke volumes, she was at least interested in a more physical relationship. Maybe friends with benefits would work...

If that is the case, she can consider the feelings mutual, he thought with a grin. He'd be lying if he said that hadn't been on his mind since he first saw her.

Walking into his room, Manuel stopped at the door, his breath catching in his throat. In all of the years he'd been on Earth, he'd never seen such a beautiful sight.

Hayley slept peacefully on her side in the center of his bed, her red hair spread out upon his comforter, surrounding her in soft curls. Her t-shirt was lifted slightly, exposing just a hint of her creamy skin to his greedy eyes. Even her jeans teased him, hugging her curves as if painted on. He listened to her steady heartbeat, her breath a whisper as it passed her slightly parted lips. His need to have her rolled through him, consuming any other thought in his mind until all he saw was her.

He didn't realize he'd moved until he found himself at the side of the bed, his hand reaching out as he prepared to crawl to where she lay. He should stop. He shouldn't pursue this. He had no right to.

Hell, he didn't even really know her, and vice versa.

As he kneeled on the edge of the bed, he paused. *I haven't woken her yet*, he thought. *I can still stop. I* should *stop.*

Shifting slightly, he continued attempting to convince himself to walk away. His heart and body yearned for her, craved her. Even his mind, through its feeble attempt to stop him, held on to the idea that, in some way, she was his. It was ridiculous because there was no way that could be true...no matter how right it felt.

Feeling a quiver in the mattress, Manuel looked up to see Hayley watching him over her shoulder. He noticed her eyes dilate slightly as her chest lifted with a deep breath.

"Manuel...," she whispered, her voice breathy.

He opened his mouth to respond, to say something, to explain why he was on the bed so close to where she lay. Then, with a sigh, she slowly licked her lips, causing any explanation that may have been forming in his mind to vanish. His words morphed into a throaty growl as his eyes followed her tongue's movement.

The smile she gave him made any uncertainty, any doubt he still had about taking her leave his body in a single shudder. That same smile was all he needed to get himself to start moving towards her.

She may not be his. He may not have any right to claim her, to even entertain the idea of having her in his life. He even knew that the time would come when she would leave, which would destroy him. But for today, for right now, she was with him, and to even have just a taste of her would be worth the heartache.

Chapter 28

Hayley held her breath as she watched Manuel slowly crawl towards her.

When she had first woken up, she was unsure why he was kneeling on the bed, tension radiating off him. She could see the rippling of the muscles in his arms, the tightening of his lips. Anyone else would have thought he was just resting, thinking as he sat on his bed. But she knew better. As she watched him, she could practically see the power rolling around him, and the sexual heat had her own body instantly taking notice.

Then there were his eyes. They were glowing as he had looked at her. Licking her lips, she had tried to curb her reaction to his closeness, but as his eyes dropped from hers and followed her tongue's movement, she had needed to squeeze her thighs together to try and ease her clit's throbbing. Of course, any time she looked at him, she could feel her muscles quivering. This was different, though.

It was wilder, more demanding. Just...more.

Shivering, she held still as he reached for her leg. Hayley was afraid if she moved, he may change his mind. When she looked over her shoulder at him, she knew he had been teetering on the edge of should he or shouldn't he. At one point, Hayley felt certain he was going to pull back, leaving her in an uncomfortable state of arousal and confusion. But, much to her delight, his obvious need to be with her, to touch her, won out.

Feeling his hands skim across her calf, she had to bite her lip to hold back a moan. God, how long had it been since she was with someone? Months? Years? Her brain tried to come up with an answer, but any conscious thought faltered when she felt his hand tighten.

His eyes took on a soft purple glow as he stared at her. She watched him lean forward, kissing a trail up her leg as he moved his body closer. She twisted slightly, lying on her back so she could watch him. So she could give him the access he wanted.

Reaching the top of her jeans, he paused. She watched him trace the edge of her pants with his finger, lightly brushing against her stomach as he moved. Her eyes followed his hand's movement. He ran his fingers slowly along the edge and then back, finally stopping at the button. How easy it would be for him to pop that button. To pull the zipper down and expose her. Goosebumps spread across her skin as her anticipation grew.

He glanced up to look at her, his fingers skillfully loosening her button, then moving to her zipper. "Is this okay?" His voice sounded husky as he smiled up at her.

Nodding, she watched as his smile widened.

With a low growl, she watched him pull back, shifting as he grasped the edges of her jeans and pulled them down her legs. The cool air in the room felt soothing to her warm skin. Manuel hummed in appreciation as his eyes traveled up her naked legs to her black lace panties.

"Beautiful," he whispered.

Hayley sighed as he moved back over her. Reaching down, she ran her hands over his t-shirt, tugging slightly at the bottom. Smirking, he reached down, pulling it off with one hand. She felt her lips part as a low moan escaped her. His muscular chest, six-pack abs, and defined V leading down into his jeans had her wiggling beneath him. Reaching up, she hovered her hand just above his skin. His power licked out around him, growing as the seconds ticked by.

Looking into his eyes, she watched as they swirled with purples and blacks. She was so caught up in their brilliance, she almost missed the slight shudder of the bed beneath her. Almost missed the rattle of the pictures on the walls.

Almost.

Oh shit! Please tell me we aren't having an earthquake.

Her mind pulled back from the thought almost immediately. There was no way anything would stop this. As she gazed into his eyes, Hayley started to comment on the matter, but was stopped as Manuel suddenly leaned forward and captured her mouth with his.

The kiss was demanding and hungry. She felt him press his body into hers, his hands roaming over her as he lifted her shirt, only breaking their kiss to pull it over her head.

Hayley reached down, blindly grabbing for the zipper on his jeans. She needed to feel him against her. After a second of fumbling, she was finally able to get his jeans open. Hayley gently bit down on his lip as she slid her hand into his pants, finding him already hard and ready for her. Smiling against his lips, she wrapped her hand around his length and squeezed. *God, he's huge!* she thought with a whimper. A shiver of excitement ran through her as she gave his dick another squeeze.

Manuel pulled his lips away from hers with a throaty moan. Closing his eyes, he rested his head upon hers as she moved her hand against him. She watched as he struggled to remain in control. Something about seeing him teeter on the edge from just her touch caused her confidence to grow.

"Manuel," she panted, feeling him grind himself into her hand. She arched her body against his, cupping him as her own body shuddered with need. Seeming to sense this, Manuel pulled back and made quick work of relieving them of the rest of their clothes.

Now naked, Hayley could feel his heat scorching her body. His muscles were hard as he wrapped one arm around her hips, hoisting her up to the head of the bed. The wood from his headboard was cool against her back as he pushed her up against it, his right hand grasping her wrists and pinning them above her head.

"Wrap your legs around me and hold onto the headboard," he demanded, his voice growling deliciously through the air.

Hayley didn't even think about it as she did what he asked. Her fingers curled around the top of the headboard as she felt his hands reach down, grabbing her thighs, positioning himself at her entrance.

With a powerful thrust, Hayley's head slammed back into the headboard as she felt him fill her. He only gave her a moment to get used to his size before he began to move. Each upward thrust had her fingers curling tighter and tighter, the wood cutting into her fingers from the force. It hurt, but the pleasure building within her canceled out any pain her hands may have been feeling.

Manuel leaned his head down into the crook of her neck. Biting gently on her shoulder, he released a low growl. It was primal and powerful, doing things to her insides that she had never felt before. The walls around them shuddered as his pace increased. Her back would be sore tomorrow from the headboard, but she didn't care. Tightening her thighs around him, she arched, pulling him in further.

Her moans echoed in her ears as she felt the heat within her core increase. His hands gripped her back as he pulled her to him, his body leaning over her as his rhythm changed.

She felt his body tensing as he moved. His eyes were shut tight, his skin slick from sweat as he brought them both closer to oblivion. Hayley wished he would open his eyes. And, just as his power licked across her skin, she got her wish. Her breath caught when he looked at her. His eyes were glowing, but not like they had when she told him about her vision. They were like a window, showing her his true power.

With a sudden rotation of his hips, Manuel's length hit that spot. The one that had her eyes rolling back as she felt her body beginning to shake. With a hard thrust, she fell apart, Manuel's name on her lips as she threw her head back.

Hayley was only somewhat aware of the lamp on the nightstand hitting the ground and the groaning coming from the wall at her back as she felt Manuel reach his own release. With a growl, he yelled her name as he slammed into her depths one last time.

Releasing her grip on the headboard, Hayley wrapped her shaking arms around his neck. Manuel pulled out of her warmth and sat back on the bed, holding her tightly in his lap as he rested his head gently against hers. Their breathing was ragged as they savored the moment.

Hayley felt a smile play across her lips as she felt Manuel's heart racing. Sliding one of her hands from around his neck, she rested it against his chest. Glancing up, she met his gaze.

"Hi," he said softly, smiling at her, tilting his head slightly to the side.

Laughing, she shook her head. "Hi." Leaning forward, she gave him quick kiss before beginning to pull out of his grasp, pausing when she noticed the shattered lamp on the ground. "Oh, your lamp broke."

"That's okay. I'll get another." His voice was filled with laughter as he pulled her back to him. Straightening his legs, he positioned her so she was straddling his lap.

"But it looked old," she commented, remembering all of the detail painted on its base. She glanced over at the nightstand. How in the world had they knocked it off anyway? The bed wasn't even touching the table. She absently tapped her finger on his stomach, shaking her head. When she realized he hadn't responded, she looked back and found him frowning. "Crap. It *was* old, wasn't it?"

"Yes." He shook his head. "It was old, but-"

"Shit. Did your parents give it to you? Please, tell me they didn't. I feel horrible. Was it an heirloom? I bet it was. Shit."

"Hayley." He reached up, rubbing a thumb over her lip to pause her rambling. He smiled at her. "Don't worry. To answer your question, though, no, it wasn't an heirloom, and no, it wasn't given to me. Stop worrying. I'll get another."

"But-"

"Hayley, listen to me. I have a gorgeous, naked woman in my arms. We've just had an incredible round of sex, which I'm sure will be even better the next time, and you want to get worked up over a broken lamp? Did I mention you're still naked? Trust me. I'm not worried about the fucking lamp."

She started to argue, stopping when she felt him shift beneath her. His hand traced a line from her face, down her neck, between the swell of her breasts, landing on her hip. Hayley watched a smirk begin to form on his gorgeous lips as he flexed his hand against her, kneading his fingers into her soft skin. Biting his lip, he hummed softly as he shifted again, his length hardening beneath her.

"See what you're doing to me?" His voice came out slightly strained. "Now, tell me, Hayley. Should I be concerning myself with that lamp? Or should I be spending my time bringing you to the point that you're screaming my name?"

With a raised eyebrow, she ground herself into him. He released a deep growl in response as he lay back, pulling her down with him until she was sprawled over his chest, her legs on either side of his hips.

Looking into his eyes, she couldn't help but run her tongue over her bottom lip and give him a slow smile. "What lamp?"

His laughter cut through the quiet room, causing his body to shake beneath her, eliciting a soft laugh from her own lips. Their laughter quickly turned into moans as their need began to grow, then was completely cut off as their mouths collided.

What lamp indeed...

Chapter 29

"What are you thinking about?"

Hayley looked over at Manuel as he closed another box. His amethyst eyes danced as they glanced her way.

After several rounds of some of the best sex she ever had, they both fell asleep for a few hours, happily exhausted. And the blissful unconsciousness that followed had probably been the best sleep she had in a long time, even if it hadn't lasted long.

Upon hearing the rustling of cardboard, she had lazily opened her eyes to find him moving quietly around the room, his bare feet hardly making a sound against the soft carpet. His jeans hung low on his hips, his chest bare for her greedy eyes. His shoulders were broad, his body rippling in all the right places as he turned to grab another box. Hayley's gaze had been traveling over the intricate cross tattooed beautifully across his back when he turned to find her staring.

Realizing she had yet to respond, Hayley felt a warm blush creep across her face. "Hmm?"

Chuckling, he stacked the box he had just closed on the pile and walked towards her. "I asked what you were thinking about."

Scooting over a bit to give him room, she smiled as he sat on the bed. "I was just admiring your tattoo. The detail is amazing."

"Thank you."

"Have you had it long?"

She watched his lips twitch as he looked away. "I've had it for a while."

"Really? The ink looks so vivid, like you just got it. It's beautiful."

"I'll have to let Cyrus know how much you like his work."

Hayley's eyes widened. "*Cyrus* did your tattoo?"

"Yeah," he laughed. "He went through a phase and took up the art."

"Some phase." She grinned. "Did he open a shop?"

"No. He mostly did work on Darren and me. There were a few people outside the family that he did some on, but not many."

"Does Darren have a back piece, too?"

"He has ink on his back, sides, and upper arms."

"Wow. I would never have taken him for an ink kind of guy."

"Yeah, well, Darren's full of surprises."

"It seems like all you boys are," she said slowly. Hayley wanted to ask him about the hunt and what he meant when he said he and his brothers were "more". She just wasn't sure how to start. Manuel promised to answer her questions, but she had a feeling he wasn't fully committed to that promise. Not that she blamed him. She had a feeling the answers all revolved around his family, and family should always be protected. Watching him closely, she noticed how tense he was all of a sudden.

Yeah, I definitely need to tread carefully here, she thought, taking a deep breath. Maybe it would be best to start small.

"Hey, Manuel. Can I ask you something?"

She heard him let out a soft sigh as he turned his head, his eyes cautious and somewhat guarded as they met hers. "Of course."

Licking her lips, she held his gaze, trying to mentally will his unease away. She knew he trusted her on a certain level. She had sensed that when he stood behind her as she faced off with the Shadow. Now if she could just get him to trust her with whatever secrets he guarded so closely. Looking at him, she realized that to get him to feel comfortable about opening up to her, she would have to open up to him.

Turning, she looked at the boxes piled around his room. She was going to help him and his family move tomorrow.

To a new place. To get a fresh start. An act that could be therapeutic and cleansing. Taking a deep breath, Hayley decided that to truly start fresh in the morning, it would be best to get everything out in the open tonight.

"Did I mention to you that my aunt raised me?"

Manuel was quiet beside her before giving a small sound of acknowledgment.

Taking that as her cue to continue, Hayley nodded. "My parents were taken from me when I was just a baby. I have no memory of them, but my aunt used to talk about them all the time. So much so, I feel like I knew them. My mom and aunt were sisters, raised around the craft." Smiling, she looked back at Manuel, who was watching her intently. "My dad, on the other hand, not so much. My aunt said it took him ages to come to terms with what my mom practiced. I'm not sure if he ever truly did, but my parents loved each other. My aunt told me she and my mom knew I would have the gift. And since they had both been raised to respect the craft and only use it to help people, they decided I would be raised the same. My dad didn't understand everything they had said, but he told my mom he trusted her to make sure I was raised right. My parents had gone out to meet some friends the night they were taken from me."

She felt Manuel reach over and begin to rub small circles on her back.

Looking over at him, she blinked a couple times. "When I got older, my aunt told me it was an accident."

"You don't believe that."

"I mean, I did at first. I was so young, I took whatever my aunt said as truth. As I got older, though, I started to question the 'accident'. I remember feeling hurt that she would lie to me. Of course, I know now that she was just trying to protect me. See, according to the police reports, my mom and dad were driving home from a friend's house late that night. It was storming...at least that's the excuse the cops used for their accident. They said between the wind and pouring rain, my dad probably didn't see how sharp the turn was as he came to it. They hit it too fast and...and went off a cliff." She felt her chest tighten as she thought about her parents' deaths. Manuel moved a little closer to her, his warmth radiating off him, soothing her nerves. "It wasn't until I was older that I started questioning my aunt about that night. The more I asked about it, the more I started getting the feeling I had been lied to."

Looking at her hands in her lap, she twisted them around. "It turns out my parents didn't die because of some accident. They had been attacked by a demon. My aunt said the smell of sulfur was so strong, it was still present in the car when she saw it in a local garage several days later. I guess my mom had been working with a local coven to locate a higher-level demon that had been rumored to have raped a woman. I'm not sure about that, though. According to my aunt, the woman in question was never located, and the demon vanished after the death of my parents."

"Is that what made you start wanting to hunt demons?"

"Well, it was that and..."

"And? And what?" Concern and curiosity laced each of his words.

Clearing her throat, she glanced at Manuel. "Um, learning about what really happened to my parents and growing up with the dream about you." Her cheeks began to heat. "I just somehow knew that hunting demons, and finding you, was what I should do."

His amethyst eyes took on a soft glow at that. His lips curled slightly into a smile as he leaned forward to place a soft kiss upon her lips. "I'm glad you found me."

"Yeah?"

"Yeah."

She smiled back at him, feeling a warmth pooling in her chest. He was glad she was there. She hoped that also meant he would trust her. "So...," she started, biting gently on her lip. "Will you tell me about you and your brothers?"

His eyes darkened slightly, searching hers as he leaned back. He was so quiet. Hayley knew he was thinking about what he promised to share with her. About answering her questions. Still willing him to be comfortable in talking to her, she decided to just remain quiet, giving him time to gather his thoughts.

Manuel's jaw ticked slightly as he looked down at the bed. She watched his abs and chest tighten and relax with each breath he took. The urge to reach out and hug him hit her strong, right along with the sudden need to tell him to just forget she said anything. But she didn't do either of those things. She somehow knew that whatever he was going to tell her was important information that would help her in her quest to help him and his family.

So she waited.

✝

Manuel concentrated on the brown speckled carpet at his feet, the feeling of the cool sheets beneath his hands as he gripped the side of the mattress, the tingling running down his back. Hell, he was trying to concentrate on everything except the beautiful woman sitting next to him with a patient, yet questioning look on her face.

He couldn't put off the inevitable forever, though. Maybe if he just gave her a slightly altered version of what he and his brothers were, something to satisfy her for now, he could get through the conversation. He hated to lie to her, though. He mentally shook his head. No. He was either going to tell her the complete truth or he would tell her nothing. Could he tell her nothing? Just change the subject, pretend the elephant in the room wasn't there?

No, he thought.

Suddenly standing, he stepped away from the bed and began to pace. He was just going to say it. He was just going to tell her that he and his brothers were angels, then go from there. Stopping abruptly, he looked at her.

Hayley's green eyes gazed warmly at him, telling him that he could trust her. Not that trusting her had been in question, but seeing that look in her eyes helped to calm his mind. Taking a step back, he cleared his throat. "My brothers and I, um..." He cleared his throat again. "Sorry."

"Don't apologize." Her voice was soft.

He nodded slowly. "It's just... I've never really talked about my brothers and myself to anyone other than Ella." He shifted his weight. "My brothers and I... We're different."

Her eyes twinkled at his comment. "I kind of figured that."

He gave a little laugh, absently running a hand through his hair. He knew she had figured that out. That was the problem. There was a reason they never had humans around them. No matter how many times they had met individuals they wished to consider a friend, or how hard they tried to hide what they were, their secret somehow found a way of slipping out. It just couldn't be helped. Powers aside, they were simply bigger, stronger, and faster than most everybody. Add all of that to the fact they didn't age, and any human around them for even a short amount of time started to have some questions, started to get a little too curious. So the fact that Hayley, being a powerful witch, had picked up on something was definitely to be expected. He suddenly realized that, deep down, he wanted her to know.

Tucking his hands in his back pockets, Manuel watched Hayley intently. *Here goes nothin'.* "Hayley, my brothers and I... We're angels."

Her eyes widened. "You're an angel?"

"Yes."

"Really?"

He nodded slowly, amusement flooding his system as he watched her try to work it out.

"Wow. That's just... Wow. So you're, like, a gold halo wearing, white-winged, harp playing angel?"

Manuel frowned. "What? No. I mean, yes, I have wings, but they're not white. They're brown. And I sure as hell don't play a harp or have a gold halo." Where did she come up with this stuff? "Oh, and before you ask, I don't wear white robes, either." He watched her stifle a smile. "Well, I don't." He grinned.

Shaking her head, Hayley moved to the edge of the bed, holding the sheet around her chest like a shawl. It curled around her seductively, cascading like a silken waterfall across her thighs. Manuel's eyes lingered on her legs as images of them wrapped around his body washed over him. Hearing Hayley hum softly, he lifted his gaze to find her smiling at him. "It's strange," she began softly. "I know I should feel shocked or concerned, but I don't. You being an angel just... I don't know. It just feels right. I'm not really sure how to explain it."

Manuel watched as her eyes traveled over him. He was impressed with how well she was taking this. Never having told anyone about being an angel before, he really hadn't known what to expect. Maybe

some denial, hysterics, laughing...
Definitely not calm acceptance. "Um, I'm
glad. I mean, I was worried you would... I
don't know..."

"Freak out?"

"Yeah." He chuckled. "Sorry. I've
never told anyone before, so I wasn't sure
how you'd react. Or if you'd even believe
me." A warmth spread through him as the
full understanding of what just happened
set in. "I'm just glad you didn't, you
know...freak out on me."

They stared at each other for a
heartbeat, a comfortable calm and sense of
understanding settling between them.
There would be no more secrets now.
Manuel felt a rightness in that knowledge
as he gazed at the beautiful woman before
him. Her green eyes sparkled with
acceptance and caring that was as foreign
to Manuel as it was welcoming.

Walking towards the bed, he slowly
dropped to his knees, pulling Hayley's legs
apart so he could nestle himself between
them. His hands slid up her calves as he
reveled in their softness. Gazing up at her,
he heard her chuckle. "What?"

"It just dawned on me." She reached
down to trail a hand delicately down his
face. "I have an angel kneeling before me."

Manuel turned his face slightly to
place a kiss on her hand and grinned.
Running his own hands up to her thighs, he

felt her shiver, goosebumps rising in the wake of his touch. Gently gripping under her thighs, Manuel pulled her closer to him. The heat from her sex caused him to moan softly as his eyes traveled up her body, greedily taking in every curve, every glimpse of her soft skin beneath the sheet.

Mine! The word thundered through him, causing his power to rise as his eyes reached hers. "I will always kneel before you, Hayley. Always."

Chapter 30

Kicking a rock across the ground, Castigo once again reminded himself to breathe. He'd just got the summons he had been dreading, finding it difficult to relax ever since. Not that he had ever been able to relax around Andras or Agalon, but ever since the last time he had disappointed Andras, well... The thought of being in the same vicinity as the demon made his skin crawl. When he got sent topside, at least he would get away from them. Besides their little "mental chats", he would be on his own, taking care of whatever business Andras asked of him. And that was fine, even great with him.

To think he had been striving to be Andras' third only months ago. Fighting to be seen and known as being more than just another disposable pawn. *And now I'm just trying to stay on his good side,* he thought with disgust.

But now they were here, on their way to see him.

Looking out over the fields, Castigo watched as several clouds gathered above him, shrouding the land in shadows. The air was deathly cold, not that he could feel it. Ever since he found out Andras and Agalon were nearby, his senses had become numb to everything around him. Actually, the gathering clouds and cold air were quite fitting. Seeing the clouds begin to grow even darker, he had to fight to suppress a shudder.

Time to get my game face on, he thought grimly.

The thought had barely crossed his mind when a rush of power crashed into him. His muscles tensed instantly, keeping himself from stumbling. Turning slowly, he found the two demons in question standing behind him.

"Castigo." Andras eyed him slowly.

"Andras," he replied with a nod. The urge to take a step back as the demons moved towards him was overwhelming and sudden, but he fought it. He'd be damned if he showed them any weakness. Castigo's eyes drifted briefly to Agalon before returning to Andras as they came to stand in front of him.

"Have you been by The 9th Circle?" Agalon asked with a growl.

"Yes, just as Andras asked me to." Frowning, his eyes shifted towards Agalon. "Everything is moving along as planned."

"Did you talk to Dev?"

The way Agalon's top lip pulled back into a sneer caused Castigo's body to tense. He would never know what the demon's deal with Dev was, but it was unsettling.

"I did," he responded.

"And?" Agalon's ice blue eyes darkened.

"And..." He looked back at Andras, who was watching him with his eerie multi-colored eyes. "He said he would help us with his brothers when the time came."

'You believe him?" Agalon tisked. "You really are a fool."

"I am no fool. He said he would, and given what happened last time he went against you two, I am inclined to believe him."

Agalon started to respond, but Andras raised a hand to stop him. Castigo watched his mouth snap shut. A single muscle in his jaw ticked, which was the only sign Andras' intervention upset him. Not that the demon would ever say anything. Nobody argued with Andras. At least nobody Castigo knew of...except Dev.

That little shit had talked a pretty big game when he was first tossed out of Heaven. It was almost like he expected to be rescued at any moment. Like his fellow angels, or God himself, would realize he wasn't meant to be down there and bring him home. Of course, that never happened. Once Andras decided to take it upon himself to break Dev, the angel never stood a chance. Not that Castigo didn't still see some fight in his eyes, but it was hidden well, buried deep within Dev's shattered mind and broken spirit. He had seen a flash of it when they were talking about his brothers. Castigo knew Dev thought he had caught himself before his reaction showed, but he'd seen it. That bit of information he would keep to himself...for now.

"What exactly did our little fallen angel say?" Andras' voice shook Castigo from his thoughts.

He blinked slowly. "He said he has not talked to the Guardians. Dev does not think any of them even know he is topside."

"So you believe he will give us whatever information we need on his brothers when we ask?"

"Yes," he responded without hesitation. Was that what he really believed? No. Not even a little. Hell, he had tried everything he knew of to warn Dev off of going against Andras, even going as far as telling him his brothers would get rid of him themselves given the chance. That wasn't something Castigo believed, but he had felt the need to plant that seed anyway. It was for Dev's own good to know it was a possibility, albeit a slim one.

"When it comes time to go after them, do you think he will play his part?"

"His part?" Bewildered, Castigo looked over at Agalon, then back at Andras. "I thought you only wanted to get information from him."

Andras smirked at him. His eyes flashed as Castigo felt the male's power begin to roll out around him. "Why, Castigo, you almost sound concerned for Dev."

"No." He shook his head, quickly smothering any concern that had been trying to work its way through him. It wasn't so much that he cared about the angel, but he wasn't a huge fan of Andras' methods of handling him. Castigo knew, without a shadow of a doubt, whatever Andras had in store for Dev, whether or not he went along with the demon's plan, would lead to nothing but pain. Given the Guardians they were up against, there was also the possibility that if all of Andras' plans fell through, Castigo was sure he could bring Dev over to his side. Of course, that would mean the foolish angel had to stay in one piece. With another shake of his head, Castigo scowled. "Why would I give a shit about that little ass? I was just under the impression you only planned to use him for information. If I had known you would want more out of him, I would have pushed him harder."

"Oh, trust me, Castigo. I plan on getting a lot more than just information out of him. After all, he knows those pesky Guardians better than anyone, so I am going to use him to get to them." Andras glanced slyly towards Agalon. "Anyway, you do not need to worry about having to deal with Dev anymore."

"No?" Castigo asked, trying to sound uncaring. However, even to his ears, that one word sounded shaky, a little too concerned.

Andras looked back at him. The sudden calmness surrounding them was almost more unnerving than having Andras' power raging against him. "No. Agalon will be in charge of handling him from here on out. I have other...plans for you. Unless there is a certain reason you do not agree. Do you feel I am making the wrong decision here? Maybe you have some knowledge, some insight that would cause you to disagree with me."

Sensing the danger in answering this wrong, Castigo quickly lowered his gaze. "Of course not, Andras. Whatever you need me to do, just say the word."

"Good. Is there anything else from your conversation with Dev you wish to tell us?"

"No," he responded, still looking at the ground.

"Really? No extra information at all?" Agalon growled.

Suppressing a growl of his own, Castigo took a deep breath. "None. He told me there has been no communication with his brothers. He has no idea where they are or what they are up to."

"He is lying." Castigo's head shot up to see Agalon looking towards Andras, the demon's ice blue eyes brightening as his power lashed out around him.

Castigo's chest tightened as he waited for his boss to respond. He waited for Andras to lash out, to turn towards Agalon, anything, but Andras' gaze was still focused on him.

"Is that true, Castigo?" Andras took a step towards him. "Are you lying to me?"

"No, Andras. Of course not."

"Because you know what happens when I am lied to...when someone disappoints me."

A chill ran through Castigo as he slowly nodded.

"Good," Andras said again. "That will be all."

Castigo only paused for a moment before turning to go.

"Oh, and Castigo?"

Stopping, he turned his head slightly to peer at Andras. "Yes, sir?"

"I will be in touch."

Without another word, Castigo dipped his chin and stepped into the shadows, his tension easing as the distance between them grew.

✝

"What do you think?" Agalon's voice hissed through the silence.

Andras clenched his jaw, not answering right away. Castigo may not have been completely lying, but he was definitely holding something back. Not that he really expected him to tell the truth. He was realistic when it came to getting information out of his demons. Demons lie. That was just how it was. The trick was knowing the difference between the lies and the truths. Sometimes this was easier said than done, especially when it came to Castigo. So the question really wasn't whether or not he believed the demon. The question was would whatever information the demon withheld interfere with his plans?

Flexing his hands, Andras shook his head. He was just going to have to wait for Castigo to fuck up. It would happen eventually. Sooner or later, if he were indeed hiding something, he would slip up, and Andras would be there to bury him. For now, he needed to focus on his next step. In order to start breaking the Guardians, he was going to need to go after what they cared about most.

"We need to get our hands on those females," Andras finally said. Turning his head skyward, he threw his power out, calling forth some of his demons.

Within seconds, six materialized in front of them. Their bodies shimmered in and out of focus as they waited for Andras to acknowledge them.

He looked at them for a moment. These demons were different than most of the ones he had under his command. They were bound to the land, destined to roam the Earth until the end of time. Normally, he would call on them to help with the corruption of some sad soul's mind. They were masters at causing an individual to go insane, leading them to commit crimes they would never normally commit, guaranteeing his claim to their soul. Right now, though, he needed them for something a little more delicate.

"You know why I called you here?" he growled, eyeing each of them in turn. They all nodded, their red eyes blazing. "You will need to immobilize them. I do not want to chance one of them being mortally injured should they fight...which they will."

"We understand," one of the demons hissed.

Agalon shifted slightly beside him as Andras offered the demons a slight nod. "Good. Get them and bring them to me."

The six demons dipped their chins. "As you wish," they responded as one.

He watched as they dematerialized. Within days, if all went as planned, he would have Ella in his hands once again. Not only would she be back where she belonged, but it was sure to weaken

Christian. Andras grinned at the thought of ending that Guardian's existence. *The first of many.* To also have the witch in his grasp was just an added bonus, one that would surely work in his favor.

"What now?" Agalon asked, breaking through his thoughts.

Glancing at his second, he watched his growing power flash through his eyes. "Now, Agalon," Andras snarled, his own power flaring, "it is time for us to pay our fallen angel a visit."

Chapter 31

"I have never moved so many boxes in my life."

Manuel chuckled as he watched Hayley flop down on his mattress. Her sigh of contentment whispered through the air, echoing exactly how he felt now that they were done. After getting up at the crack of dawn, they had successfully moved everything from their old house into the new. Everyone had been so eager, it hadn't taken long for them to start. Of course, that was almost twelve hours ago. Looking at Hayley now, her arms spread out at her side as she lay on the unmade bed among the mounds of sheets and pillows, he let out an exasperated sigh.

"Well, we would have been done sooner if you had just moved everything for us. Then we wouldn't have had to spend the whole day moving all those boxes."

He tried to suppress a laugh as she shot straight up and glared at him. "How many times do I have to tell you that I'm not going to use *my* magic to move *your* boxes? Who do you think I am anyway? That woman from *Bewitched*?"

"Oh, come on. You mean you can't twitch that cute little nose of yours and make shit happen? I bet you can." He smirked, stepping out of the way of a flying pillow. "I bet you can get all these boxes emptied and my room in order in no time flat."

"Just twitch my nose, huh?" Manuel watched her eyes glint with laughter as she tried to give him a stern look. "I'm sorry to disappoint you, but I can't just make things happen with a twitch of my nose."

"Pity," he responded. "That would have really come in handy."

"Oh, would it?"

"Yup," Manuel said with a grin. "Then we could get all this taken care of without leaving the bed."

Hayley laughed. "That does sound like a nice way to unpack your room."

He made a humming sound as his grinned widened.

She tilted her head and smirked. "I may not be able to make this go quicker, but I'm sure you can just wave your hands around and get the job done. You know, use those angelic powers of yours to take care of it."

He felt his grin waver. "My what?"

"Oh, come now, Manuel. I'm sure you can have this taken care of with just a nod of your head, maybe a flick of the wrist, and everything will just suddenly be where it's supposed to be." He shook his head. "No? Well, now, that's a pity. Looks like we'll just have to do everything the old-fashioned way," she murmured coyly.

"The old-fashioned way?"

"Yeah." She smiled. "I'll lie here and give you encouraging remarks as you put your room together."

"So you're just going to lie there while I do all the work?"

"Well, I mean, I'll help by pointing out where something will look best. I *did* help you with the heavy lifting. Poor thing. You seemed so tired after the first trip. But I'm confident you can handle the rest."

"Oh, are you?" He chuckled, moving slowly towards the bed. She seemed to immediately sense his motive because she grinned and started scooting further away from him. Manuel lunged at her, quickly pulling her towards him and pinning her to the mattress. All the while, her laughter and shrieks echoed through the room. "I think you should help me, don't you?"

Shaking her head, she laughed harder as his feathered his fingers along her side, causing her to twist beneath him. "Okay!" she yelped.

"Okay what?" He laughed as he tickled her harder.

"Okay," she gasped. "I'll help."

Manuel paused, his hands running down her side until they rested gently on her hips. "Hmm... Maybe we can take a little break before we continue."

Rolling her hips, Hayley tilted her head and gazed into Manuel's eyes. "Maybe just a little one."

He chuckled softly, leaning down to brush his lips against hers before trailing them along her jawline and down her neck. She moaned beneath him, her hands running up his arms, her nails scratching lightly against his skin. Manuel just made it to the dip between Hayley's neck and shoulder when a sudden rapping at his door made him pause.

Groaning, he glanced over his shoulder towards the door. "What?"

"Manuel, Darren wants you to install the alarm system and internet before it gets too late." Christian's voice sounded clear through the closed door.

Manuel looked back down at Hayley. "Maybe if we ignore him, he'll go away," he whispered, leaning in for another kiss.

"I heard that."

Hayley giggled and pushed gently on Manuel's chest. "You'd better go." At his frown, she pushed herself up and placed a kiss on his lips. "Don't worry... We'll continue this discussion later."

"Fine," he muttered, nipping lightly at her bottom lip before getting off the bed. "Don't go anywhere." He pointed a finger at her.

"Don't worry." She grinned, glancing around the room. "I'm sure I'll find something to keep myself occupied."

With a shake of his head, Manuel opened his door and stepped out into the hall.

"Discussion? Is that what you call it now?" Christian smirked, walking beside Manuel as they headed for the stairs.

Glancing at his brother out of the corner of his eye, he saw Christian laughing. "Oh, shut up."

"Hey, I'm just saying... Ella and I have a lot of names for what we like to do behind closed doors, but I don't think we've ever called it a 'discussion'." He made air quotes.

"I don't know what you're talking about," Manuel ground out.

"Come on, brother. There's nothing wrong with getting some action from a hot little-"

"Christian!"

He held his hands up in surrender. "All I'm saying is that if you and Hayley are starting to get to know each other better, that's okay. I mean, what you guys do in your room is your own business."

Stepping onto the bottom step, Manuel turned on Christian. "Can you please just drop this?"

Christian's chin dipped a bit. "You really like her, don't you?"

Manuel felt a warmth spread through him as he gave his brother a quick nod.

"Does she feel the same?"

"Yeah, she does. I think... I think she's it."

Christian's eyes widened. "Your soulmate?"

Manuel dipped his chin and felt his lips twitch.

"Well...," Christian said, giving his arm a light nudge. "Congrats, brother. I'm happy for you."

Manuel started to say more when he heard Darren call for him. Sighing, he began navigating his way around the boxes, Christian falling into step beside him. "Guess I should get this done. Hey, don't mention anything to the others about Hayley and me." At Christian's questioning look, Manuel rushed on. "At least for a while. I know they said they're okay with her, but I have a feeling Nicholas and Cyrus wouldn't be so keen to find out her and I are together."

"No worries, brother, although I think they will be happier for you than you think. But, until you say otherwise, I won't say a word."

Manuel grunted his appreciation, turning towards the hall that led to their office. He could hear the voices of his other brothers as he and Christian walked their way.

"I'm sure this won't take you too long," Christian muttered. Manuel glanced over at him to see a smirk pulling at his lips. "Then you can get back to your *discussion.*"

Manuel rolled his eyes as he walked into the office, Christian laughing behind him. He silently hoped his brother was right.

✝

Four hours later, Manuel growled as yet another problem flashed across his computer screen. The others had abandoned him a couple hours ago, leaving him to cuss at the computer all alone.

Christian had stopped back down a bit ago with a glass and bottle of Sailor Jerry, although he had no idea where his brother found it. However, he sure wasn't going to turn it down. His brother hadn't lingered, probably in a rush to get back to his woman. He knew the feeling.

Taking a sip of his drink, he punched in a couple more commands and sat back. The last one of his brothers he'd seen was Cyrus about a half-hour ago. He had been passing by, carrying some boxes down to the basement. He'd stopped briefly to give

Manuel shit before informing him Hayley had made her way to Christian and Ella's room...much to Christian's dismay. According to Cyrus, their brother told him she'd found her way in there to ask Ella a question...and never left. Of course, Cyrus had found it hilarious and was more than happy to share.

"Careful, brother," Cyrus had remarked as he picked his boxes back up, turning to leave. "Those two in the same room could only lead to trouble."

Even a half-hour later, his parting words were still echoing through Manuel's head. Even though Hayley was probably just talking to Ella about what happened between the two of them the other night, there was still a possibility the topic of him and his brothers could come up. He had hoped to talk to everybody about his admission to Hayley first, allowing them the chance to get used to the idea that she knew what they were before she started firing questions.

He could only imagine the look on Darren's face if she asked how he liked living on Earth. Laughing at the thought, Manuel watched as the computer slowly checked for an internet connection...again.

Manuel couldn't remember setting up their system in the last house being this difficult. Then again, he wasn't entirely focused on what he was doing at the moment. Images of red hair, creamy skin, and brilliant green eyes came to his mind. Then there was that sexy little moan Hayley made when he...

Shaking his head, Manuel took another healthy drink of his rum.

Hearing footsteps coming down the hall, he set his drink down. He knew it was Hayley before she even stepped into the room. Her very soul seemed to call out to him when they were near each other. He could feel it in his core, like a warm breeze whispering through him, pushing him closer to her.

Turning his chair slowly, he watched with growing anticipation as she made her way to him, her feet barely making a sound against the plush carpet. The soft material of her pants hugged her hips and thighs, causing his fingers to tingle with the sudden urge to touch her. To wrap his hands in the material, pulling it down her legs to reveal her gorgeous skin and wet center.

The scent of her drove him crazy as she moved closer, her green eyes flashing as she looked at him. Seeming to sense his thoughts, Hayley gave him a slow smile as she walked up to him, throwing one of her legs over him to straddle his lap.

Manuel gazed up at her. "I heard you were spending time with Ella."

Her smile widened. "I was."

"And... What were you girls talking about?"

"Oh, you know. Witchy, psychic, girly things." She laughed.

He was quiet for a minute as he took in the soft curve of her lips, the warmth in her eyes. Never, in all of his time on Earth, did he think he would find someone like her. Someone who would look at him in the same way he had seen countless couples look at each other throughout the years. Reaching up, he wrapped a strand of her red hair around his finger.

"What are you thinking?" she asked softly, turning her head to place a kiss on his hand.

"I'm thinking..." He tugged lightly on her hair, pulling her face closer to his. His other hand squeezed her ass, causing her to squirm against him. "I'm thinking it's time we finished that discussion."

Chapter 32

"Did you finally get everything all set up?"

Manuel turned from the fridge to see Darren stepping into the kitchen. After he got Hayley to fall apart on his tongue and his cock, he finished the internet and security setup. Of course, it had taken a little bit more time than he thought it would, but it was done.

Hayley had patiently watched him finish up, her gaze curious as she looked over his shoulder. Afterwards, she had gone back to his room to shower, something Manuel had hoped to join her in, but his need for something to eat had delayed his trip upstairs.

Now, glancing at Darren as he stared back at him expectantly, it looked like he may need to take a rain check.

Stifling a groan, Manuel gave his brother a short nod. "Yeah. Everything is squared away. All the sensors around the perimeter are up and functioning, as well as the security around the windows and doors. I have this place so wired up, we'll know if a demon sneezes in this direction."

"Good." Darren nodded. "With the numbers in our little group growing, the more secure our house is, the better."

Manuel didn't comment. He wasn't sure if Darren was fishing for information with the comment about their group growing. Sure, he had told his brothers Hayley would be staying with them for a bit, but there was no way Darren could know his feelings had changed. Seemingly overnight, he had gone from just wanting her around for a while to needing her with him. Just the thought of her leaving made his chest hurt.

He kept all of this to himself, though...except for Christian, who had promised to keep his secret. So there was no way Darren would know Manuel planned to ask Hayley to stay with him. Shit. He hadn't even known he wanted her to until just a few hours ago.

Staring back at Darren now, though, Manuel had a feeling Christian might have said something. He took a slow breath. "Have you been talking to Christian?"

Darren tilted his head. "No. Should I have?"

"No," he said quickly. "Just curious."

"Well, actually, I have been planning on talking to him, as well as the rest of you." Darren walked over and grabbed a glass, filling it with water. "I think it's time we all sat down to really talk about what's going on. About what we should do next."

As his brother kept talking, Manuel could only nod. *He knows, but how?! And*

*was it really such a big deal that there had
to be a household meeting about it?*
Manuel's mind whirled as he stared back at
his brother.

"This just isn't something that
should be taken lightly," Darren continued.
"I know everyone is just getting settled in,
and I would normally give you all a few
days before we get into it, but I'm sure you
agree that this is a decision that not only
should be addressed sooner rather than
later, but everyone should be able to have a
say."

"Why?" Manuel asked, his blood
starting to boil.

"Why what?"

"Why should you all have a say? I get
that it's a big step for me, but I just don't
see why my decision needs to be dissected
by everyone. Why you all need to vote on
it."

Darren's eyebrows shot up. "Of
course everyone should have a say. We
can't ignore what we all know needs to be
done. What we know needs to be... Wait."
He shook his head, taking a step towards
Manuel. "What decision?"

"What?" Manuel responded quickly,
his thoughts halting as he watched a look of
confusion cross his brother's face. Shit.
Maybe Darren had been talking about
something else.

"You said 'your decision'. What are you talking about, Manuel?"

"Um... Nothing... It's nothing. What are *you* talking about?"

Darren frowned. His blue eyes scanned over him, as if his face would give away his secrets. Seeming to find no answer, he shifted his feet. "I figured it's time for us to start hunting again. Things have been quiet lately, but that doesn't mean they aren't up to something. I understand we don't really know a lot about Andras, and everyone is a little leery about going up against him before we know more, but I doubt he's just been sitting at his desk in Hell, sipping tea."

"Hunting... Right," Manuel muttered, looking back into the refrigerator, not really seeing anything. He had little hope of Darren dropping his earlier outburst. He could feel his brother behind him, staring at him expectantly, waiting for him to explain himself. Blinking, he tried to focus on the items in front of him. Seeing the carton of milk, he grabbed it. Turning, he saw Darren had moved a couple steps closer, one eyebrow lifted questioningly. "Do we have any cereal?"

"What?"

"Cereal," he mumbled, moving past his brother to start looking through a couple partially emptied boxes for a bowl. "I'm starving."

"Manuel?"

Ignoring his brother, he continued searching through the boxes. *Just tell him, you chicken*, he thought, pulling out one newspaper wrapped item after another. Shit, why couldn't he just tell him? It really shouldn't be so hard, yet he couldn't seem to get the words past his lips. Finally finding a bowl, he set it on the counter next to the milk.

"Here."

Turning, he found Darren standing there, holding a box of Lucky Charms out to him. Manuel stared at the box before reaching for it, only to have Darren tighten his grip.

Glancing up, Manuel met his brother's eyes. "What decision, Manuel?"

Licking his suddenly dry lips, he pulled the cereal box from Darren's hand. Holding it, he felt his fingers press into the soft cardboard, denting it. Clearing his throat, he straightened his back, steadily holding Darren's gaze. "I'm going to ask Hayley to move in here. To remain with me."

The emotions rolling across Darren's face were telling. There was shock, quickly followed by flashes of uncertainty and concern. It was the final look of acceptance, then happiness that caused Manuel to release the breath he hadn't been aware he was holding.

"Does she know how you feel about her?"

"Yes. Well, I'm pretty sure she does anyway."

"Pretty sure about what?" Nicholas' voice pulled Manuel's gaze from Darren's as he entered the kitchen, Christian and Cyrus not far behind him.

Great. Because this is exactly what I need right now.

Turning to face the rest of his brothers, he met Nicholas' curious gaze. "That Hayley knows how I feel about her."

He watched the curiosity in his brother's eyes slowly turn to caution. "And how exactly *do* you feel about her, brother?"

Out of the corner of his eye, Manuel watched Christian lean against the counter, his blue eyes calmly taking in the scene around him before focusing back on Manuel. Without saying a word, he seemed to be encouraging him to continue.

Knowing he had at least one of his brothers in his corner made his shoulders straighten. "I want her to stay with me."

Nicholas' eyebrows shot up. "Permanently?"

"Yes. Permanently. At least that's what I'm hoping for."

Nicholas just shook his head. The mixed emotions flowing off him had Manuel grinding his teeth.

"I just don't understand..." Raising his hand to cut off Manuel's snarl, he continued. "The fact that she's a witch aside... You don't know her. And before you start going into your feelings, her dreams, and all that fate bullshit-"

"My feelings for her are not fucking bullshit," Manuel snapped.

"Fine," Nicholas growled. "You love her, want to be with her, whatever. The point I'm trying to make is that you are about to invite a stranger into our home. Shit, Manuel. With all the crap we've been dealing with, do you really want to bring someone we don't know into it?"

He felt the tension in the room rising. Cyrus, who had stayed quiet thus far, now made his way around Nicholas and farther into the room. His black eyes never wavered as he stared his way.

Fuck.

"You don't understand," Manuel started. Pausing, he attempted to find the right words to get his feelings across. Not that getting into an argument with one or all of his brothers was a new thing. Hell, it felt like yelling was the only way they could get through a conversation about him and Hayley lately. But he would really like to not go that route tonight.

"Then make us understand, brother," Cyrus' deep voice rumbled out.

Looking around the room, Manuel thought about Hayley. The way the light caused her green eyes to sparkle like the most brilliant gem. How even the slightest touch from her caused his heart to quicken. Shit, just having her in the same room seemed to make it easier for him to breathe.

Those things and so much more swirled through his mind as he stood there, surrounded by the only family he'd ever truly known. He wanted...needed them to understand because asking Hayley to stay with him was too big a step to take without the support of his brothers. How could they, though?

Besides Christian, none of them had felt drawn to anyone, so how could he expect them to understand? Maybe he wasn't being fair about this, but damn it. He couldn't help how he felt about her. How much he yearned for his brothers' acceptance. Having this kind of connection with a woman wasn't something he ever thought he'd have. It was actually something he'd never even considered...until Christian found Ella.

Glancing at Christian, he saw a flash of understanding in his blue eyes. He nodded, encouraging him.

Taking a deep breath, he glanced at Nicholas, then Cyrus. "She's it for me," he stated simply. "Since the first time I saw her, I felt this pull, this need to be around her. At first, I didn't know what to make of it. As I started recognizing my feelings for her, I tried to deny them. I even planned to tell her to lose my number and forget about me, but I couldn't. I *wanted* her to call me, to talk to me, to want to be around me. Because I desperately wanted to be around her. So I made up an excuse for her to stay with us for a couple days. Sure, it wasn't a total lie. She's here to help Ella, and she helped with the move, but I truly wanted her here for more selfish reasons. I told her it would only be for a couple days, but that's not enough. The thought of her leaving makes me physically ill, like I'll lose a part of myself if she goes. I know now that she was made for me, we were made for each other, and I'll be damned if I lose her now." He shrugged, glancing at Darren, who was smiling. "Hayley makes me want to be better."

"That's all well and good," Nicholas said slowly, "but what will she say when you tell her the truth about us? Have you thought of that?"

Manuel looked at him, Nicholas shifting his weight in obvious agitation. He had hoped telling them how he felt would be enough, but it was obvious he was also going to have to tell them that Hayley already knew. He had planned to tell them eventually. He just hoped to be able to put it off for a day or so.

Everyone seemed to tense, the air in the room growing heavy. He watched his brothers' eyes sweep over him, Nicholas' widening slightly, as if he already knew the answer.

"Well," Manuel started calmly. He was thankful his voice came out steady, although he knew the fact that his fingers were tapping against his jeans gave away his nervousness. "I don't have to wonder what she will say...because I already told her."

Seeing Nicholas' eyes narrow, he braced himself.

Let the fighting begin.

Chapter 33

Standing under the hot water, Hayley couldn't seem to wipe the smile off her face. Images of Manuel's solid body hovering above her, his lips curling into a sensual smile as he leaned down to capture her mouth with his, continued to play through her mind. Clenching her thighs as yet another shiver ran through her, she let out a content sigh.

For the first time she could remember since her aunt died, Hayley felt truly happy.

Sure, she'd had lovers before. Some were great in bed, while others had been duds, but Manuel was in a whole different league. She didn't have words for how he made her feel. Just... Damn.

Stepping out of the shower, she reached over and grabbed one of the large towels she had found in a cabinet. Securing it tightly around her, she walked over and glanced at the mirror. It was steamed, but with a few well-chosen words, the mirror began to clear. As her image came into view, she smiled.

Her skin, usually a creamy white, now held a soft pinkness. She knew the color spreading across her was from the hot water, but the healthy blush beneath it was all Manuel. Even her eyes, which normally held a soft green light to them, now seemed to be practically glowing.

"What is he doing to me?" she mumbled with a grin. Whatever it was, it was a good thing.

She'd never felt as alive, as wanted, as loved as she did when she was in his arms.

Turning from the mirror, Hayley made her way into Manuel's room. His many boxes were still scattered, his bed bare, save for the pillows and black sheets folded at the foot of it. Her bags still sat on his rather ornate trunk shoved against the wall.

She still couldn't believe he had just picked it up and moved it. It didn't only look heavy, she knew it was. As they had been moving items out of their old house, she had wanted to pull his trunk away from the wall to give the guys a little more room when they came back for it. She hadn't even been able to budge it. There was a faint ache in her back that reminded her how much she had tried.

Just as she had given up, Manuel walked in, picked up the trunk with ease, and carried it out of the room. Only the slight smirk on his face gave away the fact that he was aware she'd been watching him.

It had only further reminded her that he was not human. Not that him being an angel was ever far from her mind. How could it be? It wasn't every day you found the man of your dreams was an angel...literally.

She knew he was different than he had originally led her to believe. She just hadn't realized how different. Although, if she were being honest with herself, it made sense. The amount of power surrounding Manuel and his brothers was staggering, but she felt it was only scratching the surface of what power they were capable.

After slipping on her jeans, she absently reached over for one of her favorite tees. Her mind kept going over everything she had seen since meeting Manuel, everything he had told her. She knew there was more behind what she'd seen so far, an underlying concern all of the boys seemed to share. A lot of it seemed to stem from the demons they faced when they rescued Ella from Hell.

Castigo's name still rang through her mind as she had a flash of the dream that always plagued her. She had to figure out what was going on soon because she wanted, needed to be one step ahead of her dream.

But the demon that came to her in her vision, the one that had caused Manuel's power to ripple out around him, had felt different.

Chewing her lip, Hayley frowned. She really wasn't sure who it was, but she was positive it hadn't been Castigo. No, this demon's aura had felt different... Stronger.

Then there were those eyes... Hayley shuddered when she thought of them. Multi-colored and as beautiful as they were dangerous. The demon they belonged to was powerful, so much so that she wasn't even sure the boys could match it. What she needed was information on him. Who was he? Why did he put his power into Ella? What was his plan?

"One bad guy at a time," she mumbled with a shake of her head. Turning her thoughts towards Castigo again, she twisted her wet hair up into a clip. She needed to figure out where he was. Maybe if she could get to him before the events that she dreamt about took place, she could stop the threat to Manuel's life before it even had a chance to happen.

Of course, the little voice in the back of her mind kept whispering about not being able to change fate. That little voice, though, was going to have to take a back seat to the louder and more predominant one. The one that told her she needed to do all she could to do just that...change fate. Because, if her dream came to pass, there was a very real possibility that Manuel would not make it out alive.

And that just wasn't an option.

"Maybe I could just keep him from going into town until I get this figured out," she mused.

"Is that helping?"

The sound of Ella's soft voice brought a smile to Hayley's face as she turned to look at her new friend. They had only known each other a couple days, talked to each other once or twice, but she already felt a deep connection with the woman. She never had a sister, but liked to think that if she did, she would have been a lot like Ella. She was funny, sassy, and had such a sweet way about her that Hayley just adored, especially her smile, which she was sporting right now from the bedroom door.

"I find it helps...on occasion," she responded with a wink.

"And the other times?" Ella laughed.

"Let's just say there's no living with myself." She giggled.

"Well, we can't have that." Ella winked, walking into the room. "What are you talking to yourself about? Maybe I can help."

Hayley thought about it as she watched Ella sit on the edge of Manuel's bed, her elbow resting on the folded comforter. She wasn't sure if her new friend would actually be able to help, but it wouldn't hurt to find out. She was sure everyone had heard about why she reached out to Manuel in the first place, how she had been dreaming about him ever since she could remember, so there was a chance Ella would be able to help. A small chance, but still a chance.

Rolling that around in her mind, she walked over and sat next to her. "I'm not sure where to start."

"How about from the beginning."

"Well... I'm sure Christian has mentioned my dream."

"Oh, you mean the one about Manuel? The one you've been having since you were a child?" At her nod, Ella grinned. "He may have mentioned something about it."

"I figured as much. Everyone in the house has probably heard about it. However, I don't think anyone knows exactly what happens in it."

Ella frowned. "I know it's about Manuel, but you're right. I don't know any of the details. Christian doesn't, either. He would have told me if he did."

Hayley smiled. "I love that you guys don't keep secrets from each other."

She shrugged, her frown morphing into a grin. "We learned a while back that nothing good ever comes out of keeping secrets."

Nodding, Hayley sighed. "That's good. It's part of why your bond is so strong." Reaching over, she grabbed one of Manuel's pillows, pulling it into her lap. "I haven't really told anyone about the details of my dream."

"Manuel?"

"No. I mean, he knows part of it, but not all."

Seeing the encouraging look in Ella's eyes, she sighed. She knew she would eventually have to tell Manuel all of it. Truthfully, she wasn't sure what was holding her back. Okay. That was a lie. She knew the reason she hadn't given details about the dream to anyone but her aunt. She was afraid that once she did, once it was out there, it would become real.

Curling her arms around Manuel's pillow, she hugged it tightly to her chest. Taking a deep breath, she felt a warmth spread through her as his scent engulfed her senses. If she were going to save him, remain one step ahead of her dream, she was going to need help. With a nod, she turned to Ella and told her everything. The anguish she felt while running through the streets. The panic. How, when she finally came upon the alley where the fight was happening, she couldn't make out any features. At least not until she had met Manuel, seen his aura, felt his power. That, after the first meeting, she had known he was the one fighting, the one who was eventually overpowered by Castigo. How she watched as the figure with the red glowing eyes leaned over an unmoving Manuel, smiling at her. Taunting her.

It all came rushing out as she sat there, leaving her breathless and cold as she finished. A single tear trailed down her cheek as she took a shaky breath. "I don't know what to do, Ella. How do I stop this?"

Ella, who had remained quiet, reached out and laid a hand on Hayley's arm. Giving it a gentle squeeze, she released a shaky breath of her own. "I don't know, Hayley, but you will. I'm sure of it. I know we haven't known each other for long, but from what I've seen, you're a fighter. And, obviously, your bond with Manuel goes far beyond this dream and your need to stop it from becoming real. But you won't be alone. I will help you however I can. I will be right there."

Hayley smiled at her friend. This was what she needed. To know she wasn't alone. "Thank you," she stated softly, her emotions making it hard to speak.

"Now... How are things with Manuel?"

As images of earlier speared through her, Hayley felt herself blush, which deepened when Ella began to giggle. In turn, she burst out laughing. It felt good. As the laughter tapered off, she leaned towards her friend, ready to tell Ella just how great things were going, when a burst of angry male voices shook the house.

"What the hell?" she asked, jumping off the bed. As she got to the door, she leaned into the hall, listening intently to try and figure out what was going on.

"*Now* what are they fighting about?" Ella joined her, peeking around her shoulder.

Shaking her head, she tried to concentrate on what was being said, but the voices were too muffled. The power beginning to vibrate through the house started to build, crackling through the air, causing the hair on Hayley's arms to stand up.

Ella squeezed past her and started making her way towards the stairs, her strides determined as her own power began to respond. Deciding to follow, Hayley quickly took the steps behind her. As they came to the bottom, they could tell the guys were in the kitchen. Their voices became louder and louder as they headed in that direction.

"Have you lost your fucking mind?" Nicholas' voice rang out.

"Fuck you, Nicholas," she heard Manuel respond, his words practically a growl. "You told me you were going to trust me in this. That you were going to-"

"I know what I told you. I told you to spend time with her. That I was okay with her being around. I didn't think she was going to become a *permanent* fixture in this house. Truth be told, I figured you would eventually get tired of her."

Hayley stumbled a bit as she followed Ella into the kitchen. The power in the room was so strong, so angry, it was suffocating. Her lungs practically hurt from the effort to breathe. The fact they were having this argument about her hadn't escaped her notice. That Manuel had obviously told his brothers he wanted her to remain here was thrilling. Her body flooded with warmth at the thought, yet that warmth only seemed to travel so far. The realization this news was not welcome by his brothers caused her skin to go cold.

"*What...the...fuck...Nicholas?*" Manuel growled. Hayley spotted him in the center of the room.

His eyes blazed as he stared at his brother. She watched as he took a step towards Nicholas. With each one of his steps, the floor beneath her feet seemed to shudder. Bracing herself, she felt the air around her swell as a sudden gust of wind caused her hair to curl around her shoulders.

What the heck?

Glancing over at Ella, she caught the look of distress on her friend's face. Ella's own powers churned around her, answering to the building storm. Reaching over, Hayley grabbed her arm, giving a gentle squeeze, silently willing Ella's warring powers to calm. After just a moment, she felt the energy building around her ease.

Meeting Ella's gaze, she saw her smile. *Thank you*, her friend mouthed before turning back to the fight.

At this point, none of the guys had noticed they were in the room. She saw Darren, Christian, and Cyrus poised around Manuel and Nicholas. They all seemed to be ready to jump in if their brothers came to blows, although they looked anything but pleased about the argument happening before them.

Darren seemed more annoyed than anything. His blue eyes flashed as he glanced between the two. She could practically feel him warring with himself on whether or not to intervene.

Glancing at Christian, she noticed he, too, was staring intently at his brothers. His eyes were bright as he narrowed them. He was angry with the arguing, but seemed inclined to let it play out. Shit, for all she knew, this fight was a long time coming. Although she hated that she was the cause of it, she hoped they would be okay once it was over.

Looking at Cyrus, she shook her head. His black eyes scanned the scene before him, his lips curled in amusement as he leaned against the counter behind Nicholas. She was surprised he wasn't egging them on, trying to get one to take a jab at the other. He sure didn't seem like he was in a hurry to stop them. Hayley still wasn't sure where she stood with Cyrus. The few times she had found herself around him, there had been no conversation, no real acknowledgment outside of the occasional nod or glance.

His aura, his power, was so much colder than the others. It was maybe a good thing she hadn't engaged him more, although she would be lying if she said her interest in the male wasn't piqued. Now that she knew he was an angel, his coldness was even more of a mystery.

Seeming to sense her thoughts, she suddenly found those coal black eyes staring her way. Suppressing a shudder, she met his gaze. He didn't seem surprised or upset she and Ella were there, witnessing the argument. He actually looked somewhat relieved. No. That couldn't be right, could it?

With a slight quirk of his eyebrow, he smirked, then looked back towards his brothers.

She had been so lost in thought, she hadn't noticed the growing hum vibrating through the air or the occasional rattle of the cabinet doors. Shock filled her as she looked back at Manuel, finding him practically nose-to-nose with Nicholas.

Their powers now drove into her in waves as she shifted her weight, bracing herself.

"You want to run that past me again?" Manuel growled. His words came out so low, she almost missed them over the hum in the air.

How much of their argument have I missed? she thought, staring at them.

Everyone in the room seemed to hold his or her breath as the rage rolling off Manuel intensified. Watching silently, Hayley shivered as Nicholas' already blazing eyes flashed like lightning, a quick pulse of red brilliance before they narrowed at Manuel.

"I said you can't just take in some stranger because of your *feelings*, tell her about us, then expect us all to be okay with it. The fact that you took it upon *yourself* to divulge *our* secret without mentioning it to us first is utter fucking bullshit...and you know it," he seethed. "Springing her on us was one thing. Asking us to trust her and work alongside her was another. But telling her about us, wanting her to live here permanently... That's taking this shit too far, brother."

"No. You know what's taking things too far? You coming at me, attacking me because of a decision I made that has nothing to do with you. It's fucking bullshit." Manuel held up his hand before Nicholas could respond. "I had planned on talking with you all about it. Telling you guys how I felt and what I wanted to do. I just wanted to get everything straight in my head before I said anything. Shit, Nicholas. I just figured out how I felt about her a few hours ago. Yes, I told her we're angels, but I'm sure she was on her way to figuring that out anyway. And yes, I probably should have said something to you guys first, but it's done. It happened. And I don't regret it."

"Well, you will when she turns on us."

"The *fuck*, Nicholas. She isn't going to fucking turn on us. Why can't you accept the fact that she's different, better than the other witches you've known? Accept the fact that she's with me and that we care about each other?"

"Because she *won't* be different, brother. She may have you fooled now, but you'll see. When being on our side no longer suits her, she'll fucking turn and then-"

"*That's enough!*" Ella cried out, startling everyone, including Hayley. All sets of eyes turned towards them, widening at the fact that they were standing there...except for Cyrus.

Manuel's eyes locked with Hayley's as he took a couple steps towards her. The air in the room instantly calmed when he and Nicholas stepped away from each other. "Hayley...," Manuel started, his eyes showing concern, as well as embarrassment, for what she had just witnessed.

Holding up her hand, she stopped his advance. "I'm fine, Manuel. I just..." At a loss for words, she glanced at Ella.

Her friend's eyes glowed softly as she looked out over the room. Christian, who had instantly moved to be by her side, slowly rubbed her back in soothing strokes. "That is enough fighting," Ella stated calmly. She turned towards Manuel, her head tilting slightly. "You should have said something to your brothers before telling Hayley your secret." Shaking her head at him, she went on. "I get it. You know I do. That overwhelming feeling when you've finally found the one person in the world you can connect with, tell your darkest secrets to. I get it, but that secret wasn't just yours to tell, was it?"

Hayley turned back to Manuel, watching as he cast his eyes to the floor. His breath a soft sigh upon his lips, he shook his head.

"I'm happy for you both, though," she continued. Hayley looked over to find Ella looking her way. "And I trust you to keep this secret and do what is right by Manuel. Just as I trust you will do what is right by us all when the time comes."

Those ominous words sent a chill down her spine as she nodded. "Of course, Ella. You know how much I care about him. About you all. From the beginning, I've only wanted to help. I would never do anything to hurt anyone in this house."

"I know," Ella responded, reaching over for her hand and giving it a gentle squeeze. As she turned her gaze to Nicholas, Hayley heard her take a deep breath. "I'm disappointed in you, Nicholas." These words, although spoken softly, seemed to hit Nicholas like she had reached out and smacked him. "I know you have your reasons for the way you feel towards Hayley. I know there is something in your past, something you've chosen to keep to yourself, that has tainted your view of her. I had hoped you would come around, see her for who she is and not who she represents in your mind. Then you would be able to see how good she is for Manuel, as well as the rest of us. I cannot explain it, but having her with us feels right. It is knowledge that I've had since she showed up the other day, calming me as my powers threatened to grow out of control." Ella released Hayley's hand and took a step towards Nicholas. "She's here to help me just as much as she's here to help the rest of you. Now, I don't know exactly what is going on with me, but it's bad. Hayley has not only been a great help to me already, but she's offered to help me get my powers under control, stop these sudden surges. Do you want to take that hope away from me?"

The question caused Nicholas to physically pale. Hayley almost felt bad for him, but she needed the support of all Manuel's brothers. If this were the only way for Nicholas to see her as a positive asset to his family, so be it.

"Of course not," he mumbled.

Ella let out a sigh. As she walked up to Nicholas, Hayley watched him lean down and embrace her in a hug. When she whispered something to him, Hayley watched him nod a couple times. The men in the room seemed to hear her, however, because they all smiled and looked away, giving them a moment. Even Christian smiled, turning to Hayley with a wink.

Nicholas looked over the top of Ella's head, nodding at her and Manuel. "Sorry. It's just... There's a lot going on in my head, but I'll work on it."

Wanting to put this argument in the past, Hayley just smiled. "It's okay, Nicholas. I know none of you really know me, but I'm hoping that'll change and you guys will give me a chance."

"Everyone will," Manuel stated matter-of-factly, murmurs of agreement rippling through the room. Walking up to wrap his arms around her in a sideways hug, he smirked. "Like you said, they all just need to get to know you. But don't worry, darling. Once they do, I have absolute faith they will see what I do."

"Oh? And what exactly do you see, Manuel?" she asked, gazing up into his smoldering stare.

"Someone I can't live without." His words caressed across her, smothering any doubts that had begun to crawl into her head.

Smiling at him, she stretched up and placed a soft kiss upon his lips. One that was filled with all the warmth his words gave her. His eyes softened as he rested his forehead on hers, his arms tightening slightly.

After a moment, Ella broke the comfortable silence by pulling away from Nicholas and walking towards her. "I think it's time we had a girls' night."

Turning her head away from Manuel, Hayley laughed at the sudden change in topic. "What?"

"Come on. It'll be fun." Ella smiled, stopping in front of her. "There's this great little bar downtown-"

"Ella...," Christian interrupted, a blush spreading across Ella's face. When he reached out, she instantly reached for him.

"Not *that* bar," she said with a chuckle, resting her head against his chest. Her eyes gleamed as she looked back towards Hayley. "It's called Indigo, and it's absolutely adorable."

"I don't know," Hayley said, glancing up at Manuel. She could feel him tense slightly, but his face gave away none of his uncertainty over them going out alone.

"Come on. It'll be fun," Ella pressed. "It's still early, so the bar won't be crowded. Plus, the sun's still out. We'll just go grab a quick drink. Get out of the house for a bit while the guys finish getting everything unpacked."

"That does sound like fun...," she agreed slowly. As much as she wanted to stay with Manuel, the thought of getting out of the house for a little bit was rather tempting, especially after all the fighting, emotions, and powers that had been beating against her for the past couple days. A little break sounded like just the thing. "Okay," she finally said. "Let's do it."

"Yay!" Ella exclaimed, her smile widening as she wiggled in Christian's arms.

"Are you sure this is a good idea?" Manuel asked. His question was echoed by the others.

"Oh, we'll be fine," Ella said before Hayley had a chance to respond. "It's broad daylight and we'll only be gone for, like, an hour...tops. Plus, who's going to mess with a psychic and a badass witch, huh? It's not like someone's going to jump us in the middle of downtown."

"That's exactly what I'm afraid of," Manuel muttered, his eyes starting to give away his uneasiness.

Looking over, Hayley saw Christian's eyes held the same worried look. "Maybe one of us should go with you." His words came out strained.

"I second that," Darren said, coming to stand beside them.

"Seriously, guys," Ella said, looking around the group. "We'll be fine. Promise."

Nicholas shook his head. "You can't promise that because there's no way for you to know that. If you want to go out, fine, but it would definitely be safer if you took one of us with you."

"No. We need to have a little girls' time...*away* from you guys," she argued. "If we took one of you guys with us, it wouldn't really be girls' night out, would it?"

Feeling like she should weigh in on this, Hayley nodded. "I agree with Ella. We need some time to talk about girlie things, and we can't do that with you guys hovering over us. We'll be fine."

"It's settled then," Ella said sternly. "We're going out for a little bit, just the two of us, to get a drink. You guys work on getting this beautiful new house to feel like a home, and we'll be back before you know it."

"This is definitely *not* settled," Christian began to argue, although Ella had already turned to walk out of the kitchen.

"I just need to get cleaned up, then we'll get going," she yelled over her shoulder.

Hayley, too busy trying not to laugh at the look on Christian's face, didn't respond.

"That woman...," he mumbled as he quickly made his way after her. She could hear his footsteps on the stairs as he raced up them.

Darren and Nicholas chuckled as they began to move across the room, making comments about how Christian was going to sulk the whole time Ella was gone and that they wouldn't be surprised if he texted her every five minutes until she was back. Hayley let out a soft chuckle because she had a feeling they were right.

Darren glanced her way as he passed. "Don't be gone long." Even though this was said as more of a command, she knew it was because he was worried about them.

"We won't," Hayley said, smiling softly.

Seeming satisfied with her response, he turned towards Nicholas and Cyrus. "Come on, you two. I want to get the downstairs straightened up first so we can start back up on our training." Nicholas nodded towards her and Manuel as he left the room, heading towards the downstairs door, Cyrus not far behind him. "You, too, Manuel," Darren said, punching his shoulder good-naturedly as he followed. "As soon as the girls take off, get your butt downstairs to help. And bring Christian."

"You'll be careful?" Manuel said into her ear from behind as soon as they were alone, causing Hayley to shiver.

Nodding, she leaned back into him.

"I need you to say it, Hayley."

"I'll be careful," she said, turning to look up at him. "We'll be fine."

He stared down at her, his eyes searching her face as he seemed to slowly accept this was happening. "Okay, but call me if either of you see anything weird or sense anything off."

Resting her hand against his chest, Hayley laughed. "I promise to call you if anything seems off while we're out. One drink, then I'll be back."

"Okay," he said softly.

"Okay."

Chapter 34

After sifting through her bag, going through Ella's boxes, and discarding one outfit after another, they were finally ready. Before they walked out the door, Hayley had needed to repeat to Manuel a few more times that she would be careful. She definitely had an easier time of it than Ella, though, who had to practically shove Christian away from the car so she could close the door, laughing the whole time.

The laughter continued in the car as they backed out of the driveway, waving at their men...who looked like they were ready to do anything to keep them there.

Hearing Ella humming softly next to her, she looked over at her. They were a good ten minutes from the house, but her friend still had that goofy smile plastered to her face from her last teasing remark to Christian. The two of them were really perfect for each other.

"What are you humming?" Hayley asked, stretching her legs out as far as she could.

"Oh, I don't know the name of the song. It's one Christian has been listening to the last week." She laughed, turning towards downtown. "He never has the same favorite song for more than a week. He changes his playlist as often as I change my shoes." Ella paused, pursing her lips. "Okay, maybe not quite *that* often."

Hayley burst out laughing. "Sounds like me and my purses."

"Yeah?" Ella smiled. "I probably have at least fifty pair of shoes. Christian had to practically clear out his whole closet for them. And that's not even counting the room for my clothes."

"I don't think I've owned that many shoes in my whole lifetime. Although I do have, like, thirty purses grouped by size on hooks in the back of my closet."

"Good thing the new house has large closets," Ella chuckled. "Otherwise, Manuel would need to put his clothes in the attic."

Hayley's pulse quickened as she glanced out the window. "I don't know."

"Don't know what?"

"It's just, well... You saw how Nicholas reacted to Manuel wanting me to stay. The last thing I want to do is come between him and one of his brothers." Sighing, she looked back at Ella. "And I know Manuel doesn't want to have anything come between them. So maybe I shouldn't get my hopes up on staying. After all, my place isn't so bad. I'll still be nearby."

"Don't be ridiculous," Ella stated, shaking her head. "Of course Manuel wants you to stay with him, and I highly doubt you're going to come between him and any of the boys." As Hayley began to protest, Ella pushed on. "Nicholas and Manuel will be fine. Whatever Nicholas has against you staying probably doesn't even have anything to do with you."

"What do you mean?"

"His hang-ups all stem from whatever happened in his past, and you are a reminder of them. We just need for him to see you as, well, you."

"You make it sound so easy."

"That's because it is," Ella laughed. "Nicholas is a teddy bear. He'll come around."

"A teddy bear with a scary bad attitude."

Ella laughed again as she turned the wheel, pulling into the parking lot of a cute little bar. "He's not so bad. It's Cyrus who gets a little grumpy."

"Grumpy. Hmm... Not really the word I'd use."

Hayley chuckled, getting out of the car and following her friend through the parking lot. The pink neon sign of the bar glowed dimly in the bright sky. The building itself was small with a few well-placed tinted windows along the wall and a large black door at its entrance. Stepping in behind Ella, she had to blink a few times to allow her eyes to adjust to the dim light inside. It was actually rather cute. A nice bar sat on the right side of the room, the glossy wood top reflecting the lights from the back wall. Those lights illuminated an impressive double glass shelf, gleaming bottles of alcohol lining them. The rest of the bar was filled with tables and cushy black booths. She loved the place.

"I knew you'd like it here," Ella said, breaking into her thoughts.

"It's lovely," she responded with a smile, following her over to the bar.

"What can I get you ladies?" a rather handsome bartender asked, his dark brown eyes glancing between them as he smiled.

"I'll take a rum and Coke," Ella responded, her smile soft as she looked at Hayley.

"Oh, um..." She scanned the bottles behind him. "Can I get a whiskey sour?"

"Sure thing." He nodded, getting to work on their drinks.

Hayley watched him for a bit before her attention was pulled back to Ella. She was staring at her with a look of curiosity. "What?" she asked with a chuckle.

"So Manuel told you about him and his brothers, huh?"

Not really the conversation she thought would start their night off. "Um, yeah."

"How did he tell you?"

"Oh." Hayley paused as the bartender set their drinks down. "He didn't want to at first. Or maybe he just didn't know how. I don't know," she sighed, taking a sip of her drink. *Perfect.* "When he finally decided to tell me, though, he just kind of spit it out."

"He did?" Ella laughed. "Just threw it right out there? No easing you into it?"

She shook her head and joined in the laughter. "Nope. He just put it out there, then stared at me, waiting to see how I responded."

"And?" Ella giggled. "Did you freak out? Tell him he was certifiable?"

"No. I actually wasn't too surprised. I mean, I knew there was something different about them. I just hadn't been able to quite put my finger on it, you know?"

"I do. I kind of had that same *aha* moment when I found out, too."

"Oh yeah? How did Christian tell you?"

"He didn't." Hayley's face must have shown her confusion because Ella smiled and quickly went on. "I kind of found out in a more...unconventional way." She paused, taking a sip of her drink. "Let's just say having Christian show up one night and lose control of himself as he rescued me from a rather smelly drunk was, um...an eye-opening experience." She grinned over the top of her glass as she took another sip.

"Oh my," Hayley said, shifting slightly in her chair as she turned towards Ella. "Do tell."

For the next two hours, Ella talked about meeting Christian. How she thought she was losing her mind, but couldn't stop thinking about him. She talked about the night in the alley when she found Christian and Manuel facing off with Braktis, a demon that was no longer around to hurt them. As happy as Hayley was at the knowledge they could remove a demon from the Earth, killing them in a sense that they would no longer be able to come back here, it was quickly overshadowed by Ella's confession that the same could be done to the boys. To Manuel.

By the time they finished their second drink, Hayley's head was spinning, and not just from the alcohol now warming her veins. So much had been revealed to her in such a short time, information that was invaluable and worth more to her than even Ella could know.

With a better knowledge of Manuel, the boys, and Ella, and what they'd been through, she could now see a much larger picture. One that was greater and far more important than she originally thought. If she had any doubts about this being where she needed to be, Ella's story of what they had been going through and who they were up against completely squashed them.

When she saw her friend almost come to tears as she talked about her fear of losing control of her new powers and hurting those she had quickly come to love and call family, Hayley reached over and gave her arm a gentle squeeze. "I don't want you to worry about that now. I'm here and I plan on helping you, so you don't have to be afraid of what you can do anymore."

Ella looked gratefully at her, giving a small smile as she finished what was left of her drink.

Hayley followed suit, polishing off what was left of her whiskey sour as she felt her phone in her back pocket vibrate. Smirking at Ella, she reached down and retrieved it, her screen lighting up as a text from Manuel came through.

You two having a good time?

Hayley smiled, showing the screen to Ella before typing a quick response.

Yes. We're just finishing up our second drink.

Is Ella okay to drive home? Should I come get you?

"Oh god...," Ella laughed, leaning over to see the conversation. "Let him know I'm fine. We're not leaving right away anyway. I was planning on having some water and getting a basket of chips and dip to munch on."

Hayley nodded. "Water sounds good. Actually, I don't think I've had any today." She turned back to her phone as Ella waved the bartender over.

She'll be fine. We're going to have a snack and some water before we head back.

Okay. It wouldn't take me long to get there if you change your mind. Text me when you're on your way home.

Home. The fact that he had used that term made her cheeks warm.

"See," Ella said with a smirk, crunching into a chip from the basket the bartender had just set down. "Told you he was still going to have you stay."

Hayley just shook her head, trying to hide her smile as she took a sip of the water that had just been placed before her. She may be able to hide some of the giddiness she was suddenly feeling behind her glass, but the butterflies swirling around her stomach would not be denied. With just a simple statement, a single word, Manuel had made her day.

Will do. See you soon.
Can't wait, sweetheart.

The smile on her face stayed the remainder of their conversation. Ella couldn't quit gushing about Manuel calling her sweetheart, telling her how cute they looked together, and how they should go on a double date, which had Hayley smiling like a lunatic. Ella had been so animated about it that by the time they paid their bill and walked back outside, Hayley's sides hurt from all the laughing.

They huddled together, still giggling, as they walked in the cool night air. The sun had almost completely set by then, streaking the sky with soft golds and reds. Hayley glanced up, marveling at the colors.

She was just about to comment on what a great time she was having when Ella gasped beside her. When she felt her friend tense up, she turned in the direction in which she stared. Hayley instantly felt a chill run down her spine, but it had nothing to do with the cold breeze. It had to do with the demon leaning against the trunk of Ella's car.

His red eyes glowing and smile widening, he looked between them. "Well, well, well. Look at what we have here."

After forcing her brain to work, Hayley frowned. "We?"

The demon just smirked, nodding his head to the side as he glanced away from them.

Following his gaze, her breath caught as five more demons seemed to materialize out of thin air around them. Had they been looking for them? They must have, but why?

"What do you want?" Ella asked, her voice strong and even.

"It is not so much what we want," the demon snickered. "We're just following orders."

"Orders from whom?" Hayley asked, although she had a sinking feeling she knew what his answer was going to be.

The demons around them began to close in, their power churning through the air. She pulled her metaphysical wall up tight around her, throwing it around Ella, too, in the hopes she could stop the warring powers within her friend from making themselves known.

I should have told Manuel to come, she thought desperately as the demon they first saw stepped up to them. He was tall, well over six feet, so Hayley had to tilt her head back to meet his gaze. She refused to show fear in front of these evil pieces of shit. She'd never taken on demons of this level before, but that wouldn't stop her from fighting. At least until help came. Somehow, Hayley knew that help would come, and she would hold onto that hope like a lifeline.

Pushing that sense of hope into Ella, they both faced off with the demon before them. His lips twisted into a sneer as he leaned down, his breath hot and rancid against their skin. "I think you know exactly who my boss is." He laughed, his power pouring off him as the glow of his eyes began to brighten. "After all, Andras has a way of leaving an impression."

As the name Andras left his lips, Hayley felt Ella's body give a violent shudder. Her power seemed to scream out from her then, scraping across Hayley just as the demons began to move in.

With a shove of her own, Hayley began to fight back, pushing her power out around them. Calling to every God and Goddess alike, she tried to keep the demons away. As she felt her world begin to shift from the effort, she heard Ella scream. The sound was quick, piercing...and the last thing Hayley heard before her own scream tore through the air, lost in the demonic laughter around them.

Chapter 35

Dev's lungs hurt from the air he had been forcing through them for the last couple hours.

He had just returned to his office after making sure all the alcohol Trix ordered had been delivered. He trusted her to place an order for everything the bar would need. What he didn't trust were the drivers not taking a bottle or two for themselves.

What? Dishonest people? Where would I come up with that idea? he'd scoffed, making his way from the back room after finding a delivery that had, in fact, come up short.

Of course, that problem had vanished when he entered his office and found Agalon leaning against the wall...and Andras behind his desk.

I'm fucked, he thought, and it had only gotten worse after that.

Two hours later, his body practically hummed from the fear coursing through his veins. Andras had asked about the club. He wanted to know how Dev was handling everything and what still needed to get done.

Staring at the floor the whole time, Dev answered as honestly as he could, leaving out Sy's help in the club's progress. That little tidbit was going to stay with him for as long as it could.

Every moment of Andras' questioning was torturous. Every second, he knew he was a mere word away from being thrust back into a pain-filled nightmare. So he kept his answers short, he kept them as truthful as he dared, and he kept his eyes down.

"It would seem you have everything under control," Andras mused. His voice, like his power, drifted over Dev like the heat from a fire. Knowing this was said as a statement and not a question, Dev stayed silent. He heard Andras sigh. "How are things with my security team?"

"Things are going well," he answered immediately. "They have been keeping an eye on the grounds ever since they showed up. There really is little for them to do until we open, though."

He heard his chair as it scraped across the floor. Without looking, he sensed Andras rise to his feet. "I am sure I can find something for them to do in the meantime."

"Of course," Dev murmured.

"And your brothers... How are they?" Andras asked smoothly. The taping of his fingers along the desktop echoed through the suddenly quiet room.

The mention of his brothers sent Dev's world into a spin. His blood ran cold as he kept his gaze down, focusing on the floor. With a mental shudder, Dev let out a soft sigh. "I wouldn't know. I haven't seen them."

"But you *do* know they are here?"

"I had heard, but nothing concrete."

"Nothing concrete? Well, what have you heard?"

"Just rumors that there are Guardians nearby. That they have hunted down some of the lower-level demons and sent them back." Dev let each word fall from his lips with the calmness he should be feeling, yet wasn't. "That is all I know."

"Really?" Andras asked, the tips of his shoes suddenly coming into view as Dev fought the urge to flinch away. He hadn't even sensed the demon moving towards him. "See," Andras began, his voice dropping to a harsh whisper, "I have heard my own rumors, Dev. Rumors that tell me you know more than you are letting on. Rumors that say you have been a rather busy little fallen angel."

Dev shook his head, squeezing his eyes shut as he fought for calm. "I have only been doing what you asked me to. And I am holding nothing back from you now." A slight quiver in his voice gave his true emotions away.

Lies. All lies.

A soft gasp left his lips as he felt Andras' power tighten around him. It seeped quickly into his body, seeming to squeeze him from the inside. Clamping his jaw shut to keep from crying out, Dev concentrated on closing off his mind, separating himself from the pain spreading through his body. Images of chains and fire flashed through his memory as every one of his muscles tensed.

God, please..., he silently begged, fighting to keep himself standing.

A humming in his ears started, growing with every excruciating second that ticked by. Whether it was caused by the pressure building within him or Andras' power, he wasn't sure. In all honesty, he didn't really care where it was coming from or what was causing it. He only cared about making it stop.

"Dev?"

Andras' voice broke through his fevered mind, causing him to shiver as it scraped over his already tattered nerves.

Feeling the demon's power beginning to recede, he let out a soft whimper in relief. It couldn't be helped, even as his very soul cringed at this show of weakness. The gratefulness he felt as the pain eased was overwhelming, even if the relief was only slight.

"Dev, are you listening?"

Blinking a couple times, he let out a breath. The air hissed as it rushed past his teeth. "I..." He cleared his throat. "I'm sorry. I..."

His chest tightened at the sound of Andras' sigh. "Now, Dev, I really need you to pay attention. Can you do that?" His voice was a harsh whisper. At Dev's jerky nod, Andras continued. "Good. Now, I asked if there was anything you needed to tell me."

"No, Andras."

"Are you sure? Think really hard about your answer."

Dev chanced a brief glance up. His eyes collided with Andras' as the demon gazed at him, his mismatched eyes smoldering, daring him to lie. "I have only done as you've asked me to do. Nothing more."

Looking back towards the floor, Dev held his breath. The seconds ticked by as he waited for a response. A sign that Andras believed him. He needed him to because if he didn't, his time up here was going to expire sooner than he had hoped. If he didn't believe him, Dev would never get another chance to reach his brothers.

After what felt like hours, he sensed a sudden shift in the air.

"I believe you, Dev," Andras said softly. However, the demon's tone did nothing to calm his nerves. "Of course, if I find out you have lied to me..." His voice trailed off. There really was no need for him to finish that sentence. Dev knew exactly what awaited him when, not if, Andras learned the truth. "Now, I have some business I must attend to. Do make sure my club is ready on time."

"Of course," Dev responded.

"I am trusting you, Dev. Do not make me regret it."

"I will take care of everything."

Andras stood in front of him for another moment before turning to leave. Dev watched his shoes disappear from his vision, a feeling of relief slowly creeping through his system. It was short-lived, though, as he felt Agalon walk up and pause behind him. The heat from the demon's body burned against his back as Agalon leaned into him.

"I will see you soon," he whispered before following Andras out of the office. His statement came across as the threat and promise Dev was sure it was meant to.

His knees practically buckled as he heard his office door close behind them. "Fucking shit," he breathed out, making his way to his chair and flopping down in it. That had not only been a nerve-racking and unwelcome visit, but an unexpected one. He had hoped to get a heads-up that Andras was topside so he could prepare himself for the questioning, not be freaking blindsided.

Resting his head on his desk, he took a couple deep breaths. Now what? He had hoped to be able to reach his brothers before the nasty duo showed up. This was going to make things a lot more difficult. Not that they hadn't been difficult already, but damn.

Maybe he could email them. Or get someone else to email them. Or call them. Or, shit, throw a fucking paper airplane towards their front door. Groaning, Dev squeezed his eyes shut. Seeing white spots begin to explode behind his eyelids, he squeezed them tighter, willing the spots to give him some kind of insight as to what to do next. Nothing.

Sighing, he pulled his head up and leaned back in his chair, staring at the ceiling. "I know I have no right to ask this," he said softly. "I know I messed up and continue to do so, but I'm trying. I really want to be better. I just... I just need a little help."

The silence seemed to stretch out around him as he sat there. He hadn't really expected a response, none had come to all his cries for help in the past, but he still hoped this time would be different. He was obviously fooling himself.

The sharp ring of his cell phone cut through the silence, causing him to practically jump out of his seat. Reaching quickly into his pocket, he answered without even looking at the screen.

"Yeah?" he grumbled.

"Dev?" Sy's voice burst over the line.

"Listen, Sy, now really isn't a good time to-"

"It is your brothers' females," Sy cut in, his voice holding an edge to it that Dev had never heard before.

"What?" Dev frowned, his stress from a few minutes ago coming back. "Who?"

"The psychic and the witch... The ones who have been-"

"What about them?" Dev cut in.

"They are in trouble and-"

"Trouble? What are you talking about?" he growled.

"You will *stop* interrupting and responding to me like that," Sy snapped, causing Dev to straighten.

"Sorry," he murmured. It would be a good idea for him to remember to whom he was talking. "I just don't understand why you're calling to tell me this."

"If you want to help your brothers, and I know you do, now would be a good time to start," the demon responded. "Unless something has changed..."

"No. No. Nothing has changed. Where are they?"

"They are in the parking lot of the Indigo. Do you know the bar?"

"Yes. I was there when I first got here...recruiting for Andras' club," Dev said, already rising from his seat and heading to his office door.

"Good. They are surrounded by demons. I would hurry if I were you."

Locking his door from the inside, Dev turned around and scanned his office. He trusted Sy enough to know this wasn't a trap, but the demon wouldn't be telling him this without wanting something in return. "Why are you helping me?" he asked slowly.

"I have a favor to ask of your brothers. Once you are back in their good graces, so to speak, you will convince them to help me."

Frowning, Dev started to point out that there was a good chance he would never be in their "good graces", no matter what he did, but his line of thought was interrupted as Sy continued.

"We will discuss this more later," he said quickly. "You should go now." With that, the line went dead.

Dev pulled his phone away from his ear and blinked. *Well, guess the conversation is over*. Tucking it back into his pocket, he looked around one more time. Breathing deep, he could feel his power rolling through him. Conjuring up images of the bar and the area around it...more specifically, the back alley...he closed his eyes. He could feel the familiar tingling along his skin as he willed his power to grow, shifting around him as he felt his body shudder. With a soft sigh, he quietly vanished from his office.

Seconds later, the sudden chill of the air hit him as he appeared behind the bar. Blinking several times, Dev quickly adjusted to the change in light as he scanned his surroundings. It didn't take long for him to feel the power racing through the air or hear the cries of the girls. The pain and anguish in their voices spurred him into action. Taking four quick steps, he rushed around the corner of the building and paused.

With a quick glance, he noted six demons, two of which were crumpled on the ground. *Good. Four is easier to deal with.* Silently moving forward, he stopped behind a truck, peeking around it. He could make out the two females in the middle of the remaining demons. The one with the brown hair was curled up on the ground, her arms tucked around her middle as she rocked back and forth. The power curling around her was wild, unstable. Dev could practically see it in the air, jerking about as she tried to control it. Shaking his head, he realized there was more to her power than just the natural wildness that came with her slipping control. There was a darkness to it, too, which blurred through her light as it weaved around her form.

She must be the one who was in Hell, he thought, warily eyeing the warring powers. He definitely needed to get the demons away from her, and quickly.

The one standing over her was fighting the demons off as best she could. He watched in awe as she shot streams of power around them, shoving the demons around as she held them off. She was growing tired, though. He could sense it. And if he could, so could the demons.

They were definitely toying with her. Only making half-assed attacks to try and get her to wear herself out. And it was working.

He saw her arms shaking, her steps faltering as she moved closer to her friend. At that instance, he knew the demons were going to move in. Without another thought, he let free the anger that had been simmering since he spotted them. It flew through his body, pulling a growl from his lips as he felt his back spasm. In a flash of light, his wings burst out behind him. Their dark grey feathers appeared metallic as they caught what remained of the light.

Shooting forward, Dev didn't pause as he flew into the demons. Their shock at being attacked from behind made them hesitate, stumbling forward instead of fighting back. This confusion only lasted for a second, but it was long enough for Dev to grab two and toss them at the building's brick wall before the others knew what was happening. The ones he threw hit with a solid crack, their bodies crumpling to the ground. They were only stunned, but that would have to do.

Turning on the remaining two, he wasn't surprised to see that the shock of his presence had worn off. With a wild growl, they both leapt at him. He twisted, catching one in midair as the other slammed into his back. Dev was faintly aware of the startled noises from the women as he fell to the ground, grappling with the demons as they fought to pin him down. Throwing his power out around him, he smiled when he felt the demon in his hands recoil.

Meeting his eyes, Dev forced his power into him. He felt it break through his pathetic walls, crumbling beneath his attack. The demon yelled out as he reached up, grabbing his head in pain.

Dev had a quick thought of how this was always Christian's area of expertise, but that thought vanished when he felt the demon behind him slip a knife into his back.

Sonofabitch!

Yelling, he threw himself into a spin, slamming the demon against the building as he threw his wings out around him.

Twisting back and forth, he scraped the demon along the wall, as if he were trying to get gum off the side of his shoe. With a hard turn, he felt the demon's grip on him slacken, the knife falling from where it was lodged into his muscles, clattering to the ground.

It had been decades since he used his power like this and it was starting to take its toll. Gritting his teeth, he pushed on.

Pulling himself up, he spun as the demons he had tossed aside began to rise. They turned towards him with such rage, he almost couldn't make out any of their facial features around the glow of their eyes. The two at his back had also begun to get up, although their movements were slower, unsure.

Crouching down, he pulled his wings tight around him. He was getting tired. He didn't show it, but he could feel his power falter slightly. He needed them to get closer. Glancing to the side, he saw the two prone figures of the demons the women had already downed. Their forms were so still, he wondered if they would move again. He'd have to check them in a minute. For now, he was just glad there were only four demons moving in to surround him.

Thank goodness for small favors, he thought.

Holding his breath, he felt them circle him.

"You should not have come," one of the demons hissed.

"Andras will not be pleased to hear of you interfering with his plans," another growled.

"Stupid little fallen angel," a third taunted. "You will be sorry."

They had moved in closer. He could feel their presence along his skin.

Just a little bit closer.

He was only going to get one shot at this, one try to take them all out at once, so he needed them as close as possible.

Through the demons' legs, he could just make out the women. The redhead had crouched down next her friend. Both of them were shaking, staring at him with wide eyes.

He couldn't let the demons beat him. Curling his wings in closer, he met the gaze of each of the women, giving them a slow smirk as he pulled his power into his center, building it like a ball of fire in his mind.

"You ready for what is coming?" one of the demons hissed. He was now so close, Dev could feel the warmth from his breath against his face.

"Are you?" he whispered back. With that, Dev threw his wings out and released the power. He felt it as it slammed into each of the demons. They stumbled, legs buckling, as he drove his power into them.

He could feel it then. Closing his eyes, he yelled out as he felt his power curl into the darkness within the four demons, their blackness churning and withering as it tried to fight him off. His wings flexed high above him, tethering his power to that darkness, wrapping around it as he began to yank it from them.

Leaning back, his eyes flew open as the demons all let out a scream. Each one fell to his knees around him as their bodies jerked. The blackness, their oily souls, burst from their gaping mouths. Like a tornado, the darkness swirled in the air above him. Twisting his power like a net, he engulfed it and pulled it into him.

This was the part he hated. This was why he never had any problem letting Christian be the one to take demons or evil souls down.

All four demons dropped around him. Their bodies, no more than empty shells now, collapsed in on themselves. The darkness flew into him, pulled by his own light with such force, it took his breath away.

Shit!

Curling in on himself, he felt the weight of that darkness course through him. It fought, lashed out, bit into his very soul as it tried to stop what was happening.

Sweat began to drip down his face as he blinked furiously, his shudders subsiding as he felt the demons' darkness changing, succumbing to his light as he mentally rolled it into a smaller and smaller ball. Finally, the last of it winked out of existence, causing him to release a moan.

Pulling his wings back into him, Dev rested his hands upon the cool ground. His pulse finally began to slow as he pulled in one calming breath after another.

Damn, that hurt, he thought, rolling his shoulders.

"Who are you?"

The voice was so quiet, he almost missed it. Turning his head slightly, he was met with two sets of concerned, yet fearful eyes.

Licking his lips, he slowly sat back on his heels, his hands still shaking slightly as he rested them on his knees. "Are you two okay?" he asked softly, avoiding the question.

The woman with the green eyes squinted at him, her arm wrapped protectively around the other woman's shoulders. "Yes. Thank you." Her voice came out strong as she eyed him.

The beauty with the brown eyes stared at him intently. "You're like Christian," she said quietly.

Looking at the ground, Dev tried to calm his suddenly jumpy nerves. He needed to keep it together. With a shudder, he suddenly remembered the other two demons. Standing, he headed towards them without a word. Their bodies still lay motionless, eyes closed.

"I sent their souls back," came a voice from behind him.

Turning, Dev found the redhead was now standing, her hands on her hips as she looked him up and down. *Feisty.* "So I see," he smirked, turning to face her.

"You never answered Ella's question." When he raised his eyebrow, the redhead rolled her eyes. "Who are you?"

With a sigh, he glanced around. "Nobody."

"I highly doubt that. Anyone who can do what you just did most definitely is not a *nobody*," she stated matter-of-factly.

"You *are* like Christian, aren't you?" Ella asked. Getting to her feet slowly, she gazed at him, her brown eyes wide.

"Yes."

"But I've never heard them mention another." She glanced at her friend, then back at him. "Why would they not have mentioned you?"

"Because they don't know I'm here," he responded slowly. "And, like I said, I'm nobody."

"What's your name?" the redhead asked.

Shaking his head, he took a couple steps to the side. It was time for him to go. No good could come out of continuing this conversation. Then he remembered how he had been trying to figure out a way to reach his brothers. To get a message to them. Looking over at the two women before him, he blinked slowly. "My name doesn't matter." Before they could argue, he raised his hand. "It hasn't for some time, so I doubt it will now."

"But-" Ella started.

"No, please," he cut in. "I need you to tell them that Andras is here."

"He's here?" He watched as the color in Ella's face suddenly drained.

"Don't worry. I will do what I can to keep him away from you, but they need to know. Andras will be looking for both of you."

"Both of us?" Red asked in disbelief.

"Yes. He knows about you, too, Red." He smirked as she frowned at the nickname. Whatever. He liked it, so that's what he was going to call her. "You two need to get back home and stay there. Tell them he's building his army, gathering souls, finding a way to attract more."

"How?"

"He has a club that will be opening soon. And, before you ask, there's no way to stop that from happening. But maybe they can figure out a way to shut it down. To put an end to Andras and his demons."

"How do you know Christian? And you keep saying them, so you know Manuel, Nicholas, Darren, and Cyrus, too." Ella shook her head. "How?"

"It's a long story, and not one I plan on getting into right now." Dev felt a chill work down his spine as he glanced off to the side. He could just make out a figure watching them from the shadows, leaning against the side of the bar. Sy. "Listen, I have to go."

"No, wait." Ella stepped towards him.

"I have to." He looked back at them, a sadness beginning to form in his stomach. How he wished he didn't need to leave. Didn't need to go back into the darkness that he'd lived in for so long, he almost couldn't remember how it was before. Almost.

Stepping further away from them, he watched their eyes fill with worry. "Call them. Call the guys and tell them to come get you. Tell them what I told you. They'll know what to do. They'll be able to keep you safe."

Red just nodded. "We will. We'll tell them everything."

"I know you will. And Ella? Red?" He smiled softly at them as he began to pull himself back into the shadows.

"Yeah?" they both responded.

"Take care of my brothers for me." Dev said it so softly, he wasn't sure if they heard. However, their gasps rang in his ears as he pulled himself away from them.

Seconds later, tired and shaken, he appeared back in his office. With a shudder, he glanced around, relieved to find himself alone.

When his phone rang, he didn't need to guess who was on the other end. Grabbing it from his pocket, relieved to find it undamaged, he answered. "Sy."

"You lingered longer than was safe."

"Did anyone else see me?" The words came out low as he forced them past the lump forming in his throat.

"Just me."

He nodded, even though he knew Sy couldn't see him. "I saw you." He frowned. "Why were you there?"

"I just wanted to make sure you made it back safely."

"Why?"

"You owe me, my friend. I would hate for something to happen to you before I could collect."

Dev nodded again, slowly sitting on his couch. "Yes, of course."

"Do not sound so put off, Dev. Regardless of my reasons for being there, I would have still backed you up should the need have arisen." Sy tisked. "You should be thanking me."

Dev swallowed. "I am grateful that you were there, as well as for informing me about what was happening. I am sorry if I came across as ungrateful. Really. Thank you, Sy."

"You are welcome, Dev. Now, be a good little angel and keep yourself on Andras' good side. I fear your little chat with those women may come to light sooner rather than later."

"I *had* to tell them. To warn them."

"I know." Sy released a soft hiss of air. "I just hope you know what you are doing."

"Me, too, Sy," Dev said softly before hanging up. Looking around his office, he closed his eyes. "Me, too."

Chapter 36

Manuel's hands shook as he and his
brothers appeared by Indigo.

Hayley's call for help had come only
moments ago, but he and his brothers had
already been getting ready to head towards
them. Moments earlier, he had felt a rush
of fear shoot through his chest. If it hadn't
been for Darren grabbing his arm, it would
have knocked him down. The worst part
was that it happened to Christian at the
same time.

They had glanced at each other,
Manuel certain he looked as pale as
Christian. There had been no need to
wonder what the feeling was, though. With
Christian having gone through it before, he
immediately started yelling for everyone to
get ready.

That had thrown the house into
chaos. Cyrus, who was upstairs, had blasted
through the door as Christian's voice had
risen to Earth-shattering levels. Nicholas
had run in from outside, immediately on
alert as he scanned the room. Even Darren,
who was normally calm, was cussing up a
storm by Manuel's side. Although this had
all happened in a matter of seconds, it had
felt like hours. His need to get to Hayley

was so strong, he ran past his brothers before he even knew he was moving.

Manuel had been up the stairs, heading to his room for his sword, when Hayley called. Her voice had sounded scared as she told him he needed to get there. After making her repeat several times that she and Ella were okay, he had gathered the boys and they left, vanishing from the front room as quickly as their power would let them, landing in the parking lot right by the girls and the bodies of several demons.

Shaking his head, Manuel moved past the bodies to pull Hayley into a crushing hug. He needed her as close as possible. Breathing in her scent, he gripped her tight, only letting her pull away when she tapped him on the back.

"We're okay," she said, leaning up to give him a kiss. Her lips pressed to his with such passion, he knew she was feeling the need to be close to him, too. Pulling back, she smiled. "I'm glad you're here."

"I am, too," he said, resting his forehead on hers. "I don't know what I would do if anything happened to you."

Hearing a soft cry, he glanced over to see Ella pressing her face tightly into Christian's chest. His brother's eyes were filled with both relief and questions as he rubbed her back.

"What the hell happened?" Darren asked, stepping up next to them.

Hayley turned to look at him, her eyes filled with anger as she pulled away slightly. "We were just walking out here to get into Ella's car when we spotted that demon..." She pointed at one of the lumps on the ground, "leaning against it."

"The other five stepped out of the shadows," Ella said. She had turned her face so her cheek was still resting against Christian, her hands holding his sides tightly. "They worked for Andras." They all tensed at the name and watched as she turned her watery eyes up to Christian, her bottom lip quivering. "They were going to take us to him."

"Shh...," he said, kissing the top of her head. "You're safe. I won't let him get you." Ella snuggled into him, then turned to look at the rest of them.

Nicholas and Cyrus had come to stand around them, Manuel suddenly realizing Nicholas had enacted the Shade. Good thing someone had thought of that. He couldn't imagine trying to explain all the bodies to some poor human.

"I tried to fight against them, but my powers went wild. I was more afraid I'd hurt Hayley if I tried to do anything."

"She kept it together, though," Hayley jumped in. Nobody was going to give Ella a hard time for not fighting back, but Manuel could tell Hayley wanted to make it clear she did what she could. "I was able to take out two of them before they all tried to move in."

"But there are six bodies," Cyrus pointed out. "I get that you're good, but..." His voice trailed off as he looked around.

"Yeah. We all know you can handle yourself, Hayley," Nicholas chimed in slowly. "It's just..."

"No, it's okay. I get it," Hayley said with a smile. "There were a lot of them. I knew I couldn't handle them all." Looking up, Manuel watched a frown tug at the corners of her lips. "They just kept coming at me. All I could think was that I needed to keep them away from Ella, but I was getting so tired. I started worrying I wasn't going to be able to hold them back much longer."

Pulling her to him, Manuel rubbed her back. At a loss for words, he looked at Darren. His brother's blue eyes were piercing as he looked back. He could almost see the wheels in his head turning.

"But you were obviously able to," Darren remarked slowly. Mumbles of agreement rippled around the group, dying off as both Ella and Hayley shook their heads.

"No, I wasn't," Hayley said softly.

"But...," Christian began, looking between the two women.

"They were moving in," she continued, glancing over her shoulder at Ella, who gave her a slight nod. "When my powers started to fade, they came towards us. I could feel their own power like oil running over us. We were so scared." Hayley looked back up at Manuel. He started to say something reassuring, but there was a look in her eyes that gave him pause. "If he didn't show up when he did..." She shook her head, "I don't think we would be here right now."

"Who?" Manuel asked, confusion lacing his voice.

"He didn't tell us his name," Ella spoke, drawing everyone's attention. "He moved so fast."

"And his wings were *huge*," Hayley chimed in.

"Wait... What?" Nicholas exclaimed. "Wings?"

Ella nodded at him, excitement shining in her eyes. "Yes. And he took the demons out. It was really crazy. I didn't know if he was going to be able to beat them. He was fighting two at a time."

"Yeah. He knocked two of them out right off the bat, then started fighting with the other two. It was intense. And the power coming off him... Shit. I had to take a couple steps back from it." Hayley smiled, shaking her head. "Even when one stabbed a knife into his back, he... He just slammed the demon into the wall, scraping him along it with such force, he ripped the demon and the knife right off. I've never seen anything like it. Then everything changed and I was certain he was going to lose."

"Yeah," Ella jumped in. "The two he had knocked out woke up. Suddenly, he was surrounded by four. I was so worried because I thought they were going to beat him."

"Especially when they started taunting him," Hayley said. Ella nodded. "I don't know exactly what they were saying, but they just kept going, closing in on him a little at a time."

Manuel felt like he was in a tennis match, his eyes bouncing back and forth between the two women. They were getting more and more excited as the story went on. He had to admit that the fight they described sounded amazing. But, even though he was extremely thankful to the male who showed up, it just seemed a little far-fetched. Who would just show up and fight four demons? Did he know what was going on before he came? The main question, the one they should all be asking, was who in the hell was he?

"So these four demons here...," Cyrus said. Looking over, Manuel saw his brother looking down at the four bodies, nudging them with the toe of his boot. "These four had him surrounded?"

"Yes," Ella confirmed.

"And he... What? Just stood there?" Cyrus looked back at them, his eyebrows raised.

"No, no," Hayley said quickly, her fingers tightening their grasp on Manuel's shirt as he felt her excitement grow. "He was crouching on the ground, just staying still, like he was letting them move in on him."

Manuel started to get an odd feeling in his chest. Glancing around, he noticed his brothers' eyes had narrowed. "So...," he began, glancing back down at Hayley. "He was baiting them?"

She nodded, her green eyes gleaming. "I wasn't sure what he was doing at first. I thought maybe he had been injured or something. But then..." Her voice trailed off as she smiled.

"Then?" Manuel pushed.

Hayley's grin grew. "He looked over at Ella and me, made direct eye contact, and smirked."

"He smirked?" Darren asked, shaking his head as he glanced up at Manuel.

"Yup," Ella said with a laugh. "He smiled right before they lunged at him."

"Then... Shit, I've never seen anything like it." Hayley looked over at Ella.

"I have," Ella said softly before turning her gaze to Christian, her voice dropping so low, everyone moved in a bit so they could hear her. "He pulled the blackness right out of them." At Christian's gasp, she nodded. "After they collapsed, he took it all into himself...just like you did that night in the alley."

Christian's blue eyes blazed as he looked up at the rest of them. The feeling in Manuel's chest had increased to an almost painful throbbing. Rubbing a hand over it, he looked at Hayley. Her eyes filled with concern as she gazed back up at him.

"Are you okay?" she asked, resting one of her hands on top of his. He could only nod in response.

Hearing one of his brothers clear his throat, he looked up, finding Nicholas looking at him. His red eyes glowed softly as he turned his gaze to Hayley, then Ella. "Did you talk to him?"

"We did. He actually wanted us to tell you all something," Ella responded with a small smile.

"What did he say?" Christian asked, brushing some stray strands of hair out of her face.

"He said to tell you all that Andras is here." Manuel could see her body shiver when she said the demon's name. Pulling Hayley closer, he waited for Ella to continue. "He wanted us to tell you that he is building an army, gathering dark souls to him."

"He said Andras is going to use a club to bring them in," Hayley added.

"A club?" Nicholas asked.

As the question left his brother's lips, Manuel sneered. "The 9th Circle. I *knew* there was something with that club."

"Damn," Nicholas said, shaking his head and looking off into the distance. "He's moving in right under our noses."

"Shit," Darren muttered, running one of his hands over his face. "Was there anything else?" he asked, looking at the women.

"Just that you guys will be able to protect us," Hayley said softly.

"And that you'll know what to do," Ella added.

Sighing, Darren turned from them. Manuel watched as his brother seemed to weigh everything they had just learned. Looking over, he watched as Christian protectively tucked Ella under his arm. Nicholas stood there, glancing at everyone. And Cyrus had begun pacing, his black eyes gleaming as he glanced their way with every pass.

Everyone seemed to be caught up in their own thoughts, each weighing their own options on where to go from here, on what question to ask next. It was Nicholas, though, who kept drawing Manuel's attention. His brother was throwing off waves of power and emotion like fireworks. He could practically see his angst and agony flaring off his skin.

"Nicholas?" Manuel asked, noticing that everyone had turned to face him. All showed the same concern that he felt. "Are you okay?"

He shook his head, his mouth opening and closing a few times as he stood there, looking around. "It's just..." He shook his head again, staring off. Finally, he turned his glowing red eyes back to Ella and Hayley. "It's just... What you're describing, the way the male fought..." Sighing, he frowned. "Was there anything else he said? Anything at all?"

"He wouldn't tell us his name," Ella said sadly, drawing Nicholas' attention to her. "We kept asking, but he said he was nobody. That his name didn't matter and hadn't for a long time." Tears built in her eyes as she glanced around, then back at Nicholas. "Right before he left, he..."

"He what?" Cyrus asked quietly, coming to a stop right next to her and Christian. His black eyes, although as dark as onyx, managed to portray his emotional distress. And, right now, he was dealing with a lot of it.

"He..." Hayley cleared her throat, drawing their attention. "He told us to take care of his brothers." Her words seemed to wrap around them until Manuel gasped. A single tear drifted down his cheek as he turned to look away. It couldn't be. Could it?

"Holy shit," Cyrus muttered, turning away from them.

"No," Nicholas said, his voice laced with such sadness, it broke Manuel's heart.

"You said you saw his wings?" Darren slowly asked. At their nod, he looked around, finally meeting Manuel's gaze with a pain-filled one of his own. Still speaking to Ella and Hayley, he never looked away from his brother. "And what...What color were they?"

Manuel felt Hayley wrap her arms around him. His skin tingled as her power rose up around her, gliding against him. Pulling his gaze from Darren, he looked at her, seeing the sadness, the concern, the love in her gaze. He watched her bottom lip tremble a bit as she turned them up into a smile.

"They were beautiful," she said softly. Dipping her chin, she let him know she understood how hard this was for all of them. When she spoke next, it was so quiet, so low, that if it hadn't been for the utter stillness the Shade provided, he might have missed it.

With one word, the mention of a single color describing one who was lost, one who was thought to be gone forever, his world stopped.

With that one word, the pain of his past, the anguish that had rocked him and his brothers, roared to life.

Just one...simple...word.

Manuel heard Hayley let out a sigh. He saw her lips move, forming the word before the sound of her sweet voice even left her. His heart stopped as her voice reached his ears. "Grey," she said on a single breath. "His wings were the most stunning shade of grey."

Manuel closed his eyes. *Oh god... Dev.*

Chapter 37

A silence had descended upon the group ever since the revelation in the Indigo parking lot. It was like the life had been sucked out of them. The news of their brother's presence, a brother who they had all thought was lost to them, hit them like a tornado, leaving nothing but ghosts and memories in its wake.

Running a finger slowly around the lip of his glass, Manuel closed his eyes. He was sitting on their dining room floor, surrounded by their unpacked boxes. When he had stumbled in here with his now practically empty bottle of Crown and his glass, he thought he'd sit at the table. But it was not meant for dinners. It was meant for the meetings between himself and his brothers. All of his brothers.

Looking at it, he couldn't get himself to sit there. In his drunken fog, all he could think was that Dev should have been at the table, should be here now, but he wasn't.

So Manuel chose to sit on the floor and drown his memories. It had worked for a while, but not long enough. Sadly, his drunken state had faded a while ago, allowing his thoughts to twist and turn in his mind. Allowing the true gravity of what he had learned to set in.

The house was so quiet, and had been since they arrived home three hours ago. Each brother had headed off to his own corner of the house to deal with the news. In the blink of an eye, everything had changed. Ella and Hayley had sensed it immediately. He could tell because the two of them only offered sad smiles as they watched the men take care of the bodies, which had been done in a robotic fashion, each of them going through the motions in silence.

Nicholas had been the one to find the knife that had been lodged in their brother's back, still coated with his blood and taunting them as he picked it up. He held it so tight, his knuckles turned white, his red eyes blazing in anger and despair.

How many times had Dev bled for them over the past hundred years? How many times had he cried out for them, hoping they would show up to save him?

Had Dev given up? Grown to hate them? Thought they hated him?

Just thinking his name caused a sharp pain to burn through Manuel's chest. Leaning his head back against the wall, he felt the sorrow building again, but not just sorrow. There was a furious rage threatening to explode within him. Anger that they hadn't gone to find their brother. That they left him in Hell all this time, telling themselves he was lost to them.

They told themselves that so much, they truly believed it to such an extent, they hadn't even tried to find him.

God, what must he think of us?

The fact that he had saved Ella and Hayley, probably putting himself at risk by doing so, was a punch to the gut. No matter the cost, Dev had always put the rest of them first. His sin, the very thing that had caused him to be cast away from them in the first place, he'd done for them. Dev had known what he was doing could possibly cause their father cast him out, but he did it anyway. For them. He'd tried to hide why he did it, but they had all known. As soon as they had found out what happened, they'd tried to stand up for him, but it was too late. His sacrifice for them had been done, his sentence handed out with a simple nod of their father's head.

In return, they'd left him to rot.

Hearing footsteps heading his way, Manuel sighed. Opening his eyes, he watched as Nicholas walked over to him. His brother's eyes were dark as he slid down the wall, reaching for the bottle of Crown and taking a healthy drink before looking his way.

"What do we do?" he asked.

Manuel looked back at his glass. Swirling the auburn liquid around, he thought about his brother's question. What do they do? That really wasn't the question they should be asking themselves because they all knew what they were going to do. They were going to get him back. That was a given the moment Hayley confirmed Dev was there. The question they needed to ask themselves was much more complicated.

Looking at Nicholas, he tipped his head back and finished off his drink. "We're going to find him, Nicholas. What we needed to figure out is how."

"What we need are answers," Cyrus growled as he entered the room, stopping to lean against the table in front of them. Reaching down, he swiped the Crown from Nicholas' hand, finishing it off in one gulp. "We need answers and to get him the fuck away from those demons."

"Agreed," Darren said, walking in beside Christian to join them. His normally clear blue eyes were dark with anger.

"Agreed," Nicholas seconded, nodding. "But how are we going to find him? How are we going to get the answers we need so we can get Dev back? We *need* to get him back."

Manuel looked around the room as his brothers fell silent. Nicholas had turned his gaze to the floor. Sitting this close to him, he could feel the sadness and uncertainty of their situation rolling off him. They all felt the frustration at knowing their brother needed them, but not knowing where he was. For Nicholas, though, it was more intense. He and Dev had been close all those decades ago. They'd connected in a way that told everybody who came into contact with them that they were true brothers. Sure, they all had bonded with each other, growing stronger and stronger as the years passed. For Nicholas and Dev, though, it had been immediate.

Although they were all born...he guessed some would say created...at the same time, Nicholas and Dev had always been seen as the youngest in the group. Their sarcastic mannerisms and childish antics were as unforgettable as they were frustrating.

Yet they had forgotten, hadn't they? At least on some level. But they wouldn't forget again.

Looking over at Cyrus, Manuel noticed the slight glow at the edges of his onyx eyes. He knew his brother was ready to fight. To do whatever was needed to bring Dev home. They all were. The hard question was once they found him, would he want to come back with them? Would he even be happy to see them? He may have sent a warning to them, a message to point them in the right direction, but was it more than that? Or was it just a passing FYI as he disappeared from their lives once again?

Fuck.

With a mental shake, he dismissed that line of thinking. None of those questions would do them any good right now. They would just have to cross that bridge when they came to it. For now, the question that needed their immediate attention was how to gather information, which was Manuel's specialty.

Among other things, he smirked.

"I've already been looking into The 9th Circle. From what I've read, the owner of it is a huge mystery that the local newspaper hasn't been able to solve yet," Manuel said to the group. "The manager has also been unreachable. I can start doing some more digging, make some phone calls, go check out the location. I mean, it's not open yet, but I should be able to sneak around the building a bit. Sniff the place out."

"I agree that we need to get more info on this club." Darren nodded, seeming pleased that they were at least starting to come up with some sort of plan. "Granted, you are the best at gathering information and tracking, but you're not going alone." At the look of confusion on Manuel's face, Darren shook his head. "Now that we know Andras is topside, nobody is going anywhere alone. Period." He glanced around, obviously making sure the rest of them understood. "As far as finding Dev, we won't be able to get any information about where he is in a book or on the net."

"Agreed," Manuel said. The rest mumbling similar responses.

"So I figure the best way to figure out what demon is keeping our brother would be to go out and find ourselves a demon to question." Darren's eyes blazed as he let that sink in.

"So we go hunting?" Cyrus growled, his lips curling slightly.

Manuel watched Darren hold Cyrus' gaze for a heartbeat before glancing at the rest of them, pausing as their eyes met. There was so much in his brother's gaze. So many emotions building behind his eyes. However, the one that stood out was determination. Darren was determined to get the information they needed to bring their brother home.

And that was something with which Manuel couldn't agree more.

"Yes," Darren agreed slowly. Manuel could feel his brother's power start to unfurl around him as his anticipation grew. "Let's go hunting."

Chapter 38

"Are you all finished bitching?" Castigo growled at the group of demons.

They had been scouring the city for the past twelve hours, looking for humans to bring into Andras' fold. The list of qualities these humans needed to have was short. They needed to be damaged, unredeemable, and preferably unconnected to anyone else. Andras didn't want to draw too much attention to his dealings too soon, so that meant making sure the humans he took in wouldn't have anyone looking for them, worrying about where they were, ultimately missing them when they died.

Castigo had just smirked. Andras made it seem like this should be the easiest thing in the world for Castigo and the demons he sent with him to accomplish. Except this was Fhallon Heights, not Los Angeles. Sure, every town and city had their fair share of dirtbags, of undesirables lurking in the shadows of the streets, but here, well... There just weren't that many. At least none that meet with all of Andras' specifications.

Hell, most of the humans he found to be soft. Oh, they acted tough, but their souls yearned for the light, sought to be saved. And that just wouldn't do.

He had to keep searching, though. Andras had stressed that, outside of his demons, he needed at least twenty humans to do his bidding. He would accept no less. So Castigo, along with the demons he was to work with, had headed out. The four demons with him, all low-level pieces of shit, had been eager to get this over with.

Like it was going to be that easy. Castigo had been hanging around this town for a while now and knew it wasn't going to be quick. About five hours into their mission, the demons had figured this out, as well. Truthfully, he'd been surprised it had taken them that long. Castigo had expected their complaining to start almost immediately.

Now, twelve hours later, they had only found four humans who fit the mold. Not even close to the number Andras expected.

Looking around, he listened to the demons grumbling amongst themselves. He'd never worked with these particular demons before, which didn't sit well with him. However, that wasn't really surprising given the growing number of demons down in Hell. When it came to handling business for Andras, he just liked to work alone or with demons he knew.

"Oh, come on, Cas," one of the demons, he thought his name was Pret, said. "You cannot tell us you are enjoying this."

Grinding his teeth, he turned to the demons. "How many times do I have to tell you my name is Castigo, not Cas," he spit. "And it doesn't matter if I am enjoying this or not. Andras sent us out to find humans for him, and that is what we are going to do."

"But this whole thing is pointless. There is no way we are going to find twenty humans around these warehouses." Pret shuffled his feet. "Maybe we should venture further into town."

"Stop your whining," Castigo growled.

"Pret is right," another of the demons chimed in. "We have been up and down this area. There is nobody else here for us." This received grunts of agreement from the other two.

Castigo just rolled his eyes and looked off down the street. "If we cannot find any around here, what makes you all think we will have better luck downtown?"

"There are more humans downtown."

"There are bars."

"The alleys."

"It cannot hurt to look."

Castigo stood there as the demons listed one reason after another, his head hurting with each whiny comment. As much as he knew there was a chance they were right, there was one thing they hadn't thought of. The closer they got to downtown, the higher their chances of running into at least one of the Guardians.

Not that he hadn't enjoyed his last couple run-ins with them. Those fights had been the most excitement he'd seen in a long time. As much as he despised those angels, it had been exhilarating to face off with another being of worth. His pulse sped up just thinking about it.

Yet to go up against them with this sad group of demons at his back was not high on his list of what he wanted to deal with right now. That fight would be over before it even started. An uneasiness began to grow in his gut as he thought of the many different outcomes of that fight, none of which ended well for him.

He watched the demons' mouths continued to move as they released their nonsense into the air. No matter how much they might be right, the consequences of heading further into town could be more than they could handle. More than they could survive.

This is ridiculous.

"That is enough," he barked. "You all are giving me a fucking headache." Feeling a light rain beginning to fall, he shook his head. Castigo briefly glanced at the darkening sky before looking back at the demons before him. They all looked prepared to fight, pressing their need to move from this area. Raising a hand to halt any protests, he pushed on. "Fine. Let's say you are all right that we should leave this area and move further into downtown. What do we do if...*when* we come across the Guardians? Because that will happen."

"Oh, do not worry so much, *Cas*," Pret smirked, patting his coat pocket.

Clenching his jaw, Castigo attempted to move past the annoying nickname. "Do not worry? Really? Spoken like a demon that has never faced a Guardian."

Pret just laughed, causing the rest to chuckle along with him.

Fucking followers.

"Is that funny to you bunch of idiots?" Castigo snarled. "Does dying at the end of a Guardian's blade really sound like a good time to you?"

Pret's grin kept growing, his pointed teeth a stark white against his brown skin. "Like I said, you do not need to worry, my friend."

"First off, we are definitely not friends. However you got that idea in your pea-sized brain, I don't know. Secondly, what the fuck do you mean do not worry?"

Pret waved his insults away with the flick of his wrist. "Really, Cas? Do you honestly think Andras would send us out here without giving us something to use against the Guardians?" Castigo frowned, staring at the demon in confusion. "Oh, you did. I would not have expected you to be so shortsighted."

He began to take a step towards the demon, then paused. The urge to punch him in his ugly face was almost too much, but the need to see what Pret had was greater. "What did Andras give you?" Keeping his voice calm, he eyed the others as he spoke. "It must be something powerful to make you all feel like you can go up against the Guardians and win."

Instead of answering, he watched Pret reach into his coat and pull out a gun. It didn't look special, not like something that would be of any real use against a Guardian. Unless...

Castigo's mind flashed to images of the fight in Andras' office, of the power getting thrown around and the damage that was done. One thing had stood out during that fight, though. One instance that had given Castigo pause as he had fought against Nicholas... The gunshot. It was so out of place with what was happening. Andras and Agalon had barely batted an eye when the angels had made their escape and Castigo had brought up the sound. Thinking on it now, though, he couldn't help but wonder if this were the same gun. If so, what was so special about it?

"A gun?" he asked slowly. "What are you hoping to accomplish by using that? To injure them enough so you can get away?"

"Oh... No, Castigo," Pret sneered, waving the gun around. "This gun will not just injure those pesky angels. It will kill them, or the bullets that were crafted from one of Andras' cursed daggers will."

Looking at the gun, Castigo felt a stab of uncertainty. "Andras gave this weapon to you?"

"Of course," Pret snickered. "Do you really think he would have given it to *you*? After you failed him last time and lost his dagger to the very angels you were to use it against?" The others laughed beside him, causing Castigo's face to tense in anger. "I do not think so. He only sent you on this mission to get you out of the way, figuring you couldn't possibly fuck this one up."

"What the fuck?!" he roared. Why in the hell would Andras be trying to get him out of the way? None of this made any sense. Sure, he was still fighting to get back into Andras' good graces, to get back his trust, but damn them all if they thought he was just some mindless puppet. Taking a deep breath, he stared down the demons before him. "If that is the reason he sent me to find these humans for him, why did he send you four idiots?"

"Well, you see, we are here to make sure the job gets done. To, um...pick up the slack if, or should I say when you fail. Things were looking up a few hours ago, but now, well... I will venture to say Andras is rather unimpressed by your efforts so far."

"Andras is... You have been *reporting* to him?" Castigo just barely caught the gasp before it passed his lips. Not only were they his glorified fucking babysitters, but that little shit had been talking to Andras this whole time. Who knew what he had been saying. What lies he'd been telling Andras to make him look bad and the rest of them look better.

"Naturally," Pret laughed, his beady eyes looking around before landing back on Castigo. "And he feels that not only should I take charge of this mission, but it is time for us to move our search downtown. Both points I think we can all agree on that are way past due. Unless you want me to tell Andras you do not agree."

There was no way he would go against Andras, at least not in such a blatant manner. No. He was going to have to play this one smart. If Andras wanted that little shit to play leader and them to head downtown, so be it. The uneasy feeling in his gut be damned. There was nothing he could do about it now. No way he could stop the inevitable from happening. But, when he thought about it, did he want to?

Memories of Braktis' death at the hands of that Guardian sprang to his mind as he looked over the four demons. Braktis had been an idiot, but he had definitely been more of a threat than these four...even with the gun. So it was easy to assume they would not last very long in a fight with the angels. There was the slim chance they could take one of them out with those bullets...if Pret were lucky enough to get a shot off before his head was removed from his body. Would that really be such a bad thing, though? He definitely didn't see any downfall to Pret's death. He hadn't known the demon very long, but he already needed him gone. Permanently. And with the other three being Pret's followers, they wouldn't be too far behind him.

Castigo would just need to make sure none of them made it out alive so they couldn't go back and talk to Andras. Once they were gone, he would need to get out before the Guardians took him down, as well. *Yeah, that definitely wouldn't do.*

As a plan began to take root in his mind, Castigo smiled. "No, Andras is right. You all are. We will head downtown, search around the bars and alleys for the type of humans Andras needs." He watched as one of Pret's eyebrows raised slightly. "I also agree that you should take the lead," Castigo said between clenched teeth. "From here on, we go where you think is best."

"Glad to see you are not a complete idiot," Pret sneered. "We will go now, and I will let Andras know how...cooperative you can be once you know your place." He turned to head down the street. "Now, let us get out of here. I do not want to keep Andras waiting any longer than necessary You have already cost us too much time as it is. Soon, you will see that I have been right all along, Castigo. And when you do, I will accept your groveling as only a true leader should..." The other demons snarled their approval as they turned to follow Pret. The demon glanced over his shoulder at Castigo, an evil glint to his eyes. "Towering over you as you kneel before me."

Fat chance, shithead.

Pushing down the anger threatening to boil over, Castigo gave a sharp nod. Glancing up at the night sky, he felt the rain fall upon him, concentrating on the feel of it as he began to make his way after Pret and his fools. Castigo didn't know how this night would play out, but he was sure of two things.

One, by the end of this, nobody would be kneeling before anyone.

And two, he would damn well be the last demon standing.

Chapter 39

Manuel leaned against the wet brick wall of the post office. They had been wandering around the streets for a couple hours, but had yet to find a demon. They needed to find one, and soon. There were just too many questions that needed answers.

Like where was their brother? How could they get him back? What were the demons doing in Indigo's parking lot? Were they looking for the girls? What the fuck was going on at The 9th Circle? Manuel's head throbbed with all his unanswered questions. To say that being in this position was odd would be putting it lightly. He could always find answers, no matter the question, but now, with some of the most important questions needing answers, he came up with nothing.

Which is total bullshit.

He could feel his frustration growing as time ticked by, but he kept his face calm. No good would come from him losing his shit. Anyway, the girls were safe at home with Nicholas...which still floored him.

Somehow, Darren had convinced him to hang back. When the idea had been brought up, Manuel was sure there would be another fight in the house, but all it had taken was a calm stare by Darren for Nicholas to agree.

However, convincing Hayley to stay behind had been a completely different matter.

When he had told her they were going out to hunt down some demons, she freaked. She practically demanded to go with them to help, which was something he had already thought of and, just as quickly, decided against. Hayley already had more run-ins with demons than Manuel felt comfortable with. The only way he was going to be able to do what needed to be done was if he knew she was safe at home. Of course, this had gone over as well as one would imagine.

Once she reluctantly agreed to stay home, Hayley started talking to him about her dream, about the demons in it, and how they needed to stay away from downtown. By the time she got to the part about Castigo, she was sobbing. Manuel had held her tight, rubbing her back in an attempt to calm her down, soothe her fears. It wasn't until Ella promised to stay with her while they were gone that Hayley started to relax. There had been a silent conversation between the two of them before Hayley had looked back at him and made him promise to be careful.

The pain and fear in her gorgeous green eyes had nearly made him change his mind. The feel of her in his arms as she hugged him tight against her body almost had him tell the guys he was going to stay behind.

But he needed to be out here. He needed to feel like he was helping keep Hayley safe, helping take care of his brothers, and the only way that would happen would be to get some answers.

So here he was, a couple hours after leaving the house. He was frustrated, angry, and wet. All of which made for a very grumpy Manuel.

"Whatcha thinking, brother?" Christian asked, walking up and leaning against the wall next to him.

Seeing movement, Manuel looked over to see Cyrus and Darren walk around the corner. Although they were a good block away, he could see the scowls on both their faces. They'd obviously run into another dead end. With a sigh, he looked back at Christian. "There are just too many unanswered questions. Too many unknowns."

Christian just nodded as they watched Darren and Cyrus walk up. Both looked as agitated as Manuel felt.

"Nothing over by the banks or drug store," Darren sighed as he stopped in front of them. His blue eyes flashed as he looked around, absently drumming his fingers against the hilt of his broadsword.

"Save for a few drunks, there was nothing over by that shit bar, Scruples, either. Not that we should be worrying about some fucking bars and alleys," Cyrus muttered, running a hand over his face to wipe away some of the rain. "Although it was surprising to not find anything there. Figured a pit like that would be infested with demons."

Darren just shook his head, obviously deciding to ignore Cyrus' sour mood. Glancing back at Manuel, he frowned. "What about you guys?"

"Nothing over at Indigo," Christian grimaced. "I didn't really expect there to be a repeat appearance over there. Even after we cleaned up and the rain, it still reeks of sulfur. Do you guys really think Ella and Hayley are okay?" He looked at them. "I mean, I know they said they were, but... Ella just seemed so antsy, and her power felt off."

"Hayley said the demons were throwing off a lot of power. I'm sure she's just tired. Fending off that kind of energy had to be exhausting." Manuel hated that they still hadn't talked about the warring powers in Ella, but Hayley asked him for just a little more time. She felt that with the news of Dev being here and Andras being topside, they shouldn't bring anything up about the dark power in Ella until Hayley found a way to get it out of her. As much as he had wanted to argue with her, he kept his mouth shut. It made sense, but that didn't help him feel okay about keeping it from his brothers.

Plus, Hayley was really in no shape to get into an argument over anything anyway. He was telling the truth when he told Christian that she was tired. She may be trying to hide how much battling those demons took out of her, but he could see it in her eyes. "Listen, even if they dealt with a quarter of the power with those six demons that we dealt with going against Andras and the other two, I think they have the right to be a little off."

"No, you're right," Christian said slowly. "I just worry about Ella, you know? Her powers have become more unpredictable, and her moods... I just want to help her, but I don't know how."

"I know," Manuel said, reaching up and giving Christian's shoulder a squeeze. "Everything will work out."

"I agree," Darren said with a quick nod. "We'll find a way to help her. Don't worry, Christian. You're not alone in this." With a murmur of agreement from Manuel and a chin lift from Cyrus, Darren went on. "For now, though, we need to concentrate on finding a demon. Was your search any better, Manuel?"

"Not even a little, and I've been searching all over this area. I've done everything short of walking right up to the back alley of The 9th Circle itself." Manuel barely suppressed a growl. "With that place getting set to open in a matter of weeks, there's just no way there isn't a single demon around. I don't believe it."

"Maybe we should try again tomorrow night," Darren suggested. "The rain's starting to come down harder and-"

"Or... Instead of pussyfooting around out here like a bunch of newbies, we go into The 9th Circle and see what we fucking find there," Cyrus snapped.

"I don't think that'll be necessary," Christian mumbled, looking off down the road.

"Oh, I think it is *very* necessary. In fact, I think it should have been the first thing we did when we showed up here," Cyrus growled.

"Really? I didn't hear you suggesting that when we were trying to figure out where to look." Manuel rolled his eyes.

"I didn't say anything because you three already had it in your heads what we were going to do. It's not like anyone asked me what I thought." Manuel tensed as Cyrus stepped up to him. "Although I should be used to that by now, shouldn't I?"

"What the fuck, Cyrus?" Manuel said, giving his brother a light shove backwards. "What the hell is that supposed to mean?"

"You know exactly what that means. When did you ask my opinion on this, huh? When did you ask what I thought we should do? Oh, that's right. You didn't. And you know why you didn't? Because my opinion doesn't really matter. You all know best. I obviously have no idea what to do. Is that about right? I'm just the... What? House drunk? Too broken and damaged to be of any real use to the family? Well, fuck you all. And you can just stop shaking your head, Manuel."

Manuel held his hands up. "Shit, Cyrus. Nobody thinks you're broken or damaged. Of course your opinion matters-"

"Right," Cyrus barked. "You just keep telling yourself that. Who knows? Maybe you'll actually convince yourself that it's true someday. But I know how you all really feel. Ever since I was taken, you guys have treated me like a burden, like the house's dirty little secret. Go ahead. Deny it all you want, but I see the truth. I've let it slide, forgiven you all, because I *am* fucked up. I'm as damaged as you all think I am, but at least I knew where everyone stood. Now, though, things in the house have really shifted. You've all lost your focus about what we're actually here for and what our priorities are. And you know what, Manuel? You can think that I'm full of shit, but the truth of the matter is that you're just as bad as Christian. You're both so focused on some female warming your bed and wetting your dick, you've forgotten what's really important."

"What the hell are you talking about?" Christian pushed off of the wall, his eyes darkening with anger. "We know exactly what and who is important here. Maybe if you weren't so fucking selfish, you would, too." He shook his head in frustration. "Anyway, this is not the time or place for this shit. What I was about to-"

"Oh, right. I'm selfish," Cyrus cut in. "That's fucking rich. You guys are so worried about your women, you didn't stop to think that Dev, our brother who has been going through fucking hell, is probably in that fucking club." He waved his hand to the side, his voice growling through the night. "But he's not the real reason we're here looking for demons, is he? Even good old Darren is more interested in those two females than his own brother."

"Cyrus, of course we are-" Darren attempted to step in.

"No, Darren. You know what? I'm done with this shit." He looked each of them up and down in disgust. "You all go off and save your women. Focus on them and what you need to do."

"Come on, Cyrus-" Darren tried again.

"Cyrus-" Manuel started.

"I said no!" he barked, his black eyes taking on a grayish glow as his power whipped out around him. "You do what you feel is important. I'm going to go find our brother because he's family. *That's* what I feel is important." With that, he turned and stalked away. The brothers all called out to him, yelling for him to calm down and come back, but it was no use. Cyrus' anger made him deaf to all their calls.

Manuel watched him take off, his body radiating power as the shadows pulled in around him. With a last rush of power that they felt across the street, Cyrus walked into an alley, disappearing from view.

"Shit," Manuel hissed. With his hands clenched into fists at his side, he spun around to face Darren and Christian. "What the fuck was that about?" Christian was back to looking off down the street, but Darren met his frustrated gaze.

"I don't know," Darren said slowly. "I just... I know he's been upset lately and his temper has been getting worse, but... I didn't know he felt like that. Did you?"

"No. I thought he was just being... I don't know. Moody." Manuel shook his head. Now was not the time for them to be fighting amongst themselves. No matter what his brother thought, tonight did have to do with Dev. He wished he could have gotten Cyrus to see that he was needed.

Where he got the idea they all saw him as damaged and of no real use to the family was beyond him.

That was something they would have to deal with later, though. Right now, they needed to find a demon to get the answers they needed. They would just have to hope that Cyrus would be okay until they were done.

Looking at Christian, he noticed his brother frowning, his head tilted slightly as he stared away from them. "Christian?" Manuel asked, casting a brief glance at Darren before looking back. "You okay?"

"Yeah. It's just..." He paused. Still tilting his head, he gave it a soft shake. "I tried to mention it earlier, but... It's just so faint."

"What's faint?" Darren asked.

"I'm not sure. It sounds like..." His voice trailed off again.

Manuel watched as his brother's body tensed up. A sudden wave of power rolled off Christian as he turned to them, his blue eyes glowing. "Sounds like what?" Manuel asked, although he started to get the feeling he knew exactly what Christian was hearing. He could feel his power responding to the emotions rolling off his brother.

"Drumming," he said, his voice coming out strained. "It's almost too faint, though. Like if I turn my head to far to the left or right, I'll miss it."

"Which way is it coming from?" Darren asked, already pulling his broadsword from its sheath, the gold inlayed symbols along the blade catching in the soft glow from the streetlights. The cross on the handle flared in reaction to his touch.

Manuel pulled out his own blade, feeling the Sica hum to life in his hands. Its power fed off his own as he tightened his grip. "Just point me in the direction, Christian. I'll find the demon."

He watched as Christian turned, feeling the moment his brother released his powers to flow out before them, his body swaying slightly from the effort. He took a couple steps, then a couple more. Manuel stayed right at his back, Darren not far behind. They moved in a straight line down the sidewalk. The rain hitting the ground was the only sound that reached Manuel's ears.

He couldn't hear whatever Christian did. He and Ella had told him it sounded like drumming that would start off low, then get louder and stronger the closer they got to the demon...but not just any demon. That was what confused Manuel the most. It seemed to be only particular ones that set off this inner radar his brother and Ella had. Regardless, it irked Manuel that this was something he couldn't help with. He was their tracker, for fuck's sake.

Just add it to the growing list of shit I can't seem to control.

With an internal growl, he flexed his hand around the hilt of his blade. Quickening his steps, he took in one deep breath after another, hoping to catch a whiff of sulfur, a telltale sign that a demon was near. He needed to be able to track them, find the answers to everyone's questions, figure out what the demons were up to in order to get himself and his brothers one step ahead of them.

If he couldn't do this, couldn't do what he should be able to, how would he be able to help Dev? To save him from the very demons that have had their claws in him for the past several decades?

Fuck.

If he couldn't help save his brother, how in the hell would he possibly be able to protect Hayley? The answer to that was simple. He couldn't.

That knowledge left him cold. His power churned inside him as his mind fought to push that thought away.

He was so lost in his thoughts, he didn't notice Christian had stopped. Colliding into his brother, he quickly took a step back. Opening his mouth to ask what was wrong, he paused.

There it was. That smell he had been looking for. The stench clung to the air as he breathed it in, the foulness coating his tongue. Sulfur. It was faint, but it was there. Moving silently past Christian, Manuel made his way down the road, his footsteps sure as he took in one foul breath after another. Turning the corner, he didn't even look back, knowing his brothers would follow.

The rain had slowed a bit as they hit the alley. The smell of sulfur was so strong at this point, his stomach tensed. Looking between the two local shops, he was relieved to find them both already shut down for the night. The less people who could possibly stumble upon something they shouldn't, the better.

Feeling Darren and Christian come up behind him, Manuel turned to look at his brothers. "I can't tell how many there are, but there's definitely more than one demon down there," he whispered.

"Castigo has to be one of them," Christian hissed. His normally bright blue eyes darkened as black swirls began to wash through them. Manuel glanced from him to Darren before turning his attention back down the alley.

If Castigo were down there, this was about to be a lot more fun than he had originally thought. That demon had some serious power behind him. Rolling his shoulders, he took a deep breath and let his power flow out. It weaved and coiled through the air as he searched for the demons. He sent it further into the alley until it collided with a solid cold wall. Exactly what he was looking for.

Crouching lower to the ground, he let out a deep growl. "They're not too far. We should move now before they know we're here."

Darren snarled his agreement as he stepped around him. His sword glowed brighter as he held it at his side. Manuel watched his brother take several steps into the alley, his power whipping around him as he moved. Giving his shoulders another roll, Manuel began to follow. The power blazing across his back let him know Christian was not far behind.

They could hear voices now. Guttural growls rumbled through the air as they moved closer, muffled slightly by the distance. Before too long, they were finally able to make out what was being said. From the sounds of it, the demons were having quite the argument.

Instantly recognizing Castigo's voice, Manuel tensed.

"We are not supposed to kill the humans we do not use, Pret," they heard Castigo growl. "You are sloppy, and this mess will bring too much unwanted attention."

"He was whining too much. I hate whiners," came the demon's reply. "I think it would have drawn more attention to let him go. Who knows what tales he would have spun."

"Yeah. You worry too much, Castigo," another demon jeered. "Anyway, there is nothing that says we cannot have some fun while we are out here."

"And it *was* fun," Pret said. "The way his screamed and writhed about on the ground was most entertaining."

"They bleed so easily, too," another demon chimed in.

By now, the Guardians had come up behind a dumpster. Sensing the demons just on the other side, they crouched down and waited. The fact that at least one of those demons had just killed an innocent caused Manuel's blood to boil. He really wanted to just bust around this stupid bin and take the closest fucker out. And he would have if Darren hadn't held his hand up to stop them. Gripping the hilt of his Sica tighter, he ground his teeth and waited.

"Well, we are not out here to have fun," they heard Castigo snarl. "Andras sent us out here to get him humans, so that is what we are going to do. Or did you forget so quickly your determination to prove you can do this job better than I?"

"Fuck you, Castigo. I am going to do this better than you because, let's face it, I *am* better. We have already found two humans since we started looking around here. How long did it take you to find four? Hmm? That is what I thought. Maybe you should just sit back and try not to get in the way."

"Well, go on then," Castigo taunted. "What the fuck are you waiting for?"

Darren looked over at Manuel and raised his eyebrow. *What the fuck is right,* Manuel thought. He gave his brother a shrug.

"I am waiting for you to get the fuck out of my way."

As fun as it was to listen to these demons bickering, enough was enough. Stepping out from around the dumpster, Manuel let out a loud sigh. Immediately, he found himself met with five startled pairs of eyes. Well, four, seeing as Castigo didn't seem all that surprised. "It really is a sad day when even demons can't seem to get along," Manuel mocked, smirking as he met Castigo's glare. Feeling his brothers step up around him, he shifted his gaze to the other four demons, knowing Christian would keep an eye on Castigo. The other demons were a lot smaller than Castigo. Not in height, for they were all rather tall, but in build. Obviously, Andras didn't require all of his demons to be in top shape. *Pity.*

"I was wondering when you would show up," Castigo sneered.

"Sorry to have kept you waiting," Christian growled.

Manuel noticed one of the demons slowly reach into his jacket pocket, his red eyes flashing dangerously as they swept over the Guardians. "Whatcha got there?" Manuel asked, bringing the demon's focus to him.

"It is a surprise," he smirked.

"Yeah," one of the other demons chuckled. "Do you guys like surprises?"

"From you guys?" Manuel said, adjusting his grip on his sword. "I doubt there is much that would surprise us."

"We will see about that. How about you come over here and I will show you what I have." The red-eyed demon laughed. "I promise it will be a wonderful surprise."

Darren, who had been silent, barked out a laugh. "It's cute how you think this is some kind of game."

"Oh, but it is. It is the best kind of game."

"Really? And what kind is that?" Darren hissed, beginning to slowly advance towards him.

"Poker, my friend. In poker, it is always the best hand that wins." Drawing a gun from his pocket, the red-eyed demon raised it up until it was pointed at Darren's chest. "And, in this game, that would be me." Without another word, he pulled the trigger.

Manuel watched as Darren raised his broadsword in front of him, expertly deflecting the bullet and sending it off to the side. With another quick step, he reached up, shoving his power out and sending the little demon into the wall, the gun slipping from his hand and landing with a clatter upon the ground.

It was definitely game on.

At that point, they all ran at each other. Out of the corner of his eye, Manuel watched as Christian met Castigo head-on. The demon, having pulled out his own sword, swung at his brother. Their blades met with a resounding clash, the edges ringing as they glided against each other.

As much as Manuel wanted to go after Castigo himself, he figured it would be best to let Christian have a go at him first. After all, Christian had just as much anger built up against Castigo, if not more, than he did. He'd just bide his time and, once an opening presented itself, Manuel would swoop in and take him down. Rage burned through him as he heard Darren release a growl.

Darren had followed that other demon as he began to scramble up from the ground. His red eyes glowed as he lunged for the gun, only to be thrown through the air by Darren again. They didn't know what the demon thought his gun was going to do, but they all knew that they couldn't let any of them get their hands on it.

Manuel saw all of this happen in his peripheral vision, never taking his eyes off the other three slowly trying to surround him. Holding his sword in front of him, he let out a low growl as his power rushed out. The demons swayed slightly as the ground beneath them gave a hard shudder.

"What are you three waiting for?" he taunted. "An invitation?"

With that, the demons let out a snarl, which echoed through the alley as they charged. Bracing himself, Manuel felt his wings rip out of his back. With a quick flap, he flung one of the demons off to the side, the other two slamming into him.

Screams erupted from all around. Curses and shouting. Growls and grunts. The cracking of cement and crumbling brick.

And the fight was just getting started.

Chapter 40

Hayley paced around the kitchen. The guys had been gone a couple hours, but ever since they left, she had felt an uneasiness growing within her.

At first, she had chalked it up to nerves. The thought of Manuel going out there after the incident in the Indigo parking lot had left her feeling ill. She'd been physically shaken after her encounter with the demons, drained from the effort she had used to keep them at bay. Then finding out the one who had come to her and Ella's rescue had been one of Manuel's brothers, one all the boys had thought was lost to them, had been an emotional blow.

So it wasn't too surprising that she wanted Manuel close. Wanted to be wrapped up in his strong arms as she attempted to wish away the day.

But he'd gone out. She understood his need to be with his brothers, to get answers concerning Dev and the demons at the bar, but the selfish side of her had wanted him to stay. Knowing that wouldn't happen, Hayley had tried the next best thing. She'd demanded to go with them. She knew she could help. At least that was what she told herself, even as the voice in

her head said she would end up being more
of a distraction than anything.

Shit.

She hadn't even tried to do anything
with her magic since the bar. If all she
could do in this state was muster up a small
gust of wind, she could end up getting
Manuel or one of his brothers injured. So,
yeah, she had put up a fight to go with
them, but as soon as Ella said she would
stay with her, realizing Nicholas would also
stay behind, she had given in.

It was after they had been gone a
half-hour that the images of her dream
started flashing through her mind. What
was wrong with her? She had been so
wrapped up in her own needs, she hadn't
even stopped to think about what going out
to hunt some demons could mean for them.
She had warned them about the dream
again, even sobbed as the emotions of the
day and her fears for their future had
collided. But she'd still let them go because,
in the back of her mind, she hadn't really
thought it could happen tonight. God, she
was stupid. Even after she had realized her
fears could be coming true, she'd still
talked herself out of it. She would know if
her dream were going to turn into reality
tonight, right?

So, trying to get it out of her head,
Hayley had gone upstairs and taken a bath,
hoping the soothing warm water and

relaxing bath oils would calm her nerves. However, it had been anything but relaxing. With each minute that passed, her mind kept drifting back to her dream. To the smell of the rain, the details of the fight, the feeling of helplessness.

It hadn't been long after that she found herself in the kitchen, Ella and Nicholas wandering in. Ella hadn't said a word, just walked over and sat down, watching her with worried eyes as she paced. Nicholas, for all his mixed feelings towards her, had tried to calm her down. He even fixed her a cup of tea in an attempt to get her to sit. That mug was all but forgotten on the counter, only a tiny bit gone before she had set it down to continue her pacing.

Now, almost an hour-and-a-half later, she found herself more anxious than ever. Rubbing her sweaty palms on her jeans, Hayley glanced over at the kitchen table where Ella and Nicholas were sitting.

Sighing, she stopped and turned to them. "Something's wrong," she stated with a shaky breath. "I can feel it."

"Hayley, I'm sure everything is fine. It hasn't been that long, and the guys will be home-" Nicholas started.

"No, Nicholas," Hayley said, walking up to the table. "Please. I... I know you don't think much of me, believing I made up the dream I had of Manuel to get him to listen to me, but I didn't. It's real and it's happening now. I know it is. We need to do something."

Nicholas took a deep breath and stared at her, his red eyes flashing as he tapped his fingers on the table. Finally, he gave a sharp nod. "Okay, let's say that your dream, vision, whatever it was is real. Let's say that something is happening. What do we do? Do you have any idea where this fight is supposed to take place?"

Thinking hard, she shook her head. Tears of frustration threatened to fall as she looked between him and Ella. "All I know is it happens in an alley."

"Of course it's an alley," he mumbled.

"What?"

He waved one of his hands. "Nothing. Do you remember anything else?"

Glancing out one of the windows, she watched as the rain beat against it, drop after drop running down the glass until it disappeared from sight. "No. I just remember running in the rain through the streets and finding them in an alley. What if we can't find them?"

"We'll find them," Ella spoke up, her voice filled with confidence. "I have an idea."

Both Hayley and Nicholas looked at her. "What are you thinking?" he asked.

"Well, one of my powers is dowsing, the ability to find missing things, right?" At their nod, she continued. "What if, while she is focusing on her dream, I use Hayley as a focal point and see if I can find them?"

Hayley felt a spark of excitement as she thought about it. "That might just work. Hold on." Rushing out of the kitchen, she ran up to Manuel's room. Digging into her bag, she found her little black pouch tucked beneath her shirts. Reaching in, she felt the tingle in her fingertips as the object she was in need of answered her silent call. Pulling out the shiny black obsidian stone, she sent out a thank you. This was exactly what she needed.

Skipping steps as she ran back towards the kitchen, she entered to find Ella and Nicholas looking at her questioningly. "I got it."

"Got what?" Nicholas asked skeptically.

"It's an obsidian gemstone. It's used for many different things, from knife blades to jewelry. But," she said with a smile, setting the stone in the center of the table "it can also be used to help clear any unconscious blocks, sharpening internal and external vision." Seeing that they still seemed a bit confused, she rushed on. "I'm hoping that with the help of this stone, I'll be able to see details in my dream more clearly, helping Ella have a better focal point." Pleased with herself, she sat down and faced Ella. "How do you want to do this?"

"Just try and relax," she instructed. Nodding, Hayley shifted slightly in her chair. Reaching out, she palmed the cool stone before closing her eyes. Taking a deep breath, she held it for a second, then let the air leave past her lips on a soft sigh. Within seconds, she was focused on her breathing, her anxiety settled. "Okay," she heard Ella say softly. "Now, try to bring up your dream. You said you were running through the street, right?"

"Yes. The street is wet from the rain. It's so quiet."

"What do you see?"

Hayley felt the slightest pressure on her hand as Ella reached out and grasped it. "I see...lots of buildings and parked cars."

As the dream rushed back to her, she found herself on the street, her shoes slapping against the pavement as she ran. Building after building flew by her. This time, unlike before, she focused on her senses. What she felt, smelled. It wasn't long before she found herself at the opening of an alley.

She heard yelling, the voices deep and angry. She knew what she would find if she went into the alley, just as she knew the outcome. Glancing around, she spotted a street sign, its name obscured. Taking a deep breath, she reminded herself that she was back at the house, in the kitchen with Ella and Nicholas. She reminded herself that she needed to focus. Feeling a coldness in her hand, she looked down at it. Although she was in her dream, she knew that she was tightening her grip around the stone back at the house.

"Help me to see," she whispered, instantly feeling the cold stone grow warm within her palm. The heat flew through her as she looked around. It was more than the stone, though. It was Ella, her power flowing through her as she glanced at the buildings. Even though she still couldn't make out the street sign, Hayley felt a sudden certainty that they would find them. The feeling washed through her as she gave a slight shudder, blinking until she focused on the kitchen table once again.

Looking up, she saw that Ella was now looking straight ahead, her eyes glowing white, her power whipping around her. Goosebumps rose across Hayley's arms as she tightened her fingers around Ella's hand. *Please find them.* Her mind screamed for her to hurry, but she knew she needed to be patient. Ella would find them. She had to.

Seeing movement out of the corner of her eye, she watched as Nicholas stood and made his way to Ella's side. Bracing one of his hands on the table, he leaned down. She saw a faint flash of light and tore her eyes from Ella, gasping in shock as a bolt of light streaked from beneath the sleeve of Nicholas' shirt, traveling quickly down his arm, then disappearing. *Like lightning*, she thought in awe as her eyes flew up and found Nicholas staring at her. The red in his eyes wavered as a greyness flew through them. *Like a cloud in a storm.*

With a slow blink, he looked away, focusing on Ella. "What do you see, Ella?" His voice, though quiet, held a faint growl.

"I see...," she started, pausing briefly as her head tilted to the side, "brick buildings. One has a large window... Maybe a salon? No. A barber shop with red lettering in the window."

"Crews," Nicholas said, standing up. "It's the only barber shop in town. Down on Central Avenue." He looked at Hayley. She watched the storm building in his eyes until none of the red could be seen. "It's on the corner with an alley leading behind the building."

They were there.

She knew it instantly, but before she could utter a word, Nicholas was on the move, his back rigid as he left the kitchen. Looking back at Ella, Hayley noticed her eyes were back to normal, a tired look upon her face. "Go with him," she said softly. "I'll be no good to you guys in this state." Ella reached up and gripped Hayley's arm. "I felt the darkness in that alley. Something horrible is happening there. You must hurry. Go. Find the boys and bring them home. Bring them all home."

She could see Ella's fear for Christian's safety in her eyes. Feel it in the air around them. Jumping from her seat, she gave Ella a quick hug. Yelling a promise to her that they would find them in time, she ran to find Nicholas.

Following the power rolling off him like a beacon, she found him in his room, extracting an intimidating black compound bow from a case. "I'm going with you and I don't want any argument about it," she blurted out, standing in the doorway.

He glanced up at her, slinging a bag across his shoulder with arrows protruding from its top. "I figured you would," he said slowly. "After all, this is your show, princess."

"Right. Then...we should go." Glancing down the hall, she took a step away from the door. "I'll go grab my keys. Unless you want to drive." Looking back at Nicholas, she watched as his lips twitched into a small smile. "What?"

"We're not driving."

"We're not?"

"No." He shook his head. Walking towards her, he grabbed her arm and led her back downstairs and out the front door.

Feeling the cold rain hit her face, she looked up at Nicholas, unsure of what they were doing. "Well, if we're not going to drive, how do you suggest we get there?"

She watched as he took a step away from her, his eyes holding hers. "I know I have given you no reason to trust me. For that, I apologize."

"Nicholas, there's no need-"

"I'll make it up to you later, though. I promise." His face was serious as he watched her. "But I need you to trust me right now."

"Okay," she said immediately. Hayley had no reason not to trust him. No matter what he thought, she understood. She knew his reaction to her was from something he had dealt with, something in his past that had made him feel the way he did about witches. Sure, he had been a little short with her, kept himself at a distance, but at no time had she truly felt threatened. He had never made her feel like he would hurt her.

He seemed to look at her for a moment, deciding whether to believe her or not. Finally, he must have seen that she had meant it because he gave her a quick nod. Taking another small step back, she watched as his body tensed. With a growl, his shoulders curled forward as his back hunched. She was just about to ask what was wrong when a flash of light shot through the dark behind him. It was so bright, she closed her eyes, seeing spots begin to appear behind her eyelids.

"I hope you're not afraid of heights," she heard him say.

Blinking her eyes a few times, she felt her breath hitch. Never in her wildest dreams did she think she would see what she was seeing now. Sure, Manuel had told her he and his brothers were angels, but to have Nicholas standing before her now, his wings proudly spread out behind him, was something else. His wings were huge. The light from the house cast a faint glow upon them, lighting the edges so she could see the top of them towering high above his head, the bottom brushing the ground. They were black, but there was something more. Stepping closer, she smiled as she began to make out the red edges lining some of the feathers, like streaks done by a salon or brushstrokes done on a canvas.

Red, like his eyes, she mused, finally meeting his steady gaze.

Noticing his right hand stretched out to her, she reached out and grasped it. Nicholas immediately pulled her to him, wrapping his arm around her. "Now, hold on," he said calmly. "And do me a favor."

"What's that?" she asked, wrapping her arms tightly around him, barely holding back her gasp as he lifted into the air.

"When you tell Manuel how we got downtown, make sure I'm not in the room."

"Why is that?" she gasped, trying not to pay attention to how high they were or how fast they were flying. Her hair whipped around her, causing her to turn her face into his chest to keep it from stinging her eyes.

She felt his chest rumble with laughter before he answered. "Something tells me that when he finds out I held you to me and flew you across town, no matter how grateful he is, he's going to want my head." She joined in his laughter, knowing that he was probably right. "So let me get a head start before you let that cat out of the bag. Deal?"

"Deal," she laughed.

✝

What felt like mere moments later, Nicholas set them down. She looked around, spotting a building with red lettering less than a block away. Wondering why he didn't get them closer, she turned to ask him just as another flash of light streaked through the air.

"You need to warn me when you're going to do that," she grumbled, blinking to try and get her eyes to readjust.

"Sorry," he chuckled.

"Why did you put us down here?" she asked quietly, pushing her wet hair behind her shoulders.

"Any closer and the demons might have seen us coming," he said with a shrug. "Now, stay behind me." With that, Nicholas began to move down the street. She noticed how he kept himself close to the buildings, so she did the same, moving behind him like his shadow until they came to a brief stop by the edge of the barber shop. She watched him peer around the corner before turning to her. "Okay. It looks like they're around the bend at the end of the alley. Stay quiet as we make our way down there. I want to see what's going on before we rush into the fight."

Giving him a nod, she moved when he did. The need to hurry rushed over her with each step they took. She could hear them now. Voices filled with anger, grunts of pain, and the power... Oh god, the power swirling around her was like nothing she had ever felt before. As they neared another corner, she braced herself.

She felt Nicholas reach back and rest his hand against her arm. With a quick shake of his head, Hayley knew that he wanted her to wait. Standing as still as she could, she noticed that the rain had stopped. The air was now cold, the moisture still clinging to the hairs on her arm making her shiver.

As time ticked by, she began to wonder what they were waiting for. It wasn't until the tingle of his power along her skin began to grow that she looked around in wonder, noticing a light fog had begun to build along the ground. It swirled around them, growing thicker as she watched. Looking up, she saw Nicholas watching her. Raising her eyebrow in a silent question, he winked at her, causing her to shake her head as he turned back.

She could feel some confusion in the air as the fog began to reach the ongoing fight. As a snarl echoed against the walls, she blinked, practically missing when Nicholas ran around the corner.

Moving quickly, she ran after him, coming to a sudden halt as she gazed at the fight before her. Nicholas had slammed into one of the two demons that had been trying to corner Christian. Jumping back just as quickly, Nicholas reached for one of his arrows and let it fly into the demon's chest. A screech from the creature was the only sound he made before he crumbled to the ground.

Christian, in the meantime, traded blows with another demon. His dagger glowed in his right hand as he twisted it around, his arm flying through the air in a sudden move, slicing right through the demon. Blood sprayed into the air as the demon fell into the fog, his form nothing but a shadow within the gray.

Darren battled yet another, his broadsword swinging low, just missing the demon as he jumped back. As he started to run at Darren, she watched as the angel threw his hand into the air, sending the demon crashing into the wall down the alley.

Her eyes darted around quickly, noting that there were at least three demons down, leaving the one Darren had just tossed and the other... Her eyes widened when she spotted Manuel facing off with a much larger demon, their movements slow as they stared at each other, moving around much like the fight within her dream.

"Castigo," she whispered. The sudden movement of Manuel's head swinging around to face her had Hayley covering her mouth.

His eyes glowed when they met hers. She could feel the anger and confusion rolling off him. Then, just as she had feared, she saw the demon behind him lunge forward. Before she could scream, Castigo had knocked Manuel to the ground. "No!" she yelled, fear tightening her chest.

The two began to roll around beneath the fog. Moving closer, she could see Castigo snarling as he landed on top of Manuel, wrapping his hands around his neck. A darkness had begun to grow around Castigo then, its thickness slowly blocking out the boys behind him as his power intensified.

She could feel Manuel's power, too, but it was weaker. They had been fighting a long time, and with Castigo's grip around his throat, Manuel seemed to be losing steam. Hayley felt the ground shudder beneath her as Manuel attempted to call the Earth to him.

With a screech, she ran towards them, feeling tears burning her eyes as Castigo looked up at her, his silver gaze laughing as he pushed more of his power out around him. She stumbled as it hit her. Its darkness threatened to crush her, but she wouldn't stop. She would get to them, to Manuel, and prove her dream wrong. Hayley refused to believe that fate would put her on this path to find Manuel, to give her the man she loved, only to take him away. It wouldn't happen. She wouldn't allow it.

Calling on the light, the wind, and the air, she swirled her power around her, making Castigo's power shudder. "Give me strength to fight this evil," she whispered as she pushed forward. "Give me light to fight this darkness." She felt her skin warm, a glow beginning to work its way around her. A look of uncertainty filled Castigo's eyes as she got closer. "Give me power to save this life." Meeting Castigo's gaze, she pulled her power tight within her, mentally molding it into a ball of burning white light. Its heat warmed her as she stopped before them. Hearing Manuel's gasp, she watched as Castigo rose up, taking a step to the side as he growled at her.

Manuel will be okay, she thought with relief. *They all will be.*

"You are playing with fire, little girl," Castigo said, his voice growling through the building wind. Watching him take several more steps back, she smirked.

"That may be, demon," she responded, her own voice unrecognizable to her as she stepped up until she was standing protectively over Manuel. The darkness around Castigo had now dissipated, leaving him standing there in Nicholas' fog, a look of anger upon his face. "But, then again, I've never had a problem with fire. In fact, it is you who should be worried about getting burned."

Swirling her power within her, she felt the demon begin to call his own once again. *Oh, I don't think so.* Smiling, she felt her skin start to tingle as the power within her sought release. "And give me what I need to end this." With those last words, she felt her body tense as the energy within her erupted. In a ball of white light, it spread out around her, burning through the demon's power as it lit up the alley. She heard Castigo's howl as her power slammed into him. Then, just as quickly as she sensed him, he was gone.

As the power around her began to dim, she knelt down beside Manuel, his eyes blinking against the brightness. "Hey," she whispered, running her hand against his chest. The feel of his heart beating within him almost made her cry.

"Hey," he said back, his voice coming out rough as he pushed himself up. Bracing against his left hand, he reached up with his right, pulling her hand tightly to his chest. They stared at each other for a moment before movement around them drew their attention. She watched as Christian and Darren made their way over to them, gasping when she noticed Darren's cheek had been cut badly, the blood from it running down his face.

Seeing the worry in her eyes, he smiled. "I'll be fine," he said, absently wiping at the cut. "The little shit surprised me with a pocketknife. It'll be healed before we get home."

"Well, that's useful," she laughed, moving slightly as Manuel rose to his feet. He reached down and pulled her up, holding her snug against his side. "Where's Cyrus?" she asked, glancing at Christian.

"He took off right before we found the demons," he responded with a snarl. As she started to ask what happened, he raised his hand. "It's a long story. Something that would be better to get into later over a bottle of Crown."

With a smile, she nodded. She found there were certain topics that were better discussed over a strong drink, and she had a feeling anything having to do with Cyrus would definitely fall into that category. Looking up at Manuel, she blinked. "Sorry. I think Castigo got away."

"Yeah. He's kind of like a cockroach," Christian growled. "Don't worry, though. We'll get him one of these days."

"Maybe if we had gotten here sooner-" she started.

"As grateful as I am that you were here, you shouldn't have been," Manuel said with a huff. The others nodded their agreement.

"Yeah. That ball of light was no joke." Christian smirked.

Blushing slightly, Hayley just shook her head. "Thanks."

"Hey," Manuel said loudly, drawing all of their attention to him. "Where's Nicholas?"

"Nicholas!" Darren immediately called out.

"I thought he was over with Christian," Hayley said, looking around wildly.

"He was, but then he ran over to help Darren." Christian looked at Darren, who had already stepped away from them, concern building in the air around him.

"He did," Darren said, walking several steps away. "The demon I was fighting was trying to go after that gun." Glancing around, he looked up. "Nicholas!" he yelled again, his voice echoing through the alley.

"What gun?" Hayley asked in confusion.

"One of the demons was waving around a gun," Christian said absently.

Looking up at Manuel, she shook her head. "But... Can a gun even hurt you guys?"

"No. I mean, if we get shot, it'll hurt like hell, but that's about it," Manuel said, frowning. Looking from her to Darren, he shook his head. "Which a demon would know."

"True," Christian hummed. "But I don't think that was a normal gun. There must have been something special about it for the demons to have put so much faith in using it against us." Manuel and Darren both murmured their agreement as everyone got lost in their own thoughts.

Darren spun and looked at them, his eyes glowing. "In the midst of the fight, I thought I saw the demon get his hands on it. If I saw it, so did Nicholas."

"And if the demon took off to try and get away with that gun...," Christian started.

"Then Nicholas would have gone after him," Manuel finished with a growl.

"But," Hayley said, looking quickly between them. "Nicholas wouldn't have known that you guys thought there was something special with that gun. He showed up well after the fighting started."

"He would have noticed the way I reacted to seeing the demon grab it, though," Darren remarked, a look of unease crossing his face. "He would have known something was up."

"He would have gone after the demon regardless, but if he thinks that gun's important, he won't stop until he gets it back." Manuel sighed.

"Fuck!" Christian exclaimed.

Hayley watched as Darren walked past Christian and squeezed his shoulder, making his way over to the far wall. He skimmed his hand against the brick.

"Darren? What are you looking for?" Hayley asked, taking Manuel's hand in hers as they walked over to him.

"It should be...," Darren mumbled, his fingers searching over the cracked and chipped wall. He glanced over his shoulder, then back at the wall. He stepped back for a second, moved a few steps to the side, then walked back up to the wall. "If I were a stray bullet, where would I be?"

By now, Christian was standing at her other side as they watched Darren, his movements slow.

"Gotcha," he exclaimed. Reaching back, he wiggled his fingers. "Christian, let me see your dagger."

"What?" Christian asked. With a sideways glare from Darren, he shook his head and reached behind his back, pulling out his black dagger. The blade's edge glowed softly as he flipped it around in his hand, holding the hilt out to his brother.

"Thanks," he mumbled, putting the tip into a crack in the wall. With a little wiggling, Hayley watched a small piece of metal fall out, landing in his palm. Holding what remained of the bullet between his fingers, he raised it for them all to see. "This will tell us what was so special about the fucking gun."

"What do we do about Nicholas?" Hayley asked softly.

Darren looked at her, his dark blue eyes soft as he let his concern for his brother show through. "Right now, we head home. If he catches the demon, he'll show up there."

"And if he doesn't?" She hated to ask, prayed that he would be there waiting for them, but she needed to know the answer.

"If he doesn't..." Manuel paused, his fingers wrapping tightly around hers. Clearing his throat, he tried again. "If he doesn't, we go find him."

As Christian and Darren agreed, Hayley looked between them. A tightness in her chest began to grow as she thought about Nicholas. She saw the way they loved each other. Even when they were angry, the love radiated through them all.

They were truly a family, and she hoped nothing would happen to him. Looking up at the sky, she sent out a silent thank you for the help in saving Manuel, then a prayer that Nicholas would come home. This group needed to remain strong and whole, and that wouldn't happen without Nicholas by their side.

Chapter 41

Manuel leaned against the back door as he watched Hayley, Ella, and Cindy walk through the rose garden. Their fingers lightly grazed over the leaves as they chatted about what color roses might bloom in the spring. Even at this distance, he could tell that their smiles were strained. It was to be expected, though.

It had been four long days since the battle downtown and there had still been no sign of Nicholas. They had searched everywhere for him...every alley, field, bar, warehouse, and club. They'd found nothing. Not a single sign of him anywhere.

It made no sense. Even if he had been injured, they should still be able to track him, locate him. Of course, it didn't help they had found his phone on his bed. Hayley said they were in such a hurry to find them that day, Nicholas probably forgot he'd set it down.

Ella had even tried to use her powers to locate him. She'd pushed herself so hard, Christian had finally stepped in and forced her to stop, his fear for her health trumping her weak argument to keep looking. It tore her up that she couldn't find him, but none of them would allow her to come to harm by pushing herself too hard. She finally agreed to wait a few days before trying again. With her powers still at war, Hayley agreed that it would be best to not push her too hard.

Later, Manuel had overheard Cyrus ask Ella if she thought the reason she couldn't find Nicholas was because he was dead. Bracing himself against the wall, Manuel had held his breath as he waited for her answer. He feared the worst, knew his brother did, too, because the feeling of despair rolling off him was almost suffocating. Ella hadn't even blinked an eye. She'd reached out to Cyrus, grasping his face firmly between her hands as she forced him to focus on her.

"He's not dead," she said with confidence.

"Then where is he?" Cyrus had asked, his voice laced with concern and fear.

"There could be a lot of reasons why I can't sense him, Cyrus. One of the main ones is he's unconscious."

"Why would that prevent you from finding him?"

"When I look for a person, I see what they see, feel what they do. If Nicholas is unconscious, I have nothing for my power to latch onto." She'd stood, continuing to cup his face lightly as she stared into his onyx eyes. "Once he wakes, I *will* find him," she'd promised.

Manuel had gone to find Cyrus after that to see how he was. They had never talked about the argument that had happened between them all that night, or if Cyrus had found anything out when he had taken off on his own. They had all agreed to let it slide for now. He was beating himself up enough for not being there. His silence within the house had grown, as well as the brick wall he'd erected around himself. It was unnerving, horrible, and not what Manuel wanted to have happen. When he had found Cyrus in Nicholas' room, unpacking his boxes and silently hanging his movie posters on the wall, Manuel could do nothing but stare. The sadness he felt in his heart at that moment was almost too much as he watched his brother silently work. After a while, he had moved away from the door. Turning around, he slid down the wall, resting his head back as he listened to Cyrus move around the room behind him. He'd sat there for hours until Hayley had found him, pulling him gently to his feet and down the hall.

Darren had been spending every waking moment searching the news sites for signs of Dev, studying that smashed bullet, and combing the streets for Nicholas. Manuel could tell that the fact Nicholas had taken off with no backup ate at him. Nobody blamed him, though. Nicholas always had a mind of his own when it came to fighting. He would do whatever it took to protect his brothers. If that meant chasing after some demon by himself, that was what he'd do. There was nothing Darren could have done to stop him. They had all told him as much, but he would just shrug off their words.

Last night, Manuel had glanced out the window and found Darren sitting alone in the middle of the yard, gazing angrily at the sky. He never spoke a word, though. Manuel had waited for him to yell, curse, or threaten the heavens for the safe return of their brothers. He'd expected it, fully understood if he did. To know Dev was out there somewhere, possibly in pain, was horrible, but to now have Nicholas also missing was like a nail in the coffin. The anger building in all of them as the days passed was becoming physically noticeable. So Manuel would not have blamed Darren if he had lost it, cursing everything they believed. But he hadn't. Manuel had watched him for a while, debating on heading out to see if he was okay. Then he caught movement out of the corner of his eye. As he'd looked over, he watched Cindy make her way from the side of the house towards Darren.

She still didn't know exactly what they were or what had happened, but she wasn't stupid. When she came over and found them all in a dark mood, Cindy had only asked a few questions. When she walked through the door the next morning and found out Nicholas was missing, she hadn't left. Instead of harping on them about what they should be doing or asking questions they couldn't answer, she had taken it upon herself to start unpacking the house. She began in the kitchen. By the time she moved into the living room, Ella and Hayley had both stepped in to help. Having her around had proved invaluable as they had all begun to deal with this in their own way.

Manuel had watched Cindy cross the yard last night with a calm understanding. Her curly blond hair glowed softly from the light of the moon as she quietly came to a stop beside Darren. She never said anything. Just stood there for a moment before gracefully sitting down on the grass. They didn't touch or talk, but Manuel saw the tension slowly slip from his brother's shoulders. That was all he needed to see before leaving them to find their silent comfort in each other.

Watching the girls now, he had to smile. Just as he and his brothers worked together during this time of uncertainty, these beautiful women had not only stood by them, offering their unwavering support, but had found a calming strength in each other.

Hayley had agreed to move in with him. Well, it hadn't really been discussed. She told him yesterday morning that she wanted to get her stuff out of the apartment. He wasn't sure what different scenarios she had thought of, what reaction she was expecting, but her laughter told him that throwing her over his shoulder and heading out to the car wasn't one of them. He had just shrugged and told her he wanted to do it before she changed her mind.

Last night, he'd asked her how she'd ended up in Fhallon Heights. She'd just laughed, saying she'd pulled up here and just knew this was the town she was supposed to be in.

"Just like that?" Manuel had asked with a chuckle.

"Just like that. And then, when I saw you in the library that night-"

"Ah, you mean the night I scared you and made you drop all those books?"

"Yes." She playfully smacked his arm. "Anyway, when I saw you, I just knew you were the one I'd been looking for."

"You were looking for me?" Manuel had smirked.

"I've always been looking for you, Manuel." Her eyes began to fill with tears. "You've always been it for me. I didn't understand it when I was younger, but when I saw you, I just knew that fate had been leading me towards you. Had brought me here, to this town, to be with you."

He'd pulled her close, kissing her as if his life depended on it. "Well, you're stuck with me now," he whispered as their lips parted. "I'm in this with you until the end, so don't think you'll be able to shake me anytime soon."

"Oh, I won't try." She'd smiled, a soft light beginning to glow in her eyes as she gazed lovingly at him. "I've been dreaming about you for as long as I can remember, Manuel. And now that I've found you..." She cleared her throat. "Now that I have you in my life, in my arms, I never plan on letting you go."

That moment would forever be burned in his mind. For all of the years he'd been here on Earth, all of the amazing sights he'd seen, beautiful words he'd heard, nothing would ever come close to what she'd said to him that day.

She was everything he'd always hoped to find. She was his happiness. His reason for being here. She was his.

And, fuck, he loved her.

He hadn't told her yet, but he was sure she knew. With everything that had been going on, the right moment just hadn't happened. Even the night he had been just about to say it, they had been interrupted. That was okay, though. He knew the time would come eventually.

When it did, he would profess not only his undying love for her, but his want...his need to make their union an everlasting one. To make up for not saying it yet, he'd put his love for her into every hug, every soft word, every stolen kiss, every passing caress. At night, when they lay in each other's arms and he held her tight as she silently cried, he willed his love to flow into her. To soothe her as her very presence soothed him. She was the light in his dark world. The anchor that caused him to hold on and focus, even as he felt his world falling apart.

"I wonder where they are," she'd said quietly that morning as they sat in the early light. Her worry for Nicholas and, even though she'd only seen him that one time, her fear for Dev's safety were apparent in everything she did. As much as it pained him to see her like this, it also warmed his heart to know that she cared for his family as much as he did, accepting them into her heart...imperfections and all.

As much as Manuel wanted to say something to her to ease her worry, he hadn't responded because he didn't have an answer. There were no words he could've said that would take the sadness from her voice or make Nicholas and Dev appear. So he'd just sat there, staring at the sky quietly, shifting slightly as he'd reached over and pulled her close. Her shoulders gave a shake as a soft sob escaped her lips. His throat tightened as he fought to stay strong. That question needed an answer. If not from him, from somebody.

Even now, hours later, that question still burned in his mind.

Feeling Christian move up beside him, he looked over. His brother's normally bright blue eyes were dull and bloodshot from several sleepless nights and long days. With a nod, Christian offered him a cup of coffee.

"Thanks," Manuel murmured, lifting the mug to his lips. The coffee rolled over his tongue as he took a healthy drink.

"I think we need to buy stock in this," Christian said, raising his own mug up in a mock salute before taking a sip.

"I agree. With how much we've been going through, it's a wonder the stores around here still have any on their shelves."

"Speaking of... I think we're going to need some more."

"Shit. Really?"

"Yup. Damn, I don't think I've ever drank this much coffee."

"Me, either," Manuel stated. Turning back to watch the girls, they had now moved over to where Ella wanted to plant her lilies. She was waving her hand around as Cindy just looked on and nodded. However, Hayley had turned to look for him. She had begun to count on him being nearby, and as their eyes met, he saw the relief wash over her face. With a little wave, she turned back to Ella.

"Do you think Nicholas will be okay?" Christian's voice broke through the silence.

"Of course," Manuel said with a lot more confidence than he actually felt.

"I mean, he has to be, right? We'd know by now if he..." Christian's voice trailed off. With a shake of his head, he took another drink of his coffee before setting the mug down on the wooden table, the muscles in his jaw ticking as he rolled his shoulder. "I'm going to see if the girls are getting hungry yet." His voice sounded tired as he walked away.

Manuel watched him go. Watched as he walked up behind Ella, resting his head softly against hers. Ella reached up, running one of her hands through his hair as she turned in his arms. He saw Hayley and Cindy share a look with each other before silently walking away, heading farther down the path to give the couple some space.

Christian's statement of knowing whether or not Nicholas was still alive hit him hard. Manuel rubbed his hand over his chest, closing his eyes as he sent out a silent prayer. But even as he hoped for Nicholas' safe return, the voice in his head told him to prepare for the chance that he won't.

He knew that the possibility of these fights not having a happy ending were very real. The fact they could go out at any time and find themselves on the wrong end of a blade was an undeniable truth. That this may have happened to Nicholas was unimaginable, unthinkable, but...

With a mental shake, he reached out a hand as Hayley walked towards him. She grabbed it, immediately stepping into his embrace. Kissing the top of her head, Manuel made himself stop that line of thinking. Sure, it could happen, but until they knew anything for sure, he would continue to believe Nicholas was fine.

He was a fighter, and if the tables were turned and it was one of them missing, he would never give up. The proof of that was how hard he had fought to get Cyrus back when he had been taken all those years ago.

Just like then, they would find their brother...both of them.

Even with the many uncertainties forcing their way into their thoughts, causing them all to replay that night over and over, wondering what would have happened had they done something different, Manuel refused to give up.

One thing was certain. If Nicholas didn't come home of his own accord, if Dev wasn't able to reach out again, they would find them and bring them home. None of them would stop looking for their brothers. Ever.

Want to know what happened to
Nicholas?
Or whether Dev will ever be reunited
with his brothers?
To get the answer to these questions
and more, be sure to keep on the
lookout for...

Faithfully Entangled
The Fallen Guardians Series,
Book 3

Coming 2017

Acknowledgments

I want to start by sending out a huge thank you to all of my family and friends. It's crazy, you know? When you're in the midst of writing - knee deep into the storyline, character drama, and plot twists - that you don't always notice all of the little things that people do to show their support. All of the kind words, smiles and hugs. The messages from an online friend saying "Hi", just because. The friend that shows up with a bottle of wine on the weekend because they know you had a tough week. These things, these amazing signs of support and love, may not always be noticeable right away, but when you stop and look back, you realize that all those little things were exactly what you needed...even if you didn't know it at the time.

So, with that being said...

To Nyki, Ashley, Winter, Michelle, Rissa, Tory, and everyone else that supported me throughout this last year - you know who you are... I thank you. Seriously, I couldn't have done this without you guys in my corner.

To my Mom, Dad, Katie, John, Mary, and Lacey... You guys aren't just my family but you've been my sounding board and my rock throughout all of this. Thank you for listening to my rambles, for forgiving my silence when I'm concentrating too hard, and for dealing with all of my stressed out craziness. I love you guys!

To my girl Diana, at Diana M. Photography... Thank you for yet another gorgeous cover. It is exactly what I had in mind for Manuel's cover, and I still can't stop staring at it. You're the best girl and I love you to pieces.

To my amazingly awesome, always-there-when-I-need-her, I-don't-know-what-I'd-do-without-her, editor Kim...woman, you are the best. You take my words and make them better...and for that I will forever be grateful.

And last, but definitely by no means least, to you...the readers! I know it is always said, that we as authors wouldn't be here without you, but it is an absolute fact. You guys are the drive behind my writing. Every time you reach out to me, every time you review my work, and every time you tell your friends about my writing, you push me to work a little harder. I can't tell you what having all of your support means to me, I truly can't. What I can say, is that I look forward to writing many many more books for you, and that I so hope you enjoyed reading Bound in Fate. It was a real joy to write Manuel and Hayley's story,

and just as with Christian and Ella's, I have a feeling their journey isn't quite done yet.
So until next time my luvs...
Dance like nobody can see you...
Laugh like you can't get enough... And never, ever, stop reaching for your dreams!

"You are my drive, my inspiration, and the life behind my words!" ~ E.F. Rose xx

About the Author

E.F. Rose lives in the Central Valley of California, surrounded by her family, friends and boyfriend. She has always enjoyed writing and considers herself to be a multi genre author, with urban fantasy and dark romance being her main focus. If she isn't writing up a storm, than Emily can probably be found either online chatting with friends, reading a good book, or out enjoying life.

My Work

Echoes (A Book of Poetry)

The Fallen Guardian's Series

Divinely Entwined (Book 1)
Bound in Fate (Book 2)

And look for the release of *Faithfully Entangled* (The Fallen Guardians Series, Book 3)
coming 2017

Contact Information

You can email me at...
emily@efrose.com

or follow me on....

Facebook @
www.facebook.com/DarkestRose13

Twitter @
www.twitter.com/Emily_F_Rose